UNTOLD COMIC TALES FROM THE HIT TV SERIES ON THE CW

RIVERDALE®

SEASON THREE

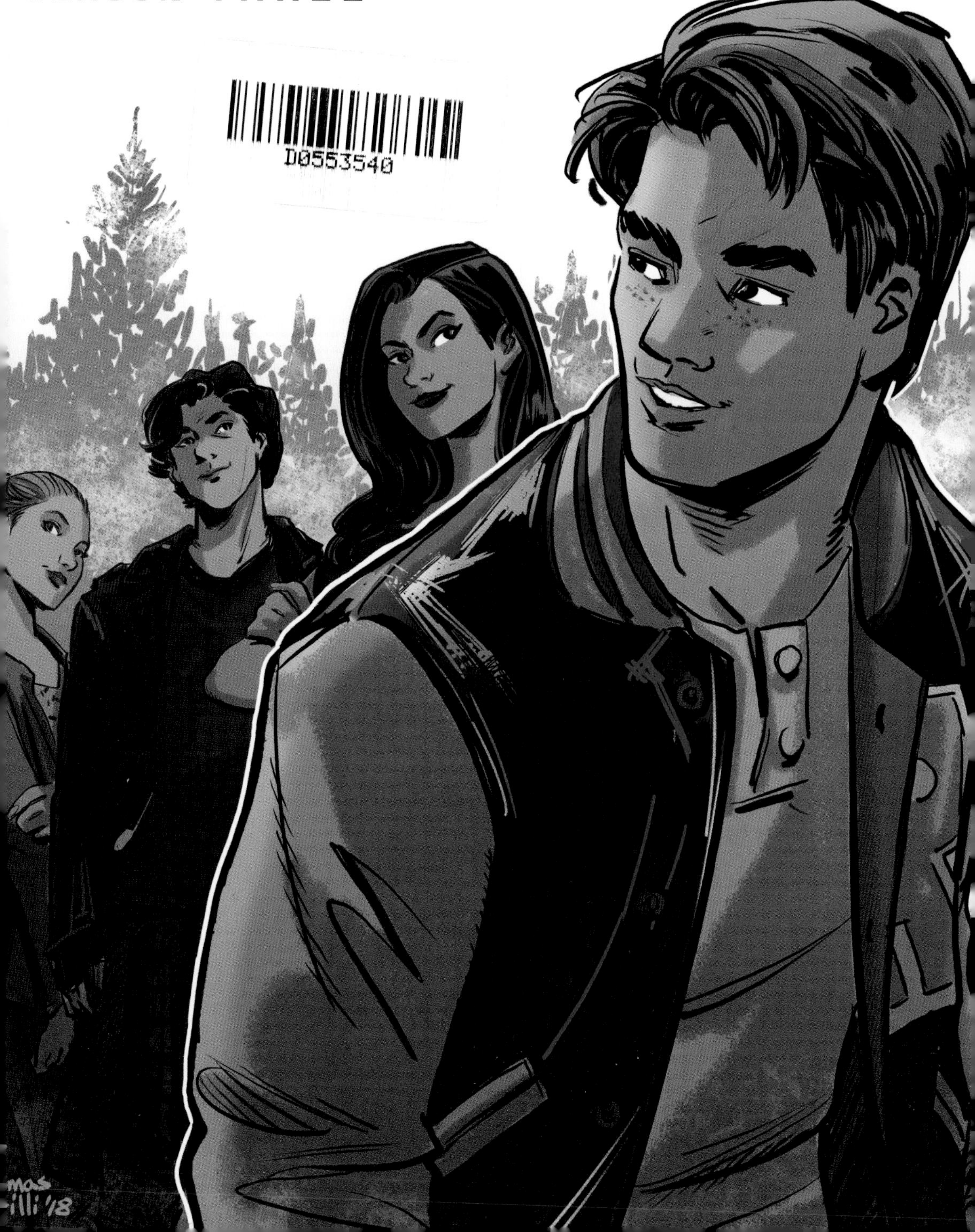

UNTOLD COMIC TALES FROM THE HIT TV SERIES ON **CW**

RIVERDALE®

WRITTEN BY:

MICOL OSTOW

WITH ART BY:

**THOMAS PITILLI, JOE EISMA,
ANDRE SZYMANOWICZ, MATT HERMS,
JANICE CHIANG & JOHN WORKMAN**

CHIEF EXECUTIVE OFFICER/PUBLISHER:

JON GOLDWATER

CHIEF CREATIVE OFFICER:

ROBERTO AGUIRRE-SACASA

EDITOR-IN-CHIEF:

VICTOR GORELICK

LEAD DESIGNER:

KARI MCLACHLAN

With this collection of all five issues of *Riverdale: Season 3* out in the world, I've had a chance to reflect on one of the most unexpected turns my writing career has taken—and one of the most fun turns, too. I can honestly say I never planned to write comics, but in retrospect, the signs were there.

From my earliest days as a reader (which always included Archie Comics), to my first job in publishing where, among other media tie-ins, we published old-school *Sabrina The Teenage Witch* books and eventually even *Betty and Veronica Mad Libs*... this iconic brand was all around me. And when Roberto Aguirre-Sacasa's genre-blending, retro-modern noir spin on the Riverdale universe came to my TV screen, I was hooked. The show, it felt, had been created just for me.

(Apparently, I wasn't alone in feeling that way.)

So when the team at Archie approached me about making the jump from writing *Riverdale* novels to tackling the comics, there was no question. They assured me that more integral to the comic than experience in the format, was knowledge of and affection for the characters, and that I had by the (maple) barrelful.

I'm grateful that my editors Alex Segura and Jamie Rotante, artists Joe Eisma and Thomas Pitilli, and everyone else involved in the creation and production of these comics were endlessly patient with me. I'm grateful that readers appreciated my own attempts to bring classic tropes and stories to the *Riverdale* crew (I'd like to think Hitchcock would have approved of Jughead Jones reimagined in the image of Jimmy Stewart a la *Rear Window*). I'm grateful to the *Riverdale* team for creating a world where organ-harvesting cults, demonic role-playing games, underground prison fight clubs, and poisoned cheerleaders are just business as usual for Archie Andrews and his gang.

It's been a blast putting my own spin on this tiny corner of the Archie universe. If you, like me, can't get enough of the *Riverdale* world, I hope these stories hit the spot. Raise a milkshake and settle in!

Micol Ostow
Writer

CHAPTER ONE

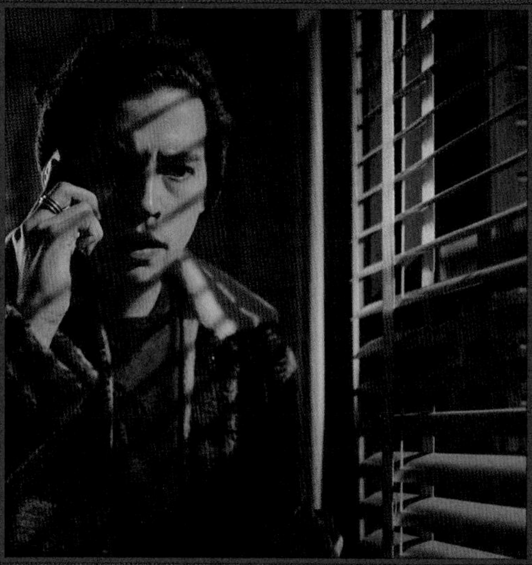

REAR WINDOW

WRITER:
MICOL OSTOW

ART:
THOMAS PITILLI

COLORS:
ANDRE SZYMANOWICZ

LETTERS:
JOHN WORKMAN

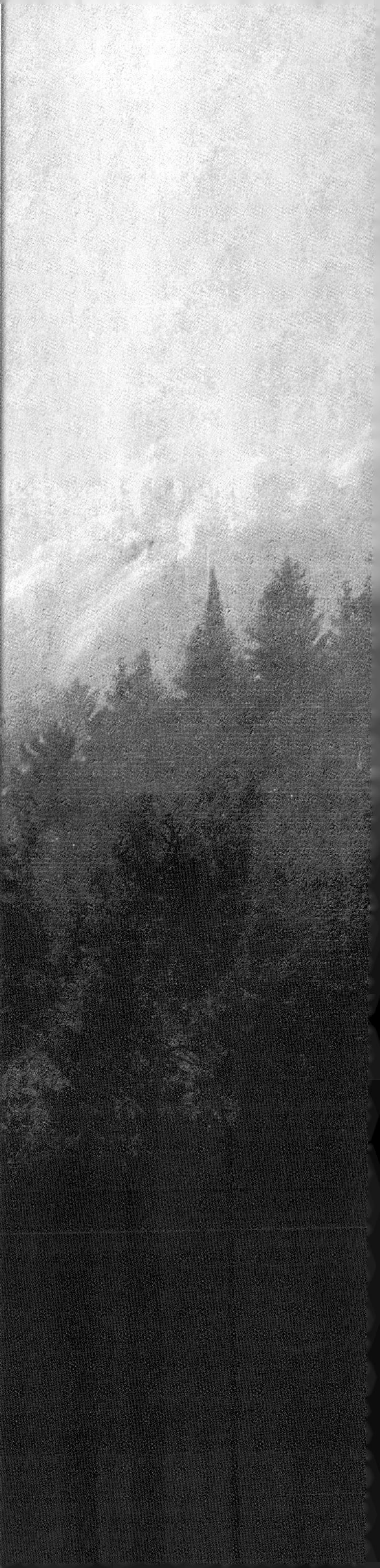

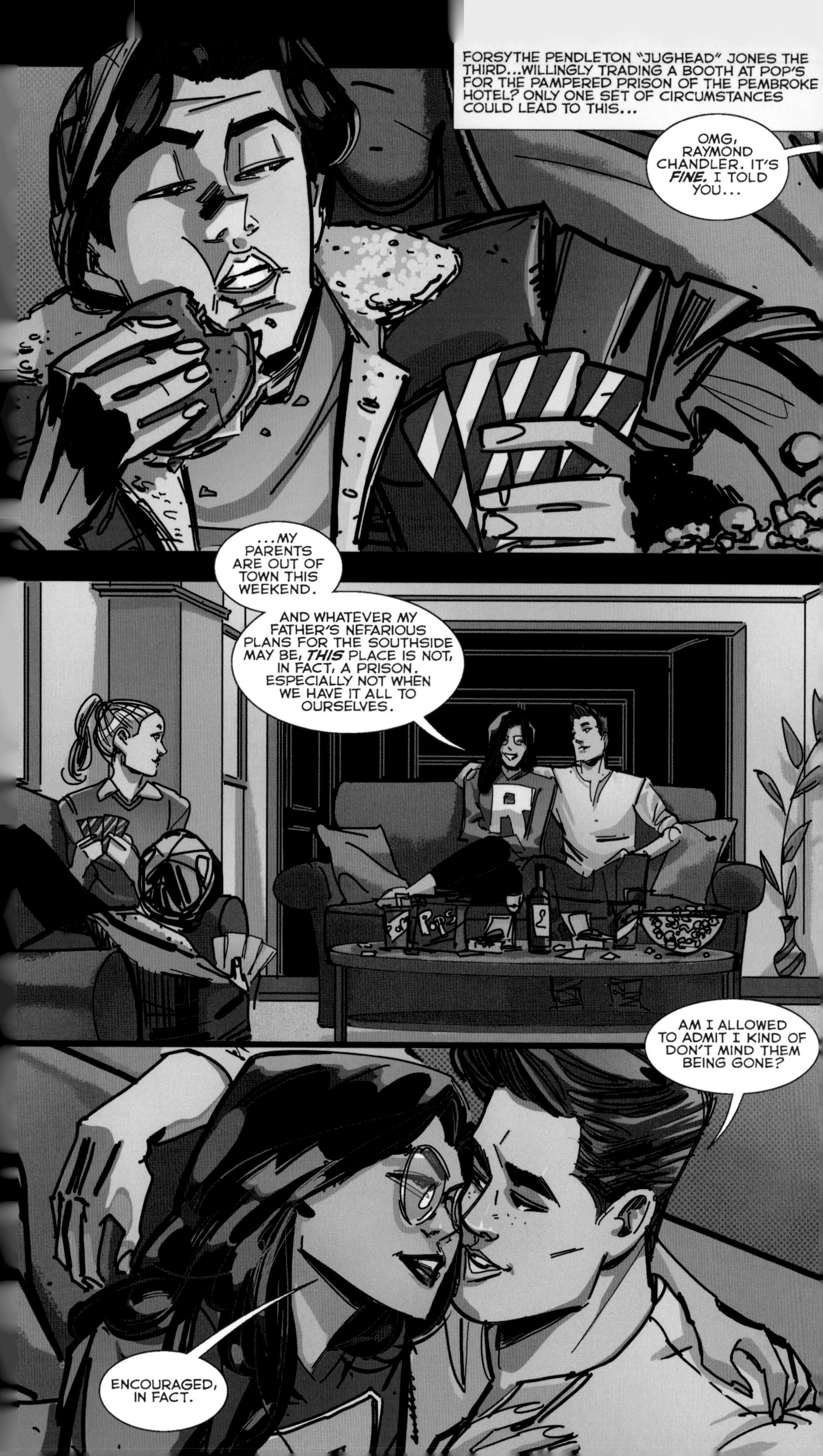
FORSYTHE PENDLETON "JUGHEAD" JONES THE THIRD...WILLINGLY TRADING A BOOTH AT POP'S FOR THE PAMPERED PRISON OF THE PEMBROKE HOTEL? ONLY ONE SET OF CIRCUMSTANCES COULD LEAD TO THIS...
OMG, RAYMOND CHANDLER. IT'S *FINE.* I TOLD YOU...
...MY PARENTS ARE OUT OF TOWN THIS WEEKEND.
AND WHATEVER MY FATHER'S NEFARIOUS PLANS FOR THE SOUTHSIDE MAY BE, *THIS* PLACE IS NOT, IN FACT, A PRISON. ESPECIALLY NOT WHEN WE HAVE IT ALL TO OURSELVES.
AM I ALLOWED TO ADMIT I KIND OF DON'T MIND THEM BEING GONE?
ENCOURAGED, IN FACT.

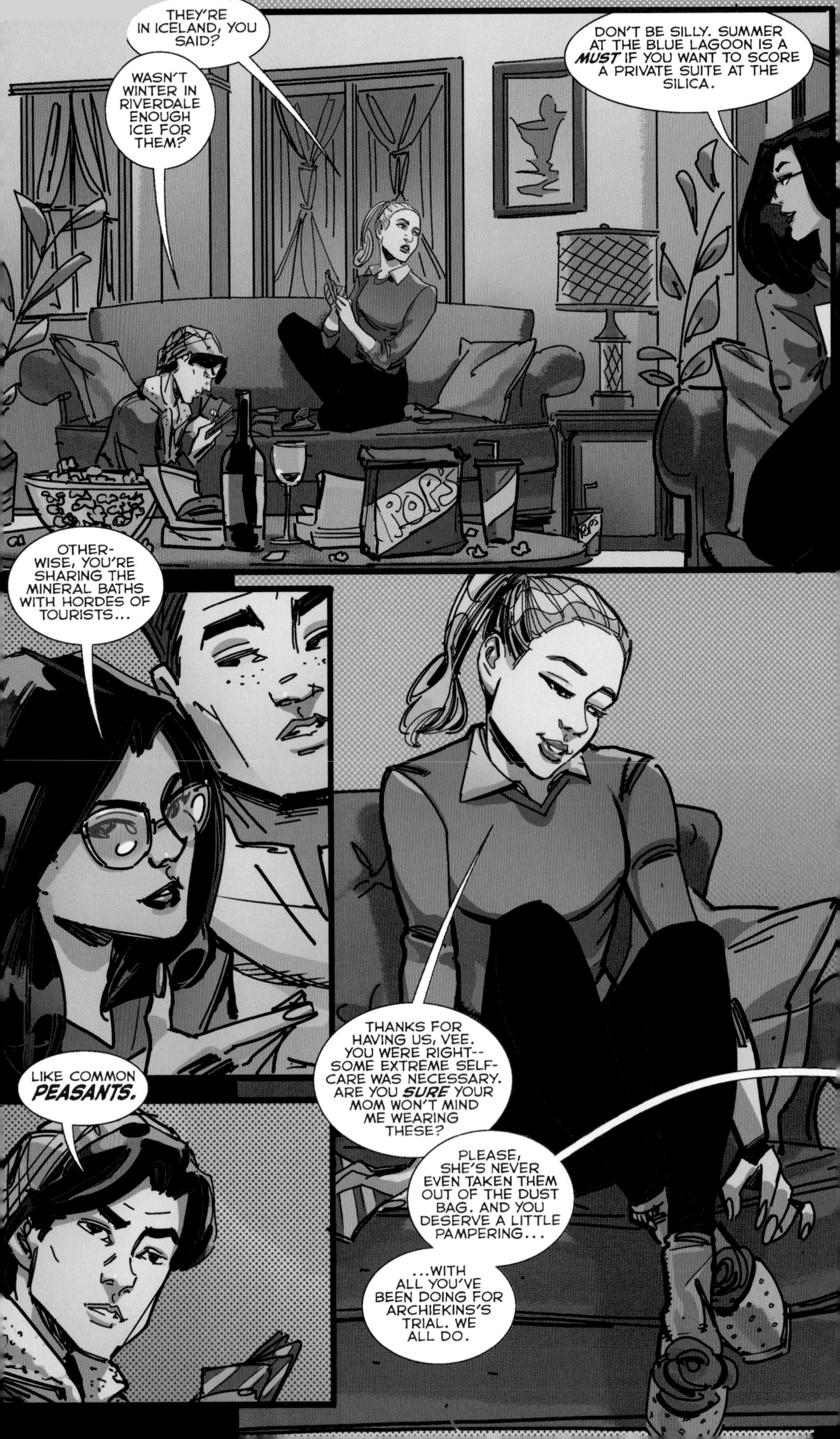
THEY'RE IN ICELAND, YOU SAID?
WASN'T WINTER IN RIVERDALE ENOUGH ICE FOR THEM?
DON'T BE SILLY. SUMMER AT THE BLUE LAGOON IS A *MUST* IF YOU WANT TO SCORE A PRIVATE SUITE AT THE SILICA.
POP'S
OTHER-WISE, YOU'RE SHARING THE MINERAL BATHS WITH HORDES OF TOURISTS...
LIKE COMMON ***PEASANTS.***
THANKS FOR HAVING US, VEE. YOU WERE RIGHT-- SOME EXTREME SELF-CARE WAS NECESSARY. ARE YOU ***SURE*** YOUR MOM WON'T MIND ME WEARING THESE?
PLEASE, SHE'S NEVER EVEN TAKEN THEM OUT OF THE DUST BAG. AND YOU DESERVE A LITTLE PAMPERING...
...WITH ALL YOU'VE BEEN DOING FOR ARCHIEKINS'S TRIAL. WE ALL DO.

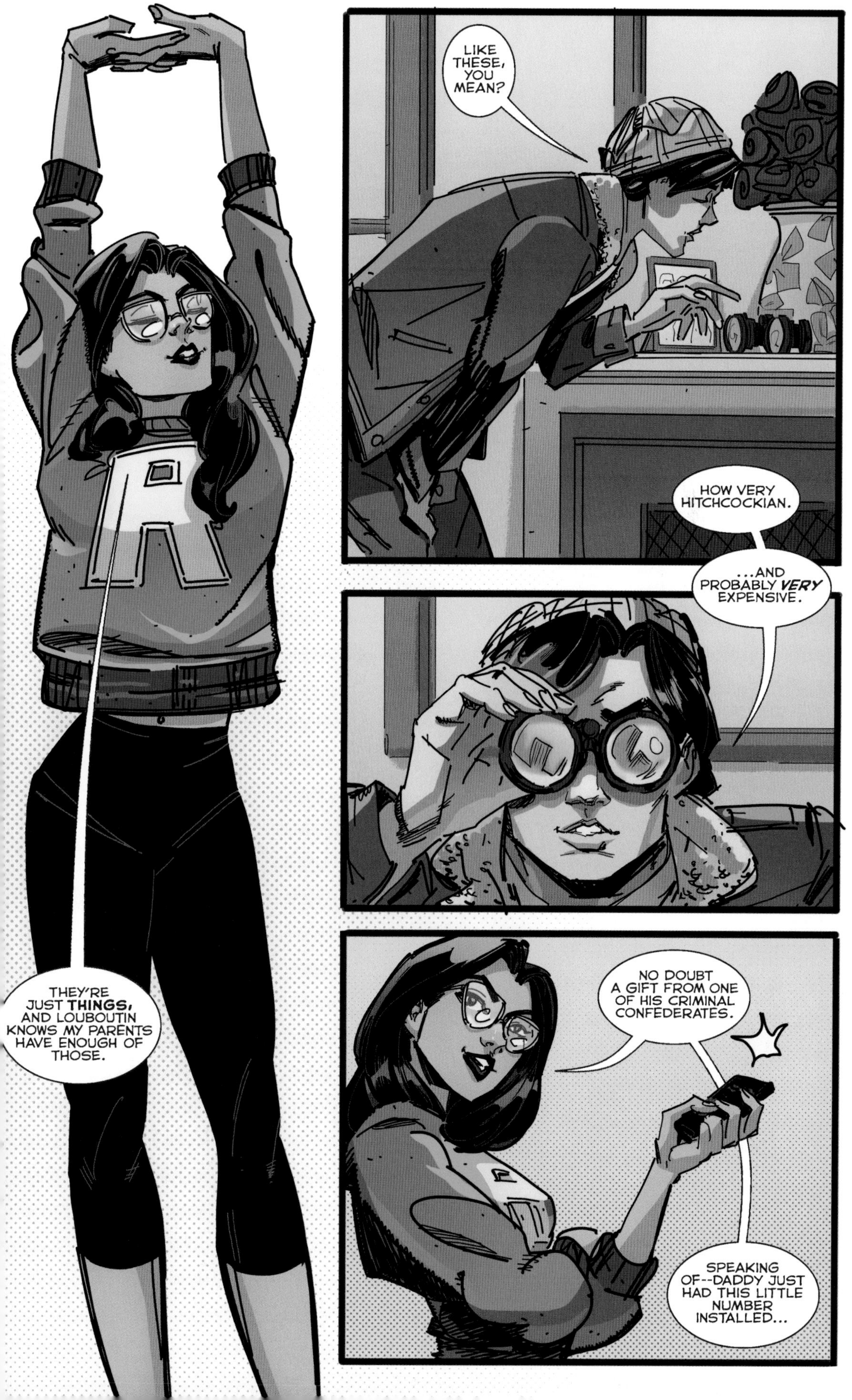
LIKE THESE, YOU MEAN?
HOW VERY HITCHCOCKIAN.
...AND PROBABLY VERY EXPENSIVE.
THEY'RE JUST THINGS, AND LOUBOUTIN KNOWS MY PARENTS HAVE ENOUGH OF THOSE.
NO DOUBT A GIFT FROM ONE OF HIS CRIMINAL CONFEDERATES.
SPEAKING OF--DADDY JUST HAD THIS LITTLE NUMBER INSTALLED...

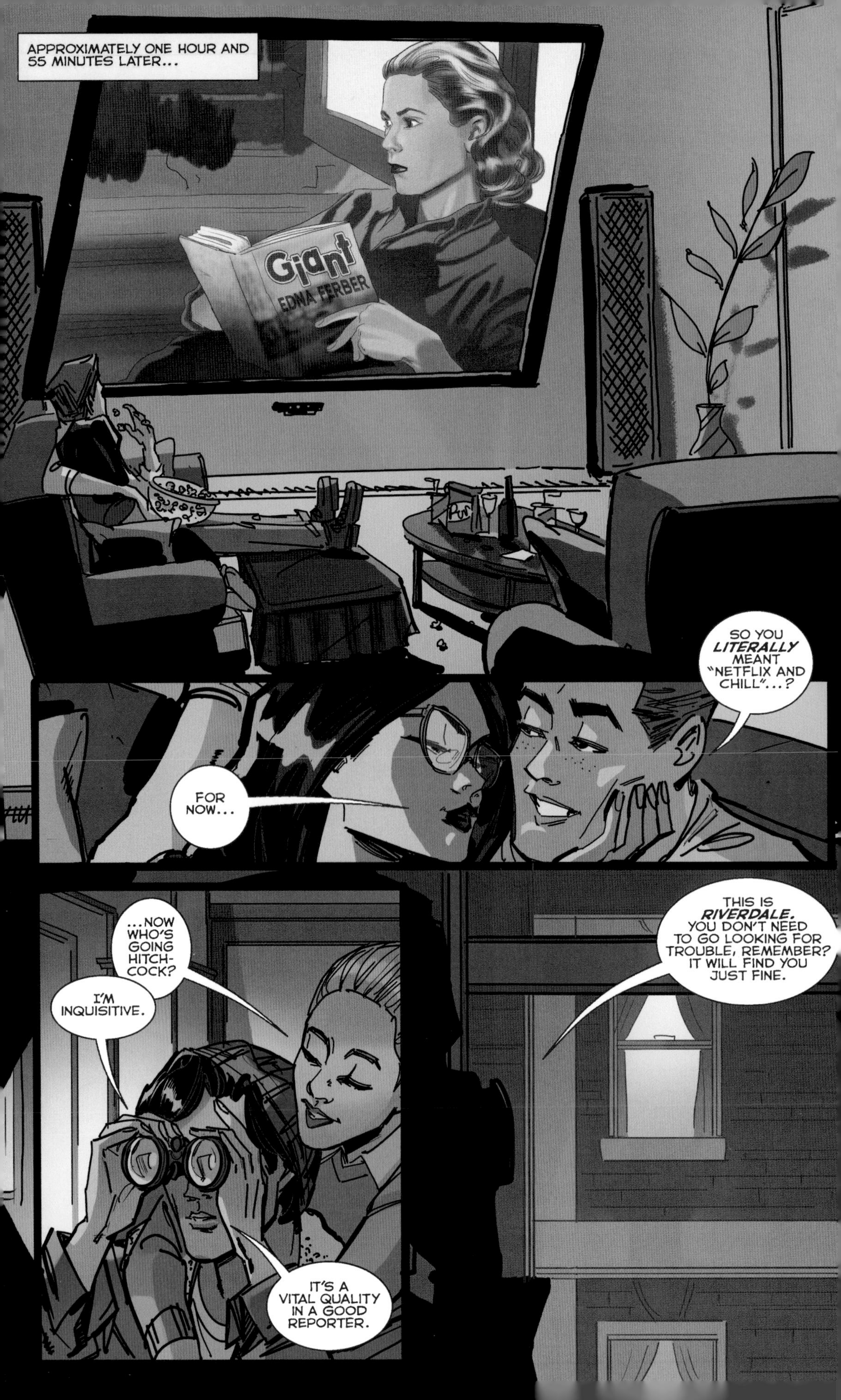
APPROXIMATELY ONE HOUR AND 55 MINUTES LATER...
Giant
EDNA FERBER
SO YOU LITERALLY MEANT "NETFLIX AND CHILL"...?
FOR NOW...
...NOW WHO'S GOING HITCH-COCK?
I'M INQUISITIVE.
IT'S A VITAL QUALITY IN A GOOD REPORTER.
THIS IS RIVERDALE. YOU DON'T NEED TO GO LOOKING FOR TROUBLE, REMEMBER? IT WILL FIND YOU JUST FINE.

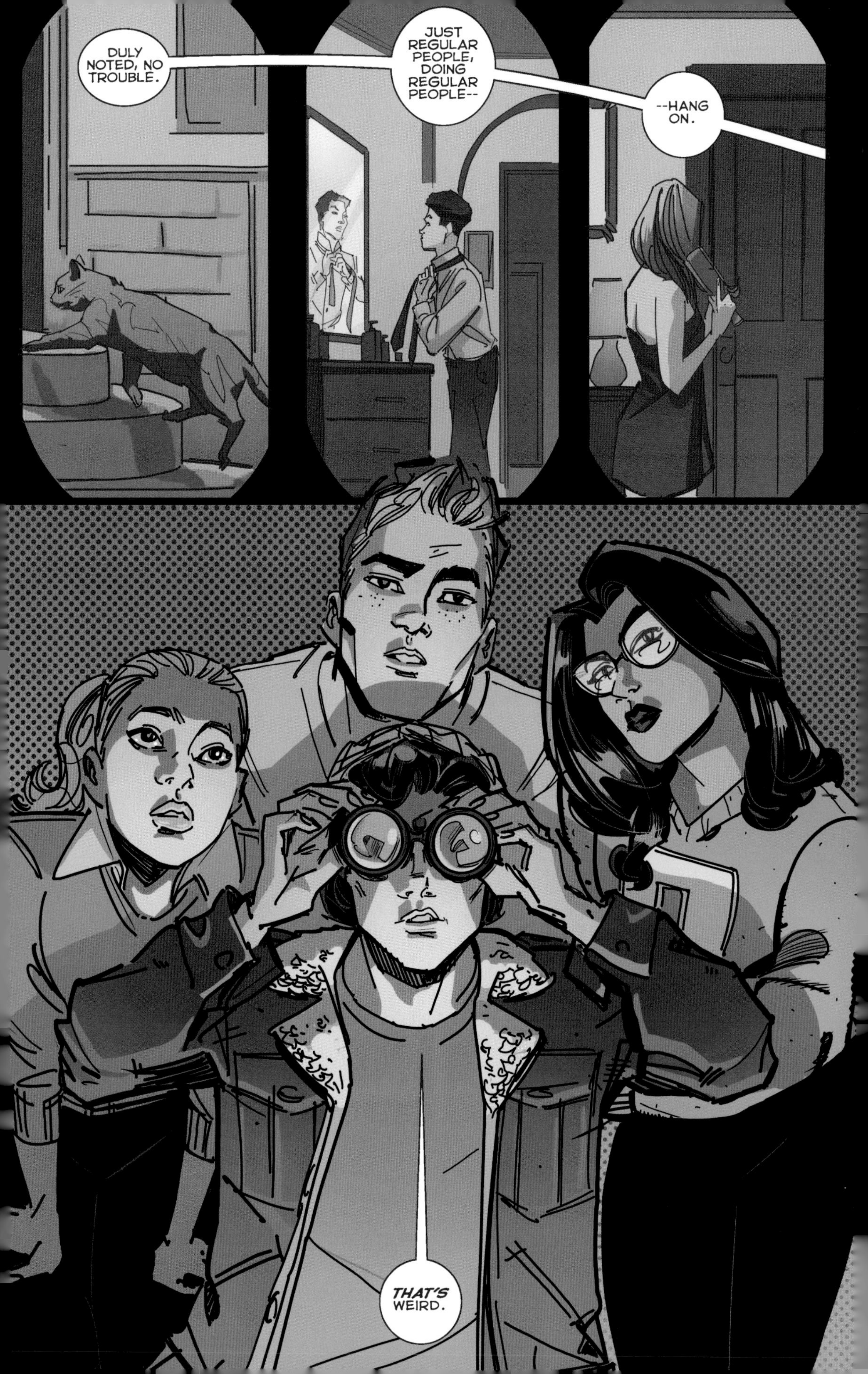
DULY NOTED, NO TROUBLE.
JUST REGULAR PEOPLE, DOING REGULAR PEOPLE--
--HANG ON.
THAT'S WEIRD.

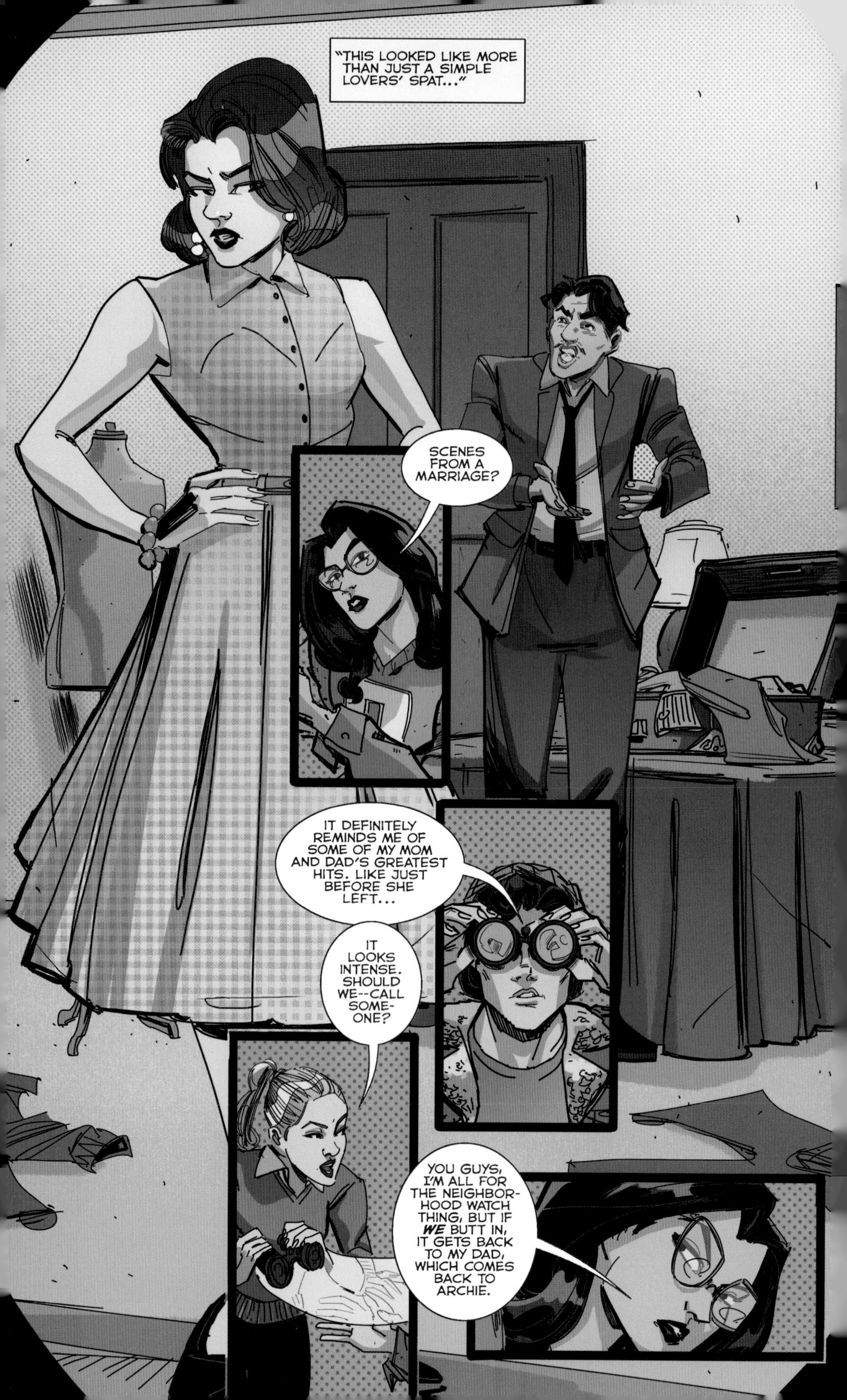
"THIS LOOKED LIKE MORE THAN JUST A SIMPLE LOVERS' SPAT..."
SCENES FROM A MARRIAGE?
IT DEFINITELY REMINDS ME OF SOME OF MY MOM AND DAD'S GREATEST HITS. LIKE JUST BEFORE SHE LEFT...
IT LOOKS INTENSE. SHOULD WE--CALL SOME-ONE?
YOU GUYS, I'M ALL FOR THE NEIGHBOR-HOOD WATCH THING, BUT IF WE BUTT IN, IT GETS BACK TO MY DAD, WHICH COMES BACK TO ARCHIE.

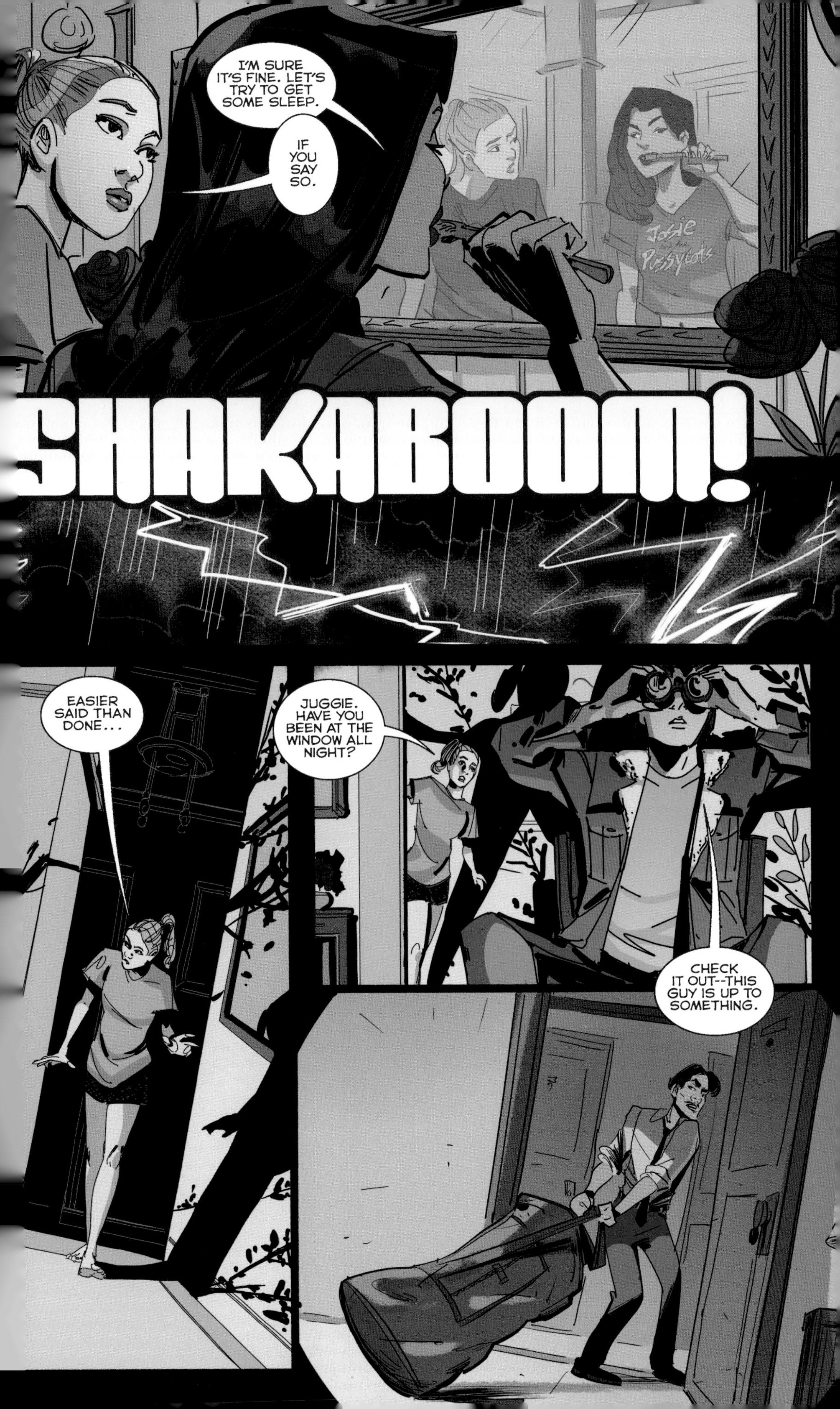
I'M SURE IT'S FINE. LET'S TRY TO GET SOME SLEEP.
IF YOU SAY SO.
Josie and the Pussycats
SHAKABOOM!
EASIER SAID THAN DONE...
JUGGIE. HAVE YOU BEEN AT THE WINDOW ALL NIGHT?
CHECK IT OUT--THIS GUY IS UP TO SOMETHING.

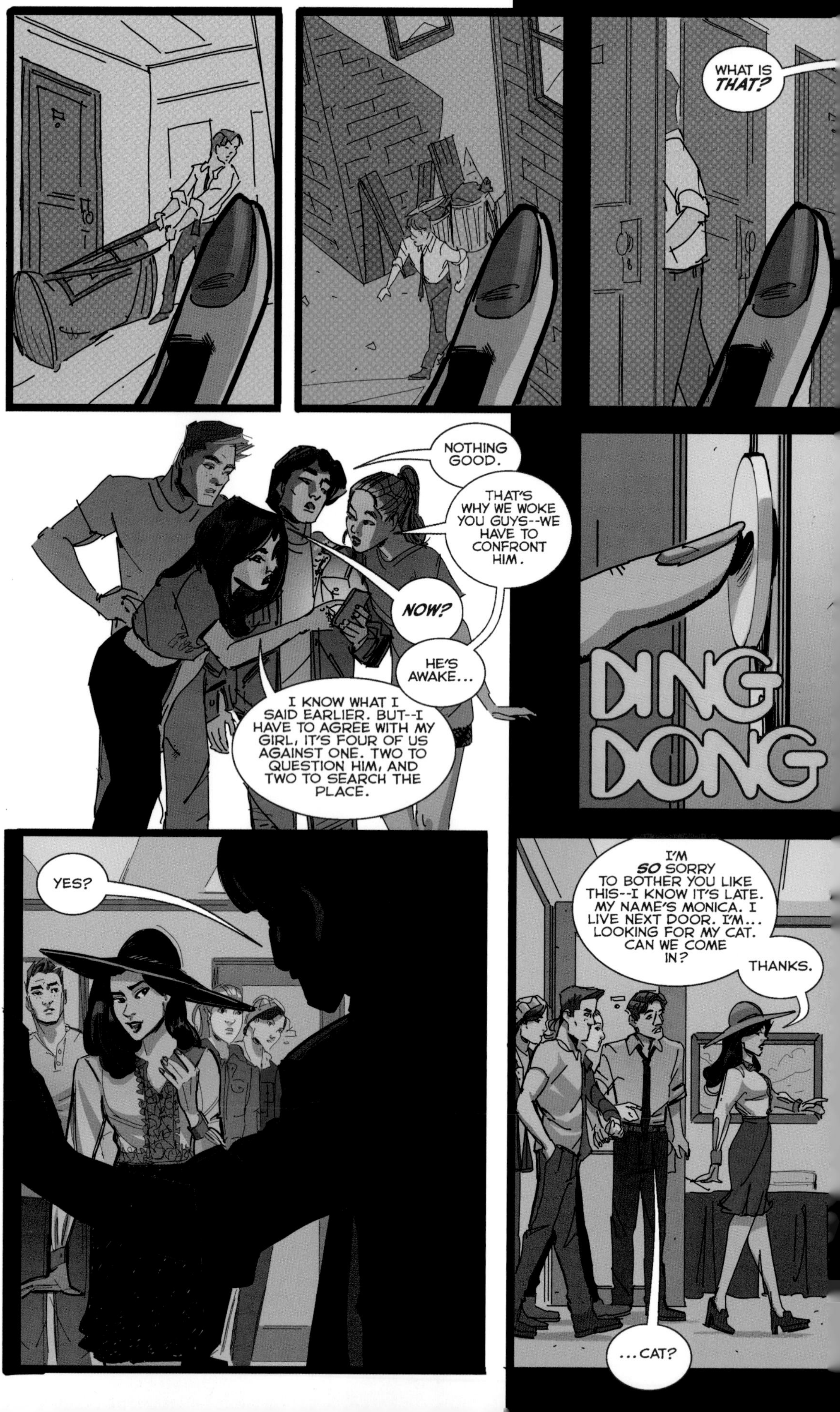

WHAT IS THAT?
NOTHING GOOD.
THAT'S WHY WE WOKE YOU GUYS--WE HAVE TO CONFRONT HIM.
NOW?
HE'S AWAKE...
I KNOW WHAT I SAID EARLIER. BUT--I HAVE TO AGREE WITH MY GIRL, IT'S FOUR OF US AGAINST ONE. TWO TO QUESTION HIM, AND TWO TO SEARCH THE PLACE.
DING DONG
YES?
I'M SO SORRY TO BOTHER YOU LIKE THIS--I KNOW IT'S LATE. MY NAME'S MONICA. I LIVE NEXT DOOR. I'M... LOOKING FOR MY CAT. CAN WE COME IN?
THANKS.
...CAT?

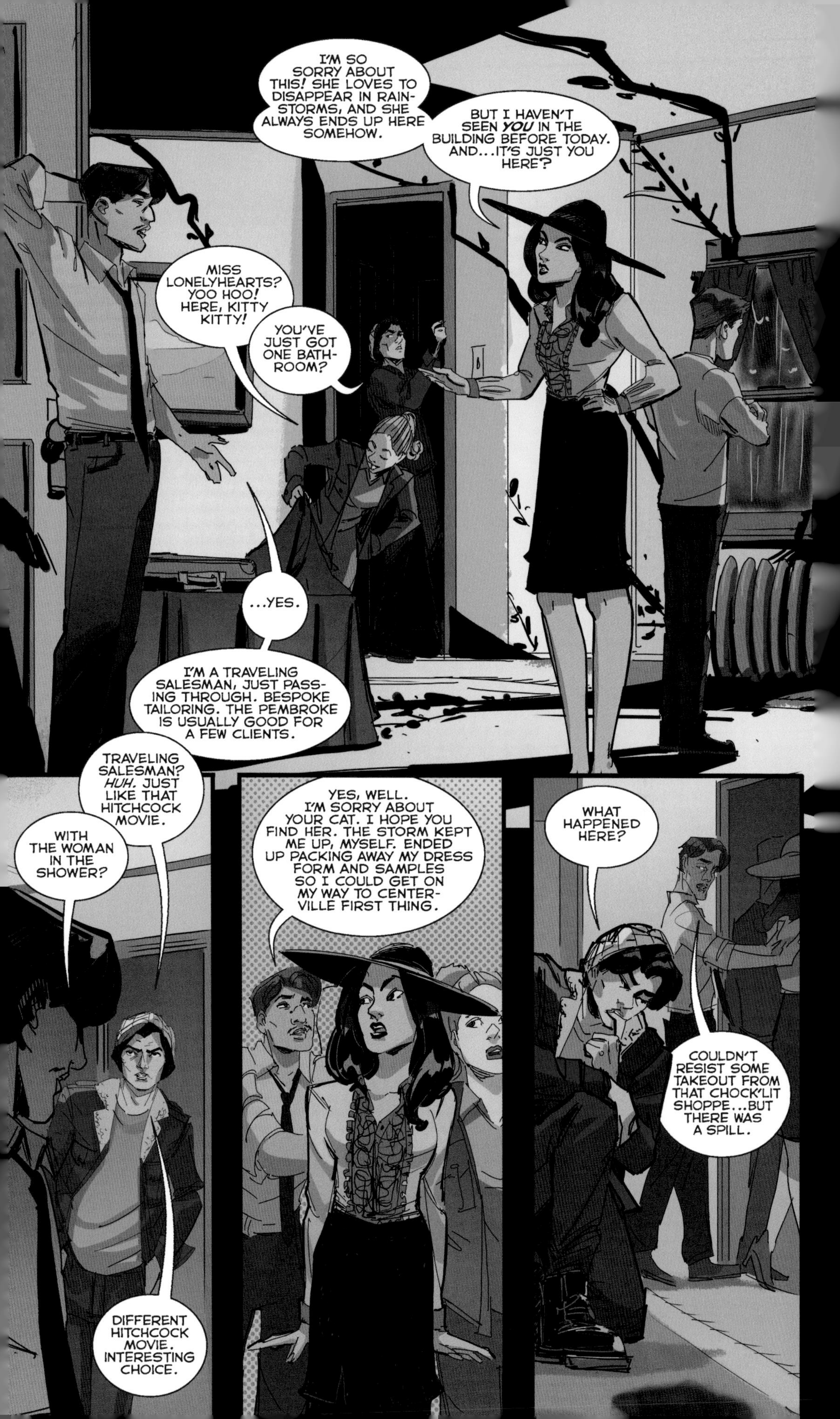
I'M SO SORRY ABOUT THIS! SHE LOVES TO DISAPPEAR IN RAIN-STORMS, AND SHE ALWAYS ENDS UP HERE SOMEHOW.
BUT I HAVEN'T SEEN *YOU* IN THE BUILDING BEFORE TODAY. AND...IT'S JUST YOU HERE?
MISS LONELYHEARTS? YOO HOO! HERE, KITTY KITTY!
YOU'VE JUST GOT ONE BATH-ROOM?
...YES.
I'M A TRAVELING SALESMAN, JUST PASS-ING THROUGH. BESPOKE TAILORING. THE PEMBROKE IS USUALLY GOOD FOR A FEW CLIENTS.
TRAVELING SALESMAN? *HUH.* JUST LIKE THAT HITCHCOCK MOVIE.
WITH THE WOMAN IN THE SHOWER?
DIFFERENT HITCHCOCK MOVIE. INTERESTING CHOICE.
YES, WELL. I'M SORRY ABOUT YOUR CAT. I HOPE YOU FIND HER. THE STORM KEPT ME UP, MYSELF. ENDED UP PACKING AWAY MY DRESS FORM AND SAMPLES SO I COULD GET ON MY WAY TO CENTER-VILLE FIRST THING.
WHAT HAPPENED HERE?
COULDN'T RESIST SOME TAKEOUT FROM THAT CHOCK'LIT SHOPPE...BUT THERE WAS A SPILL.

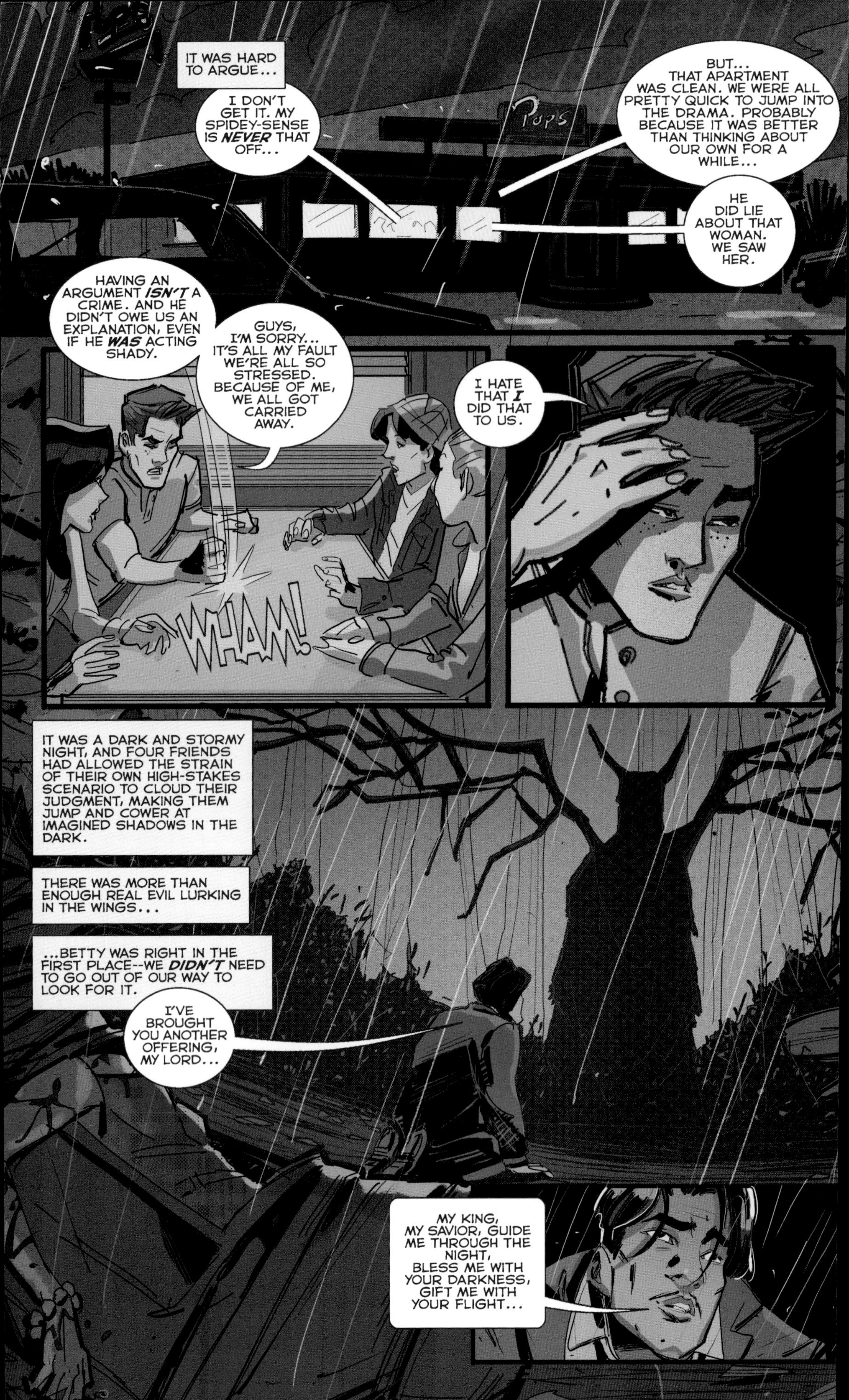
IT WAS HARD TO ARGUE...
I DON'T GET IT. MY SPIDEY-SENSE IS NEVER THAT OFF...
Pop's
BUT... THAT APARTMENT WAS CLEAN. WE WERE ALL PRETTY QUICK TO JUMP INTO THE DRAMA. PROBABLY BECAUSE IT WAS BETTER THAN THINKING ABOUT OUR OWN FOR A WHILE...
HE DID LIE ABOUT THAT WOMAN. WE SAW HER.
HAVING AN ARGUMENT ISN'T A CRIME. AND HE DIDN'T OWE US AN EXPLANATION, EVEN IF HE WAS ACTING SHADY.
GUYS, I'M SORRY... IT'S ALL MY FAULT WE'RE ALL SO STRESSED. BECAUSE OF ME, WE ALL GOT CARRIED AWAY.
WHAM!
I HATE THAT I DID THAT TO US.
IT WAS A DARK AND STORMY NIGHT, AND FOUR FRIENDS HAD ALLOWED THE STRAIN OF THEIR OWN HIGH-STAKES SCENARIO TO CLOUD THEIR JUDGMENT, MAKING THEM JUMP AND COWER AT IMAGINED SHADOWS IN THE DARK.
THERE WAS MORE THAN ENOUGH REAL EVIL LURKING IN THE WINGS...
...BETTY WAS RIGHT IN THE FIRST PLACE--WE DIDN'T NEED TO GO OUT OF OUR WAY TO LOOK FOR IT.
I'VE BROUGHT YOU ANOTHER OFFERING, MY LORD...
MY KING, MY SAVIOR, GUIDE ME THROUGH THE NIGHT, BLESS ME WITH YOUR DARKNESS, GIFT ME WITH YOUR FLIGHT...

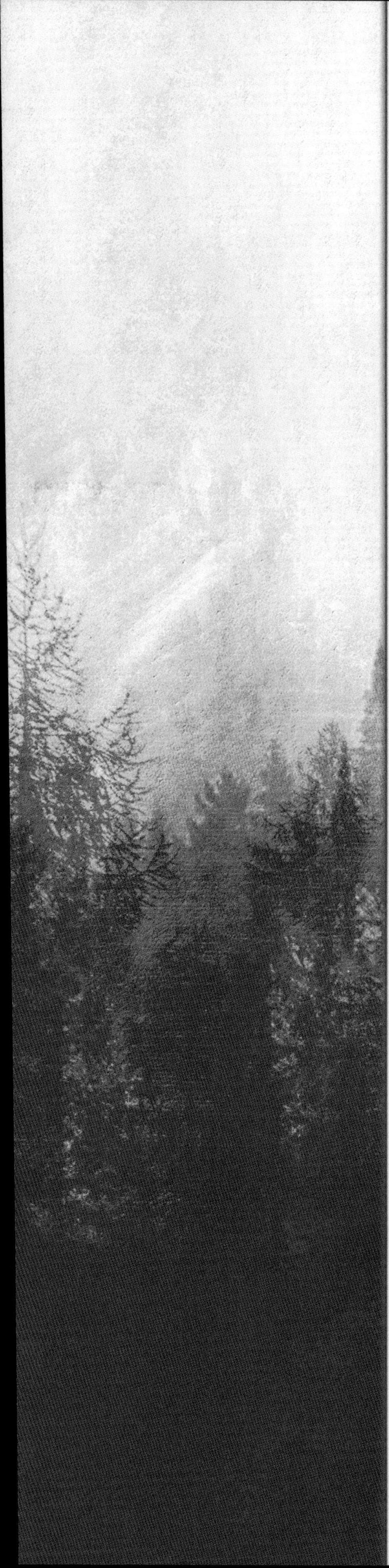

CHAPTER TWO

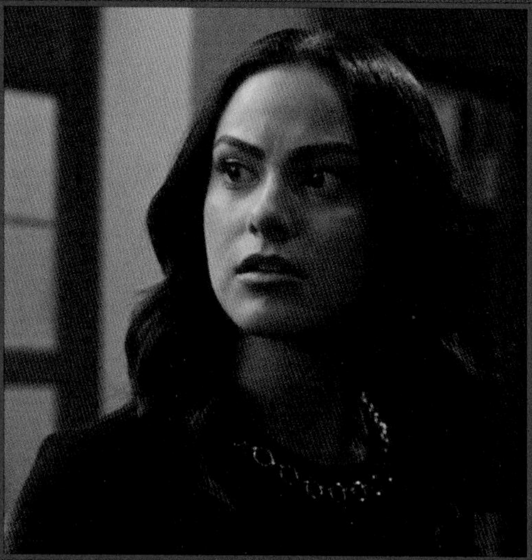

MOMMIE DEAREST

WRITER:
MICOL OSTOW

ART:
JOE EISMA

COLORS:
MATT HERMS

LETTERS:
JANICE CHIANG

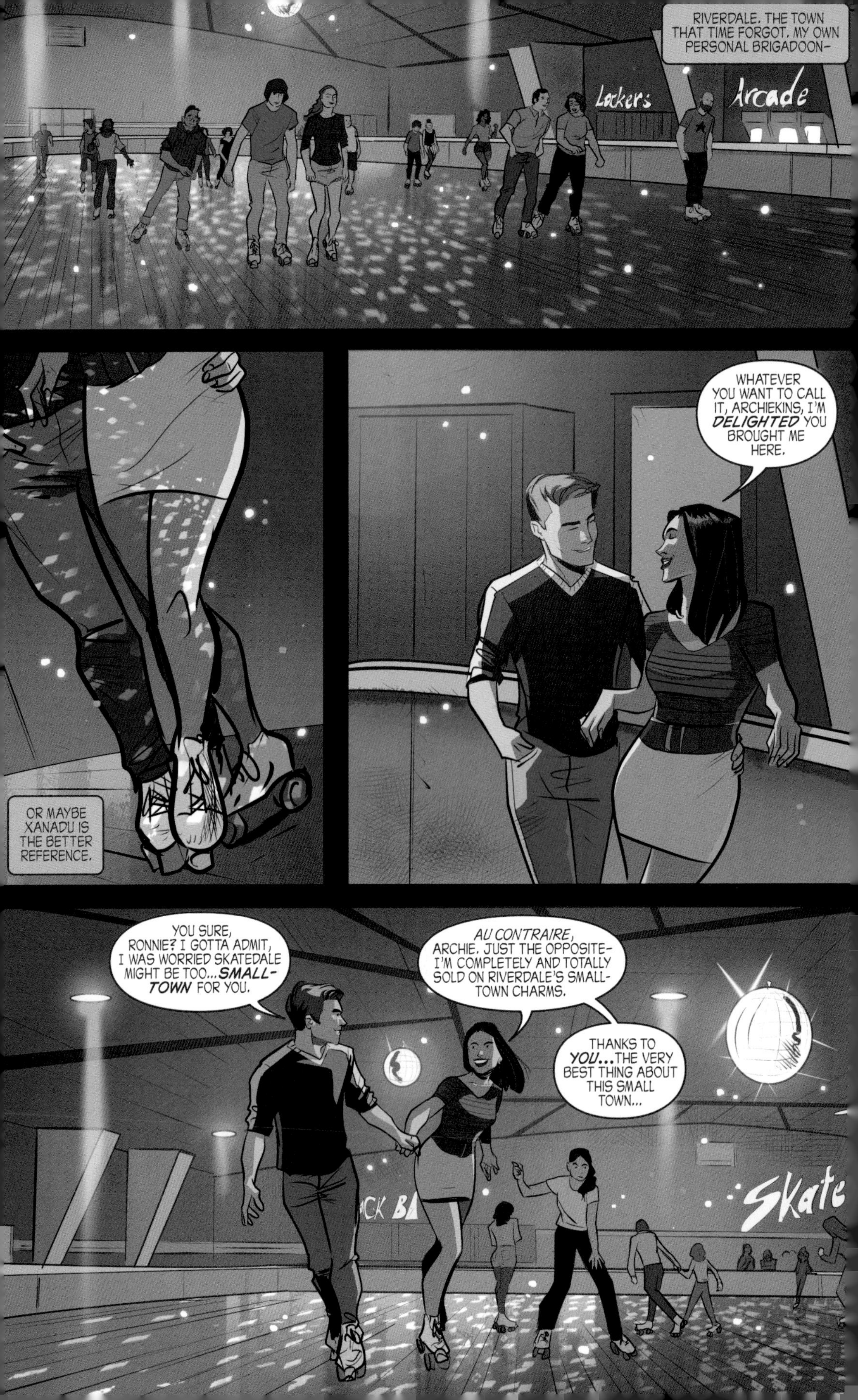
RIVERDALE. THE TOWN THAT TIME FORGOT. MY OWN PERSONAL BRIGADOON–
Lockers
Arcade
OR MAYBE XANADU IS THE BETTER REFERENCE.
WHATEVER YOU WANT TO CALL IT, ARCHIEKINS, I'M *DELIGHTED* YOU BROUGHT ME HERE.
YOU SURE, RONNIE? I GOTTA ADMIT, I WAS WORRIED SKATEDALE MIGHT BE TOO...*SMALL-TOWN* FOR YOU.
AU CONTRAIRE, ARCHIE. JUST THE OPPOSITE–I'M COMPLETELY AND TOTALLY SOLD ON RIVERDALE'S SMALL-TOWN CHARMS.
THANKS TO *YOU*...THE VERY BEST THING ABOUT THIS SMALL TOWN...
Skate

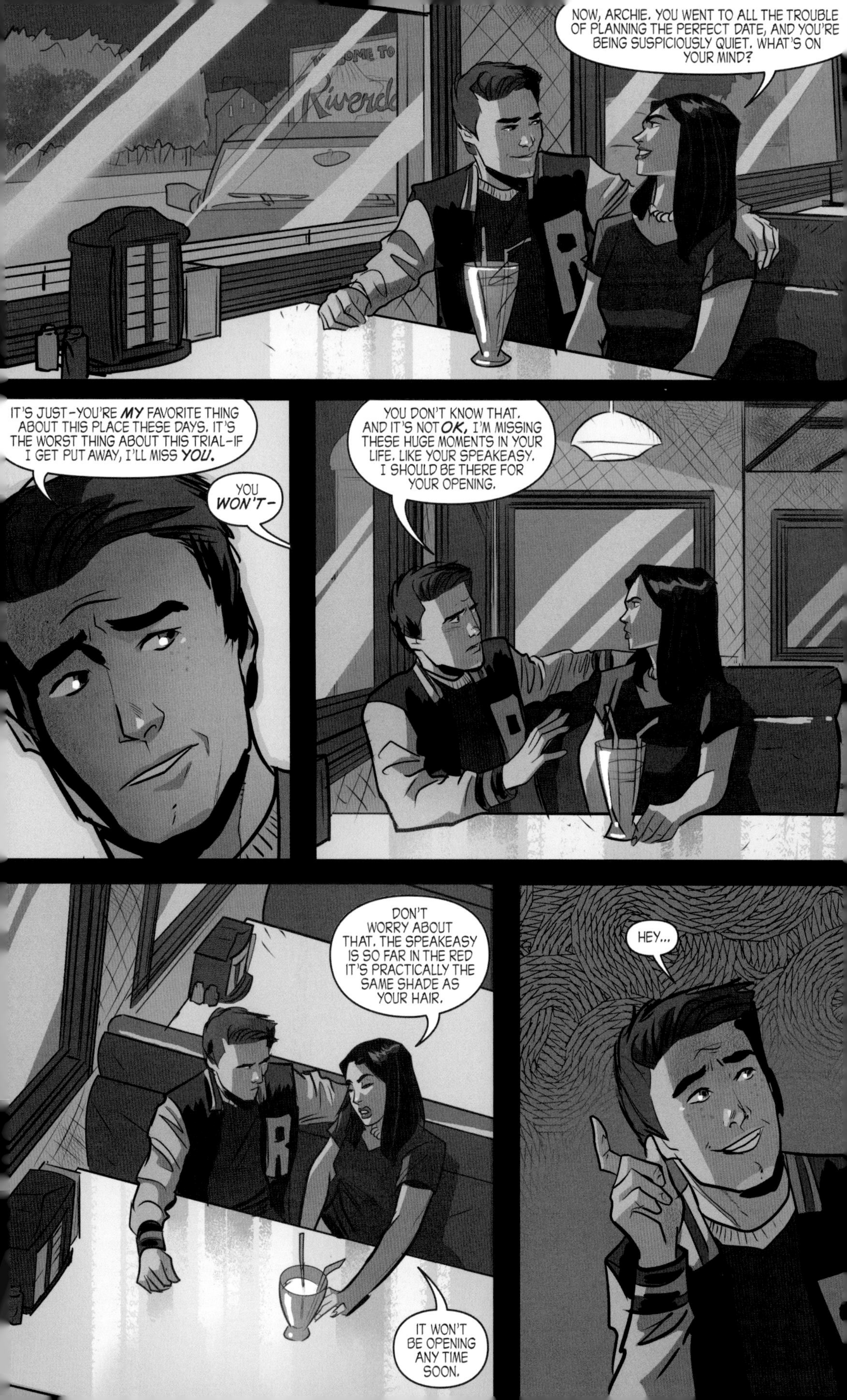
NOW, ARCHIE. YOU WENT TO ALL THE TROUBLE OF PLANNING THE PERFECT DATE, AND YOU'RE BEING SUSPICIOUSLY QUIET. WHAT'S ON YOUR MIND?
IT'S JUST-YOU'RE *MY* FAVORITE THING ABOUT THIS PLACE THESE DAYS. IT'S THE WORST THING ABOUT THIS TRIAL-IF I GET PUT AWAY, I'LL MISS *YOU.*
YOU *WON'T-*
YOU DON'T KNOW THAT. AND IT'S NOT *OK,* I'M MISSING THESE HUGE MOMENTS IN YOUR LIFE. LIKE YOUR SPEAKEASY. I SHOULD BE THERE FOR YOUR OPENING.
DON'T WORRY ABOUT THAT. THE SPEAKEASY IS SO FAR IN THE RED IT'S PRACTICALLY THE SAME SHADE AS YOUR HAIR.
IT WON'T BE OPENING ANY TIME SOON.
HEY...

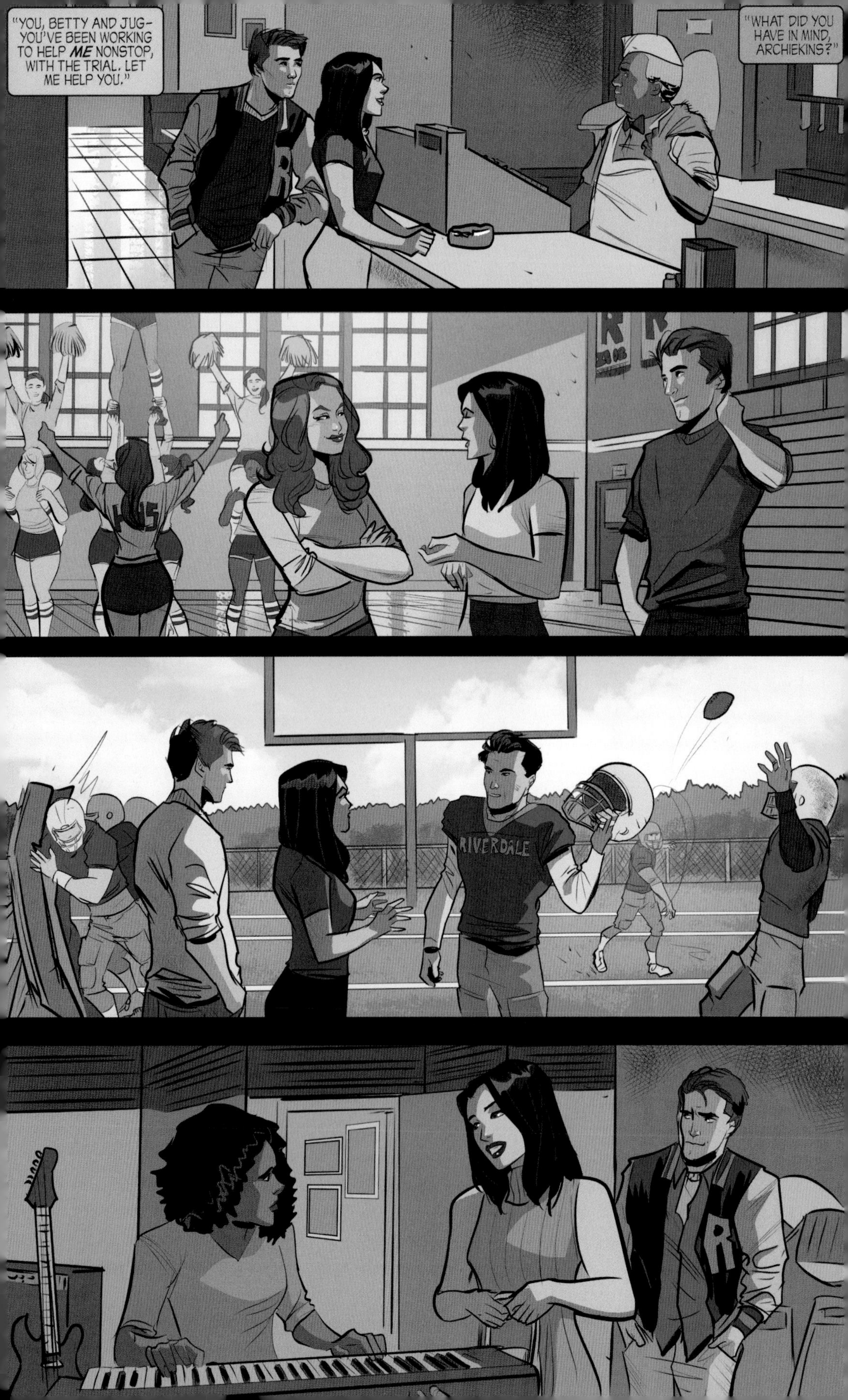
"YOU, BETTY AND JUG-YOU'VE BEEN WORKING TO HELP *ME* NONSTOP, WITH THE TRIAL. LET ME HELP YOU."
"WHAT DID YOU HAVE IN MIND, ARCHIEKINS?"
RIVERDALE

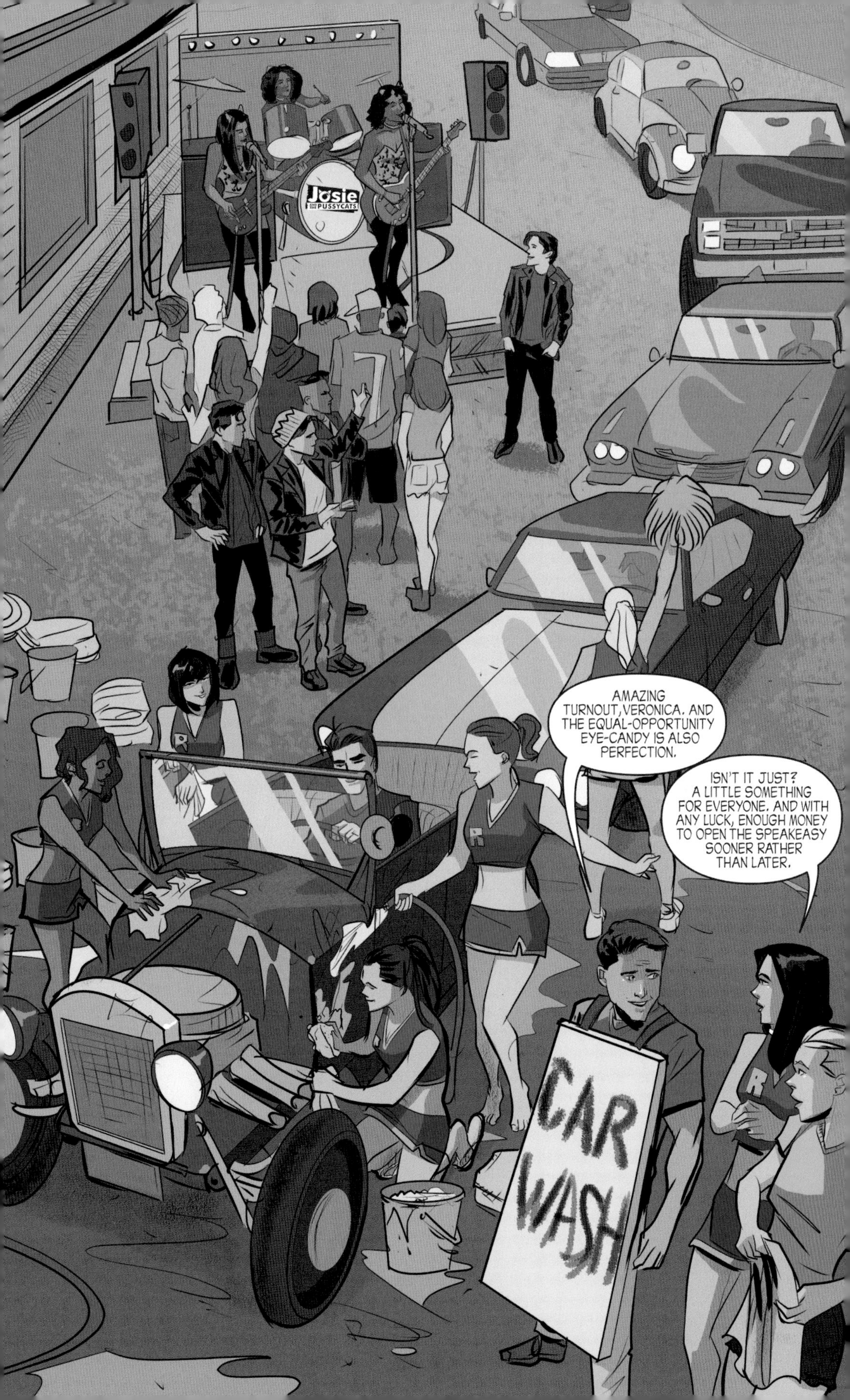
Josie AND THE PUSSYCATS
AMAZING TURNOUT, VERONICA. AND THE EQUAL-OPPORTUNITY EYE-CANDY IS ALSO PERFECTION.
ISN'T IT JUST? A LITTLE SOMETHING FOR EVERYONE. AND WITH ANY LUCK, ENOUGH MONEY TO OPEN THE SPEAKEASY SOONER RATHER THAN LATER.
CAR WASH

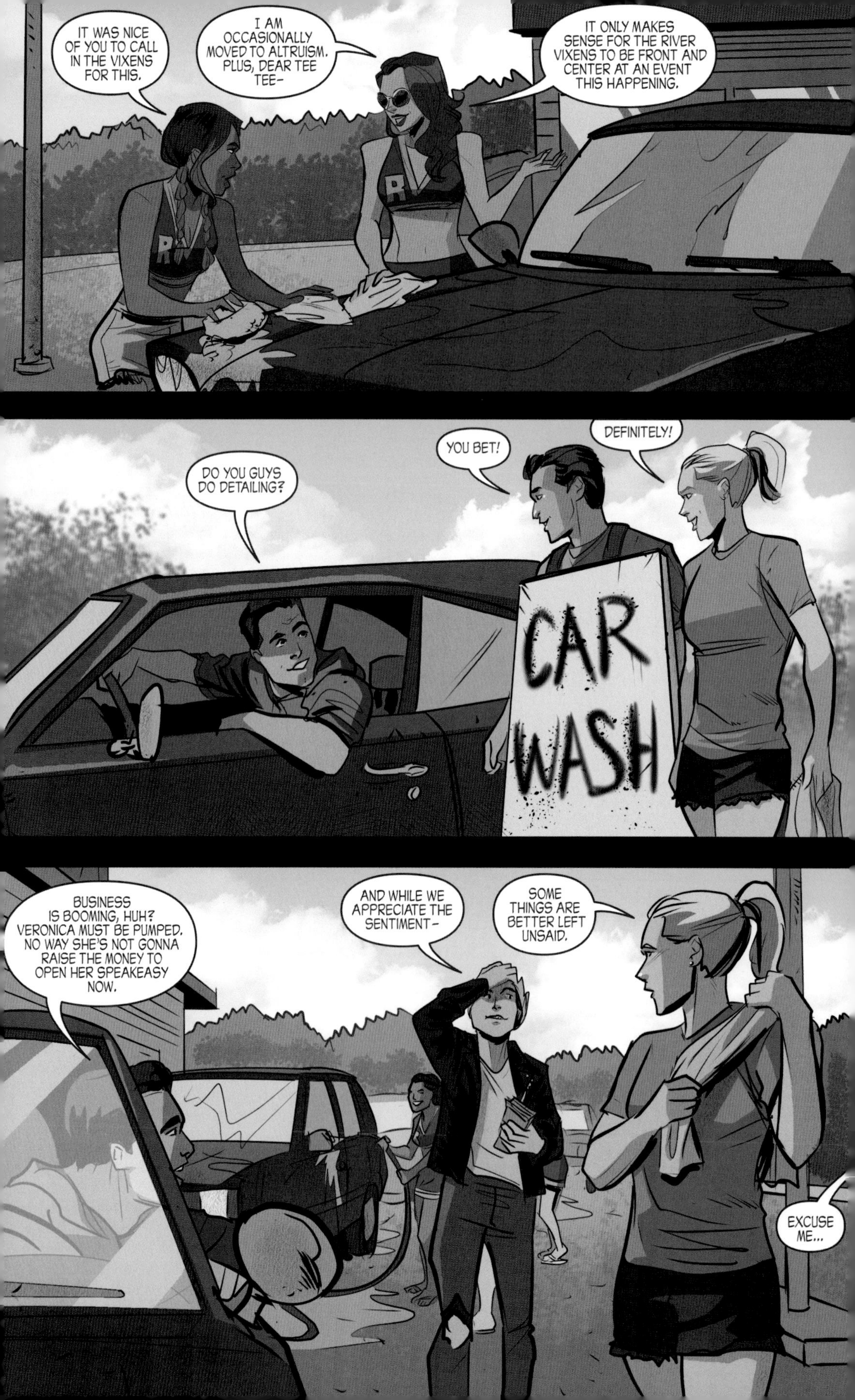
IT WAS NICE OF YOU TO CALL IN THE VIXENS FOR THIS.
I AM OCCASIONALLY MOVED TO ALTRUISM. PLUS, DEAR TEE TEE-
IT ONLY MAKES SENSE FOR THE RIVER VIXENS TO BE FRONT AND CENTER AT AN EVENT THIS HAPPENING.
DO YOU GUYS DO DETAILING?
YOU BET!
DEFINITELY!
CAR WASH
BUSINESS IS BOOMING, HUH? VERONICA MUST BE PUMPED. NO WAY SHE'S NOT GONNA RAISE THE MONEY TO OPEN HER SPEAKEASY NOW.
AND WHILE WE APPRECIATE THE SENTIMENT-
SOME THINGS ARE BETTER LEFT UNSAID.
EXCUSE ME...

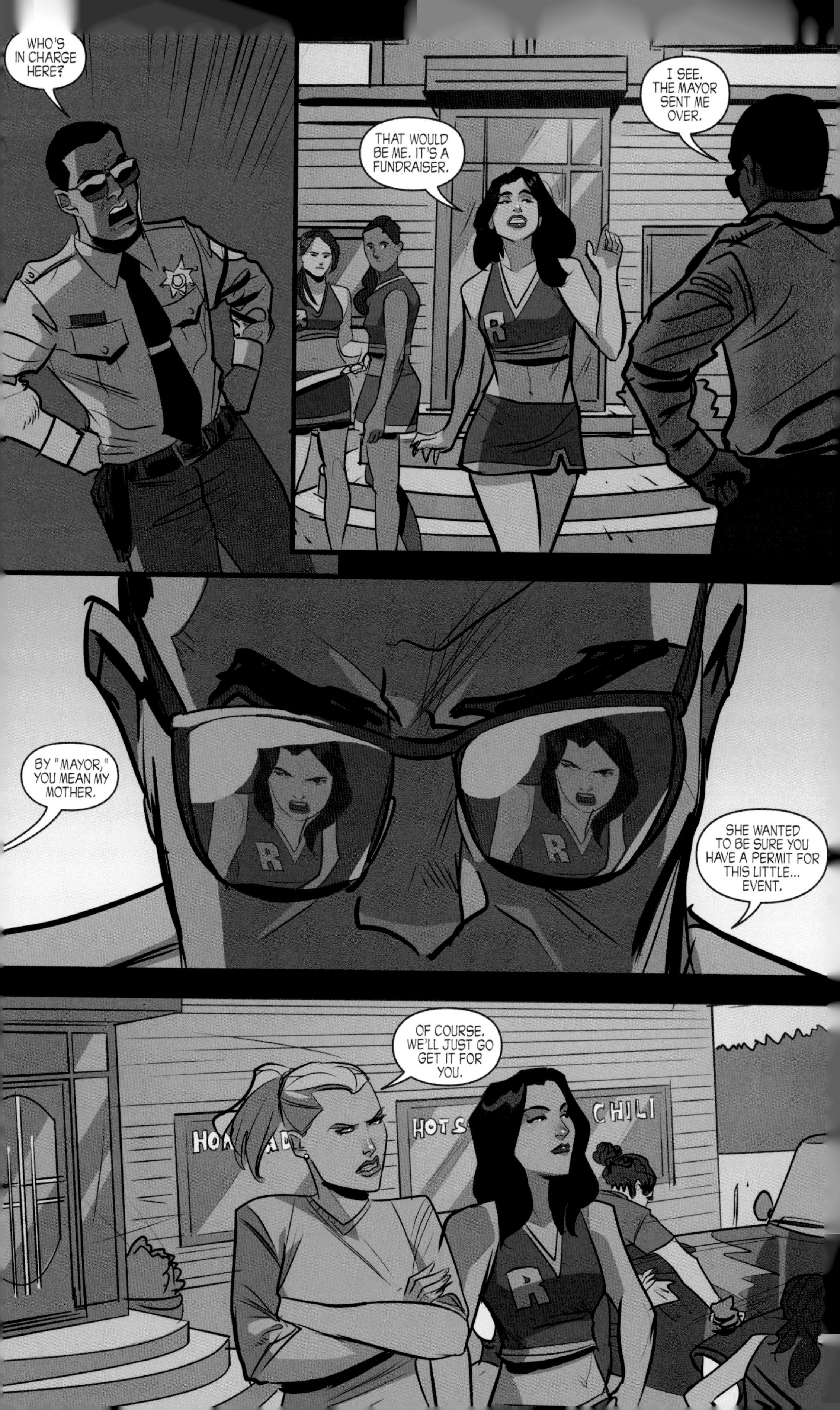
WHO'S IN CHARGE HERE?
THAT WOULD BE ME. IT'S A FUNDRAISER.
I SEE. THE MAYOR SENT ME OVER.
BY "MAYOR," YOU MEAN MY MOTHER.
SHE WANTED TO BE SURE YOU HAVE A PERMIT FOR THIS LITTLE... EVENT.
OF COURSE. WE'LL JUST GO GET IT FOR YOU.
CHILI

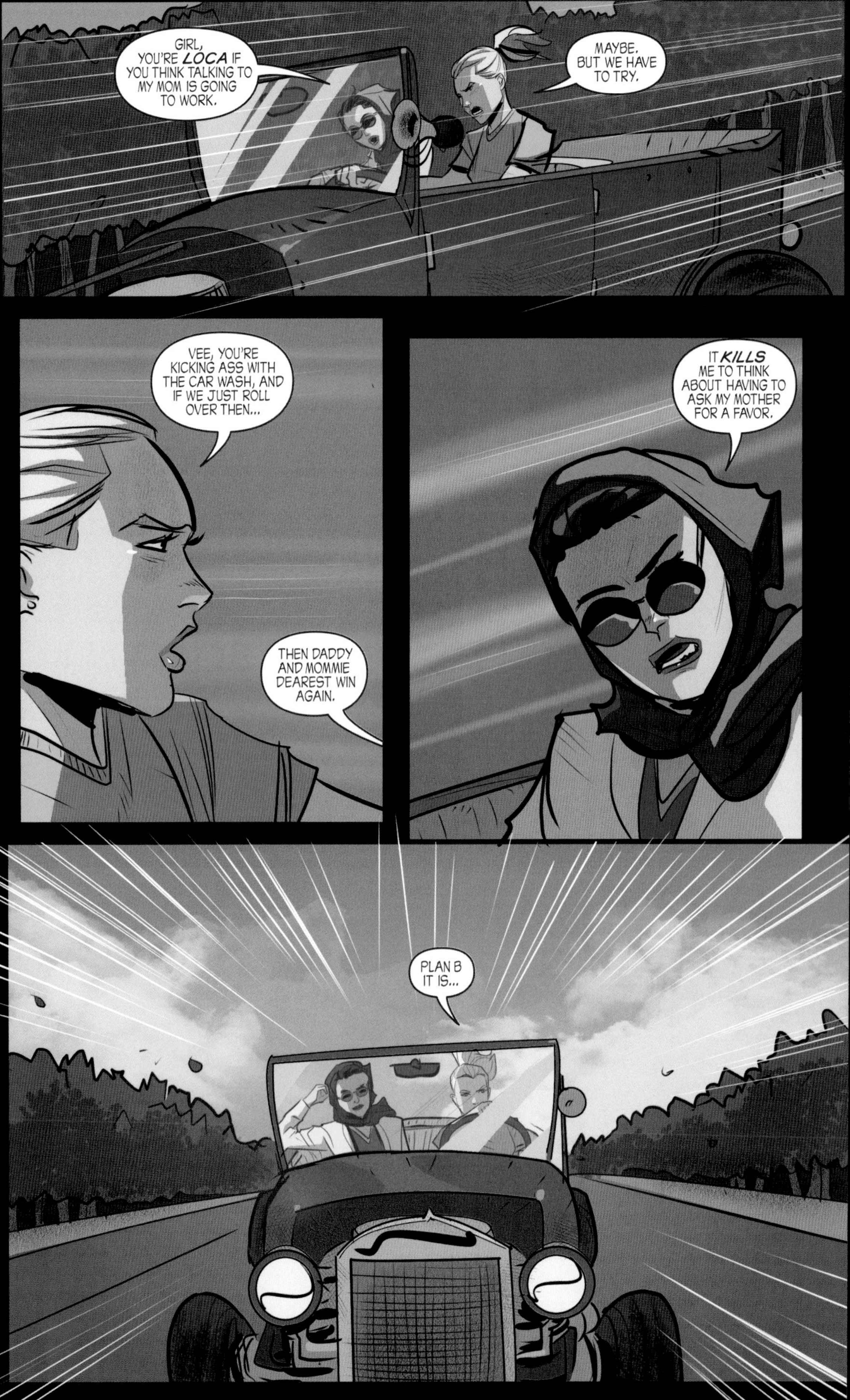
GIRL, YOU'RE LOCA IF YOU THINK TALKING TO MY MOM IS GOING TO WORK.
MAYBE. BUT WE HAVE TO TRY.
VEE, YOU'RE KICKING ASS WITH THE CAR WASH, AND IF WE JUST ROLL OVER THEN...
THEN DADDY AND MOMMIE DEAREST WIN AGAIN.
IT KILLS ME TO THINK ABOUT HAVING TO ASK MY MOTHER FOR A FAVOR.
PLAN B IT IS...

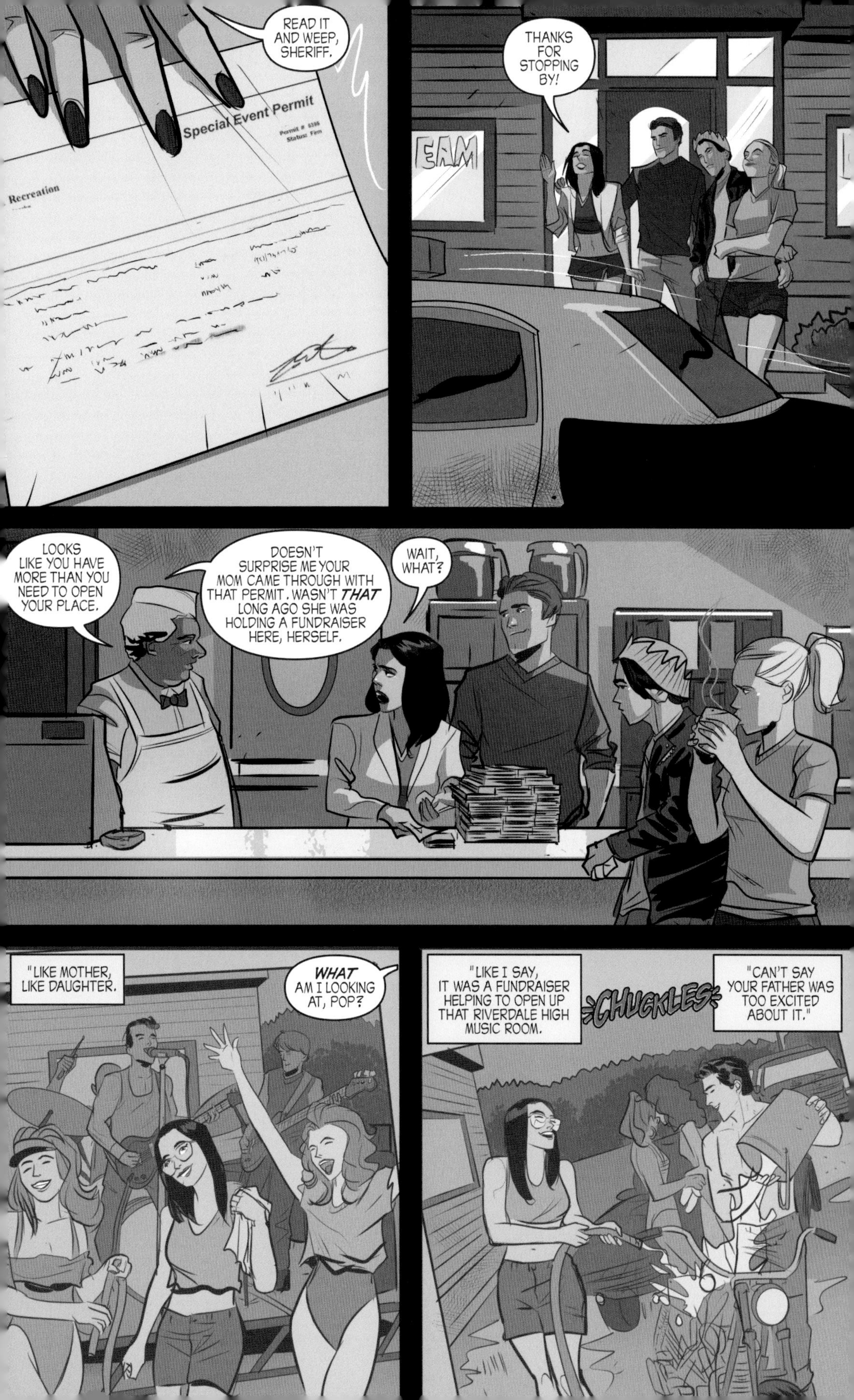

READ IT AND WEEP, SHERIFF.
Special Event Permit
Recreation
THANKS FOR STOPPING BY!
LOOKS LIKE YOU HAVE MORE THAN YOU NEED TO OPEN YOUR PLACE.
DOESN'T SURPRISE ME YOUR MOM CAME THROUGH WITH THAT PERMIT. WASN'T *THAT* LONG AGO SHE WAS HOLDING A FUNDRAISER HERE, HERSELF.
WAIT, WHAT?
"LIKE MOTHER, LIKE DAUGHTER.
WHAT AM I LOOKING AT, POP?
"LIKE I SAY, IT WAS A FUNDRAISER HELPING TO OPEN UP THAT RIVERDALE HIGH MUSIC ROOM.
CHUCKLES
"CAN'T SAY YOUR FATHER WAS TOO EXCITED ABOUT IT."

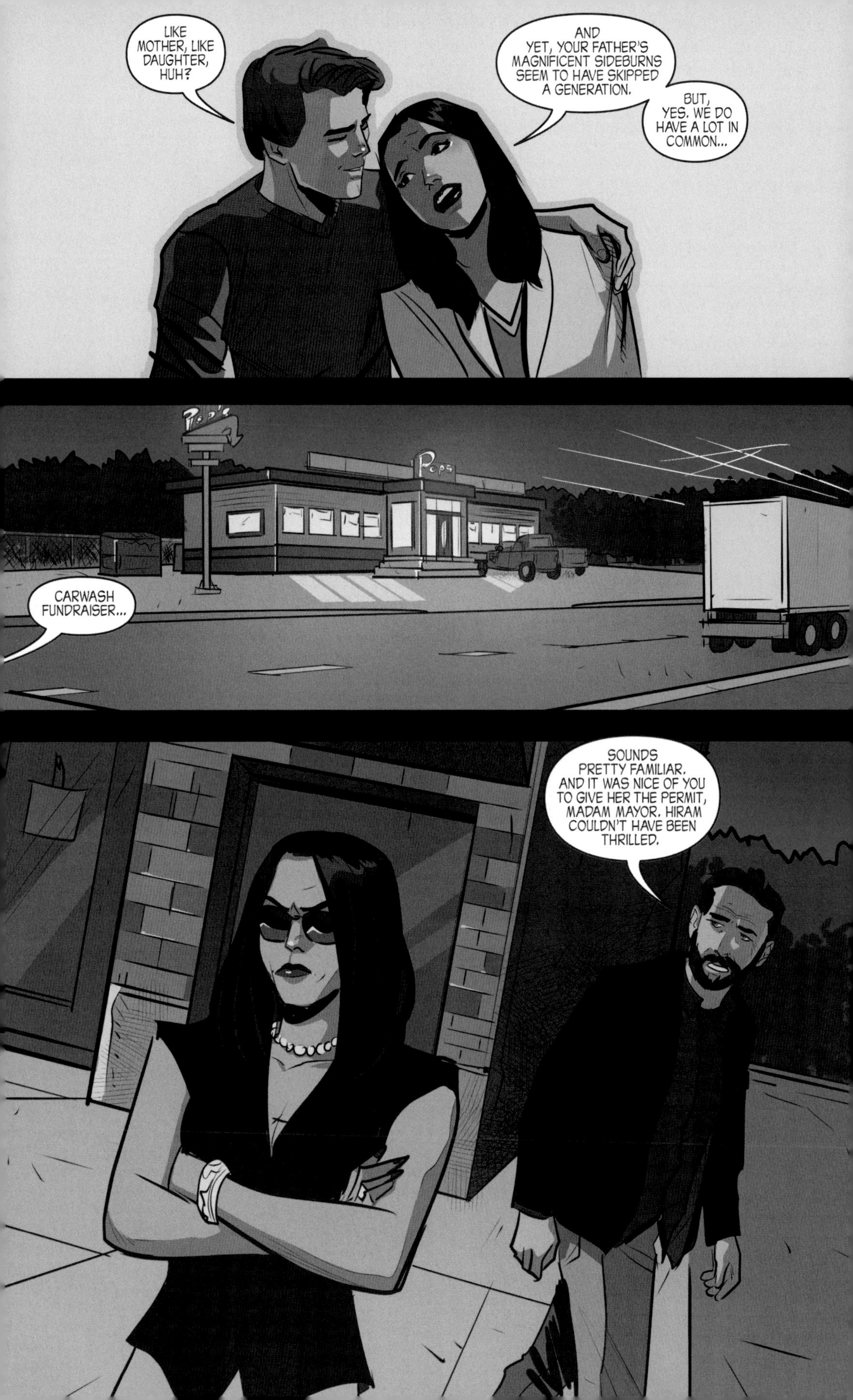
LIKE MOTHER, LIKE DAUGHTER, HUH?
AND YET, YOUR FATHER'S MAGNIFICENT SIDEBURNS SEEM TO HAVE SKIPPED A GENERATION.
BUT, YES. WE DO HAVE A LOT IN COMMON...
CARWASH FUNDRAISER...
SOUNDS PRETTY FAMILIAR. AND IT WAS NICE OF YOU TO GIVE HER THE PERMIT, MADAM MAYOR. HIRAM COULDN'T HAVE BEEN THRILLED.

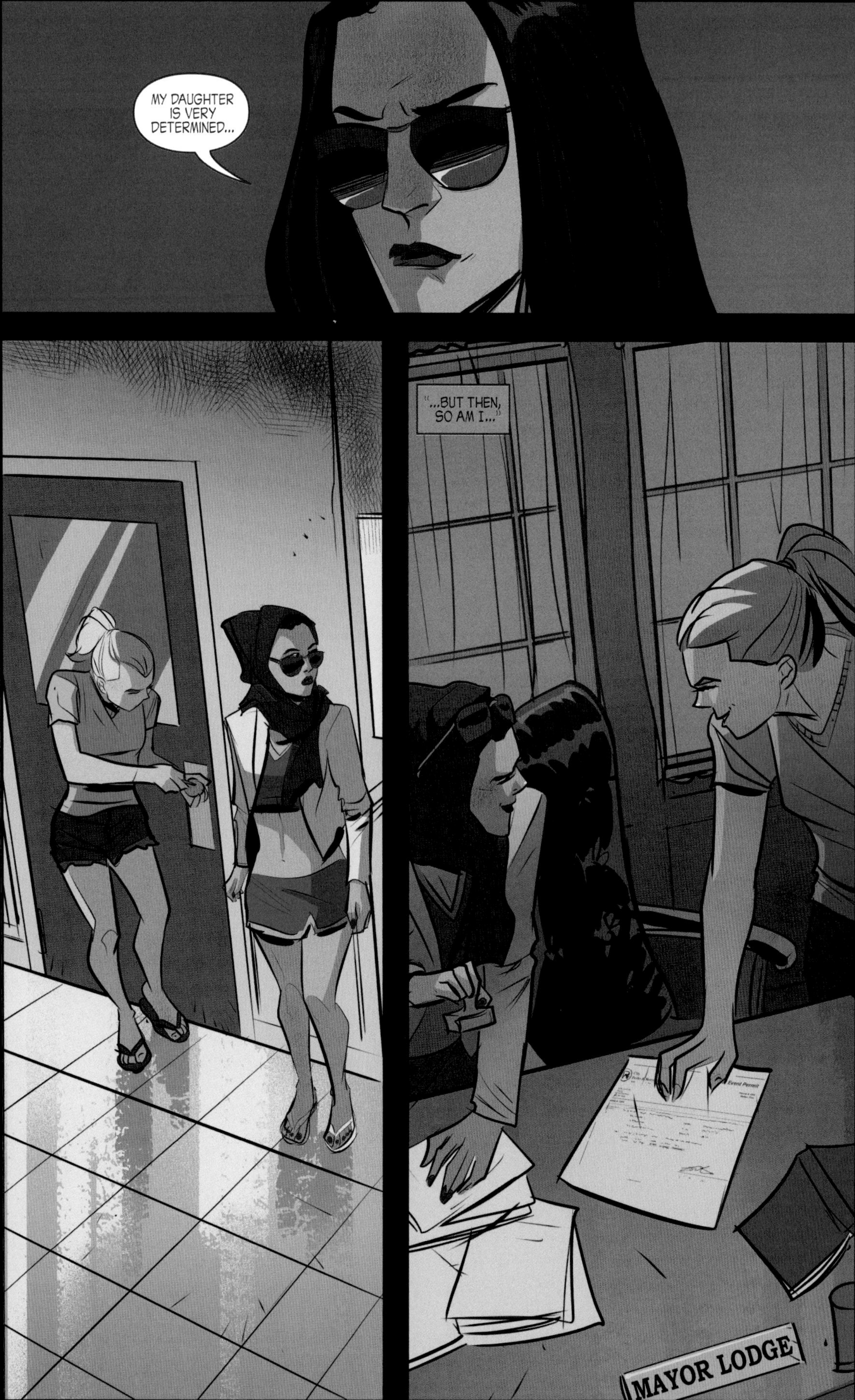
MY DAUGHTER IS VERY DETERMINED...
"...BUT THEN, SO AM I..."
Event Permit
MAYOR LODGE

CHAPTER THREE

COLD COMFORT
FARM

WRITER:
MICOL OSTOW

ART:
THOMAS PITILLI

COLORS:
ANDRE SZYMANOWICZ

LETTERS:
JOHN WORKMAN

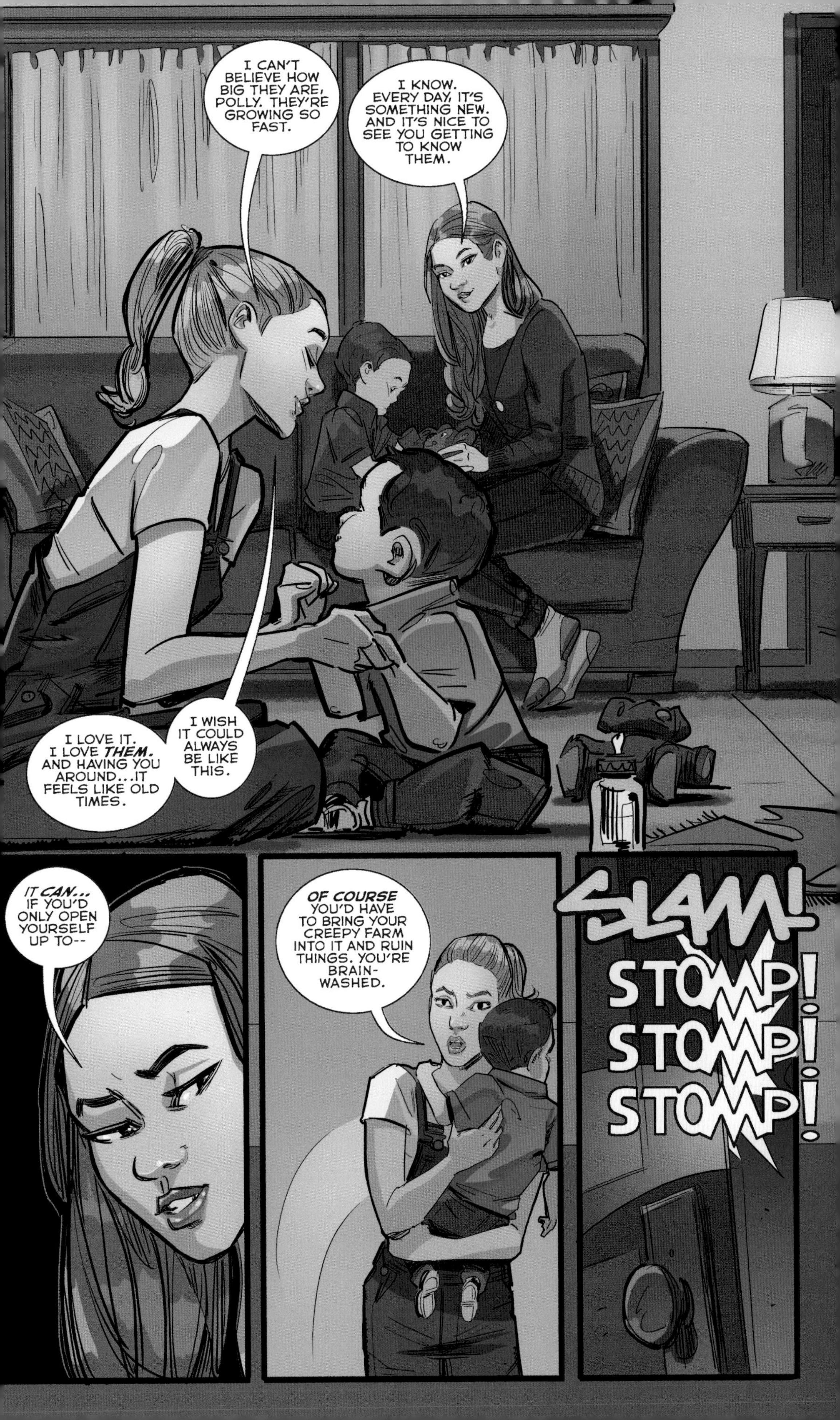
I CAN'T BELIEVE HOW BIG THEY ARE, POLLY. THEY'RE GROWING SO FAST.
I KNOW. EVERY DAY, IT'S SOMETHING NEW. AND IT'S NICE TO SEE YOU GETTING TO KNOW THEM.
I LOVE IT. I LOVE *THEM.* AND HAVING YOU AROUND...IT FEELS LIKE OLD TIMES.
I WISH IT COULD ALWAYS BE LIKE THIS.
IT *CAN...* IF YOU'D ONLY OPEN YOURSELF UP TO--
OF COURSE YOU'D HAVE TO BRING YOUR CREEPY FARM INTO IT AND RUIN THINGS. YOU'RE BRAIN-WASHED.
SLAM!
STOMP! STOMP! STOMP!

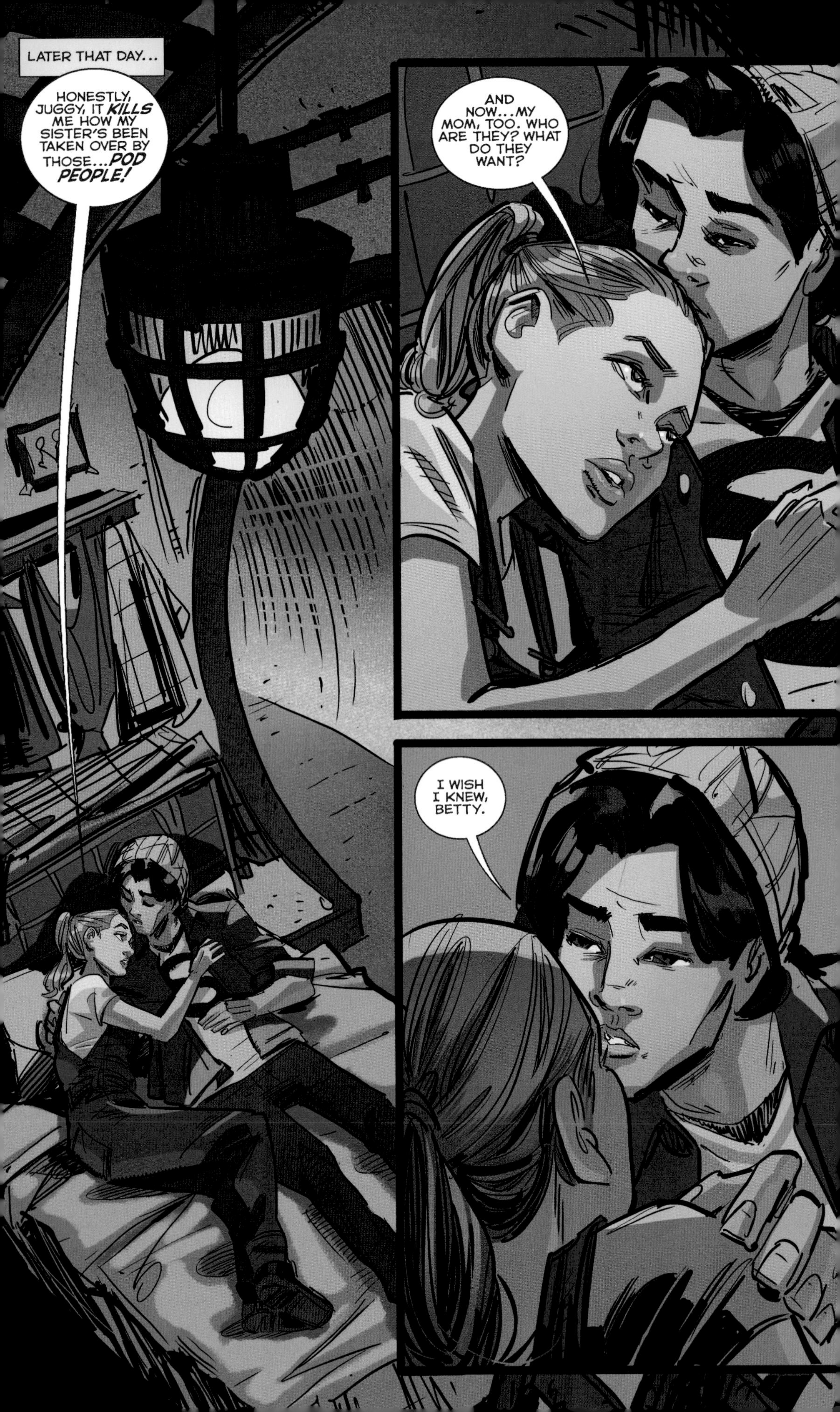
LATER THAT DAY...
HONESTLY, JUGGY, IT KILLS ME HOW MY SISTER'S BEEN TAKEN OVER BY THOSE...POD PEOPLE!
AND NOW...MY MOM, TOO. WHO ARE THEY? WHAT DO THEY WANT?
I WISH I KNEW, BETTY.

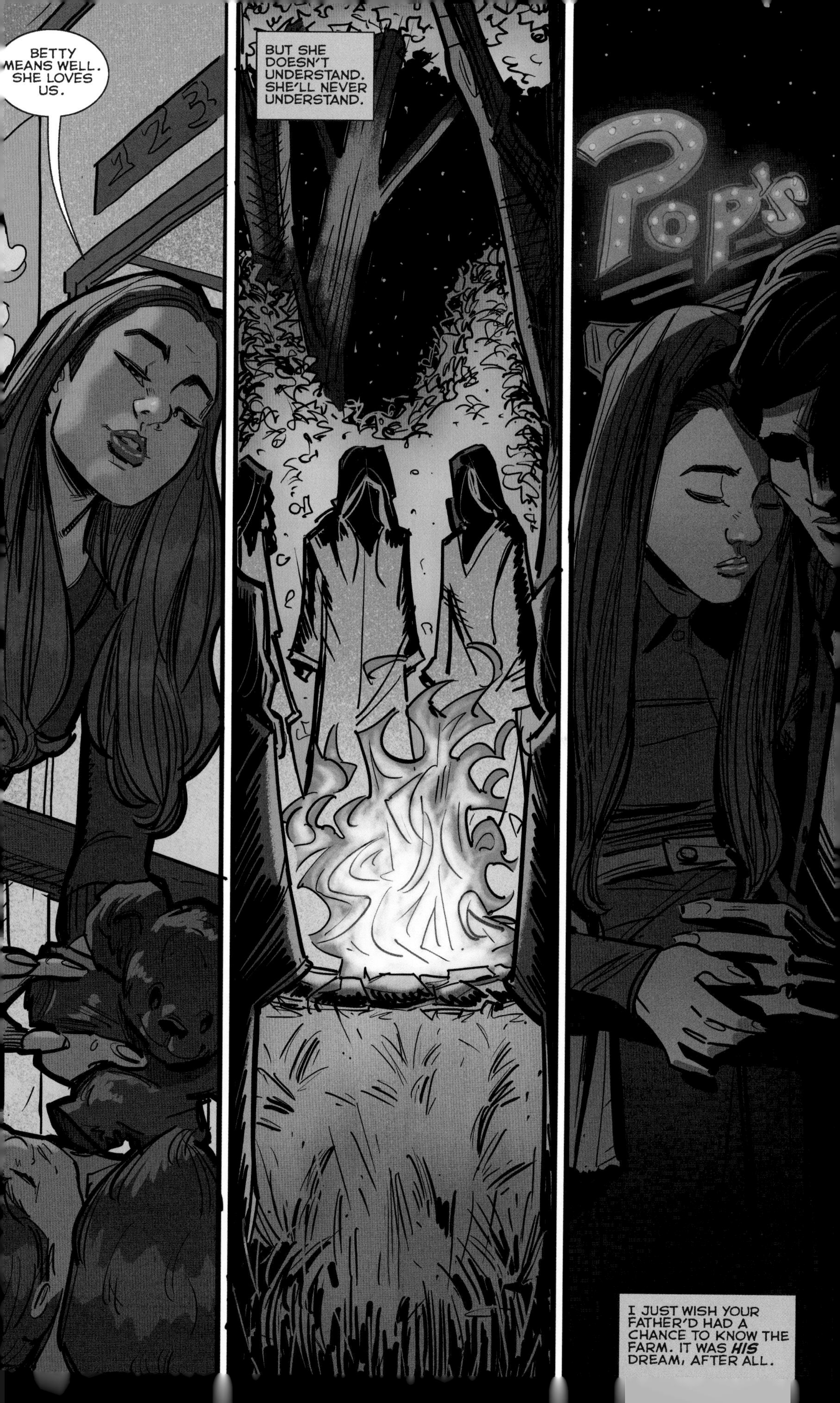
BETTY MEANS WELL. SHE LOVES US.
BUT SHE DOESN'T UNDERSTAND. SHE'LL NEVER UNDERSTAND.
I JUST WISH YOUR FATHER'D HAD A CHANCE TO KNOW THE FARM. IT WAS *HIS* DREAM, AFTER ALL.

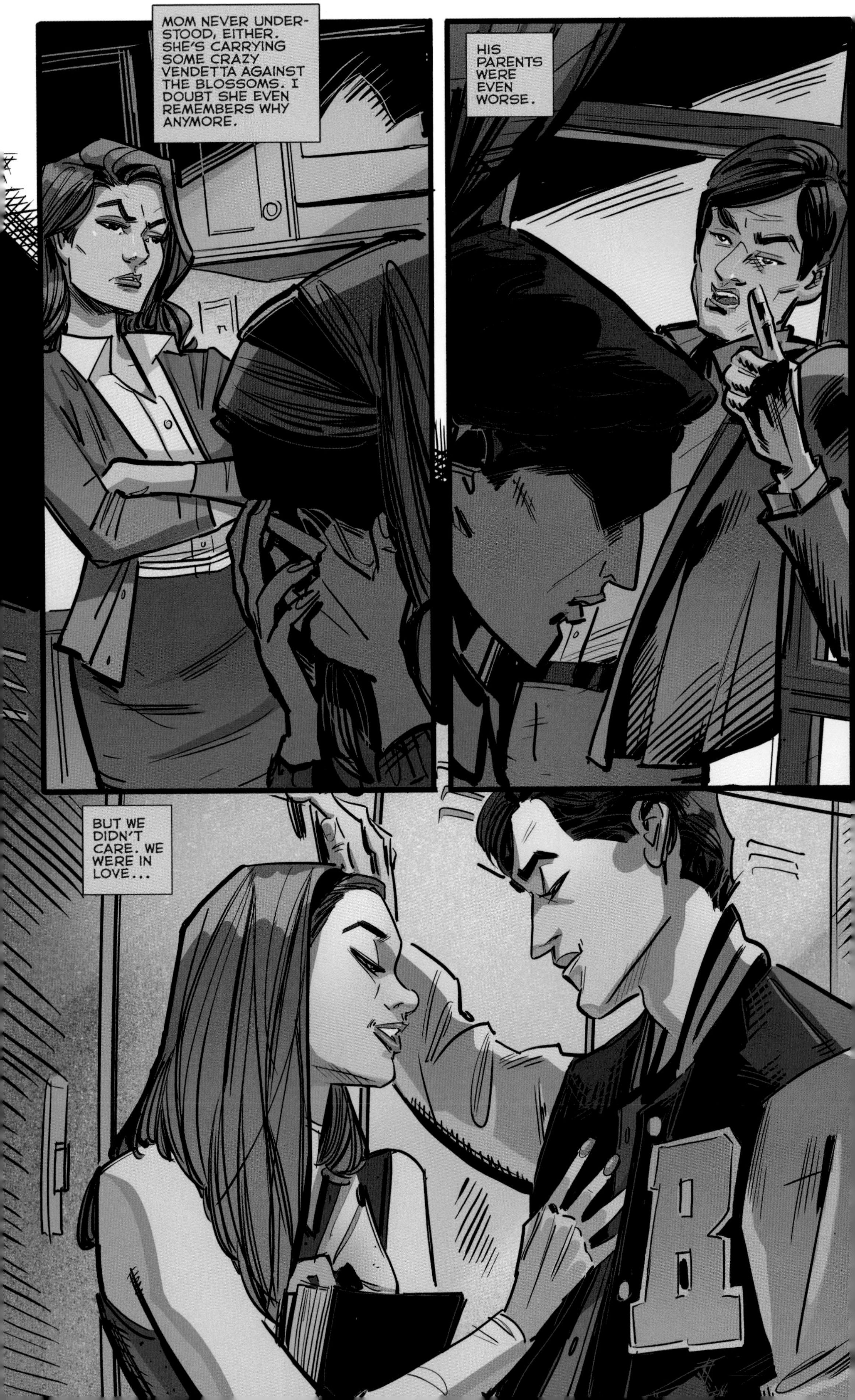
MOM NEVER UNDERSTOOD, EITHER. SHE'S CARRYING SOME CRAZY VENDETTA AGAINST THE BLOSSOMS. I DOUBT SHE EVEN REMEMBERS WHY ANYMORE.
HIS PARENTS WERE EVEN WORSE.
BUT WE DIDN'T CARE. WE WERE IN LOVE...

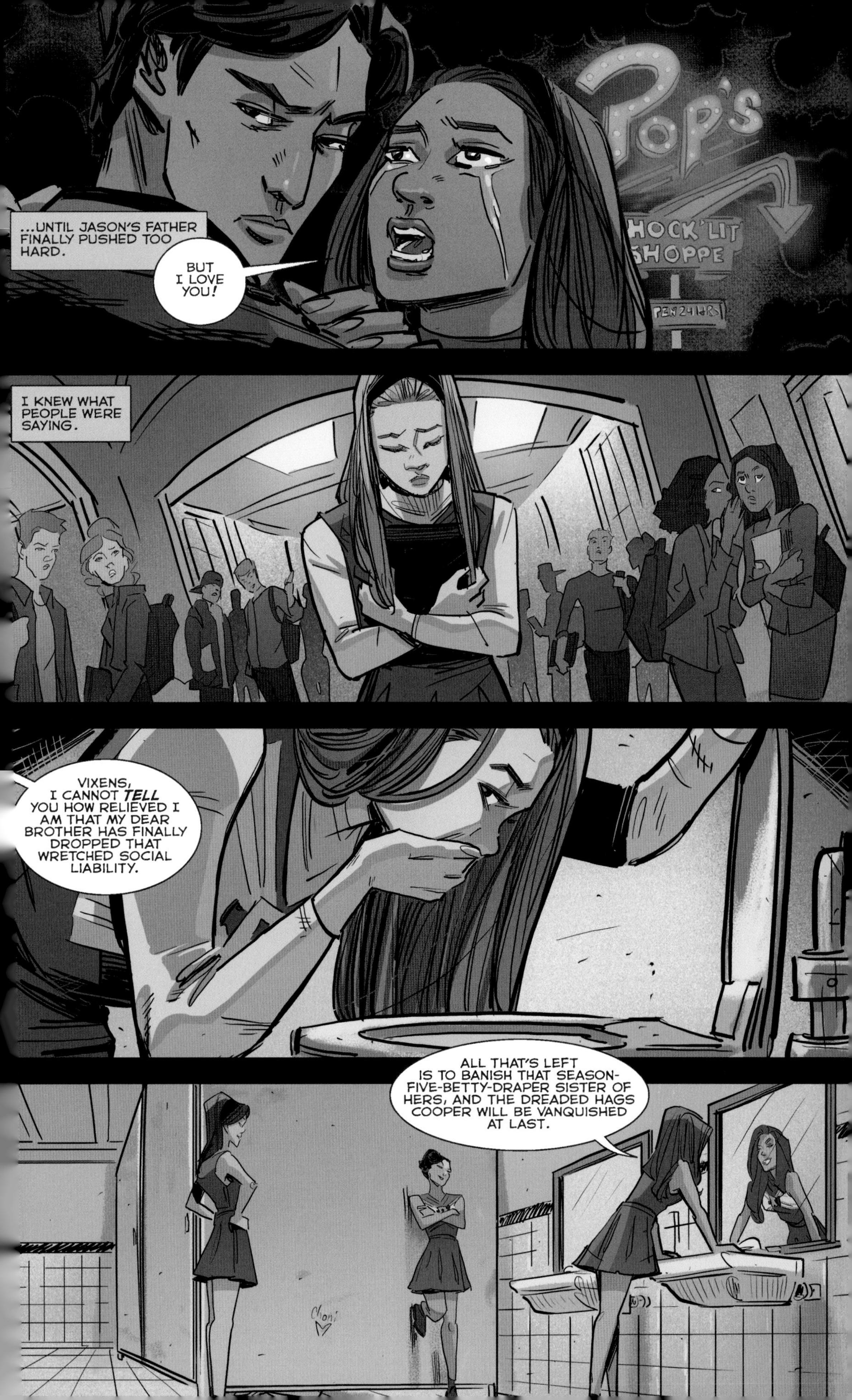

POP'S
CHOCK'LIT SHOPPE
...UNTIL JASON'S FATHER FINALLY PUSHED TOO HARD.
BUT I LOVE YOU!
I KNEW WHAT PEOPLE WERE SAYING.
VIXENS, I CANNOT TELL YOU HOW RELIEVED I AM THAT MY DEAR BROTHER HAS FINALLY DROPPED THAT WRETCHED SOCIAL LIABILITY.
ALL THAT'S LEFT IS TO BANISH THAT SEASON-FIVE-BETTY-DRAPER SISTER OF HERS, AND THE DREADED HAGS COOPER WILL BE VANQUISHED AT LAST.
Choni

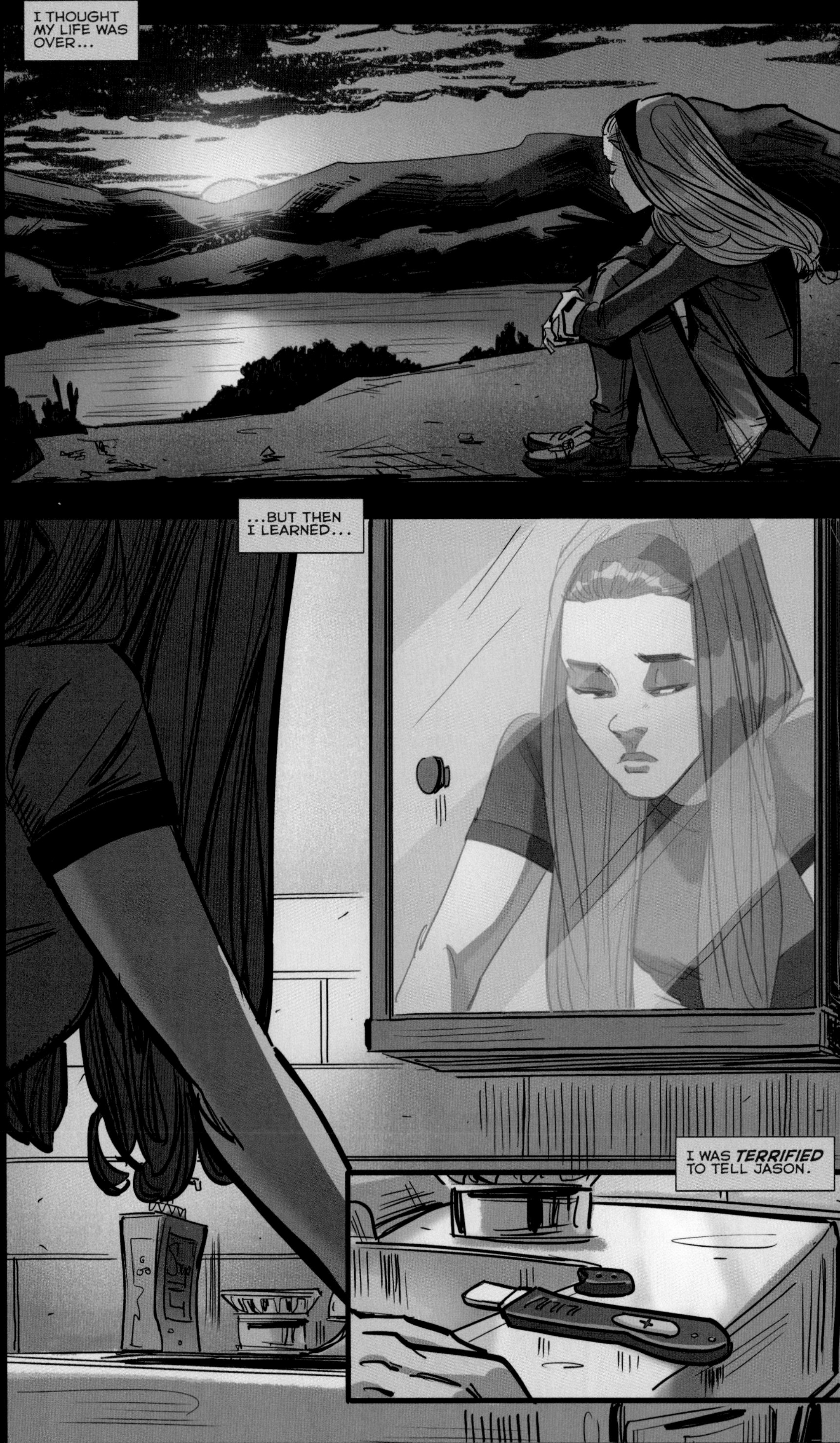
I THOUGHT MY LIFE WAS OVER...
...BUT THEN I LEARNED...
I WAS *TERRIFIED* TO TELL JASON.

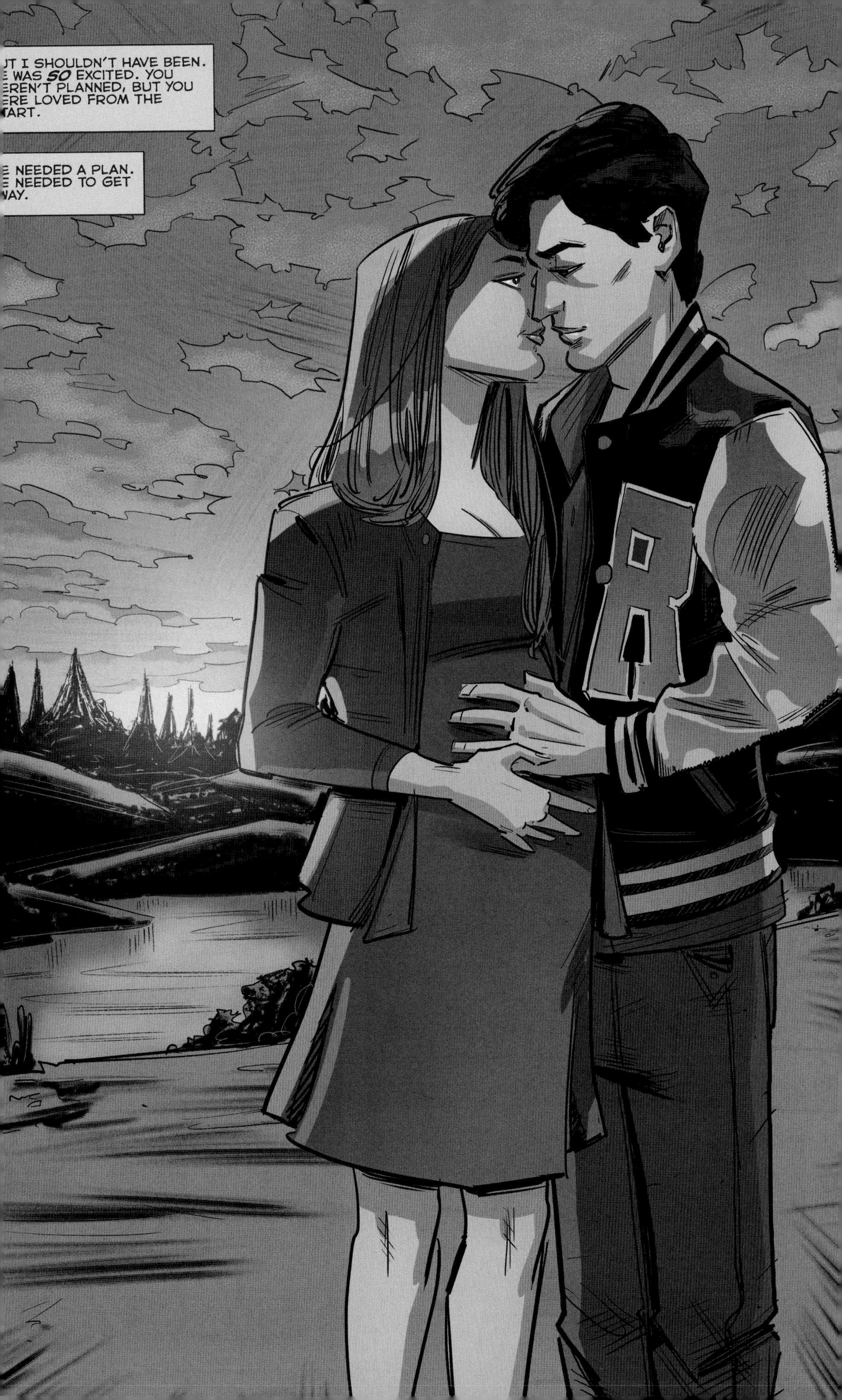

UT I SHOULDN'T HAVE BEEN. E WAS SO EXCITED. YOU ERENT'T PLANNED, BUT YOU ERE LOVED FROM THE TART.
E NEEDED A PLAN. E NEEDED TO GET WAY.

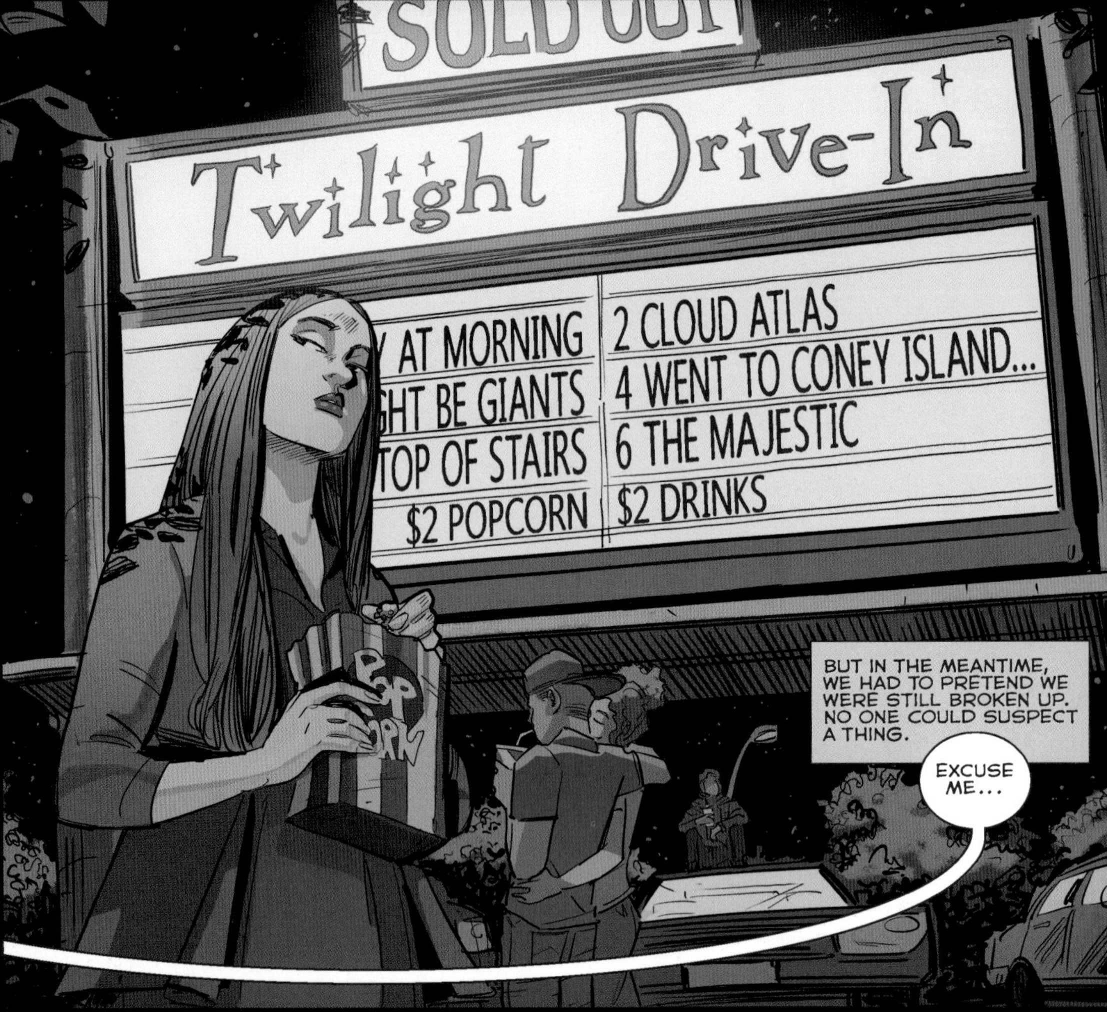
SOLD OUT
Twilight Drive-In
Y AT MORNING
GHT BE GIANTS
TOP OF STAIRS
$2 POPCORN
2 CLOUD ATLAS
4 WENT TO CONEY ISLAND...
6 THE MAJESTIC
$2 DRINKS
POP CORN
BUT IN THE MEANTIME, WE HAD TO PRETEND WE WERE STILL BROKEN UP. NO ONE COULD SUSPECT A THING.
EXCUSE ME...

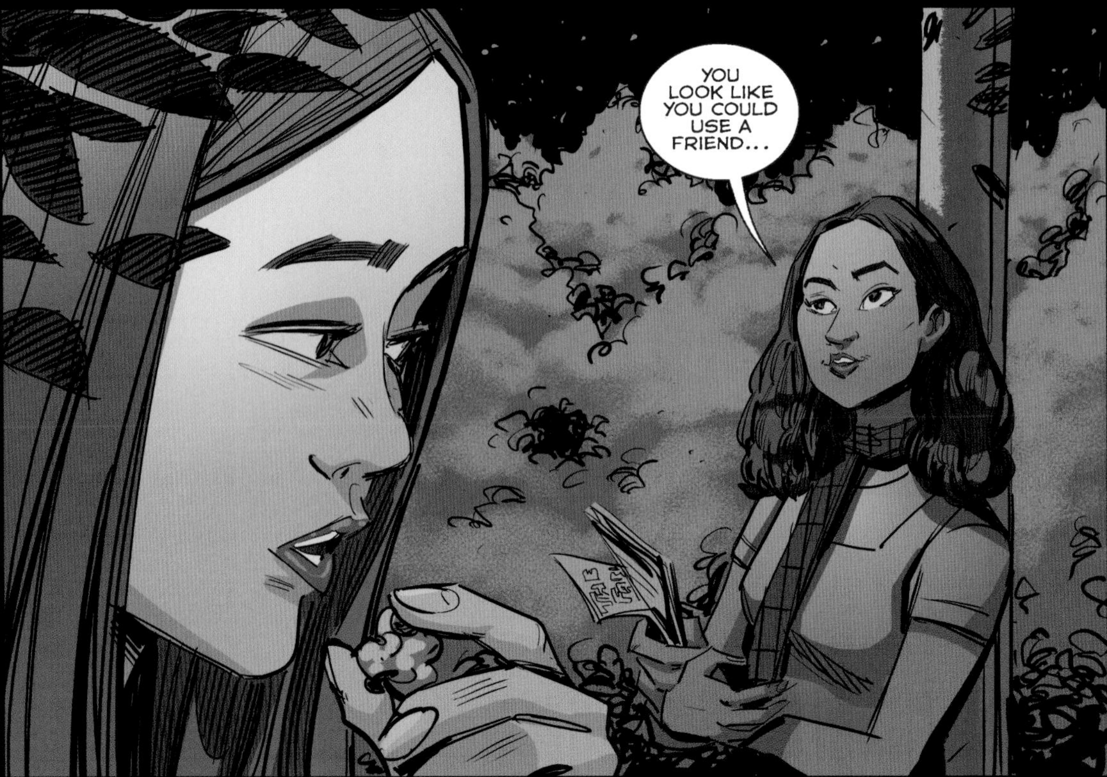
YOU LOOK LIKE YOU COULD USE A FRIEND...

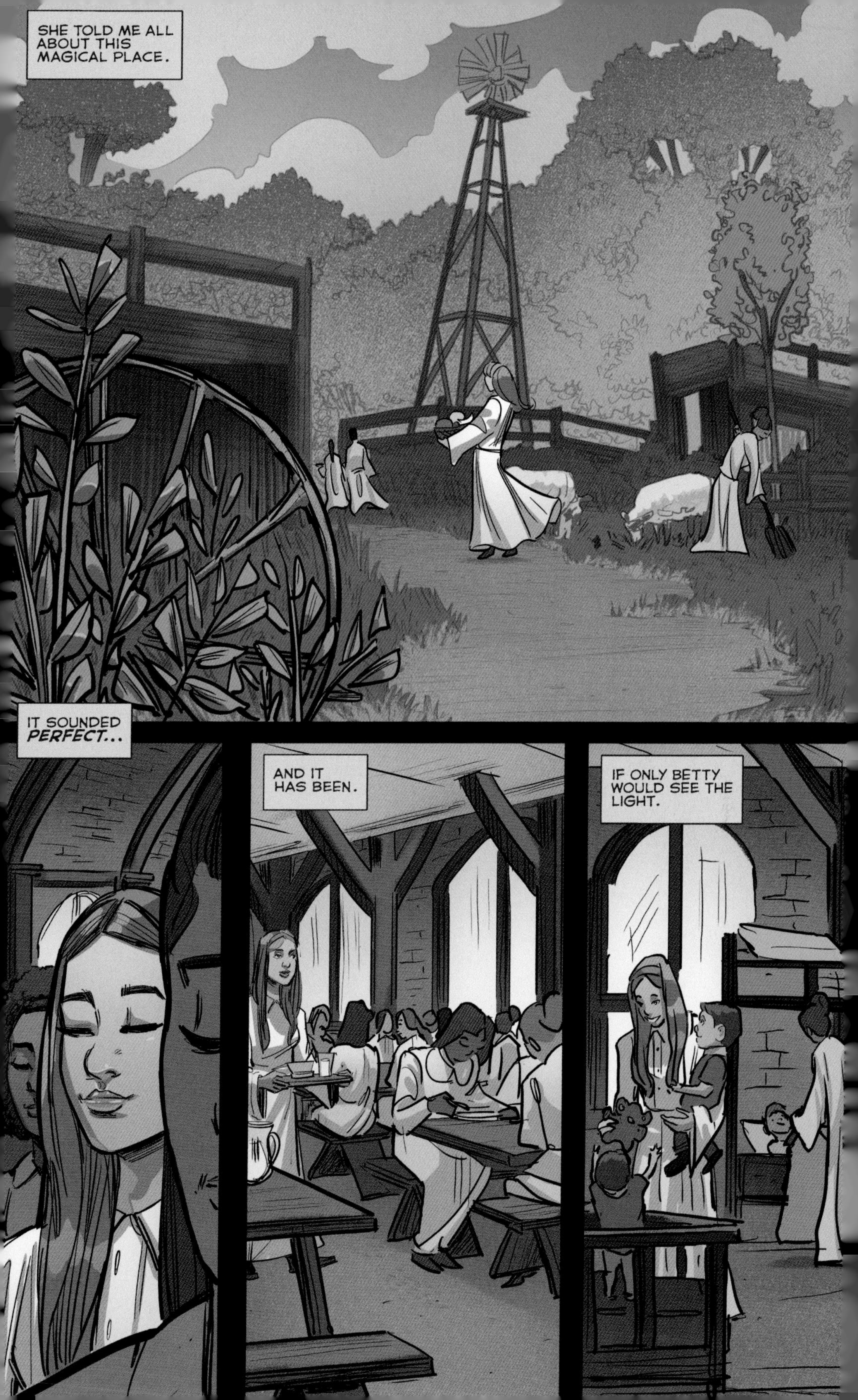
SHE TOLD ME ALL ABOUT THIS MAGICAL PLACE.
IT SOUNDED *PERFECT*...
AND IT HAS BEEN.
IF ONLY BETTY WOULD SEE THE LIGHT.

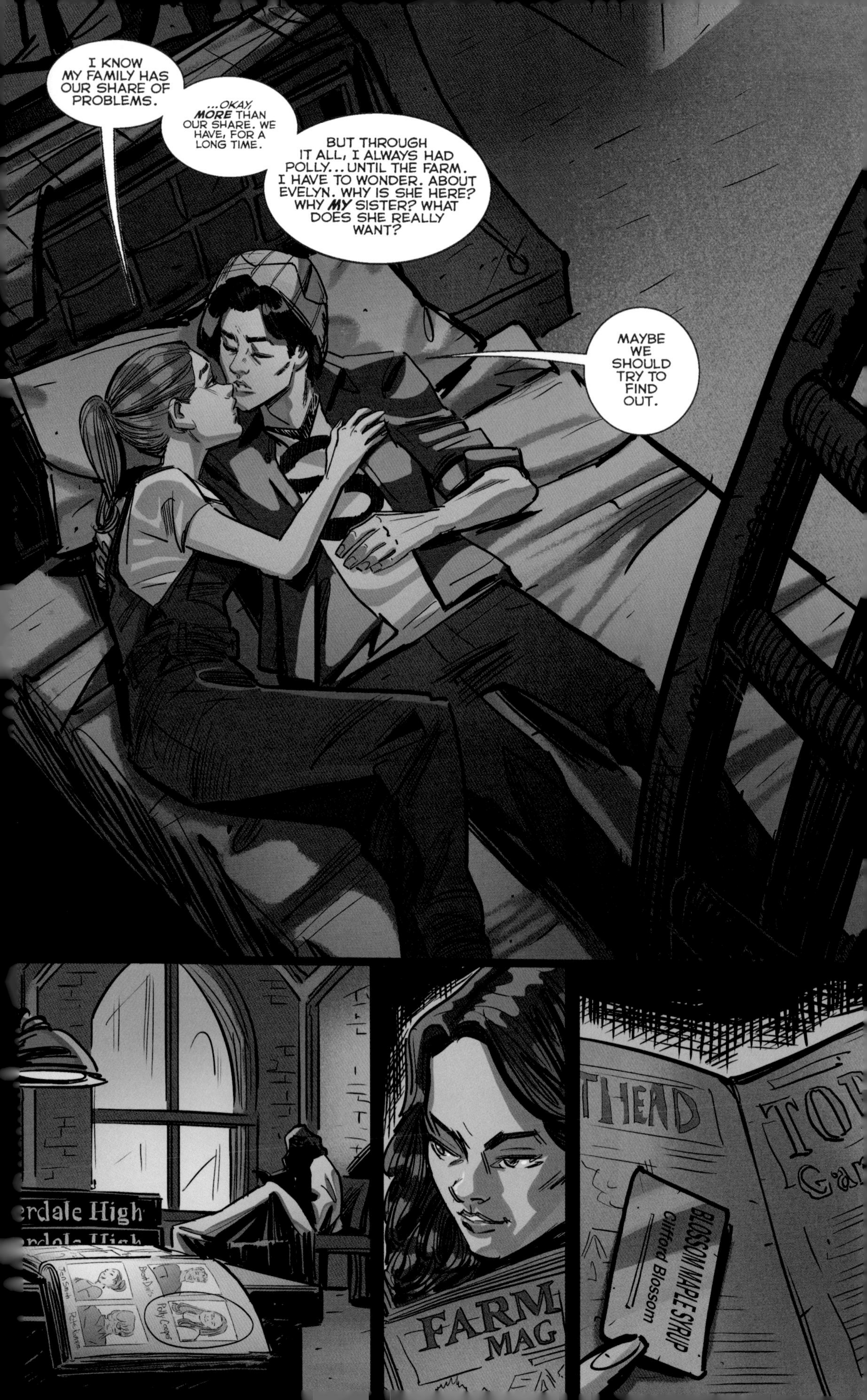
I KNOW MY FAMILY HAS OUR SHARE OF PROBLEMS.
...OKAY, **MORE** THAN OUR SHARE. WE HAVE, FOR A LONG TIME.
BUT THROUGH IT ALL, I ALWAYS HAD POLLY... UNTIL THE FARM. I HAVE TO WONDER. ABOUT EVELYN. WHY IS SHE HERE? WHY ***MY*** SISTER? WHAT DOES SHE REALLY WANT?
MAYBE WE SHOULD TRY TO FIND OUT.
FARM MAG
BLOSSOM MAPLE SYRUP
Clifford Blossom

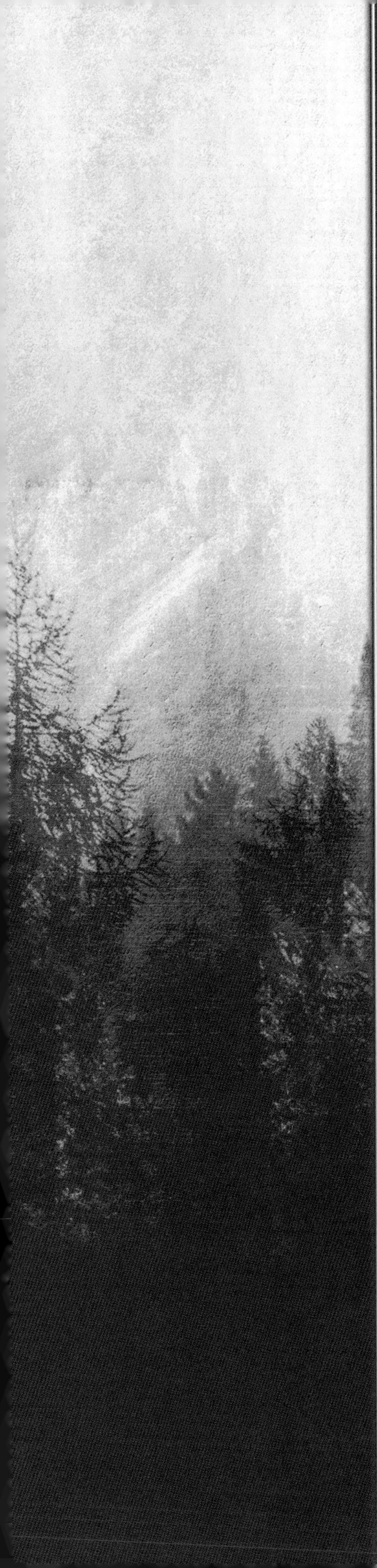

CHAPTER FOUR

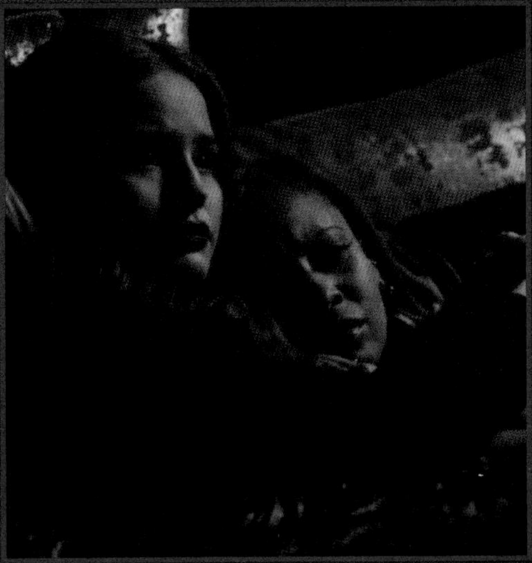

CHONI GOES WEST

WRITER:
MICOL OSTOW

ART:
JOE EISMA

COLORS:
MATT HERMS

LETTERS:
JANICE CHIANG

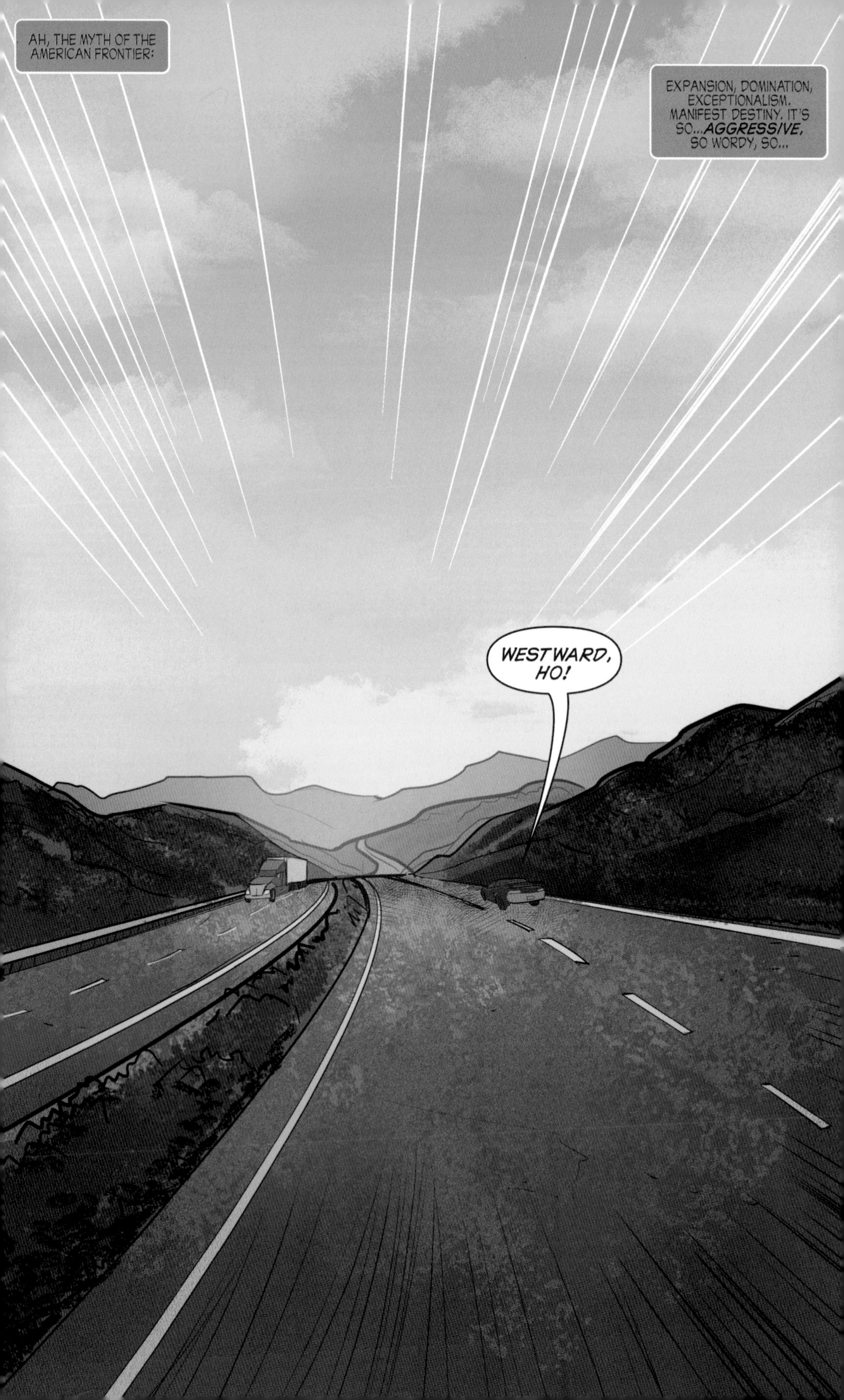
AH, THE MYTH OF THE AMERICAN FRONTIER:
EXPANSION, DOMINATION, EXCEPTIONALISM. MANIFEST DESTINY. IT'S SO...AGGRESSIVE, SO WORDY, SO...
WESTWARD, HO!

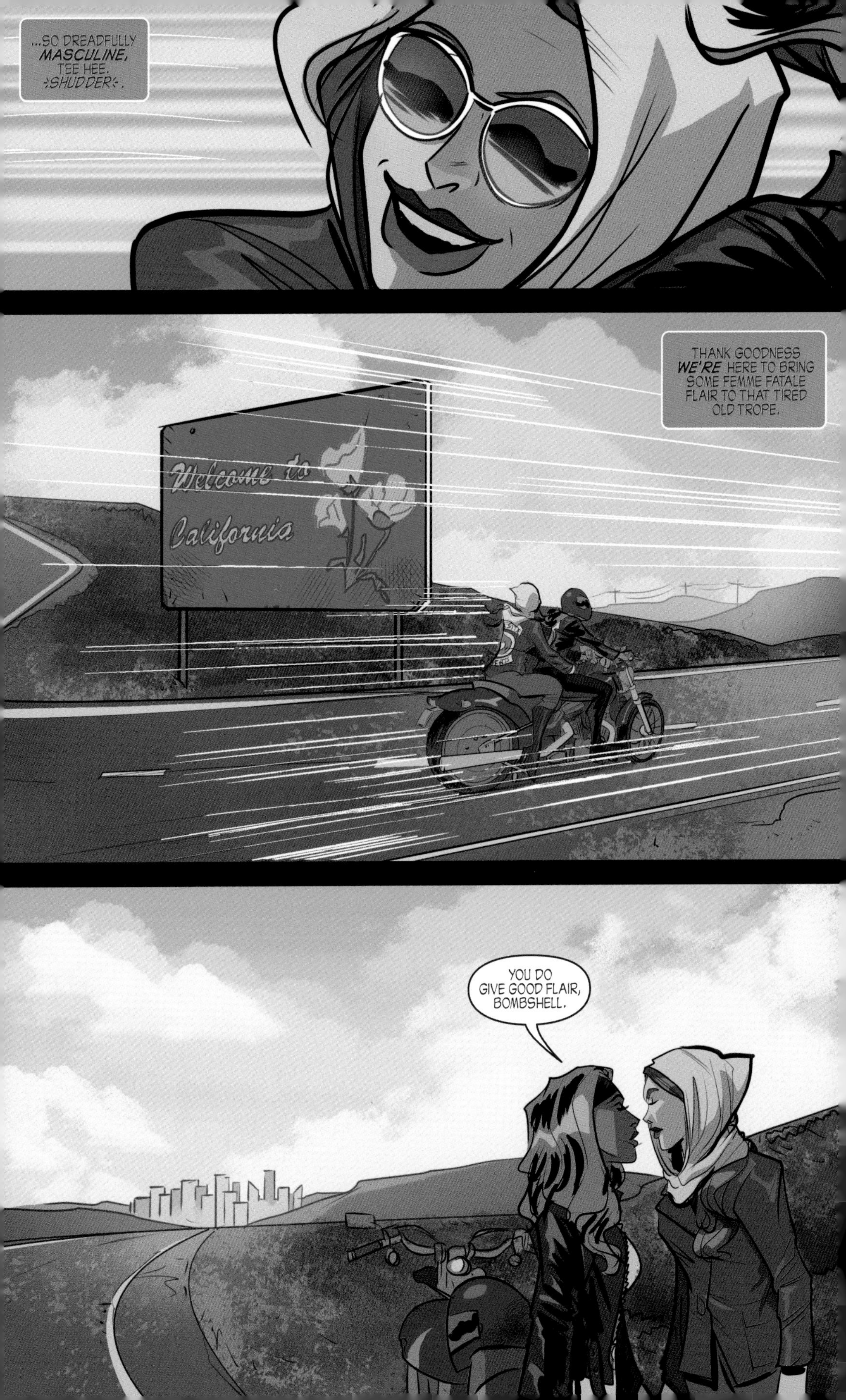
...SO DREADFULLY MASCULINE, TEE HEE. ⊰SHUDDER⊱.
THANK GOODNESS WE'RE HERE TO BRING SOME FEMME FATALE FLAIR TO THAT TIRED OLD TROPE.
Welcome to California
YOU DO GIVE GOOD FLAIR, BOMBSHELL.

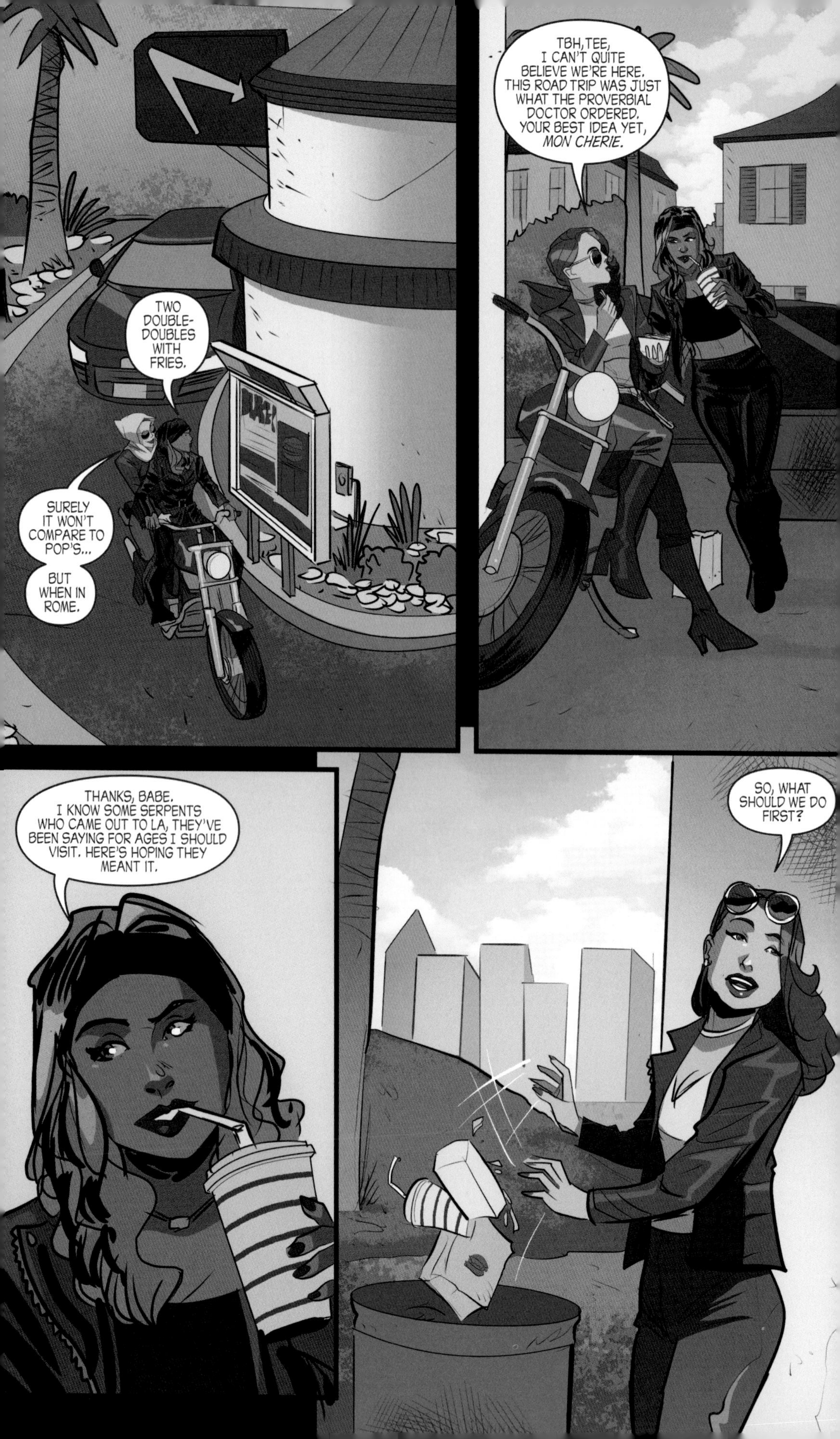
TWO DOUBLE-DOUBLES WITH FRIES.
SURELY IT WON'T COMPARE TO POP'S...
BUT WHEN IN ROME.
TBH, TEE, I CAN'T QUITE BELIEVE WE'RE HERE. THIS ROAD TRIP WAS JUST WHAT THE PROVERBIAL DOCTOR ORDERED. YOUR BEST IDEA YET, *MON CHERIE.*
THANKS, BABE. I KNOW SOME SERPENTS WHO CAME OUT TO LA, THEY'VE BEEN SAYING FOR AGES I SHOULD VISIT. HERE'S HOPING THEY MEANT IT.
SO, WHAT SHOULD WE DO FIRST?

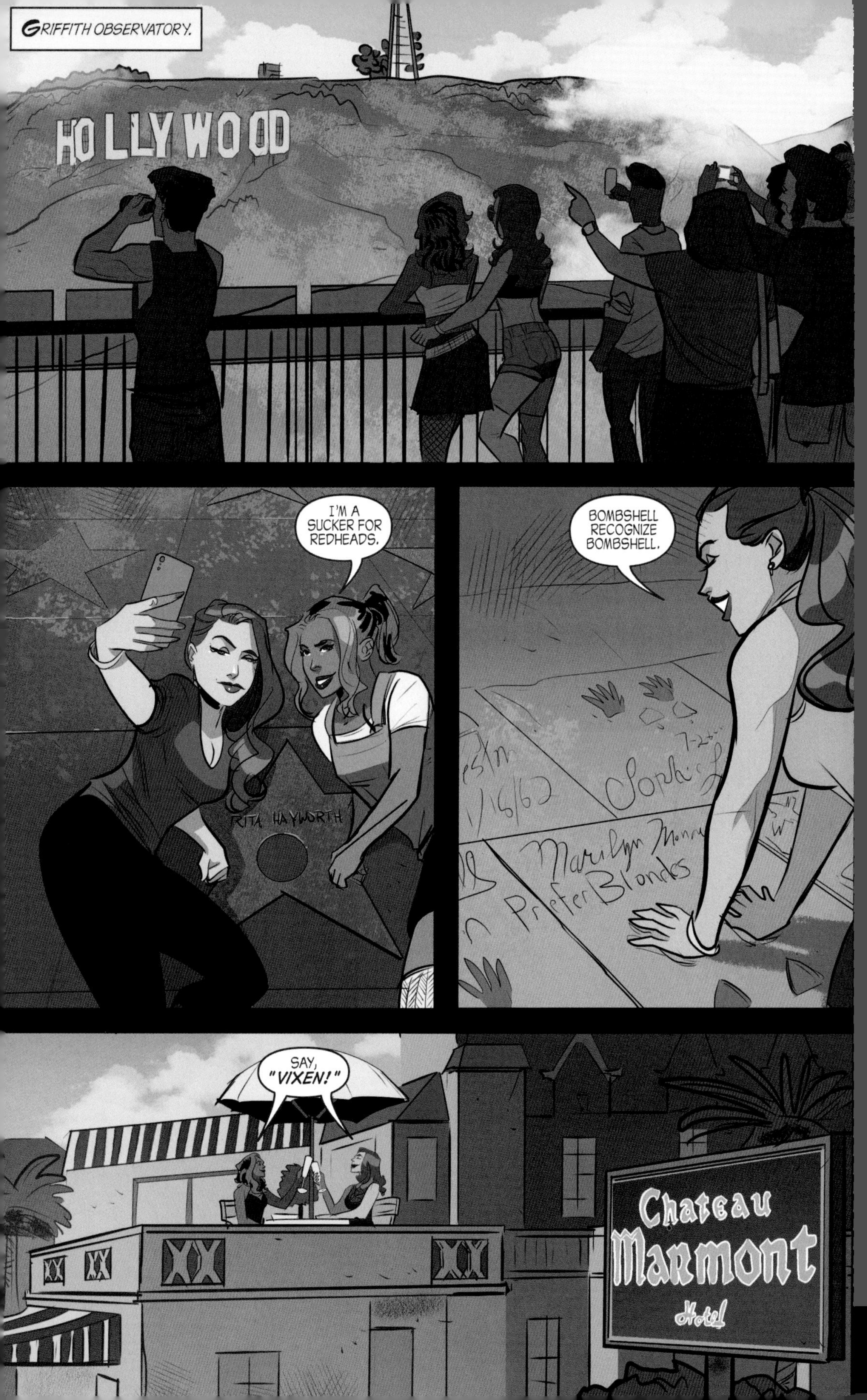
GRIFFITH OBSERVATORY.
HOLLYWOOD
I'M A SUCKER FOR REDHEADS.
RITA HAYWORTH
BOMBSHELL RECOGNIZE BOMBSHELL.
Prefer Blondes
SAY, "VIXEN!"
Chateau Marmont
Hotel

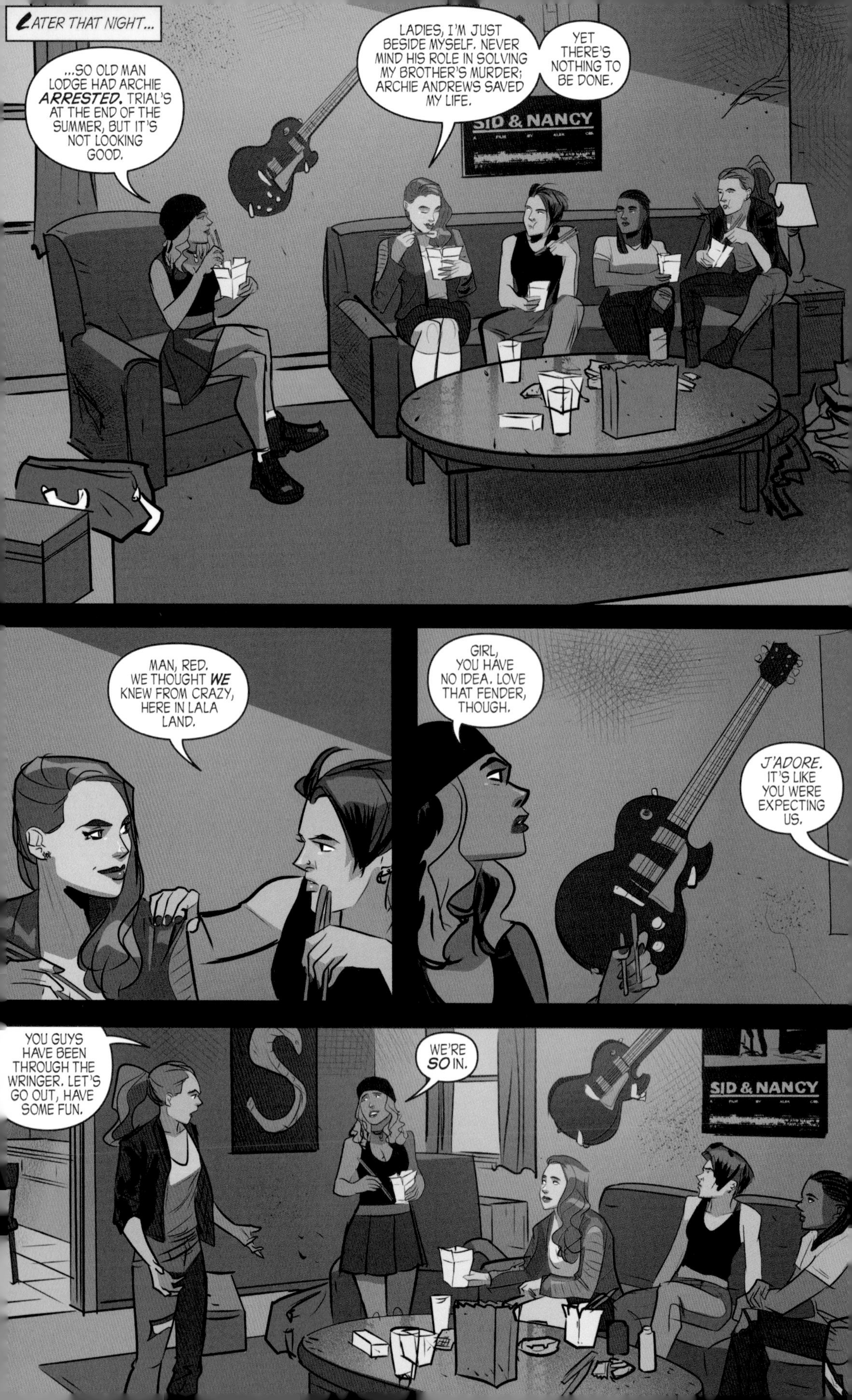
LATER THAT NIGHT...
...SO OLD MAN LODGE HAD ARCHIE ARRESTED. TRIAL'S AT THE END OF THE SUMMER, BUT IT'S NOT LOOKING GOOD.
LADIES, I'M JUST BESIDE MYSELF. NEVER MIND HIS ROLE IN SOLVING MY BROTHER'S MURDER; ARCHIE ANDREWS SAVED MY LIFE.
YET THERE'S NOTHING TO BE DONE.
SID & NANCY
MAN, RED. WE THOUGHT WE KNEW FROM CRAZY, HERE IN LALA LAND.
GIRL, YOU HAVE NO IDEA. LOVE THAT FENDER, THOUGH.
J'ADORE. IT'S LIKE YOU WERE EXPECTING US.
YOU GUYS HAVE BEEN THROUGH THE WRINGER. LET'S GO OUT, HAVE SOME FUN.
WE'RE SO IN.
SID & NANCY

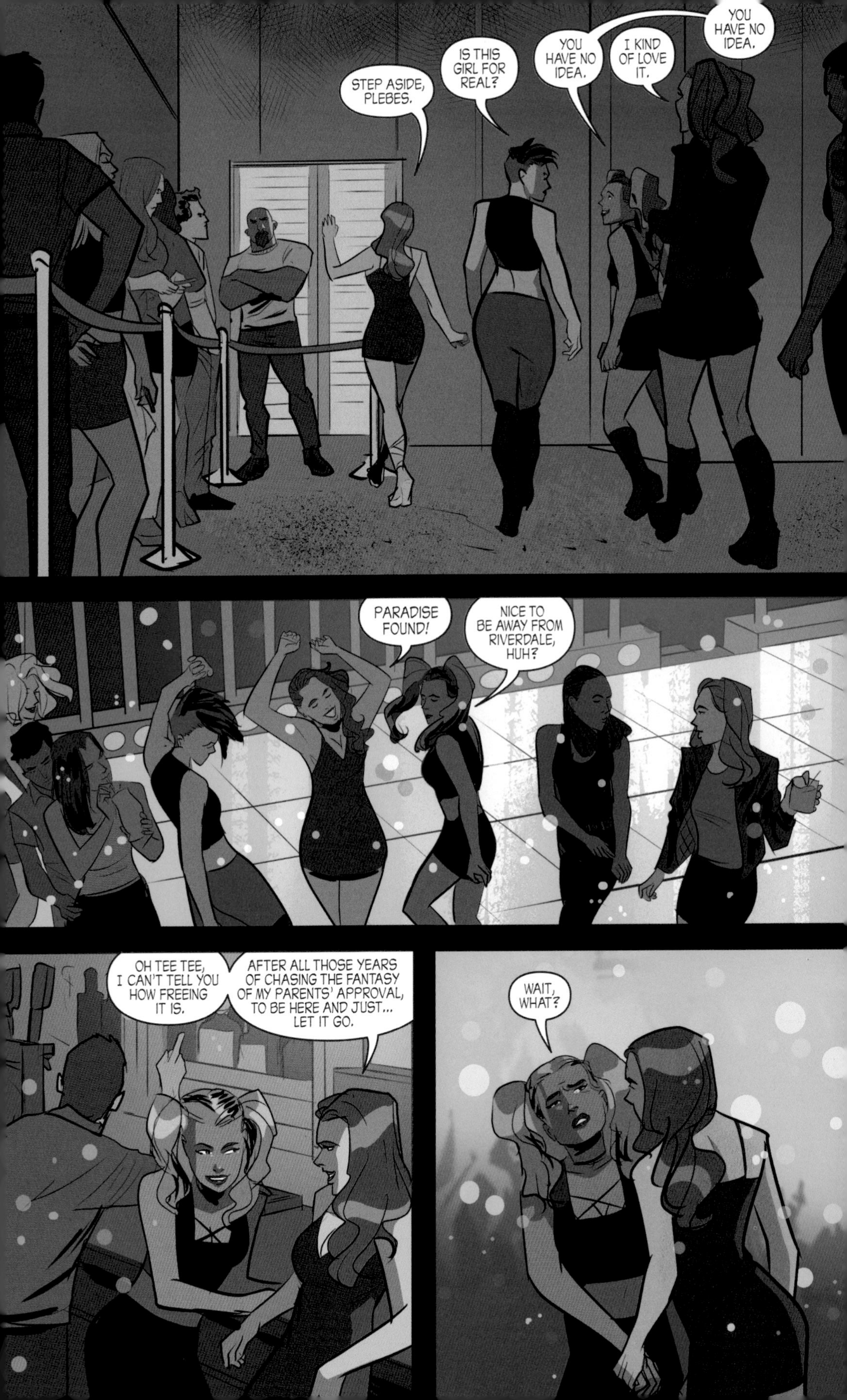
STEP ASIDE, PLEBES.
IS THIS GIRL FOR REAL?
YOU HAVE NO IDEA.
I KIND OF LOVE IT.
YOU HAVE NO IDEA.
PARADISE FOUND!
NICE TO BE AWAY FROM RIVERDALE, HUH?
OH TEE TEE, I CAN'T TELL YOU HOW FREEING IT IS.
AFTER ALL THOSE YEARS OF CHASING THE FANTASY OF MY PARENTS' APPROVAL, TO BE HERE AND JUST... LET IT GO.
WAIT, WHAT?

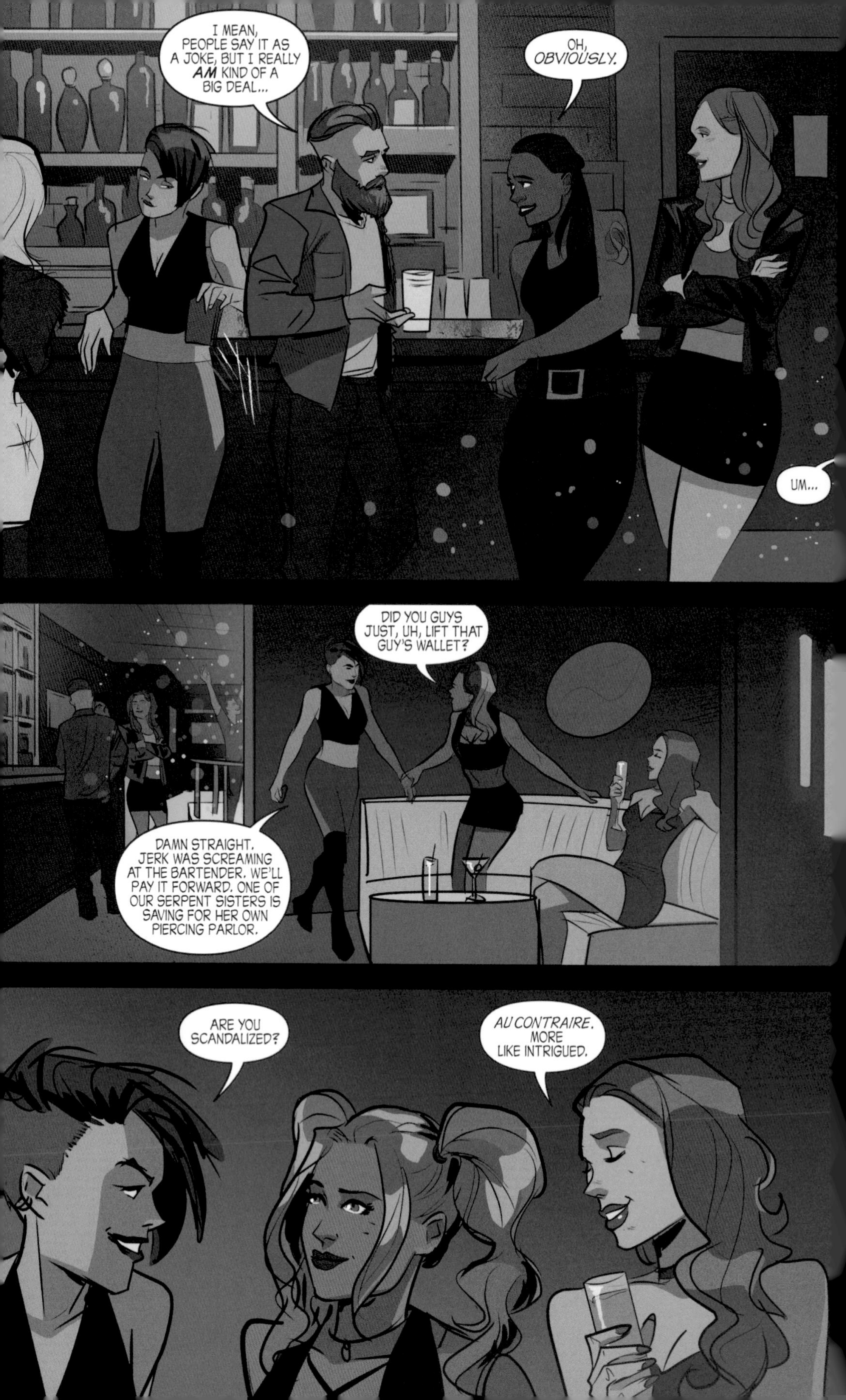
I MEAN, PEOPLE SAY IT AS A JOKE, BUT I REALLY AM KIND OF A BIG DEAL...
OH, OBVIOUSLY.
UM...
DID YOU GUYS JUST, UH, LIFT THAT GUY'S WALLET?
DAMN STRAIGHT. JERK WAS SCREAMING AT THE BARTENDER. WE'LL PAY IT FORWARD. ONE OF OUR SERPENT SISTERS IS SAVING FOR HER OWN PIERCING PARLOR.
ARE YOU SCANDALIZED?
AU CONTRAIRE. MORE LIKE INTRIGUED.

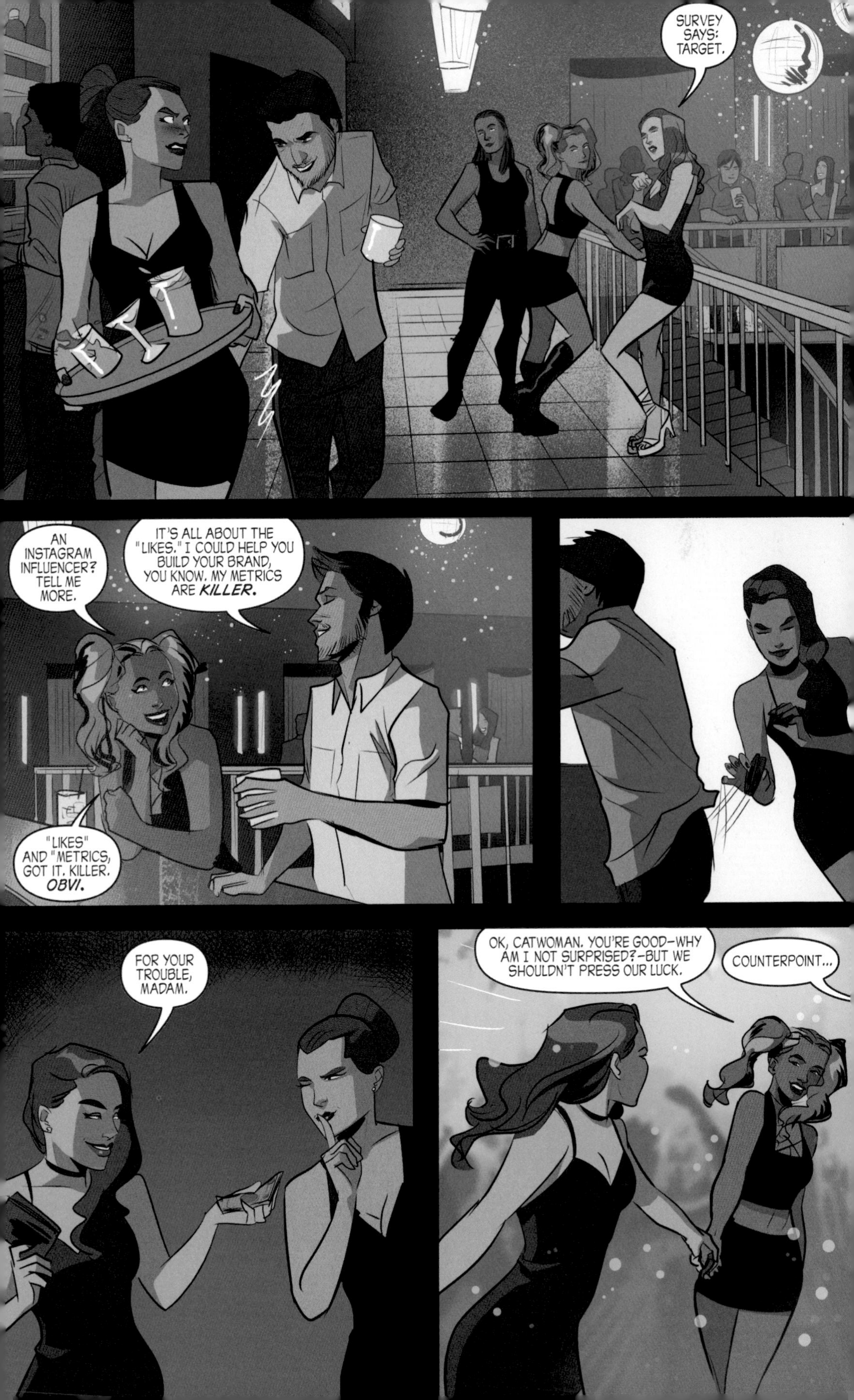
SURVEY SAYS: TARGET.
AN INSTAGRAM INFLUENCER? TELL ME MORE.
IT'S ALL ABOUT THE "LIKES." I COULD HELP YOU BUILD YOUR BRAND, YOU KNOW. MY METRICS ARE KILLER.
"LIKES" AND "METRICS, GOT IT. KILLER. OBVI.
FOR YOUR TROUBLE, MADAM.
OK, CATWOMAN. YOU'RE GOOD—WHY AM I NOT SURPRISED?—BUT WE SHOULDN'T PRESS OUR LUCK.
COUNTERPOINT...

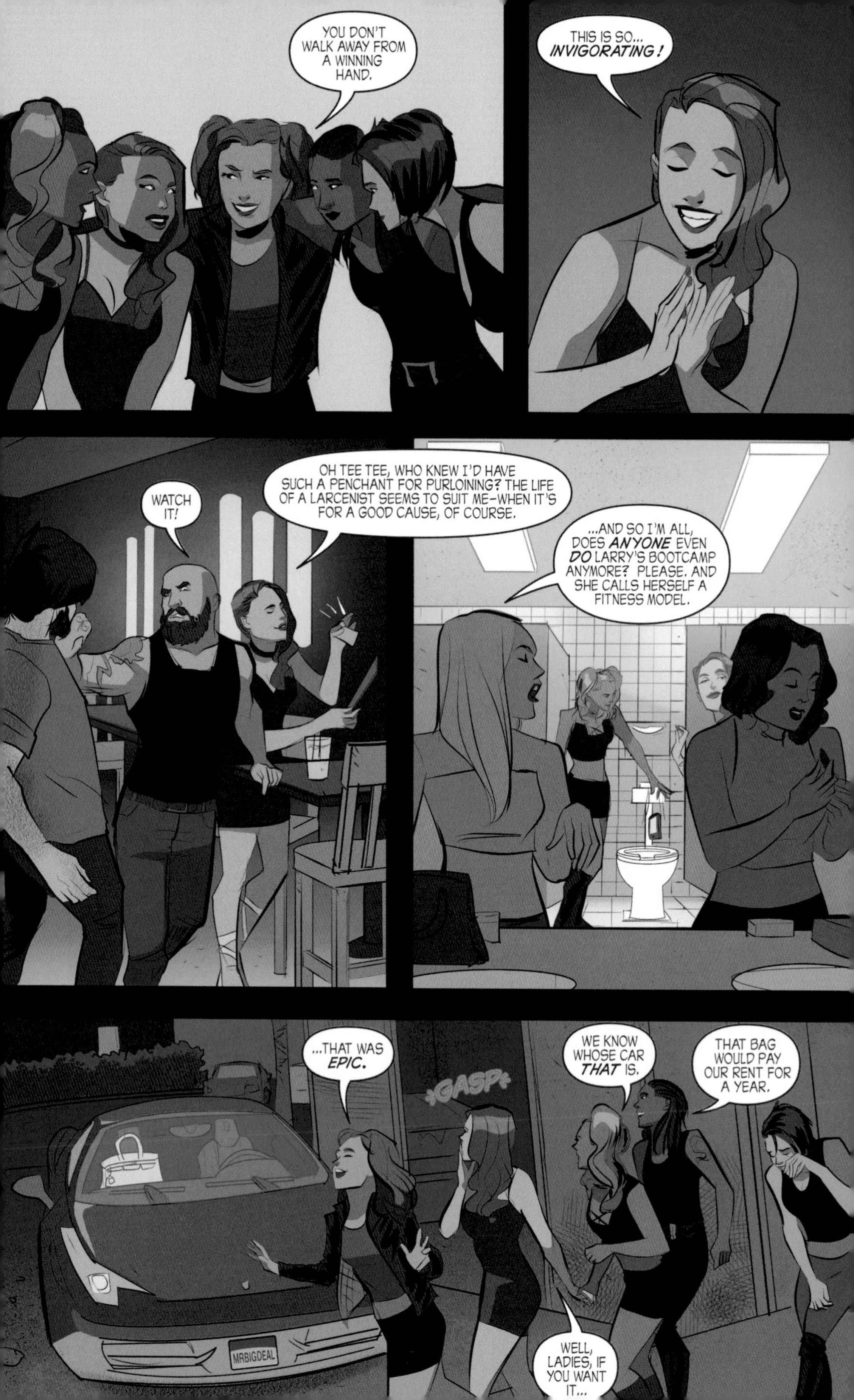
YOU DON'T WALK AWAY FROM A WINNING HAND.
THIS IS SO... INVIGORATING!
WATCH IT!
OH TEE TEE, WHO KNEW I'D HAVE SUCH A PENCHANT FOR PURLOINING? THE LIFE OF A LARCENIST SEEMS TO SUIT ME—WHEN IT'S FOR A GOOD CAUSE, OF COURSE.
...AND SO I'M ALL, DOES ANYONE EVEN DO LARRY'S BOOTCAMP ANYMORE? PLEASE. AND SHE CALLS HERSELF A FITNESS MODEL.
...THAT WAS EPIC.
GASP
WE KNOW WHOSE CAR THAT IS.
THAT BAG WOULD PAY OUR RENT FOR A YEAR.
MRBIGDEAL
WELL, LADIES, IF YOU WANT IT...

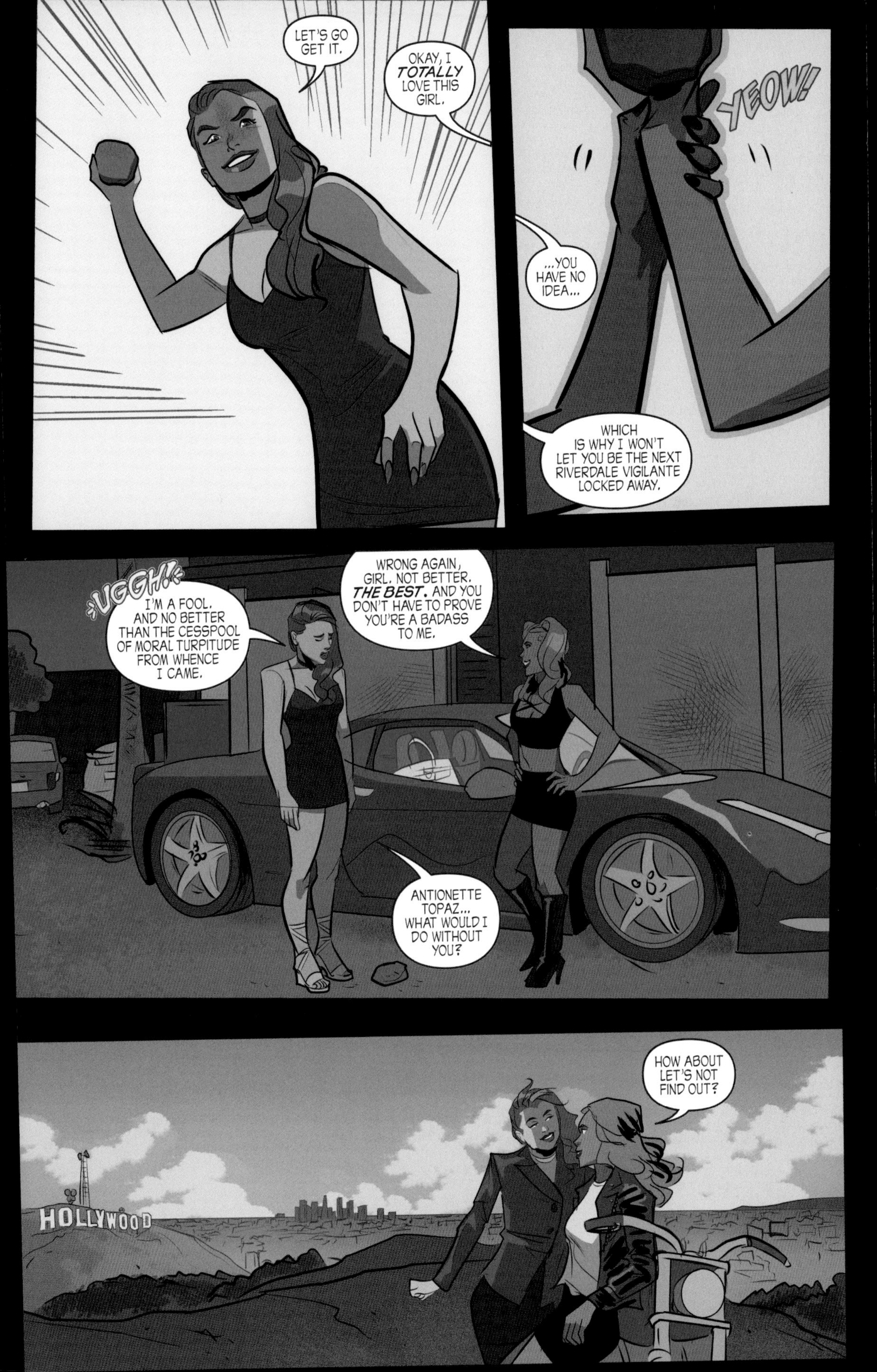
LET'S GO GET IT.
OKAY, I *TOTALLY* LOVE THIS GIRL.
YEOW!
...YOU HAVE NO IDEA...
WHICH IS WHY I WON'T LET YOU BE THE NEXT RIVERDALE VIGILANTE LOCKED AWAY.
UGGH!
I'M A FOOL. AND NO BETTER THAN THE CESSPOOL OF MORAL TURPITUDE FROM WHENCE I CAME.
WRONG AGAIN, GIRL. NOT BETTER. *THE BEST*. AND YOU DON'T HAVE TO PROVE YOU'RE A BADASS TO ME.
ANTIONETTE TOPAZ... WHAT WOULD I DO WITHOUT YOU?
HOLLYWOOD
HOW ABOUT LET'S NOT FIND OUT?

CHAPTER FIVE

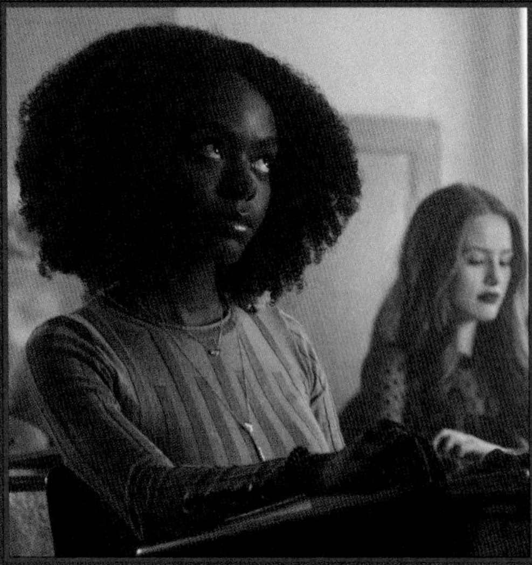

YOU'VE GOT MAIL

WRITER:
MICOL OSTOW

ART:
THOMAS PITILLI

COLORS:
ANDRE SZYMANOWICZ

LETTERS:
JOHN WORKMAN

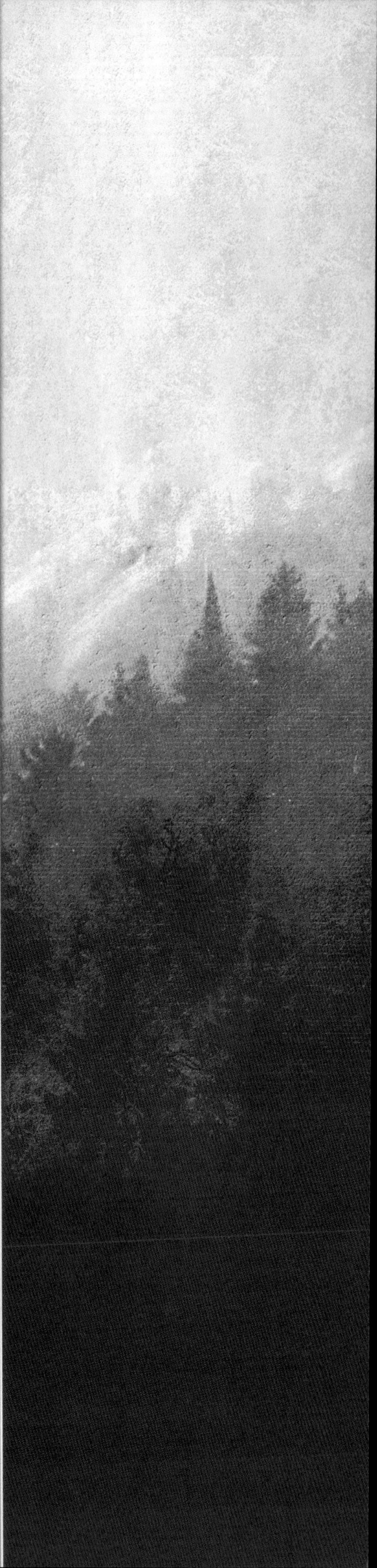

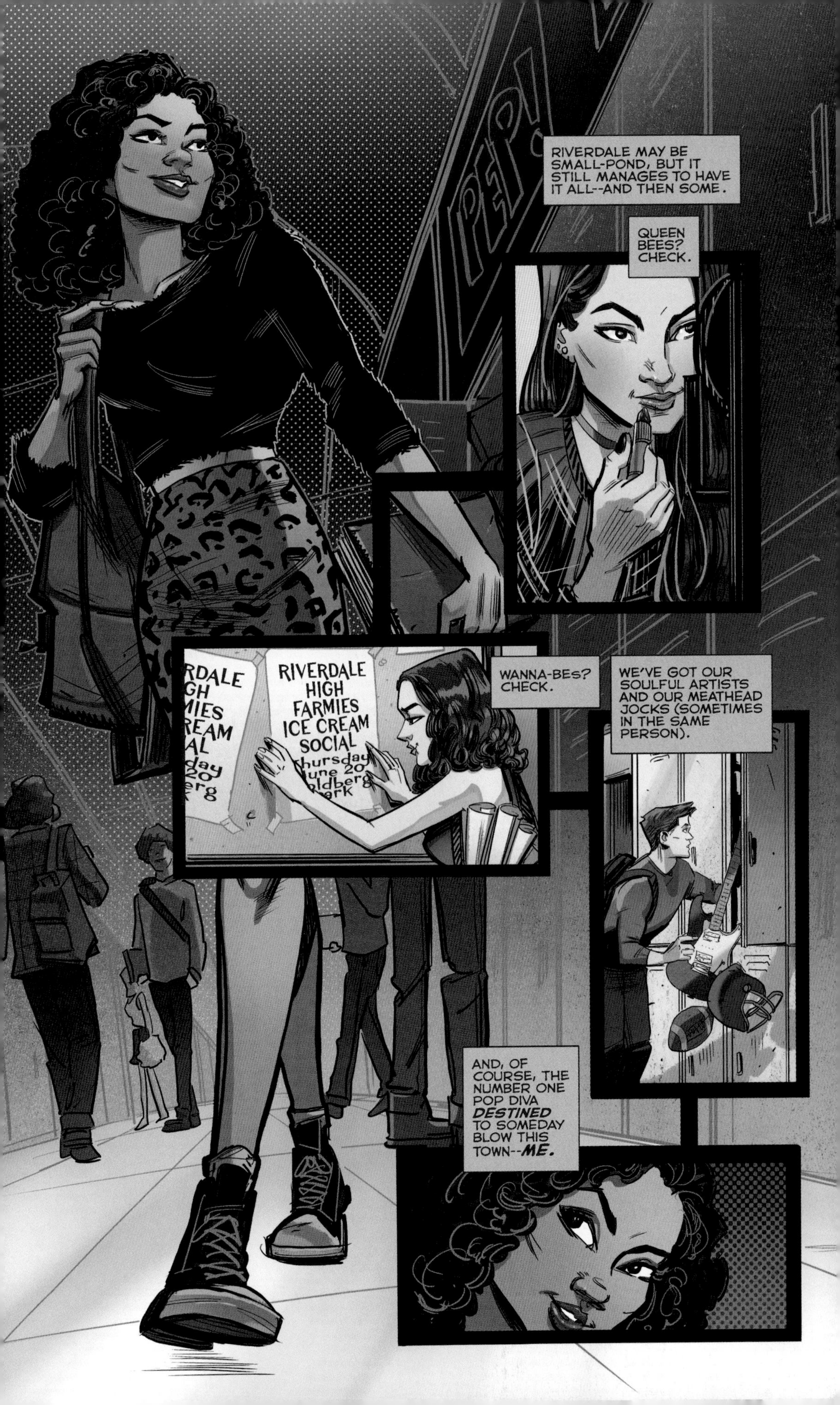
RIVERDALE MAY BE SMALL-POND, BUT IT STILL MANAGES TO HAVE IT ALL--AND THEN SOME.
QUEEN BEES? CHECK.
RIVERDALE HIGH FARMIES ICE CREAM SOCIAL Thursday June 20
WANNA-BEs? CHECK.
WE'VE GOT OUR SOULFUL ARTISTS AND OUR MEATHEAD JOCKS (SOMETIMES IN THE SAME PERSON).
AND, OF COURSE, THE NUMBER ONE POP DIVA *DESTINED* TO SOMEDAY BLOW THIS TOWN--*ME.*

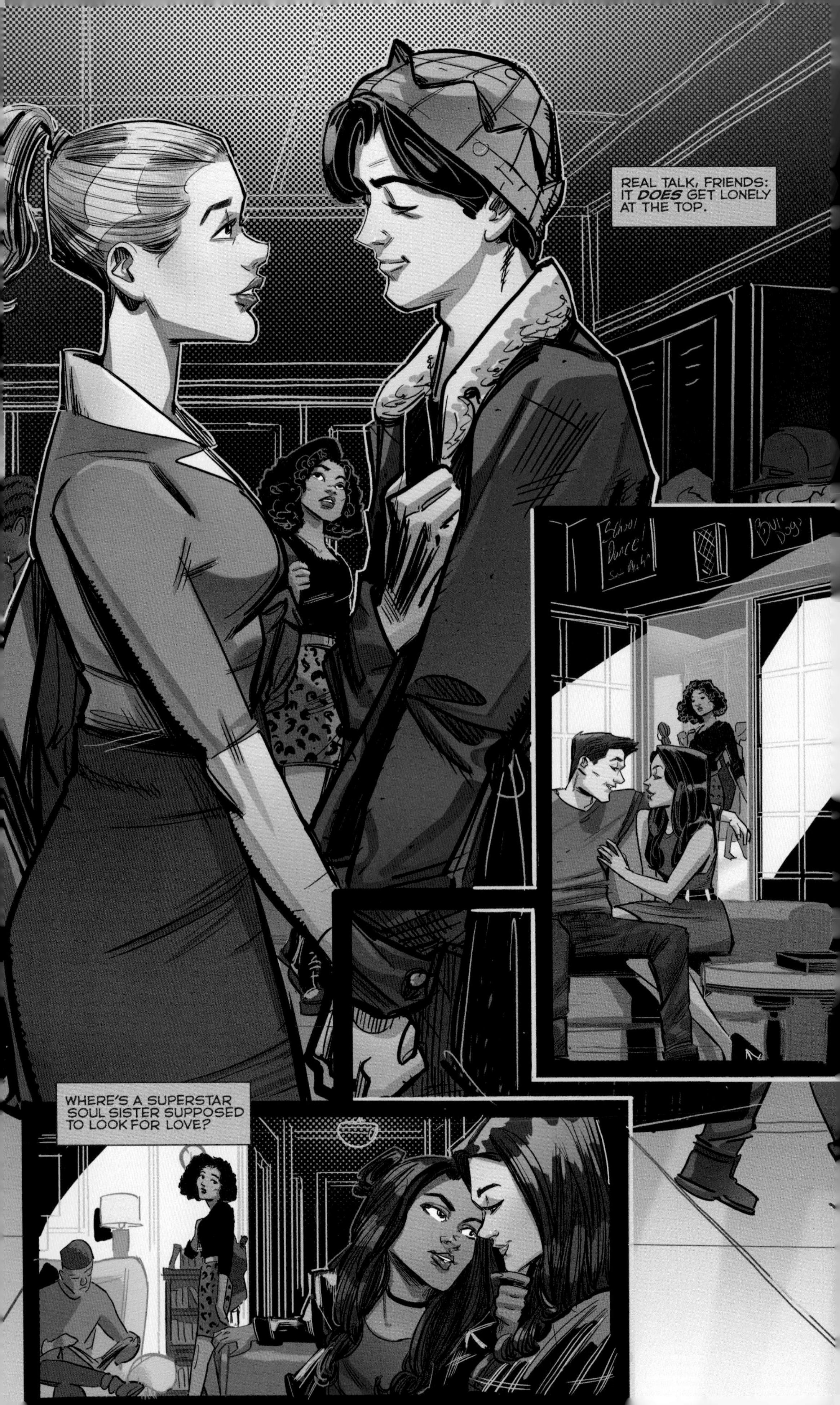
REAL TALK, FRIENDS: IT *DOES* GET LONELY AT THE TOP.
School Dance!
Bulldogs
WHERE'S A SUPERSTAR SOUL SISTER SUPPOSED TO LOOK FOR LOVE?

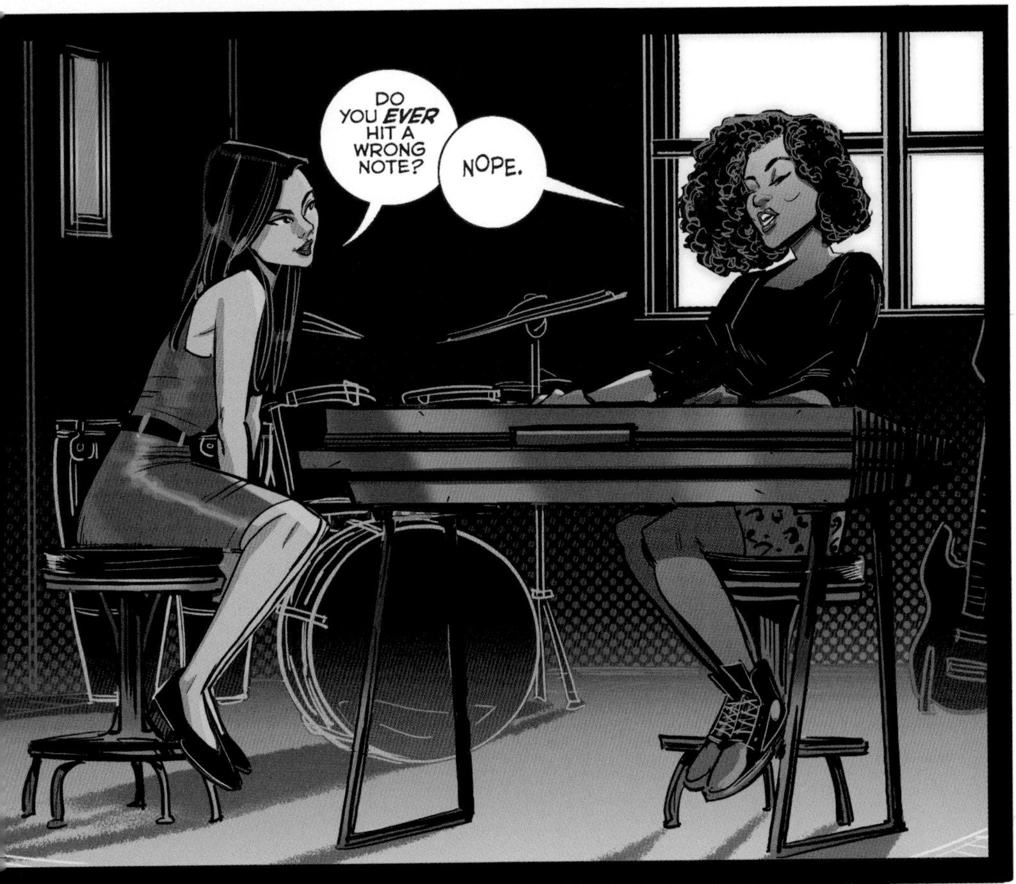
DO YOU *EVER* HIT A WRONG NOTE?
NOPE.

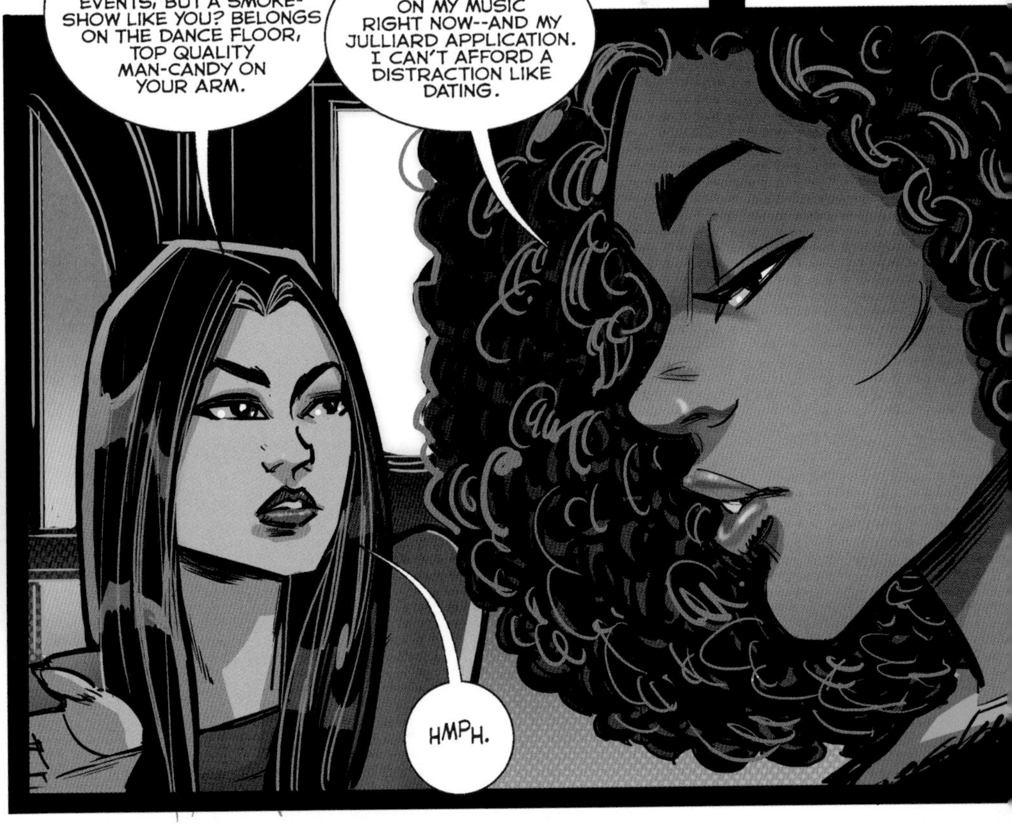
GIRL, I KNOW YOU'RE USUALLY TOO BUSY HEADLINING SCHOOL EVENTS, BUT A SMOKE-SHOW LIKE YOU? BELONGS ON THE DANCE FLOOR, TOP QUALITY MAN-CANDY ON YOUR ARM.
I'VE GOTTA STAY FOCUSED ON MY MUSIC RIGHT NOW--AND MY JULLIARD APPLICATION. I CAN'T AFFORD A DISTRACTION LIKE DATING.
HMPH.

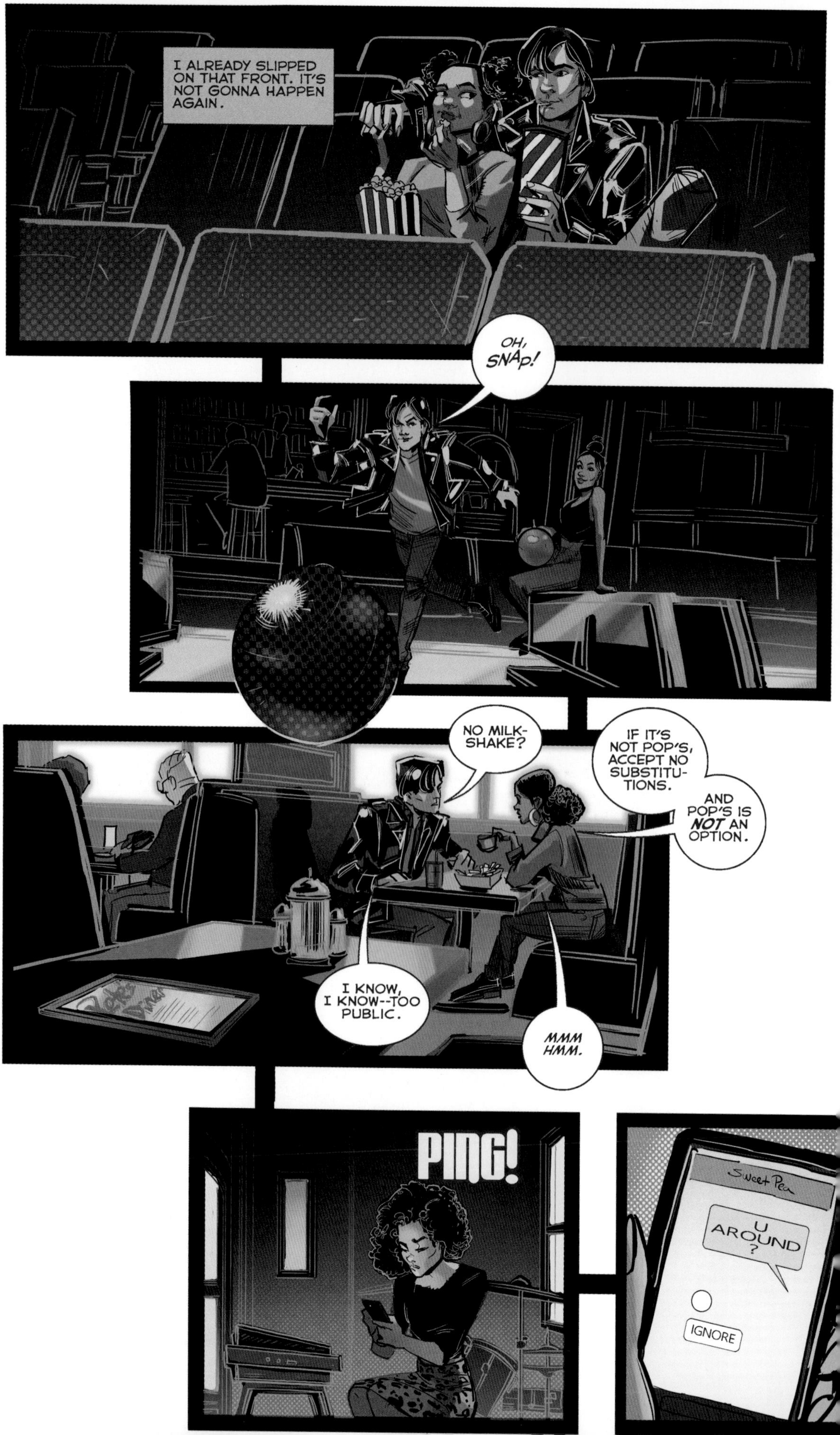
I ALREADY SLIPPED ON THAT FRONT. IT'S NOT GONNA HAPPEN AGAIN.
OH, SNAP!
NO MILK-SHAKE?
IF IT'S NOT POP'S, ACCEPT NO SUBSTITU-TIONS.
AND POP'S IS NOT AN OPTION.
I KNOW, I KNOW--TOO PUBLIC.
MMM HMM.
PING!
Sweet Pea
U AROUND ?
IGNORE

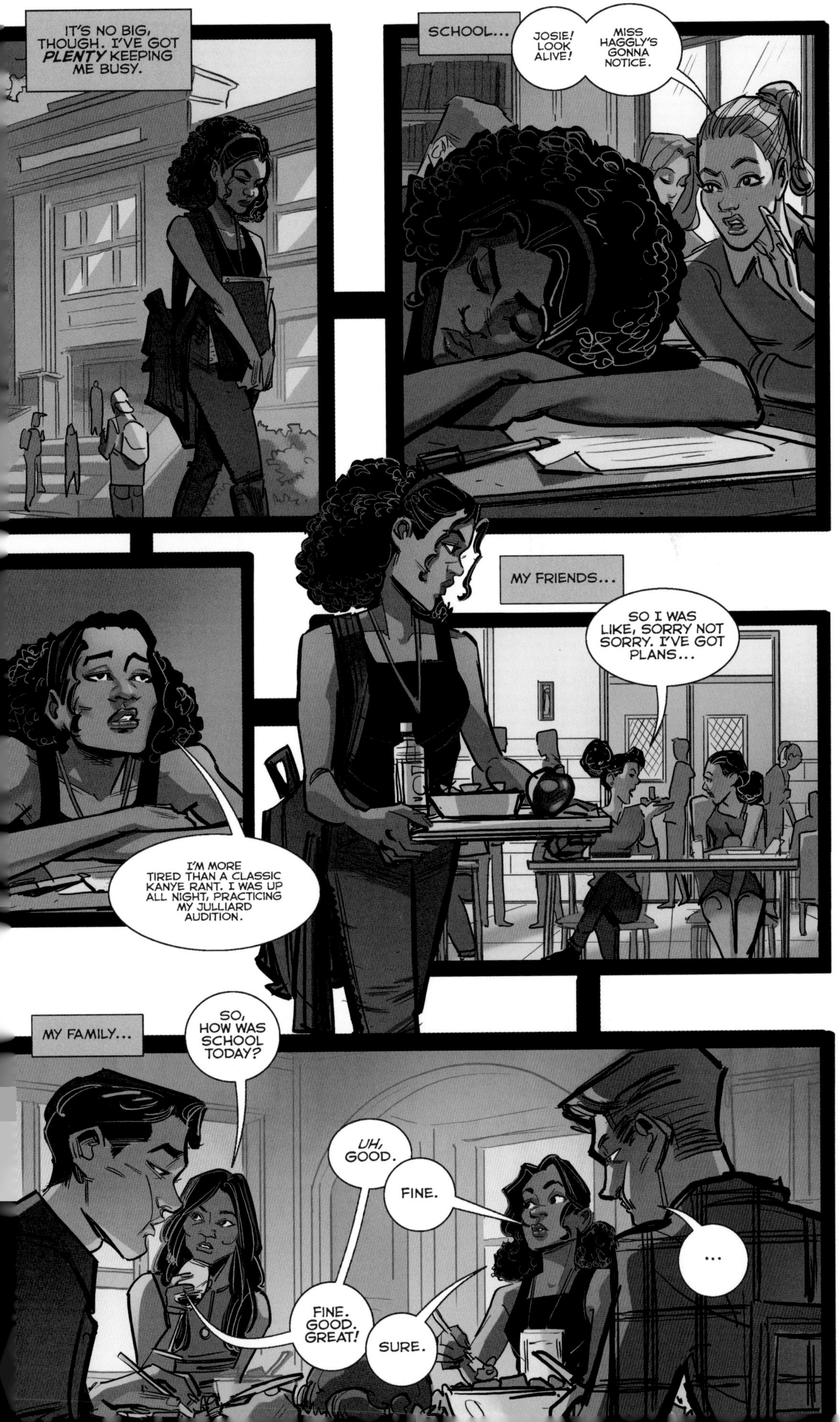
IT'S NO BIG, THOUGH. I'VE GOT *PLENTY* KEEPING ME BUSY.
SCHOOL...
JOSIE! LOOK ALIVE!
MISS HAGGLY'S GONNA NOTICE.
I'M MORE TIRED THAN A CLASSIC KANYE RANT. I WAS UP ALL NIGHT, PRACTICING MY JULLIARD AUDITION.
MY FRIENDS...
SO I WAS LIKE, SORRY NOT SORRY. I'VE GOT PLANS...
MY FAMILY...
SO, HOW WAS SCHOOL TODAY?
UH, GOOD.
FINE.
...
FINE. GOOD. GREAT!
SURE.

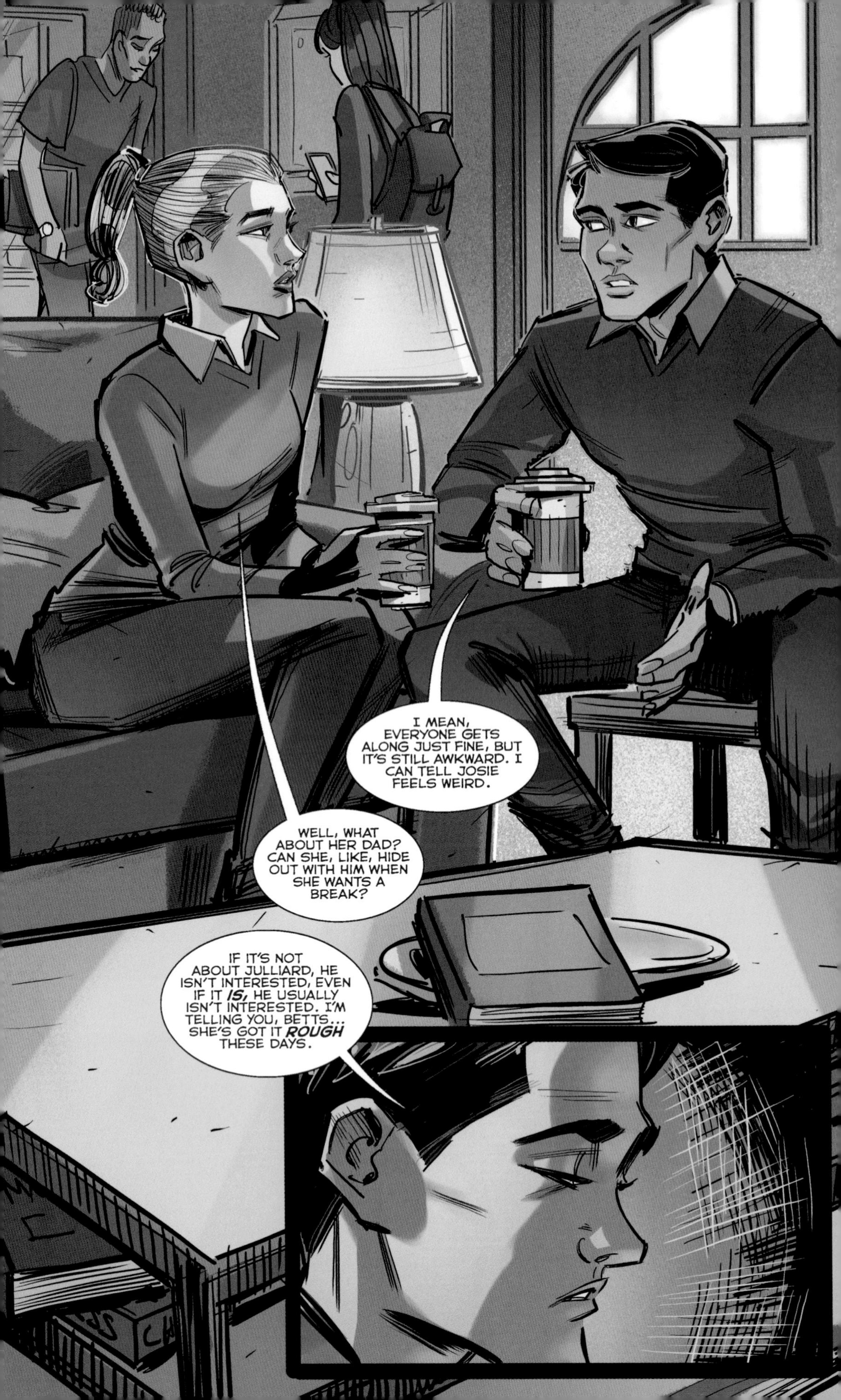
I MEAN, EVERYONE GETS ALONG JUST FINE, BUT IT'S STILL AWKWARD. I CAN TELL JOSIE FEELS WEIRD.
WELL, WHAT ABOUT HER DAD? CAN SHE, LIKE, HIDE OUT WITH HIM WHEN SHE WANTS A BREAK?
IF IT'S NOT ABOUT JULLIARD, HE ISN'T INTERESTED. EVEN IF IT *IS*, HE USUALLY ISN'T INTERESTED. I'M TELLING YOU, BETTS... SHE'S GOT IT ***ROUGH*** THESE DAYS.

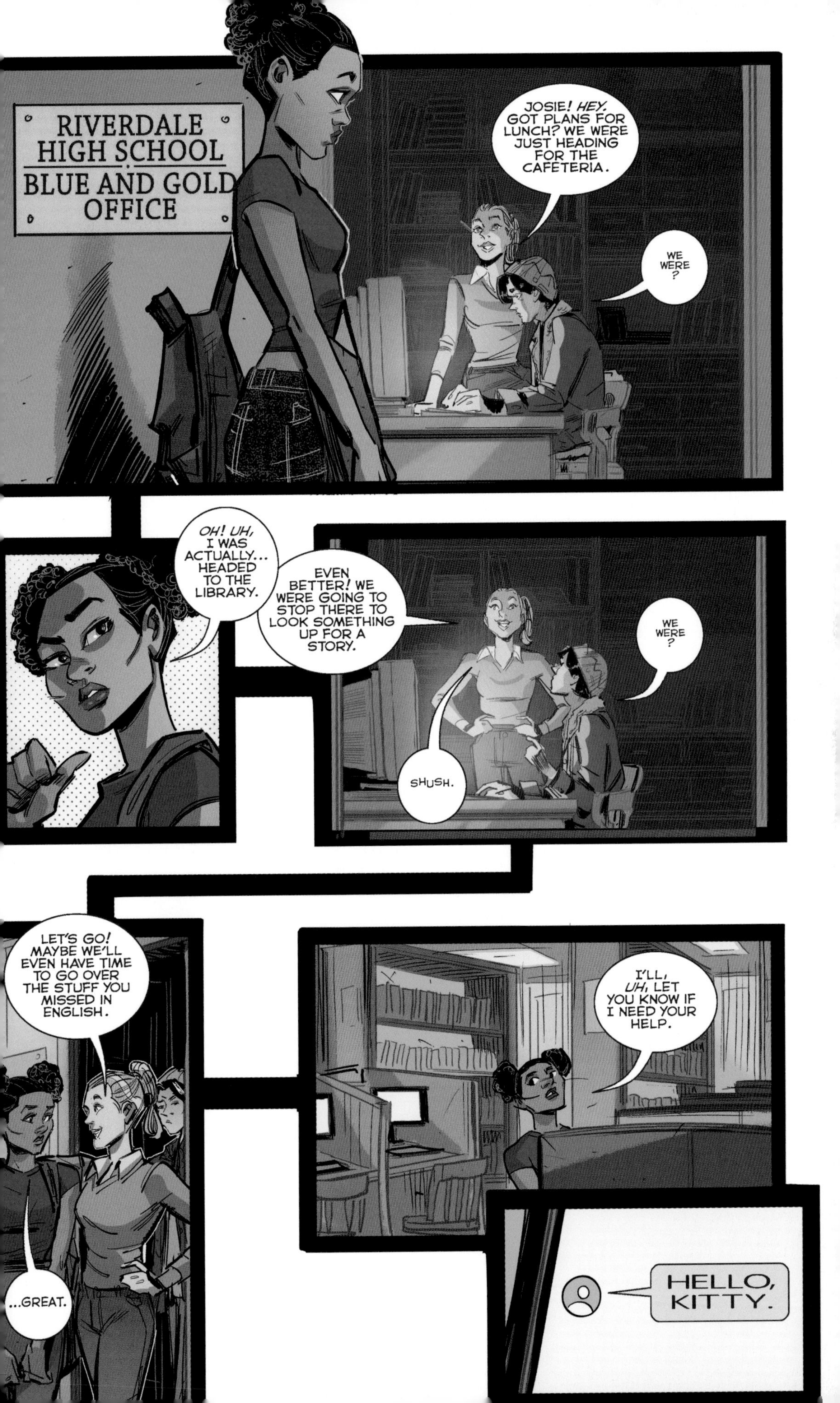
RIVERDALE HIGH SCHOOL
BLUE AND GOLD OFFICE
JOSIE! HEY. GOT PLANS FOR LUNCH? WE WERE JUST HEADING FOR THE CAFETERIA.
WE WERE?
OH! UH, I WAS ACTUALLY... HEADED TO THE LIBRARY.
EVEN BETTER! WE WERE GOING TO STOP THERE TO LOOK SOMETHING UP FOR A STORY.
WE WERE?
SHUSH.
LET'S GO! MAYBE WE'LL EVEN HAVE TIME TO GO OVER THE STUFF YOU MISSED IN ENGLISH.
...GREAT.
I'LL, UH, LET YOU KNOW IF I NEED YOUR HELP.
HELLO, KITTY.

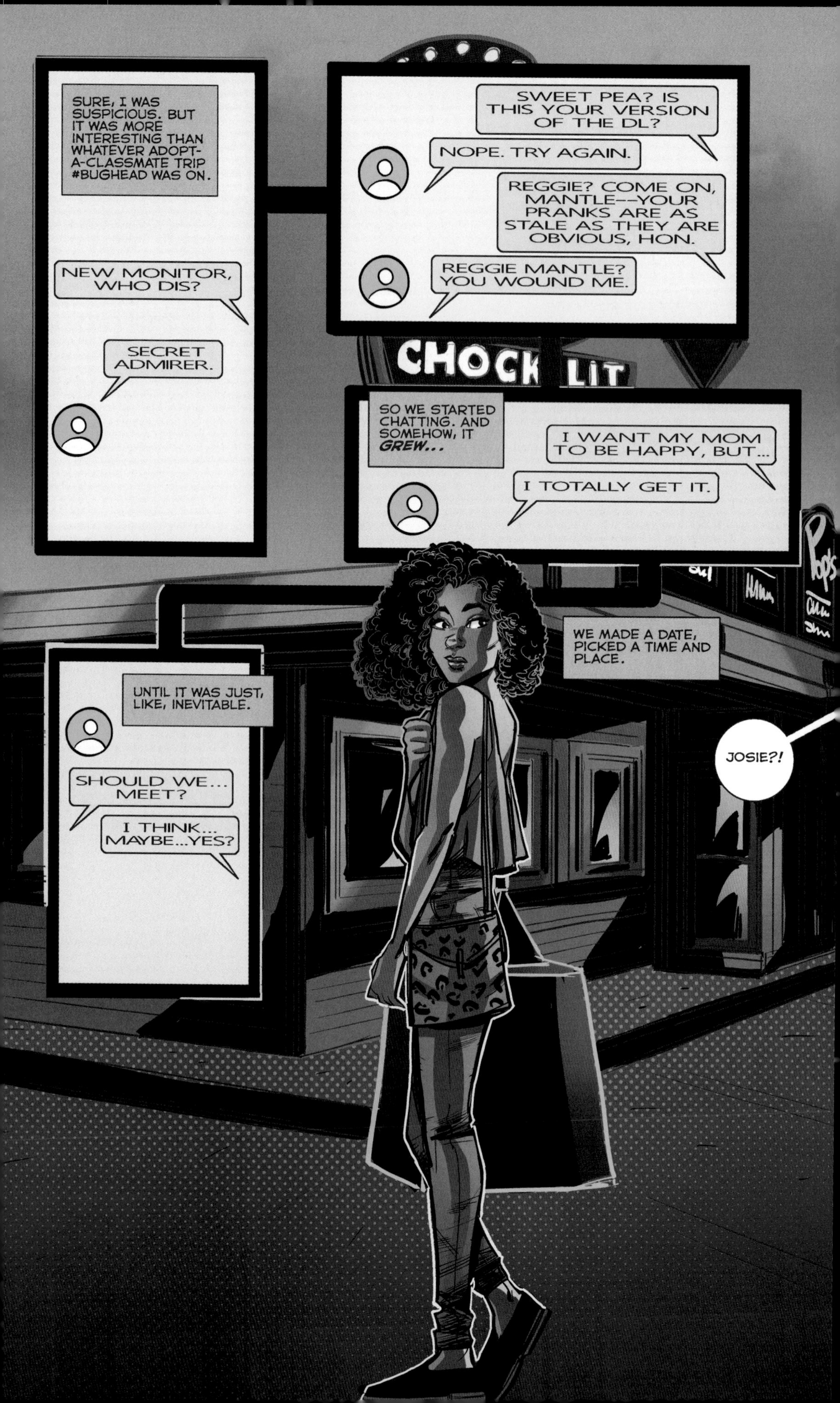
SURE, I WAS SUSPICIOUS. BUT IT WAS MORE INTERESTING THAN WHATEVER ADOPT-A-CLASSMATE TRIP #BUGHEAD WAS ON.
NEW MONITOR, WHO DIS?
SECRET ADMIRER.
SWEET PEA? IS THIS YOUR VERSION OF THE DL?
NOPE. TRY AGAIN.
REGGIE? COME ON, MANTLE--YOUR PRANKS ARE AS STALE AS THEY ARE OBVIOUS, HON.
REGGIE MANTLE? YOU WOUND ME.
CHOCK LIT
SO WE STARTED CHATTING. AND SOMEHOW, IT *GREW...*
I WANT MY MOM TO BE HAPPY, BUT...
I TOTALLY GET IT.
UNTIL IT WAS JUST, LIKE, INEVITABLE.
SHOULD WE... MEET?
I THINK... MAYBE...YES?
WE MADE A DATE, PICKED A TIME AND PLACE.
JOSIE?!

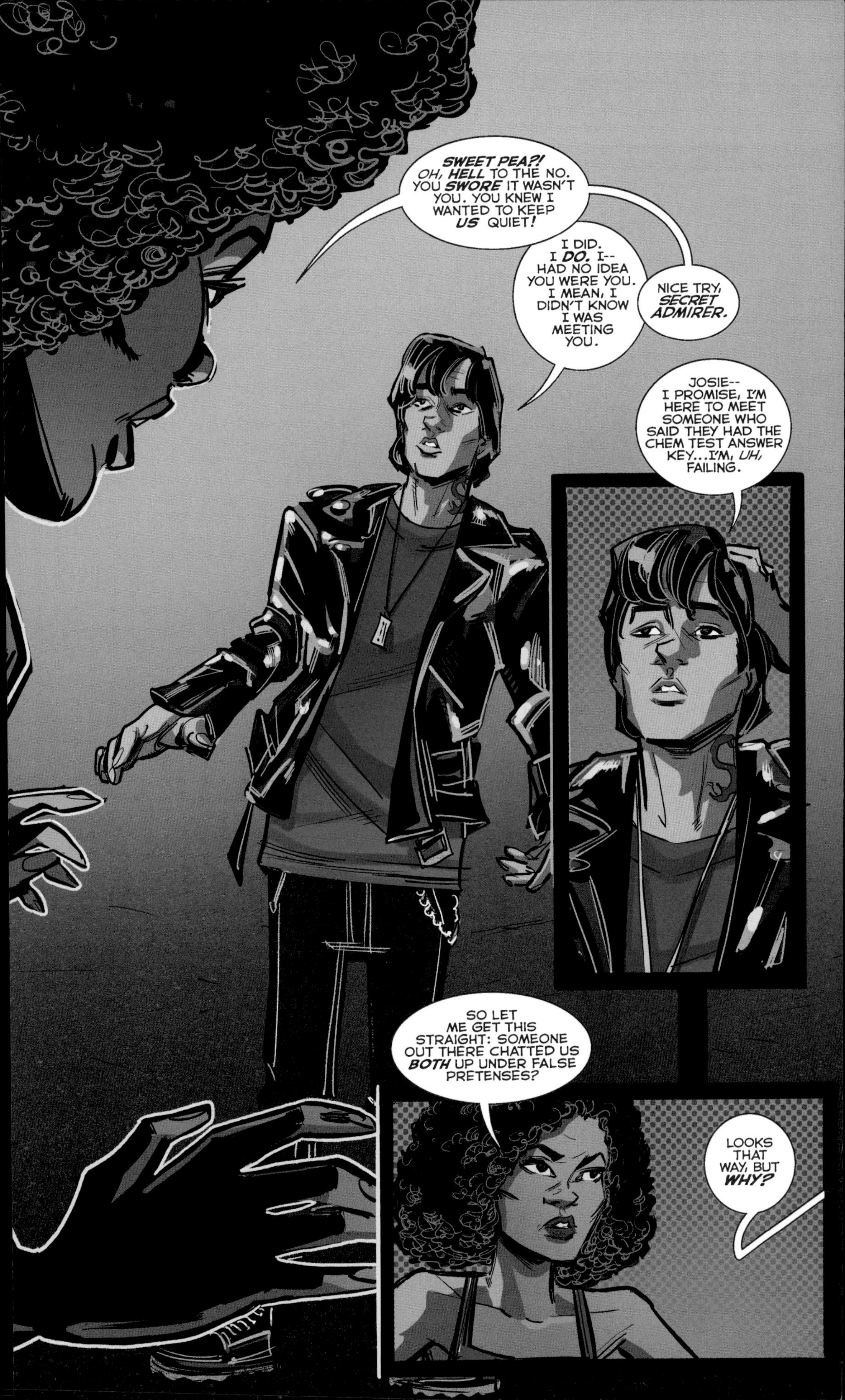
SWEET PEA?! OH, HELL TO THE NO. YOU SWORE IT WASN'T YOU. YOU KNEW I WANTED TO KEEP US QUIET!
I DID. I DO. I-- HAD NO IDEA YOU WERE YOU. I MEAN, I DIDN'T KNOW I WAS MEETING YOU.
NICE TRY, SECRET ADMIRER.
JOSIE-- I PROMISE, I'M HERE TO MEET SOMEONE WHO SAID THEY HAD THE CHEM TEST ANSWER KEY...I'M, UH, FAILING.
SO LET ME GET THIS STRAIGHT: SOMEONE OUT THERE CHATTED US BOTH UP UNDER FALSE PRETENSES?
LOOKS THAT WAY, BUT WHY?

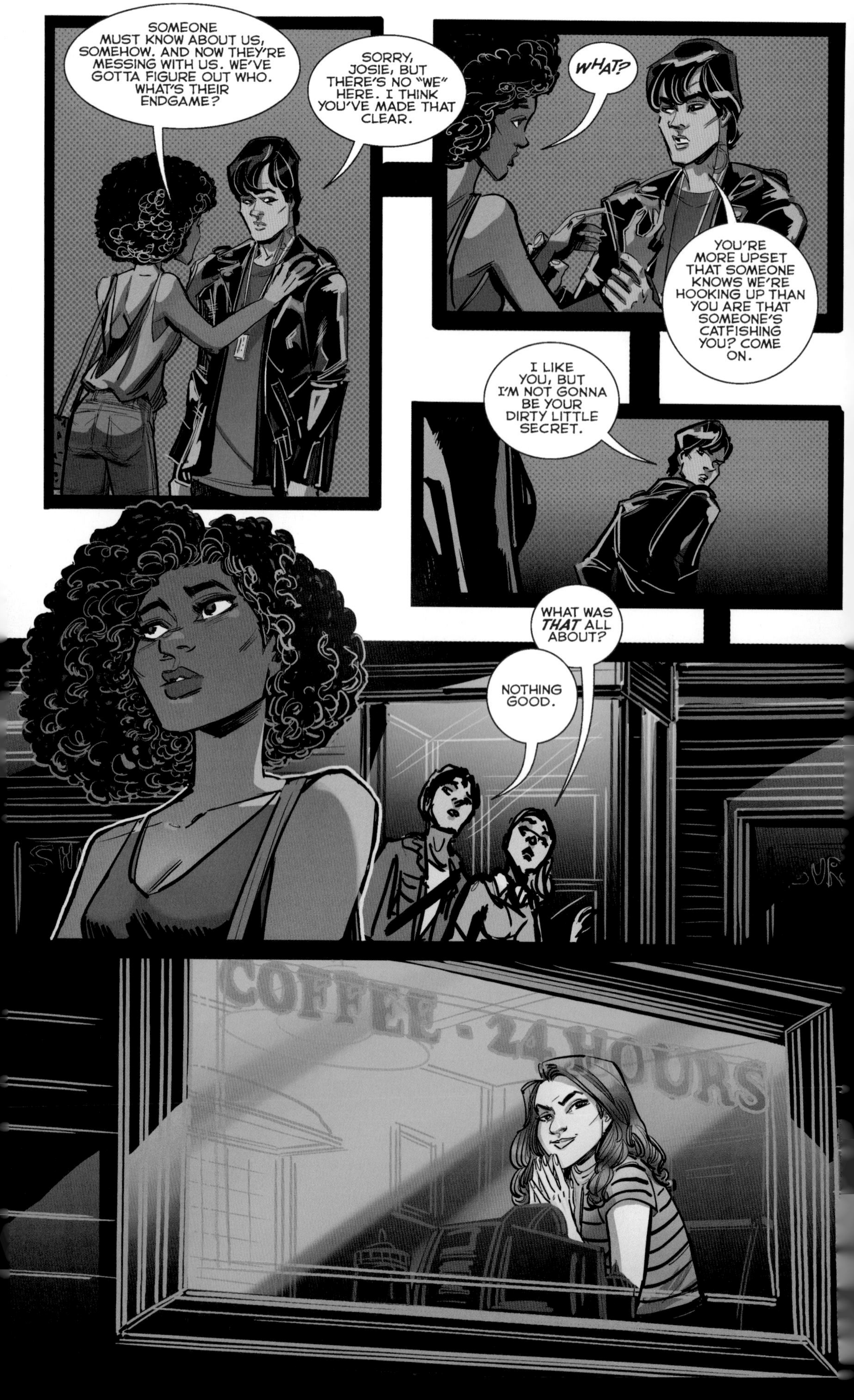
SOMEONE MUST KNOW ABOUT US, SOMEHOW. AND NOW THEY'RE MESSING WITH US. WE'VE GOTTA FIGURE OUT WHO. WHAT'S THEIR ENDGAME?
SORRY, JOSIE, BUT THERE'S NO "WE" HERE. I THINK YOU'VE MADE THAT CLEAR.
WHAT?
YOU'RE MORE UPSET THAT SOMEONE KNOWS WE'RE HOOKING UP THAN YOU ARE THAT SOMEONE'S CATFISHING YOU? COME ON.
I LIKE YOU, BUT I'M NOT GONNA BE YOUR DIRTY LITTLE SECRET.
WHAT WAS *THAT* ALL ABOUT?
NOTHING GOOD.
COFFEE - 24 HOURS

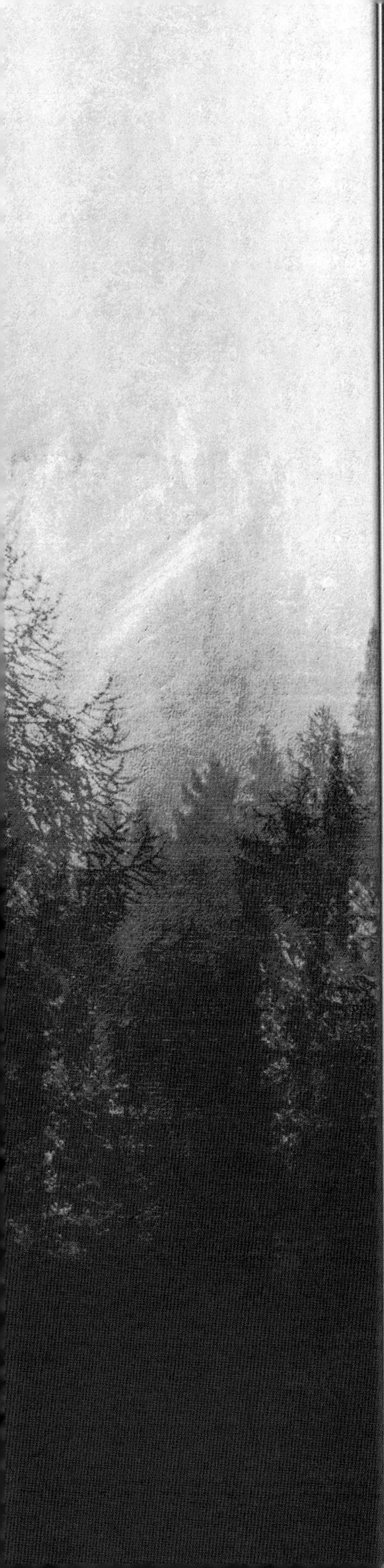

CHAPTER SIX

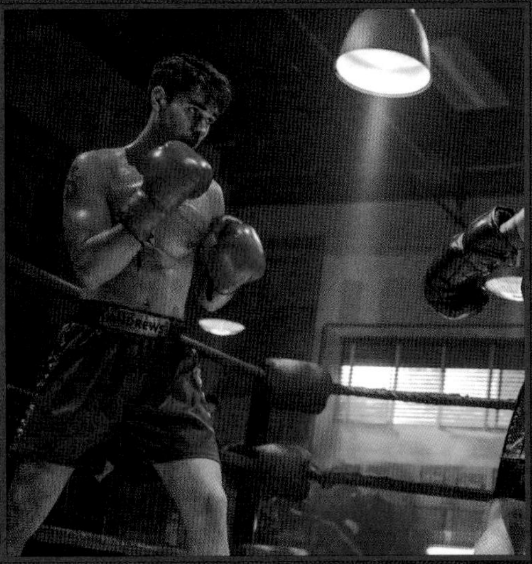

FUNNY GAMES

WRITER:
MICOL OSTOW

ART:
JOE EISMA

COLORS:
MATT HERMS

LETTERS:
JANICE CHIANG

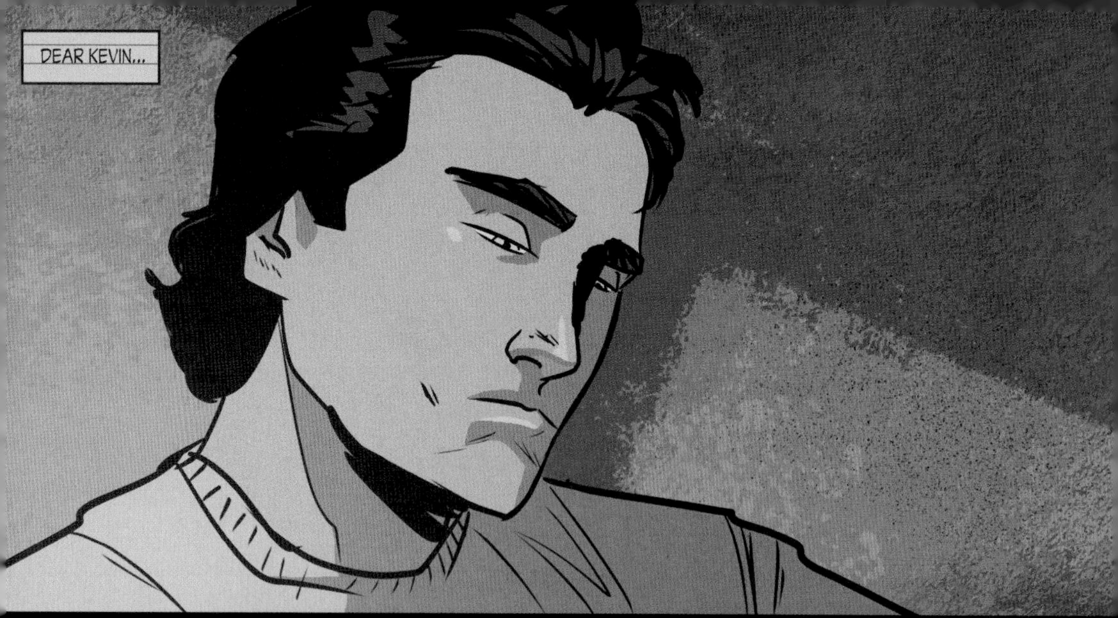
DEAR KEVIN...

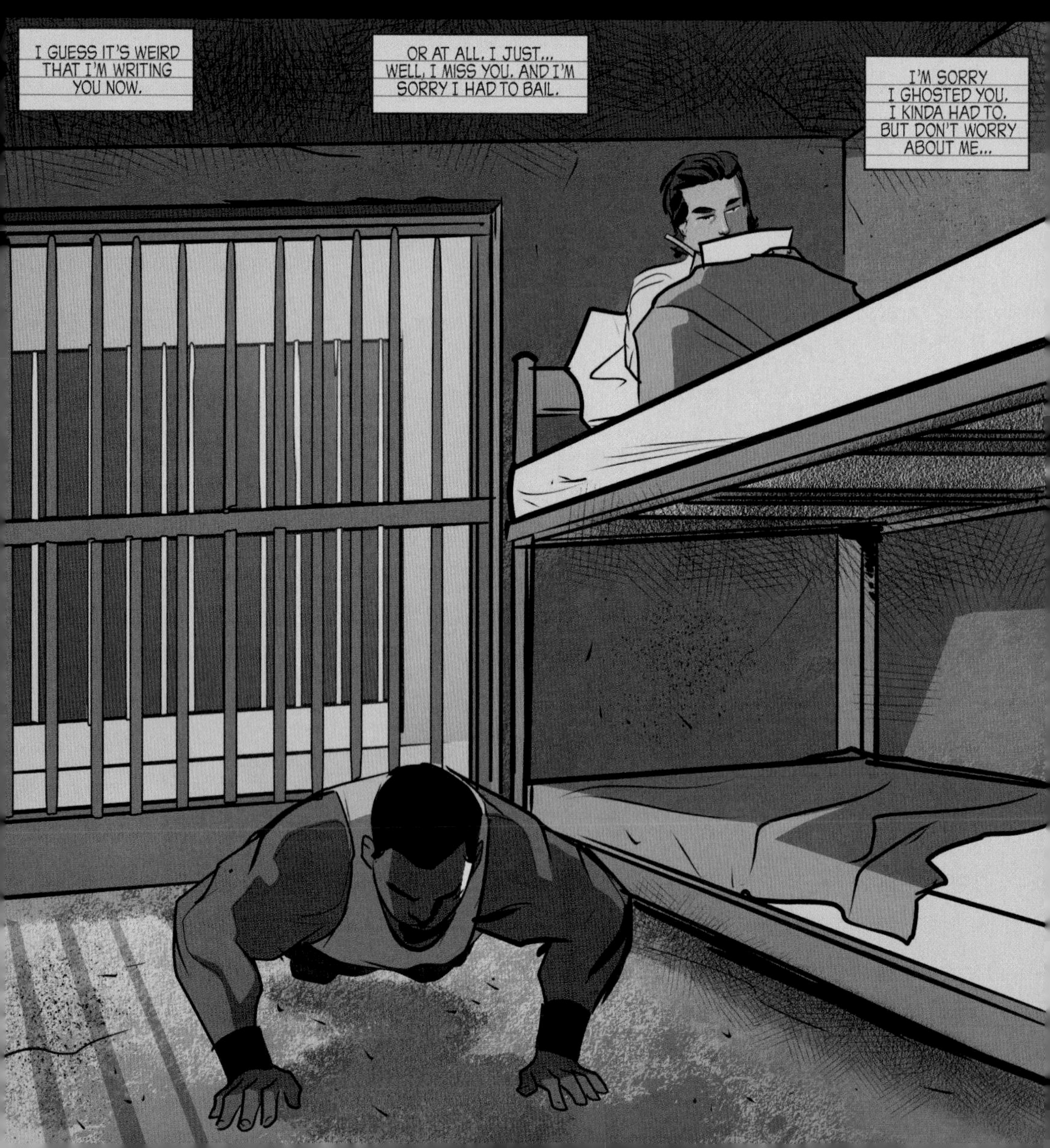
I GUESS IT'S WEIRD THAT I'M WRITING YOU NOW.
OR AT ALL. I JUST... WELL, I MISS YOU. AND I'M SORRY I HAD TO BAIL.
I'M SORRY I GHOSTED YOU. I KINDA HAD TO. BUT DON'T WORRY ABOUT ME...

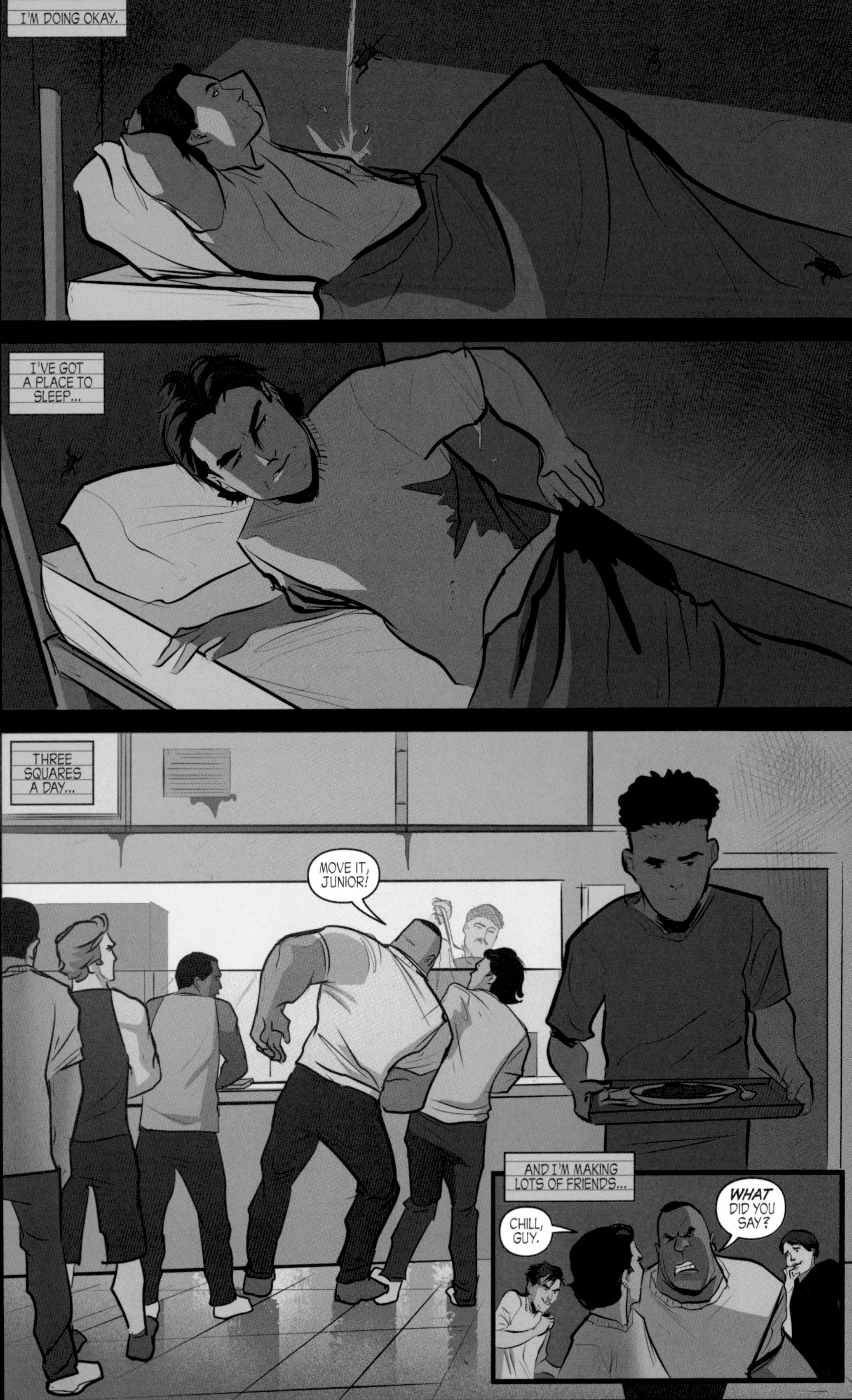

I'M DOING OKAY.
I'VE GOT A PLACE TO SLEEP...
THREE SQUARES A DAY...
MOVE IT, JUNIOR!
AND I'M MAKING LOTS OF FRIENDS...
CHILL, GUY.
WHAT DID YOU SAY?

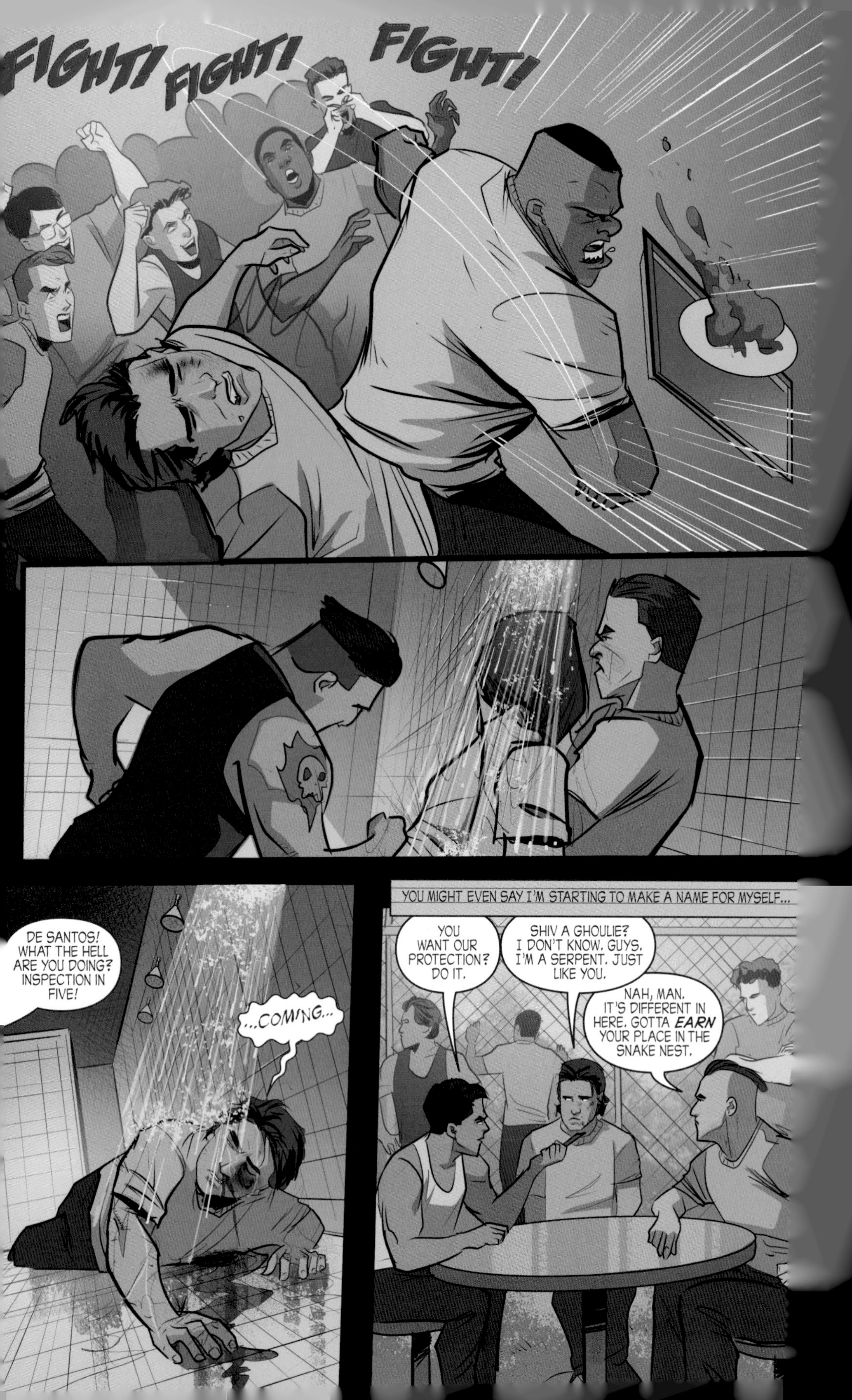
FIGHT! FIGHT! FIGHT!
DE SANTOS! WHAT THE HELL ARE YOU DOING? INSPECTION IN FIVE!
...COMING...
YOU MIGHT EVEN SAY I'M STARTING TO MAKE A NAME FOR MYSELF...
YOU WANT OUR PROTECTION? DO IT.
SHIV A GHOULIE? I DON'T KNOW, GUYS, I'M A SERPENT, JUST LIKE YOU.
NAH, MAN. IT'S DIFFERENT IN HERE. GOTTA EARN YOUR PLACE IN THE SNAKE NEST.

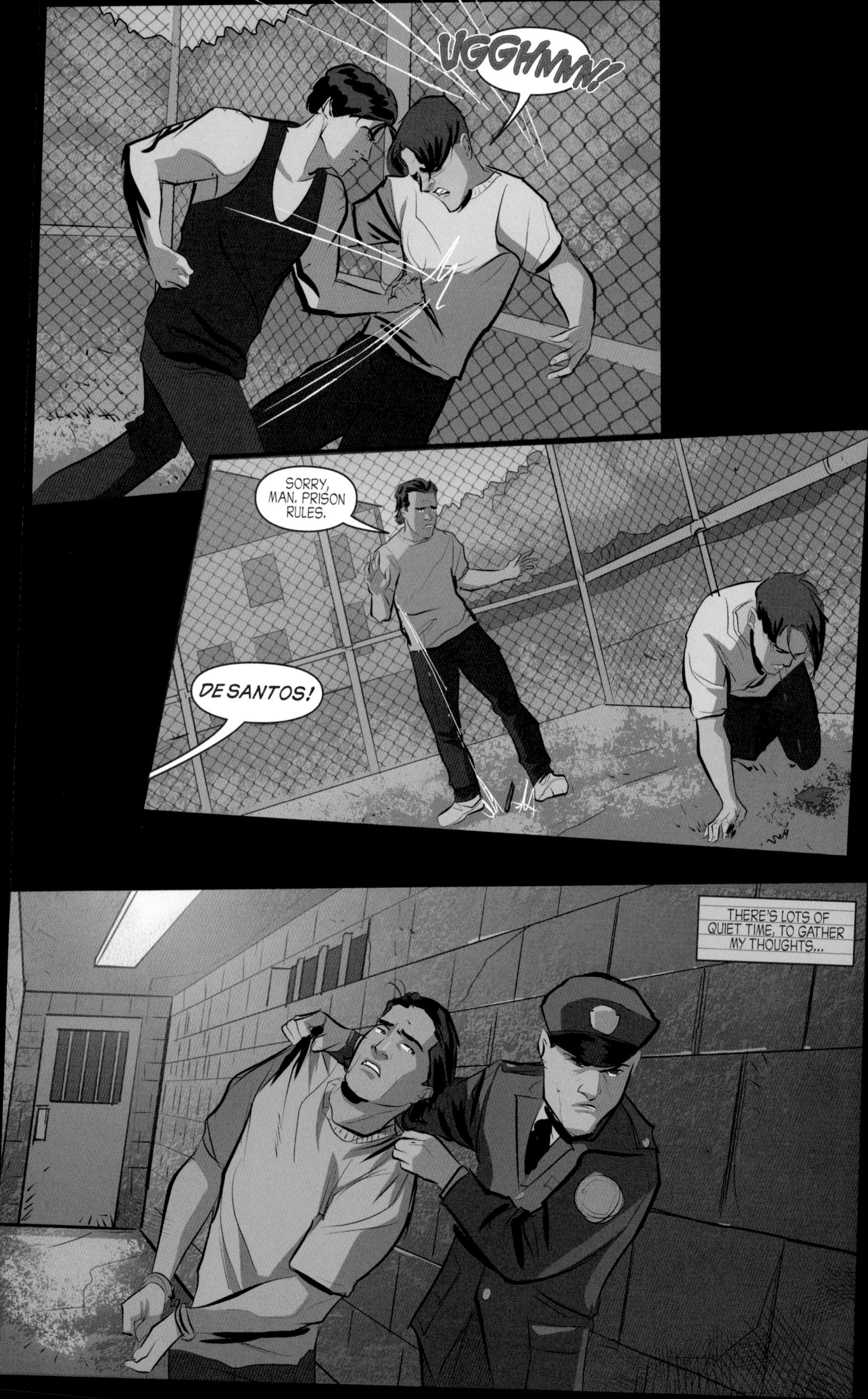
UGGHMMN!
SORRY, MAN. PRISON RULES.
DE SANTOS!
THERE'S LOTS OF QUIET TIME, TO GATHER MY THOUGHTS...

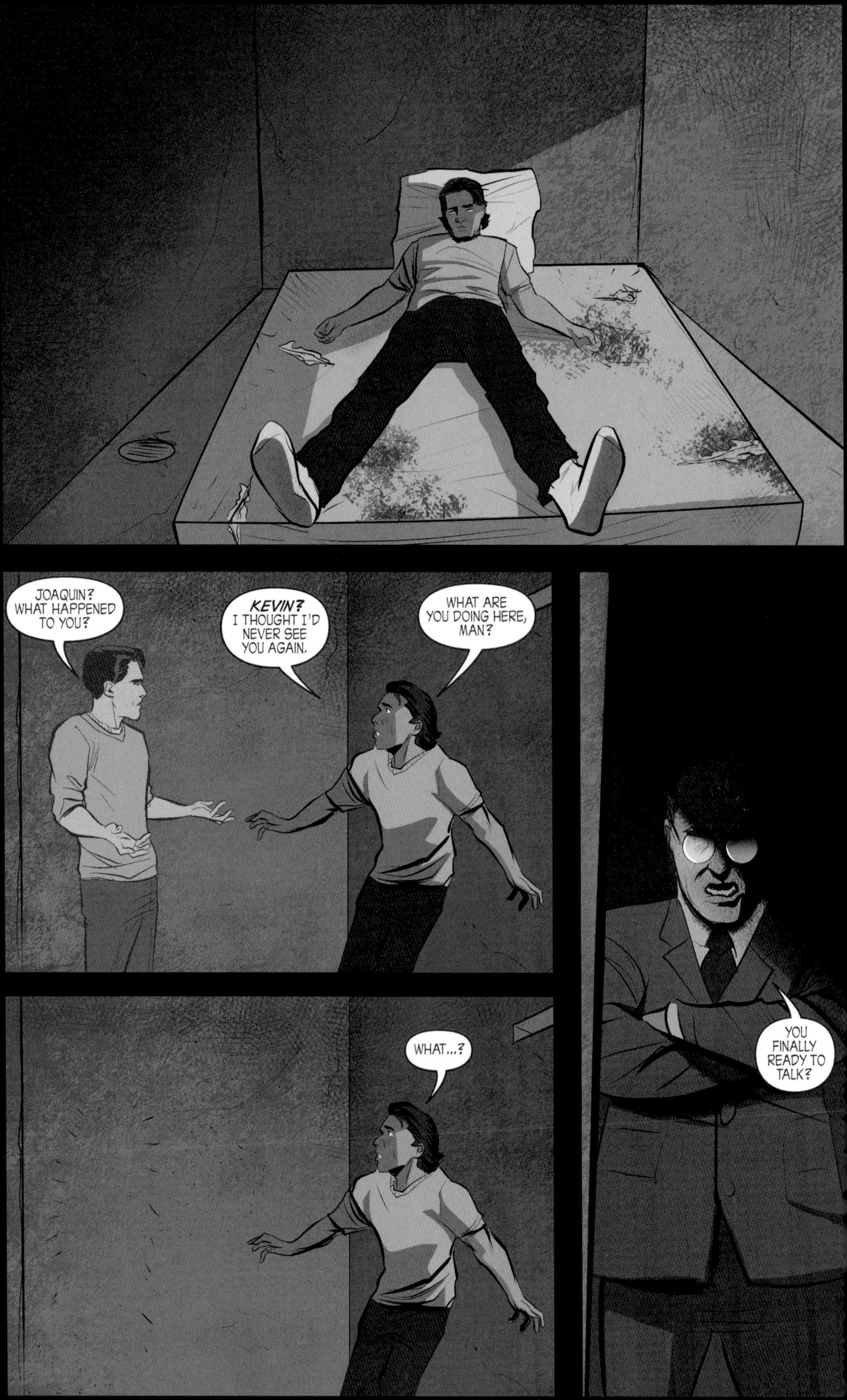
JOAQUIN? WHAT HAPPENED TO YOU?
KEVIN? I THOUGHT I'D NEVER SEE YOU AGAIN.
WHAT ARE YOU DOING HERE, MAN?
WHAT...?
YOU FINALLY READY TO TALK?

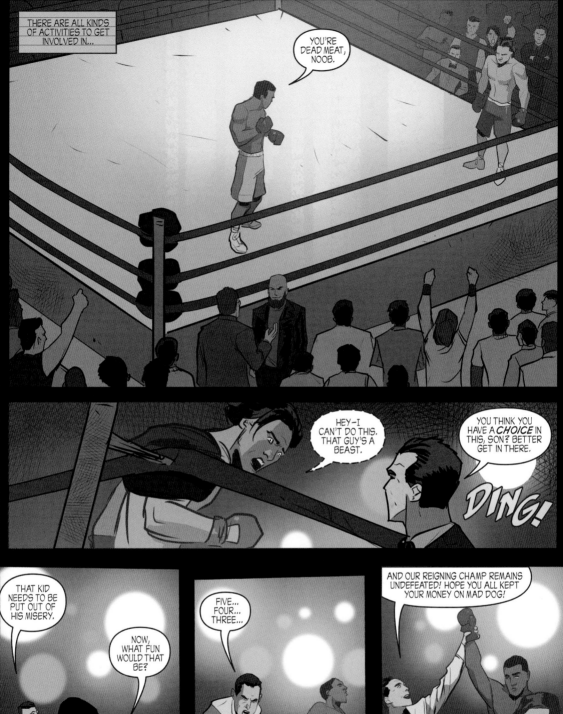

THERE ARE ALL KINDS OF ACTIVITIES TO GET INVOLVED IN...

YOU'RE DEAD MEAT, NOOB.

HEY—I CAN'T DO THIS. THAT GUY'S A BEAST.

YOU THINK YOU HAVE A *CHOICE* IN THIS, SON? BETTER GET IN THERE.

DING!

THAT KID NEEDS TO BE PUT OUT OF HIS MISERY.

NOW, WHAT FUN WOULD THAT BE?

FIVE... FOUR... THREE...

AND OUR REIGNING CHAMP REMAINS UNDEFEATED! HOPE YOU ALL KEPT YOUR MONEY ON MAD DOG!

JOAQUIN?...

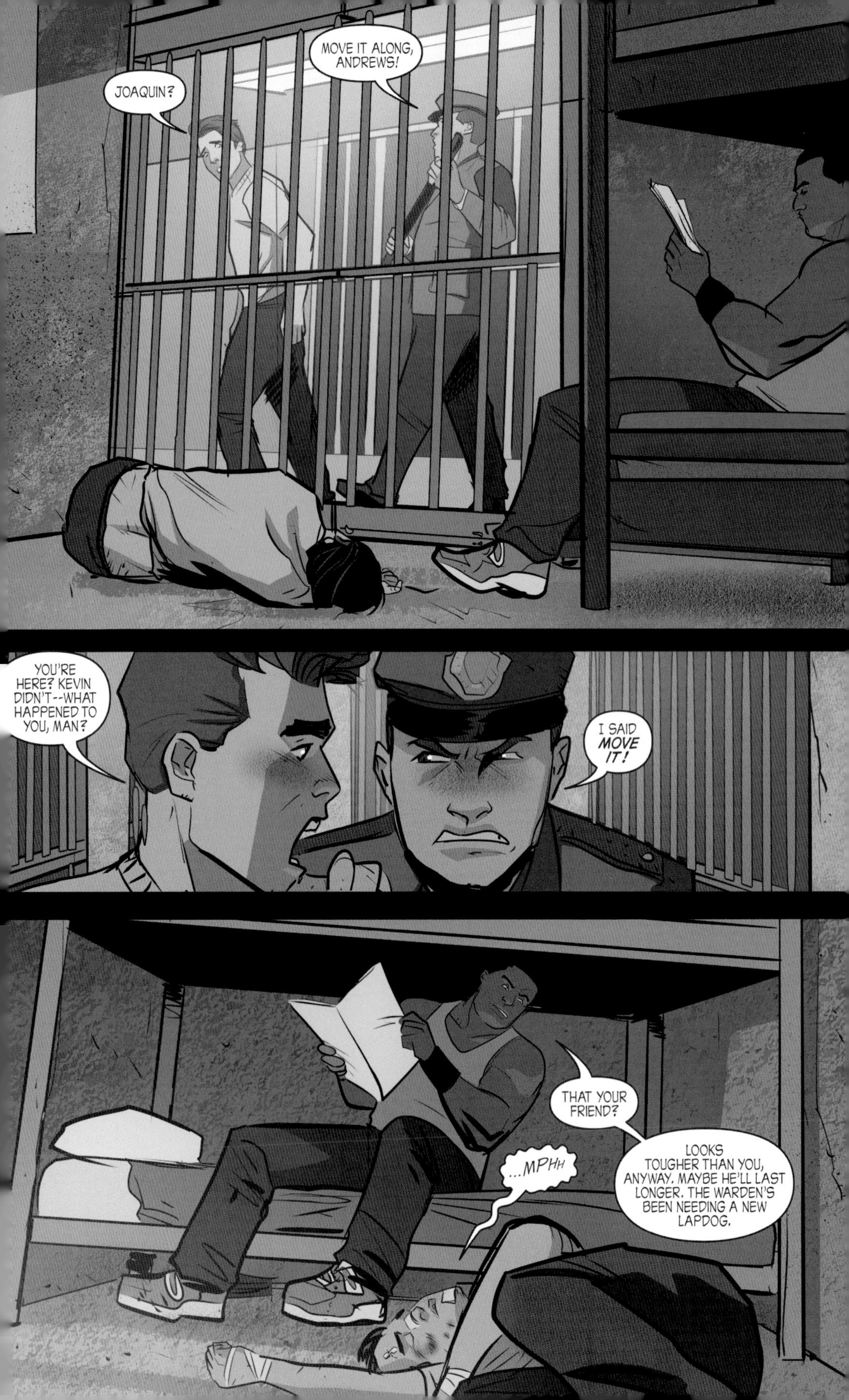
JOAQUIN?
MOVE IT ALONG, ANDREWS!
YOU'RE HERE? KEVIN DIDN'T--WHAT HAPPENED TO YOU, MAN?
I SAID *MOVE IT!*
THAT YOUR FRIEND?
LOOKS TOUGHER THAN YOU, ANYWAY. MAYBE HE'LL LAST LONGER. THE WARDEN'S BEEN NEEDING A NEW LAPDOG.
...MPHH

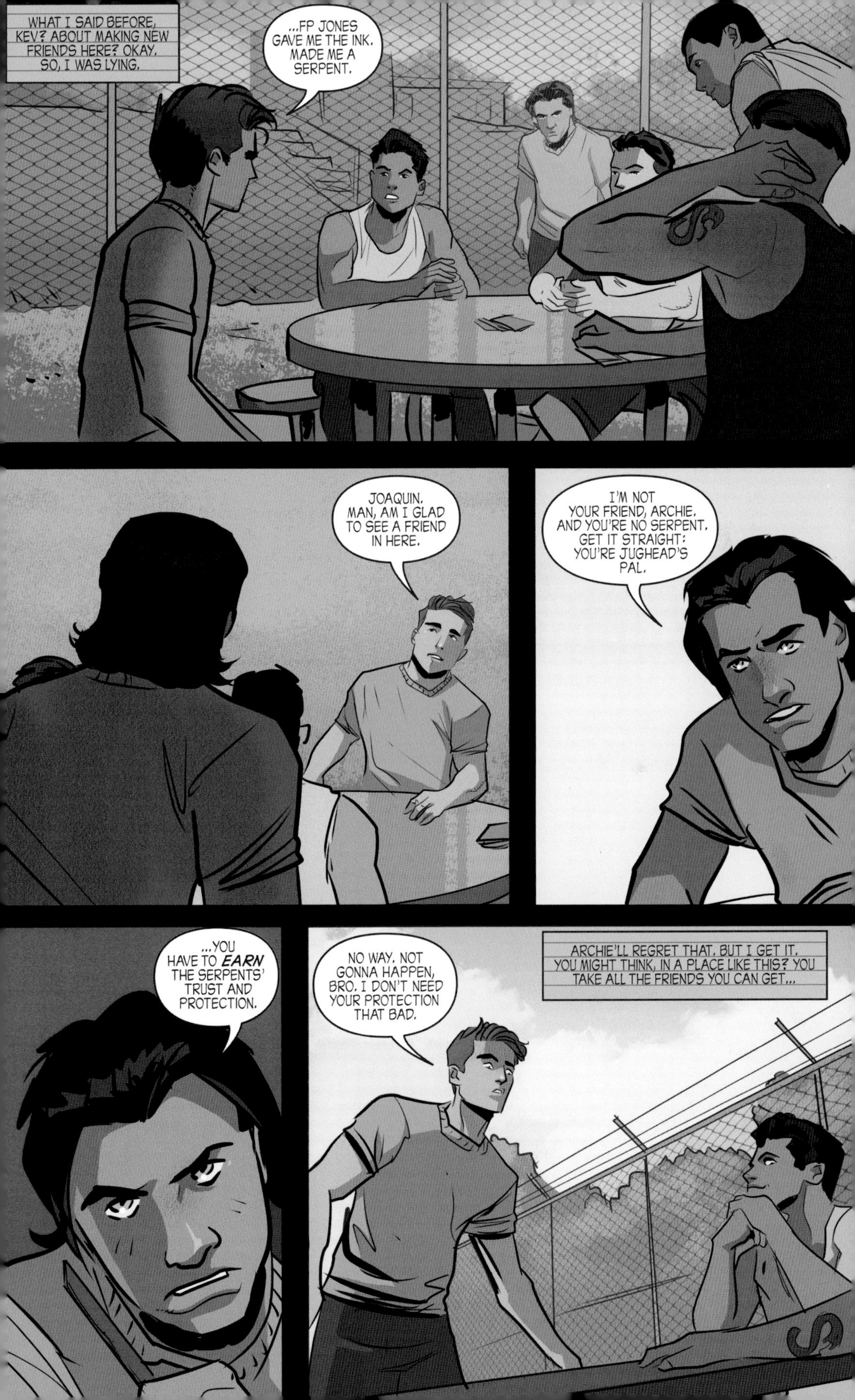
WHAT I SAID BEFORE, KEV? ABOUT MAKING NEW FRIENDS HERE? OKAY. SO, I WAS LYING.
...FP JONES GAVE ME THE INK. MADE ME A SERPENT.
JOAQUIN. MAN, AM I GLAD TO SEE A FRIEND IN HERE.
I'M NOT YOUR FRIEND, ARCHIE. AND YOU'RE NO SERPENT. GET IT STRAIGHT: YOU'RE JUGHEAD'S PAL.
...YOU HAVE TO *EARN* THE SERPENTS' TRUST AND PROTECTION.
NO WAY. NOT GONNA HAPPEN, BRO. I DON'T NEED YOUR PROTECTION THAT BAD.
ARCHIE'LL REGRET THAT. BUT I GET IT. YOU MIGHT THINK, IN A PLACE LIKE THIS? YOU TAKE ALL THE FRIENDS YOU CAN GET...

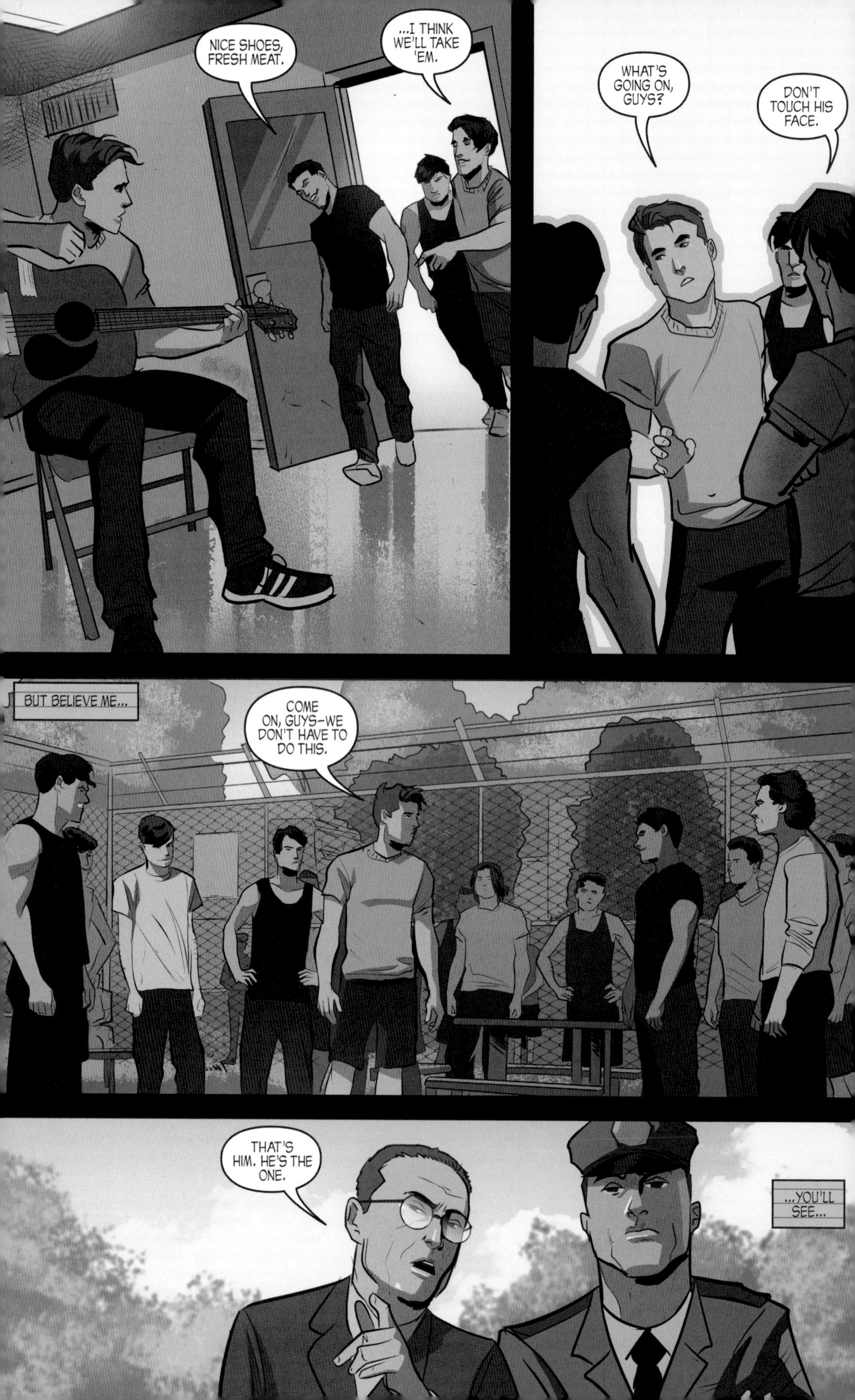
NICE SHOES, FRESH MEAT.
...I THINK WE'LL TAKE 'EM.
WHAT'S GOING ON, GUYS?
DON'T TOUCH HIS FACE.
BUT BELIEVE ME...
COME ON, GUYS—WE DON'T HAVE TO DO THIS.
THAT'S HIM. HE'S THE ONE.
...YOU'LL SEE...

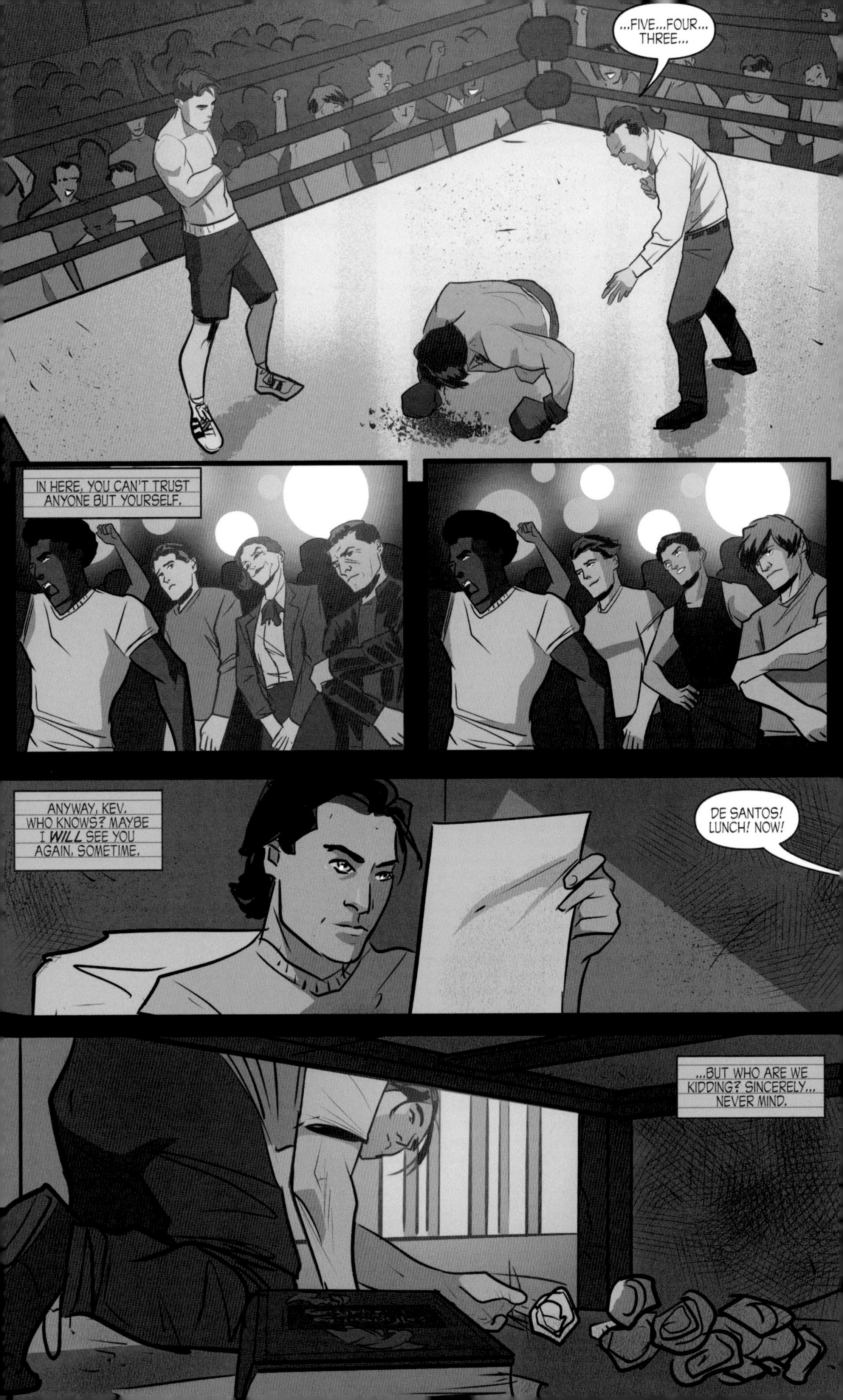
...FIVE...FOUR... THREE...
IN HERE, YOU CAN'T TRUST ANYONE BUT YOURSELF.
ANYWAY, KEV. WHO KNOWS? MAYBE I *WILL* SEE YOU AGAIN, SOMETIME.
DE SANTOS! LUNCH! NOW!
...BUT WHO ARE WE KIDDING? SINCERELY... NEVER MIND.

CHAPTER SEVEN

STRANGERS AT THE BUS STOP

WRITER:
MICOL OSTOW

ART:
THOMAS PITILLI

COLORS:
ANDRE SZYMANOWICZ

LETTERS:
JOHN WORKMAN

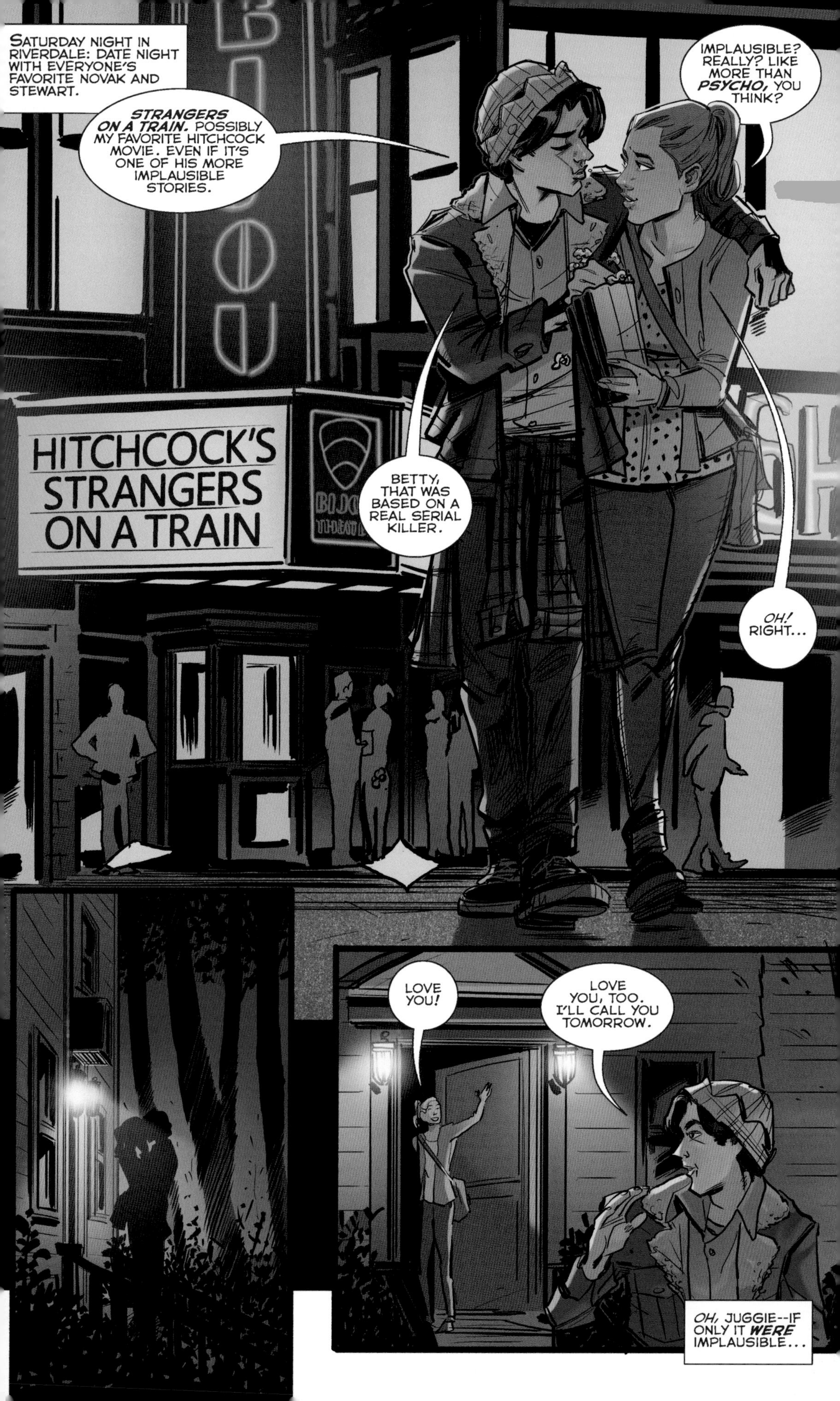
SATURDAY NIGHT IN RIVERDALE: DATE NIGHT WITH EVERYONE'S FAVORITE NOVAK AND STEWART.
STRANGERS ON A TRAIN. POSSIBLY MY FAVORITE HITCHCOCK MOVIE. EVEN IF IT'S ONE OF HIS MORE IMPLAUSIBLE STORIES.
IMPLAUSIBLE? REALLY? LIKE MORE THAN PSYCHO, YOU THINK?
HITCHCOCK'S STRANGERS ON A TRAIN
BETTY, THAT WAS BASED ON A REAL SERIAL KILLER.
OH! RIGHT...
LOVE YOU!
LOVE YOU, TOO. I'LL CALL YOU TOMORROW.
OH, JUGGIE--IF ONLY IT WERE IMPLAUSIBLE...

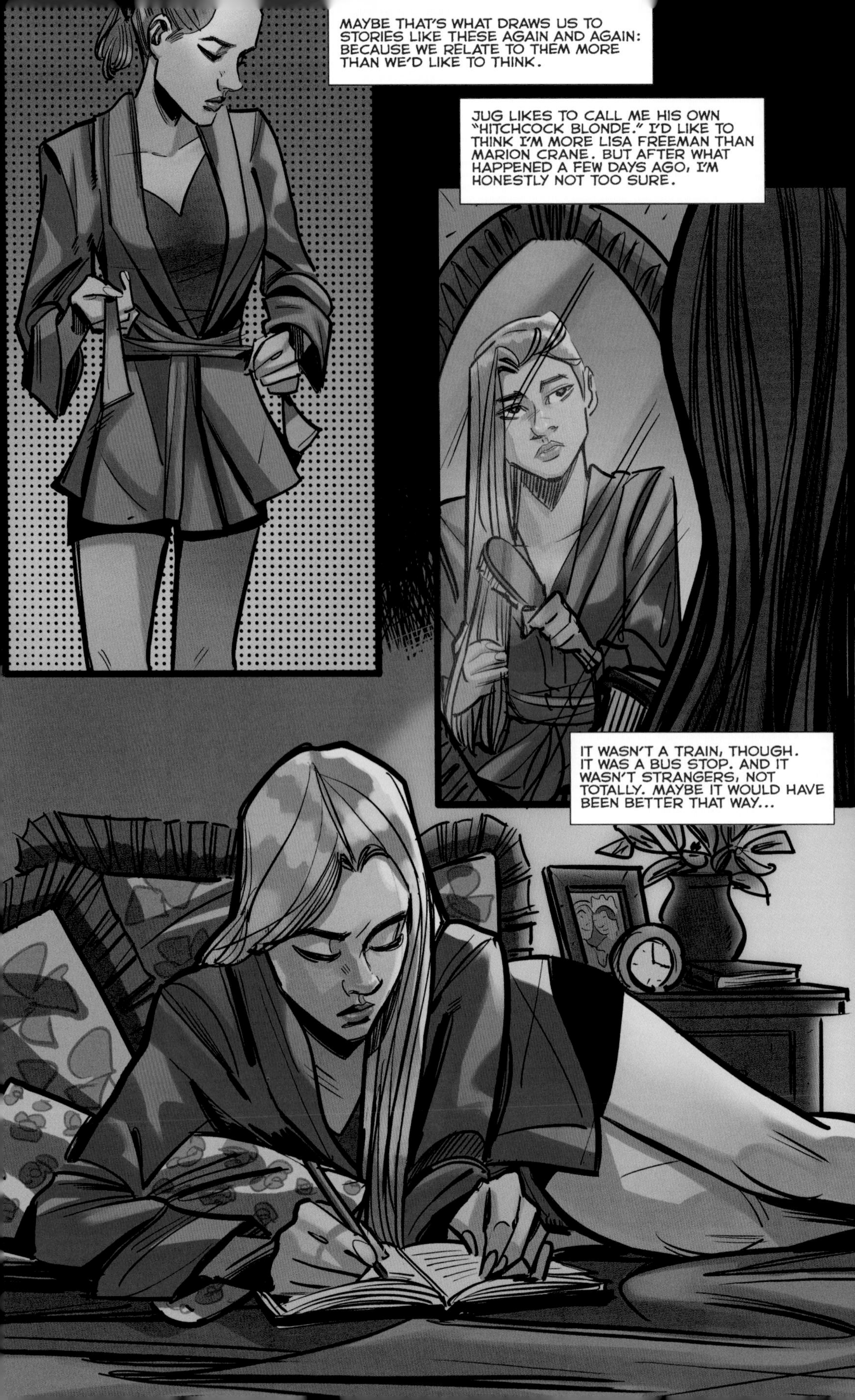
MAYBE THAT'S WHAT DRAWS US TO STORIES LIKE THESE AGAIN AND AGAIN: BECAUSE WE RELATE TO THEM MORE THAN WE'D LIKE TO THINK.
JUG LIKES TO CALL ME HIS OWN "HITCHCOCK BLONDE." I'D LIKE TO THINK I'M MORE LISA FREEMAN THAN MARION CRANE. BUT AFTER WHAT HAPPENED A FEW DAYS AGO, I'M HONESTLY NOT TOO SURE.
IT WASN'T A TRAIN, THOUGH. IT WAS A BUS STOP. AND IT WASN'T STRANGERS, NOT TOTALLY. MAYBE IT WOULD HAVE BEEN BETTER THAT WAY...

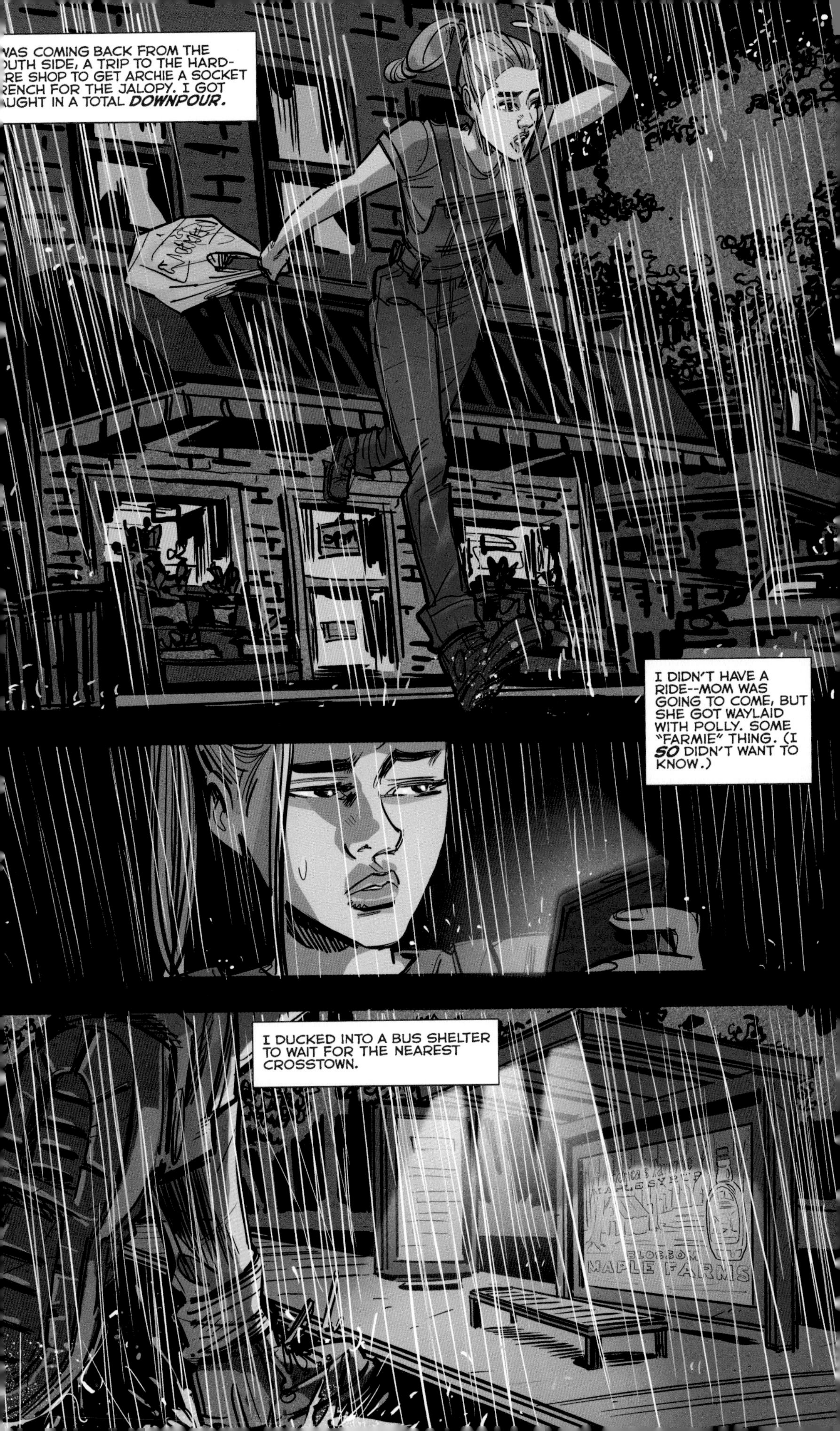

WAS COMING BACK FROM THE SOUTH SIDE, A TRIP TO THE HARD-RE SHOP TO GET ARCHIE A SOCKET RENCH FOR THE JALOPY. I GOT UGHT IN A TOTAL DOWNPOUR.
I DIDN'T HAVE A RIDE--MOM WAS GOING TO COME, BUT SHE GOT WAYLAID WITH POLLY. SOME "FARMIE" THING. (I SO DIDN'T WANT TO KNOW.)
I DUCKED INTO A BUS SHELTER TO WAIT FOR THE NEAREST CROSSTOWN.
BLOSSOM MAPLE FARMS

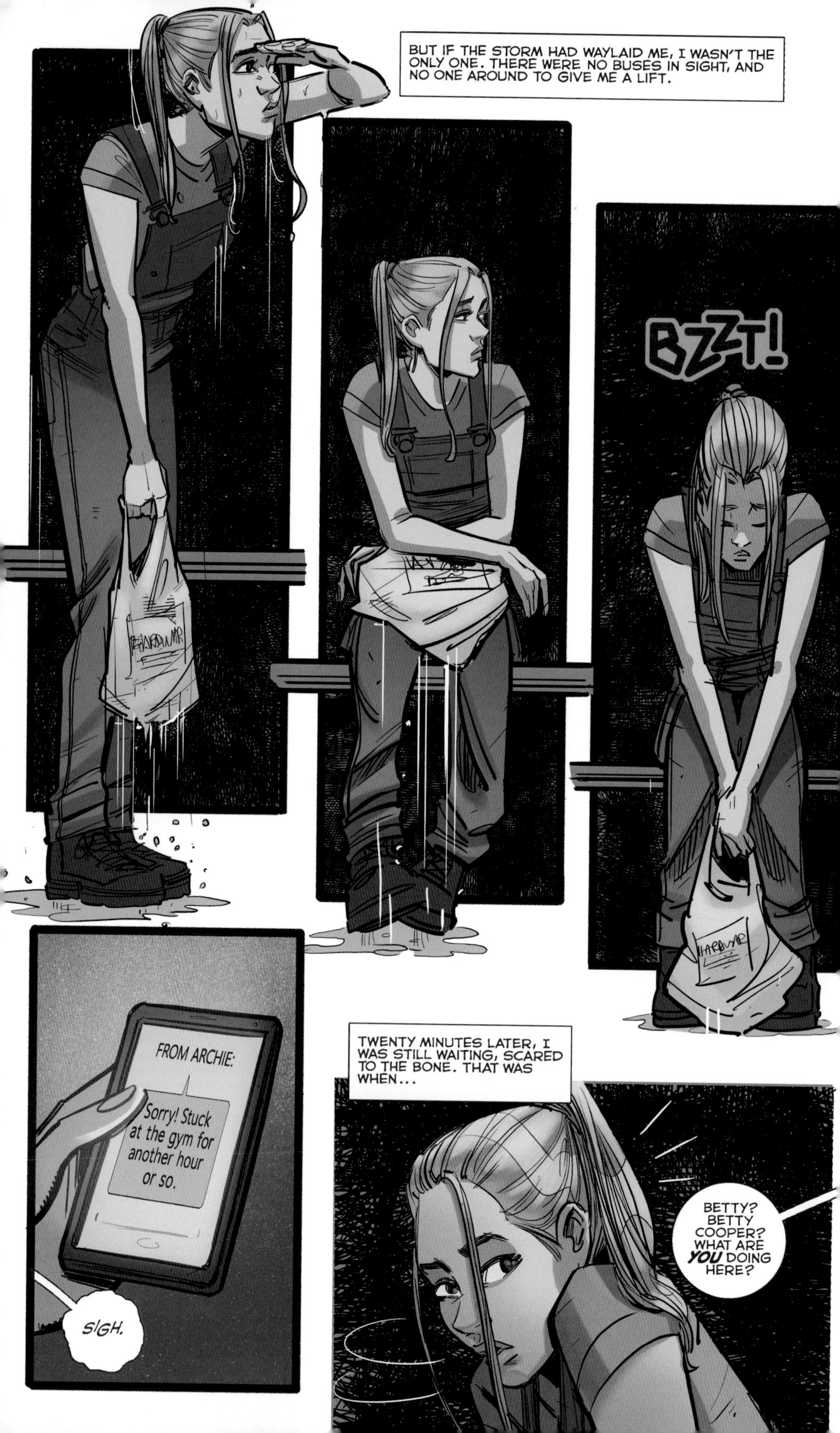
BUT IF THE STORM HAD WAYLAID ME, I WASN'T THE ONLY ONE. THERE WERE NO BUSES IN SIGHT, AND NO ONE AROUND TO GIVE ME A LIFT.
BZZT!
FROM ARCHIE:
Sorry! Stuck at the gym for another hour or so.
SIGH.
TWENTY MINUTES LATER, I WAS STILL WAITING, SCARED TO THE BONE. THAT WAS WHEN...
BETTY? BETTY COOPER? WHAT ARE YOU DOING HERE?

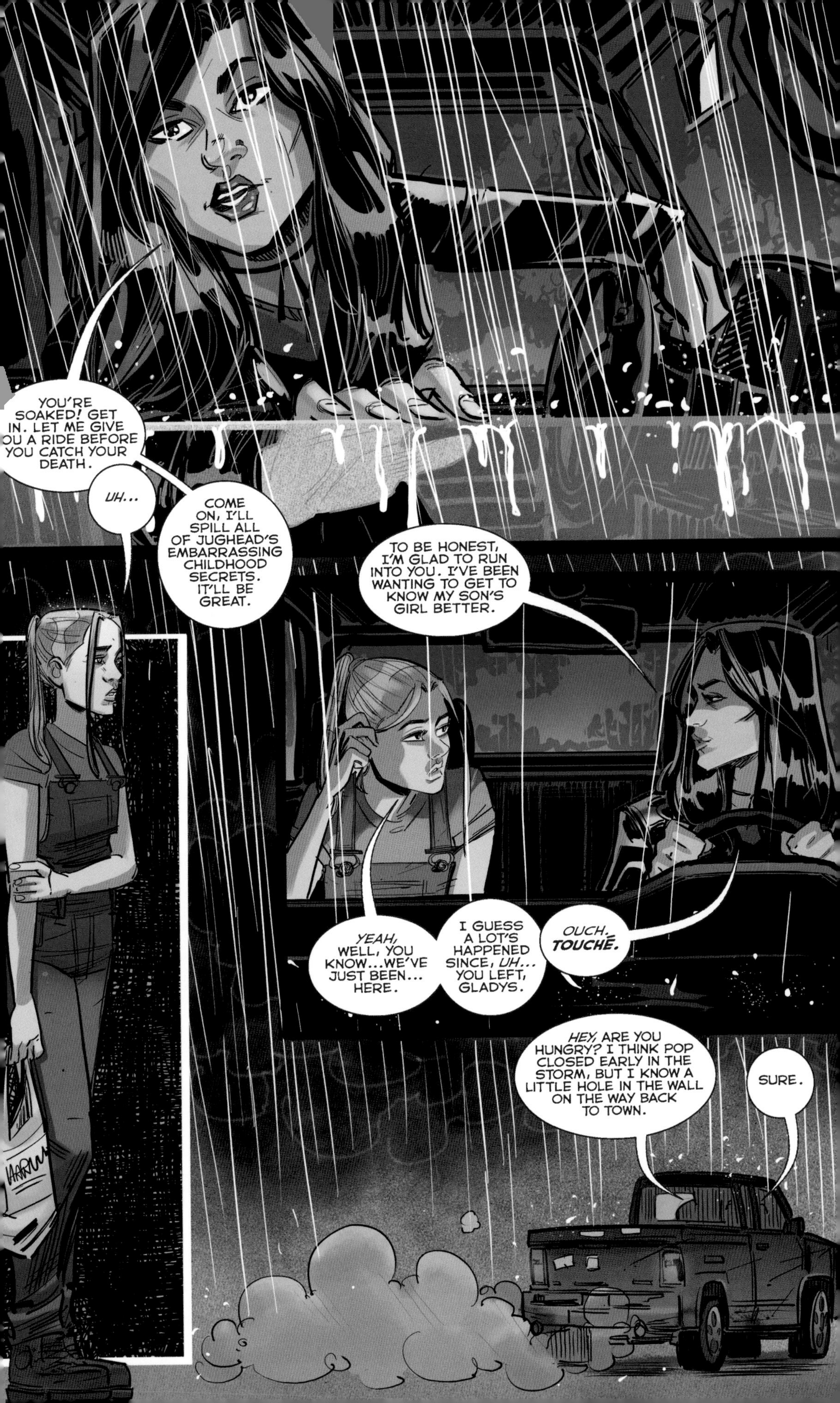
YOU'RE SOAKED! GET IN. LET ME GIVE OU A RIDE BEFORE YOU CATCH YOUR DEATH.
UH...
COME ON, I'LL SPILL ALL OF JUGHEAD'S EMBARRASSING CHILDHOOD SECRETS. IT'LL BE GREAT.
TO BE HONEST, I'M GLAD TO RUN INTO YOU. I'VE BEEN WANTING TO GET TO KNOW MY SON'S GIRL BETTER.
YEAH, WELL, YOU KNOW...WE'VE JUST BEEN... HERE.
I GUESS A LOT'S HAPPENED SINCE, UH... YOU LEFT, GLADYS.
OUCH. TOUCHÉ.
HEY, ARE YOU HUNGRY? I THINK POP CLOSED EARLY IN THE STORM, BUT I KNOW A LITTLE HOLE IN THE WALL ON THE WAY BACK TO TOWN.
SURE.

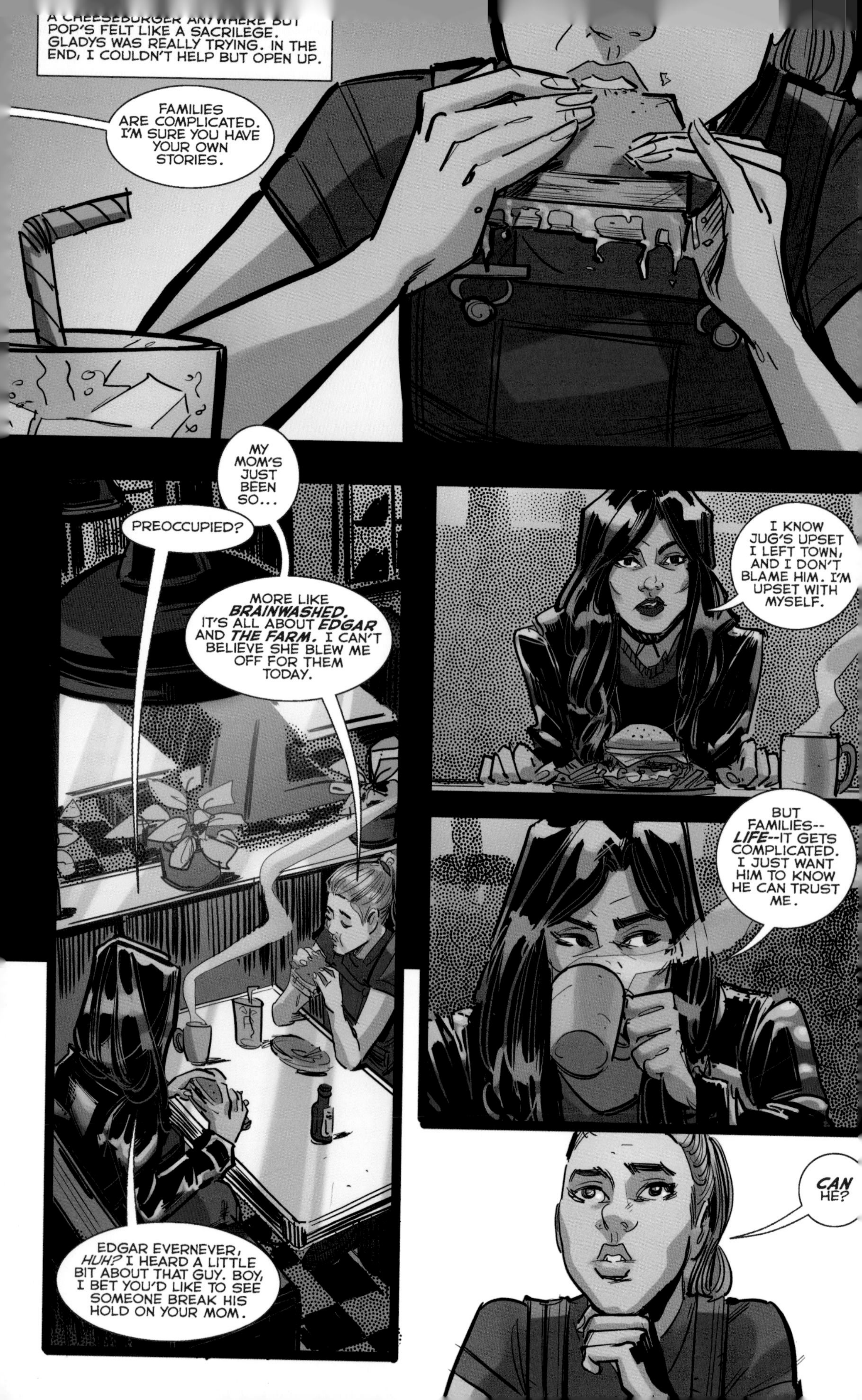
A CHEESEBURGER ANYWHERE BUT POP'S FELT LIKE A SACRILEGE. GLADYS WAS REALLY TRYING. IN THE END, I COULDN'T HELP BUT OPEN UP.
FAMILIES ARE COMPLICATED. I'M SURE YOU HAVE YOUR OWN STORIES.
MY MOM'S JUST BEEN SO...
PREOCCUPIED?
MORE LIKE ***BRAINWASHED.*** IT'S ALL ABOUT ***EDGAR*** AND ***THE FARM.*** I CAN'T BELIEVE SHE BLEW ME OFF FOR THEM TODAY.
EDGAR EVERNEVER, *HUH?* I HEARD A LITTLE BIT ABOUT THAT GUY. BOY, I BET YOU'D LIKE TO SEE SOMEONE BREAK HIS HOLD ON YOUR MOM.
I KNOW JUG'S UPSET I LEFT TOWN, AND I DON'T BLAME HIM. I'M UPSET WITH MYSELF.
BUT FAMILIES-- ***LIFE***--IT GETS COMPLICATED. I JUST WANT HIM TO KNOW HE CAN TRUST ME.
CAN HE?

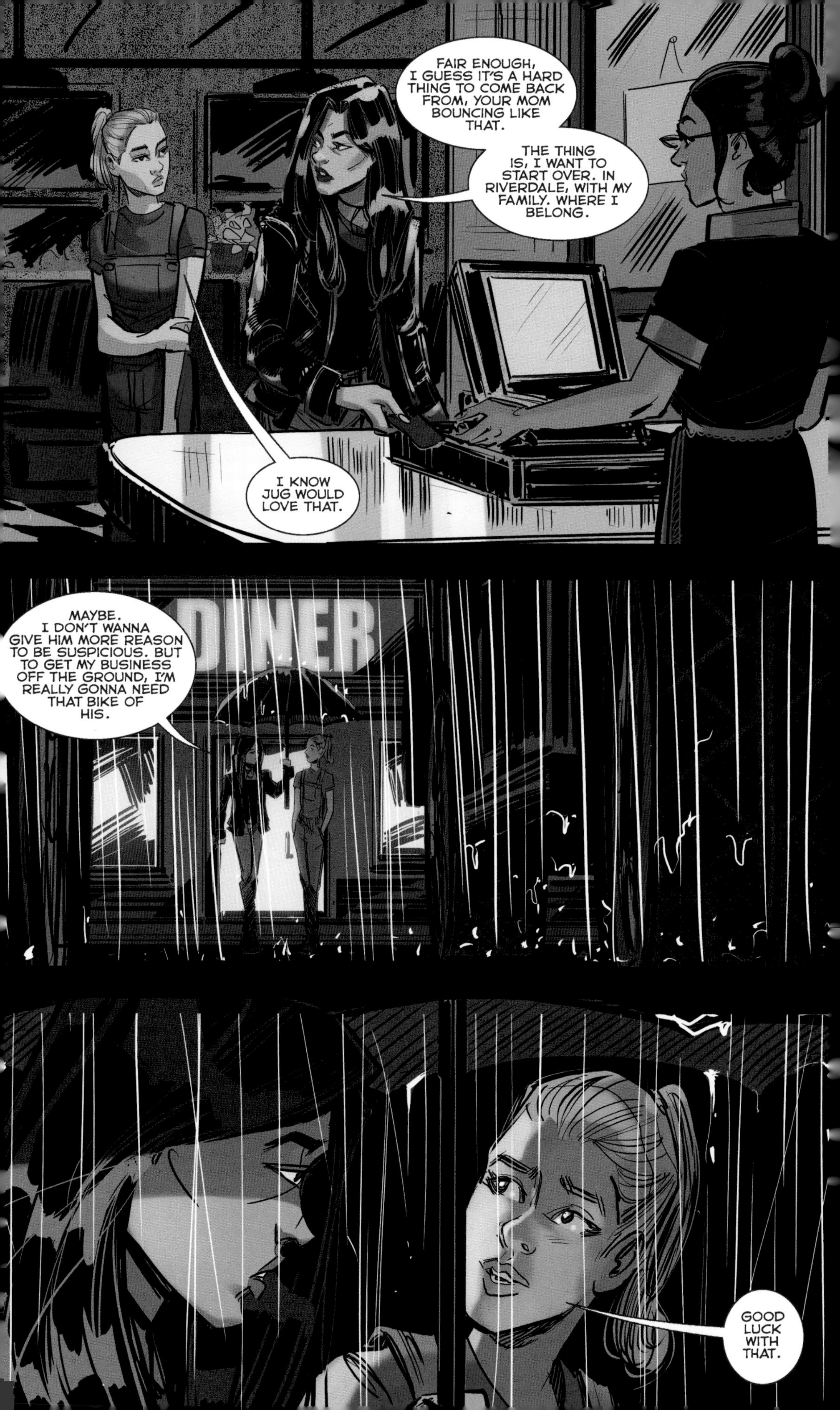
FAIR ENOUGH, I GUESS IT'S A HARD THING TO COME BACK FROM, YOUR MOM BOUNCING LIKE THAT.
THE THING IS, I WANT TO START OVER. IN RIVERDALE, WITH MY FAMILY. WHERE I BELONG.
I KNOW JUG WOULD LOVE THAT.
DINER
MAYBE. I DON'T WANNA GIVE HIM MORE REASON TO BE SUSPICIOUS. BUT TO GET MY BUSINESS OFF THE GROUND, I'M REALLY GONNA NEED THAT BIKE OF HIS.
GOOD LUCK WITH THAT.

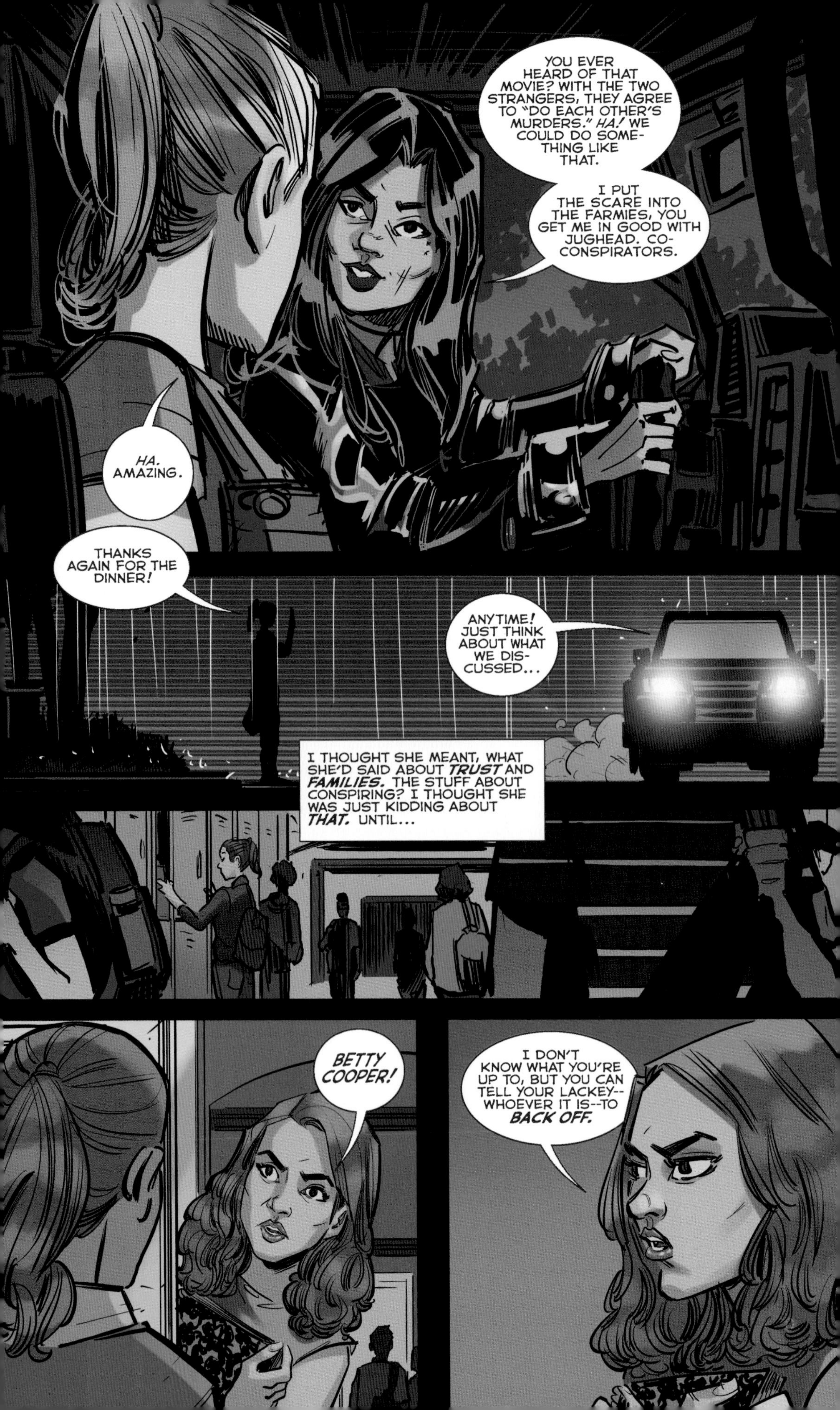

YOU EVER HEARD OF THAT MOVIE? WITH THE TWO STRANGERS, THEY AGREE TO "DO EACH OTHER'S MURDERS." HA! WE COULD DO SOMETHING LIKE THAT.
I PUT THE SCARE INTO THE FARMIES, YOU GET ME IN GOOD WITH JUGHEAD. CO-CONSPIRATORS.
HA. AMAZING.
THANKS AGAIN FOR THE DINNER!
ANYTIME! JUST THINK ABOUT WHAT WE DISCUSSED...
I THOUGHT SHE MEANT, WHAT SHE'D SAID ABOUT TRUST AND FAMILIES. THE STUFF ABOUT CONSPIRING? I THOUGHT SHE WAS JUST KIDDING ABOUT THAT. UNTIL...
BETTY COOPER!
I DON'T KNOW WHAT YOU'RE UP TO, BUT YOU CAN TELL YOUR LACKEY--WHOEVER IT IS--TO BACK OFF.

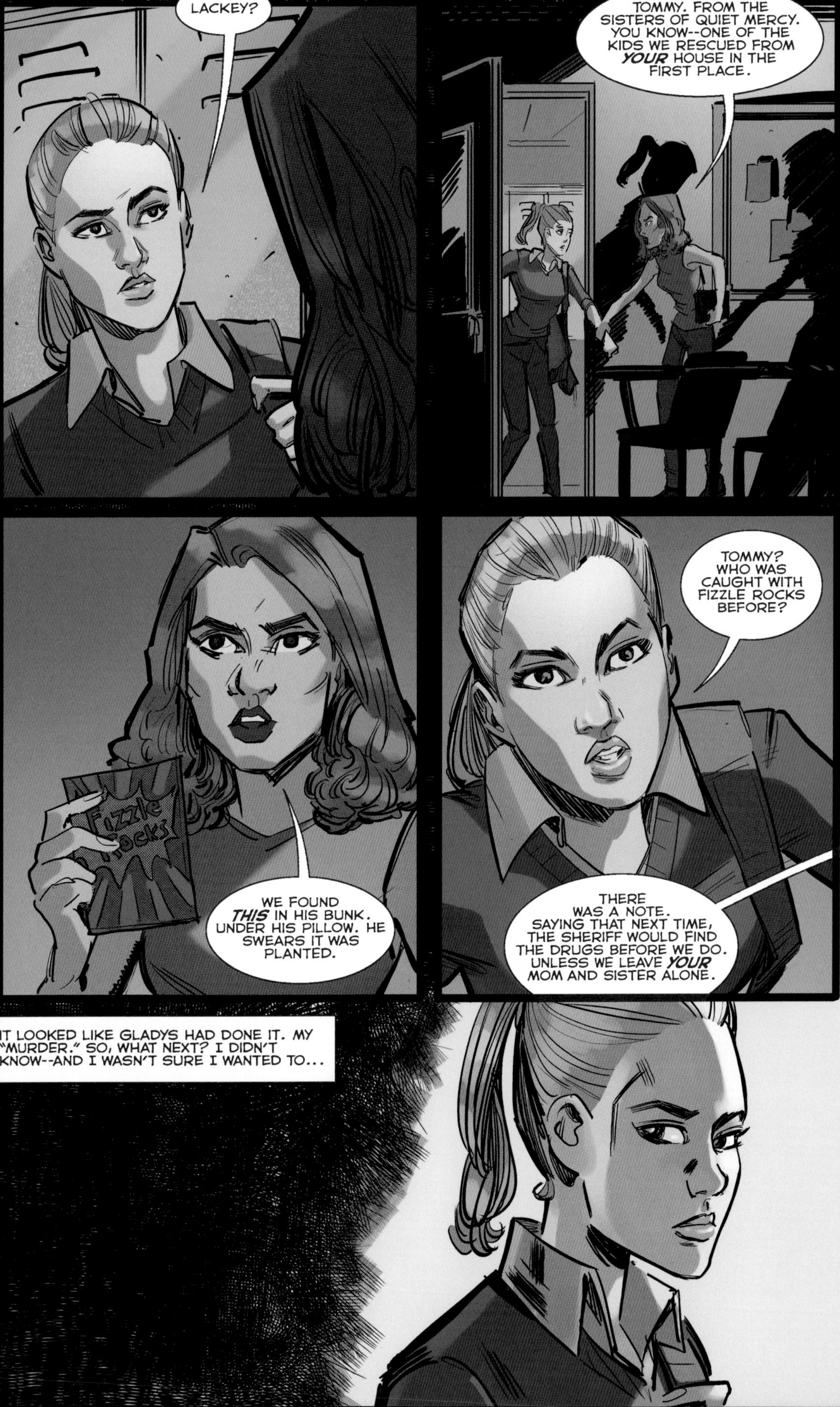
LACKEY?
TOMMY. FROM THE SISTERS OF QUIET MERCY. YOU KNOW--ONE OF THE KIDS WE RESCUED FROM *YOUR* HOUSE IN THE FIRST PLACE.
Fizzle Rocks
WE FOUND *THIS* IN HIS BUNK. UNDER HIS PILLOW. HE SWEARS IT WAS PLANTED.
TOMMY? WHO WAS CAUGHT WITH FIZZLE ROCKS BEFORE?
THERE WAS A NOTE. SAYING THAT NEXT TIME, THE SHERIFF WOULD FIND THE DRUGS BEFORE WE DO. UNLESS WE LEAVE *YOUR* MOM AND SISTER ALONE.
IT LOOKED LIKE GLADYS HAD DONE IT. MY "MURDER." SO, WHAT NEXT? I DIDN'T KNOW--AND I WASN'T SURE I WANTED TO...

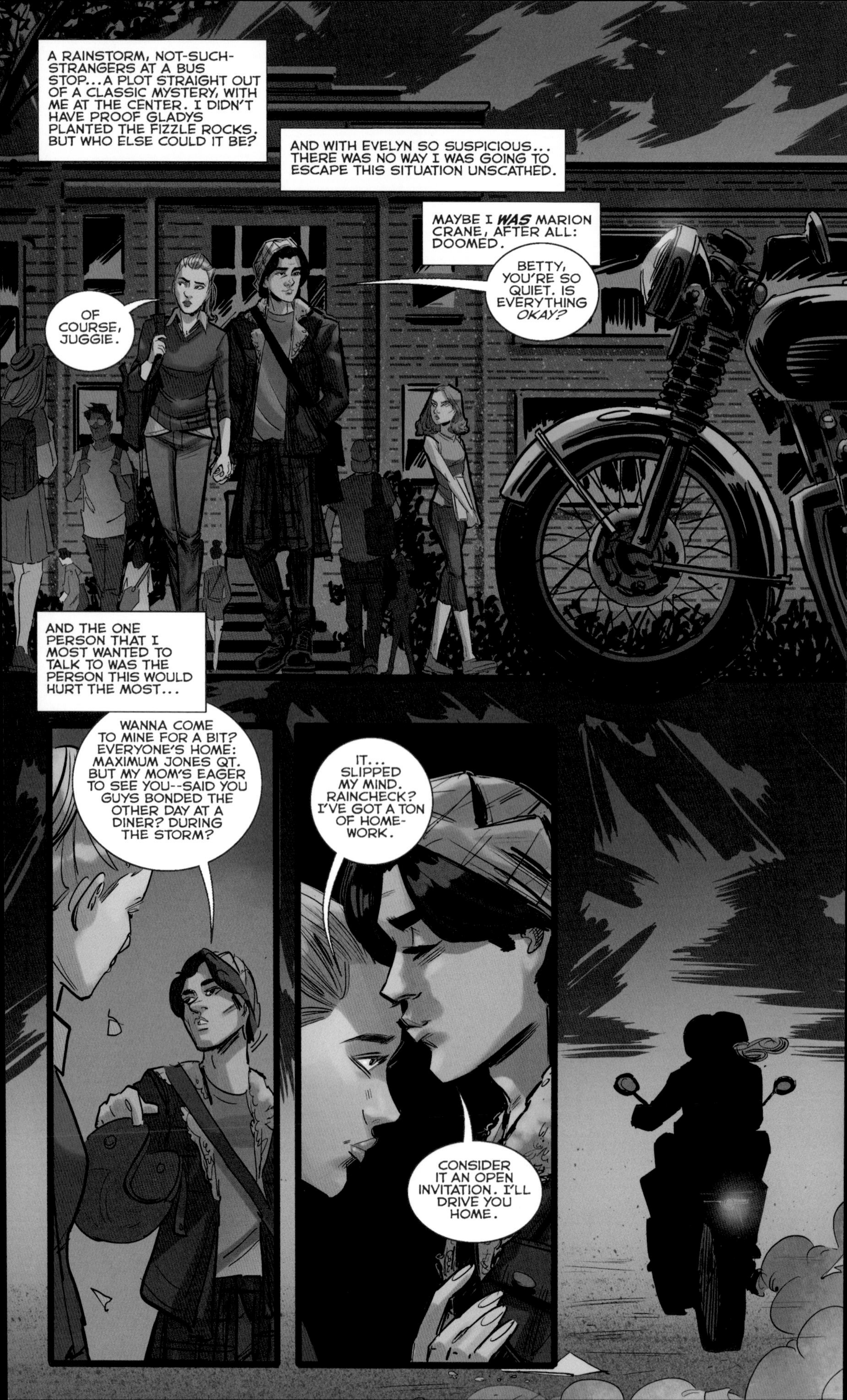
A RAINSTORM, NOT-SUCH-STRANGERS AT A BUS STOP...A PLOT STRAIGHT OUT OF A CLASSIC MYSTERY, WITH ME AT THE CENTER. I DIDN'T HAVE PROOF GLADYS PLANTED THE FIZZLE ROCKS. BUT WHO ELSE COULD IT BE?
AND WITH EVELYN SO SUSPICIOUS... THERE WAS NO WAY I WAS GOING TO ESCAPE THIS SITUATION UNSCATHED.
MAYBE I ***WAS*** MARION CRANE, AFTER ALL: DOOMED.
BETTY, YOU'RE SO QUIET. IS EVERYTHING *OKAY?*
OF COURSE, JUGGIE.
AND THE ONE PERSON THAT I MOST WANTED TO TALK TO WAS THE PERSON THIS WOULD HURT THE MOST...
WANNA COME TO MINE FOR A BIT? EVERYONE'S HOME: MAXIMUM JONES QT. BUT MY MOM'S EAGER TO SEE YOU--SAID YOU GUYS BONDED THE OTHER DAY AT A DINER? DURING THE STORM?
IT... SLIPPED MY MIND. RAINCHECK? I'VE GOT A TON OF HOME-WORK.
CONSIDER IT AN OPEN INVITATION. I'LL DRIVE YOU HOME.

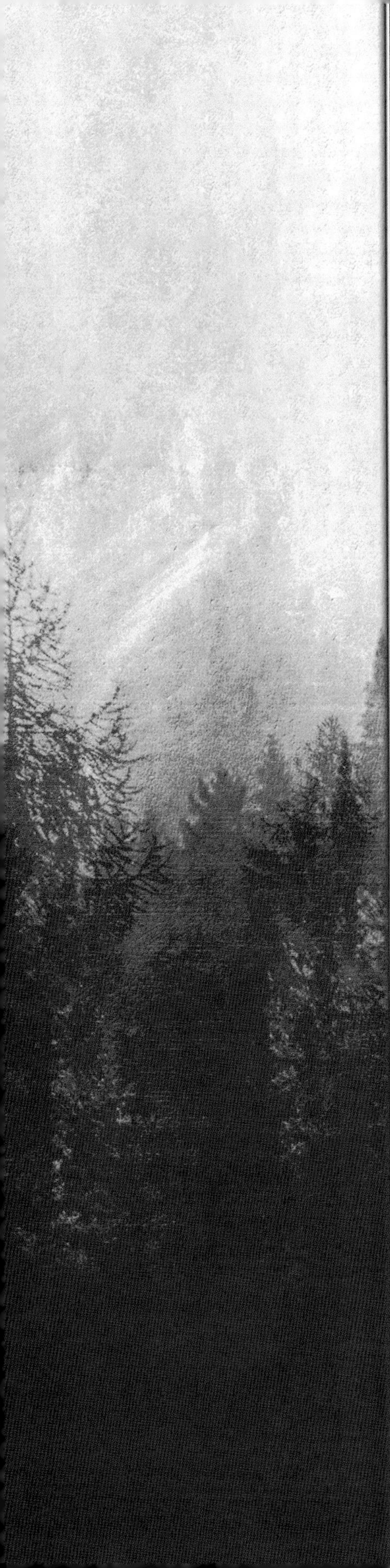

CHAPTER EIGHT

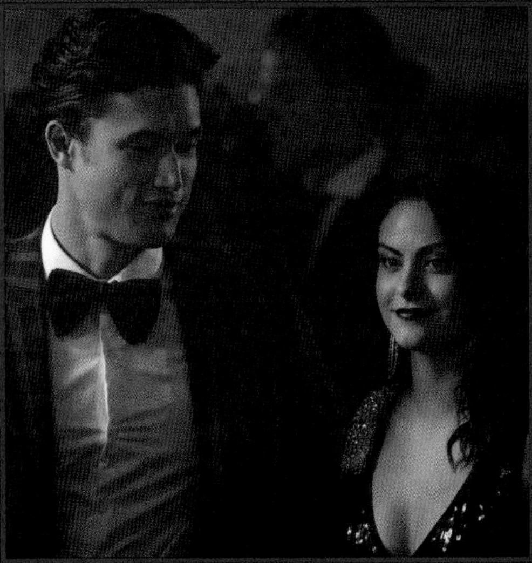

DEAD CALM

WRITER:
MICOL OSTOW

ART:
JOE EISMA

COLORS:
MATT HERMS

LETTERS:
JANICE CHIANG

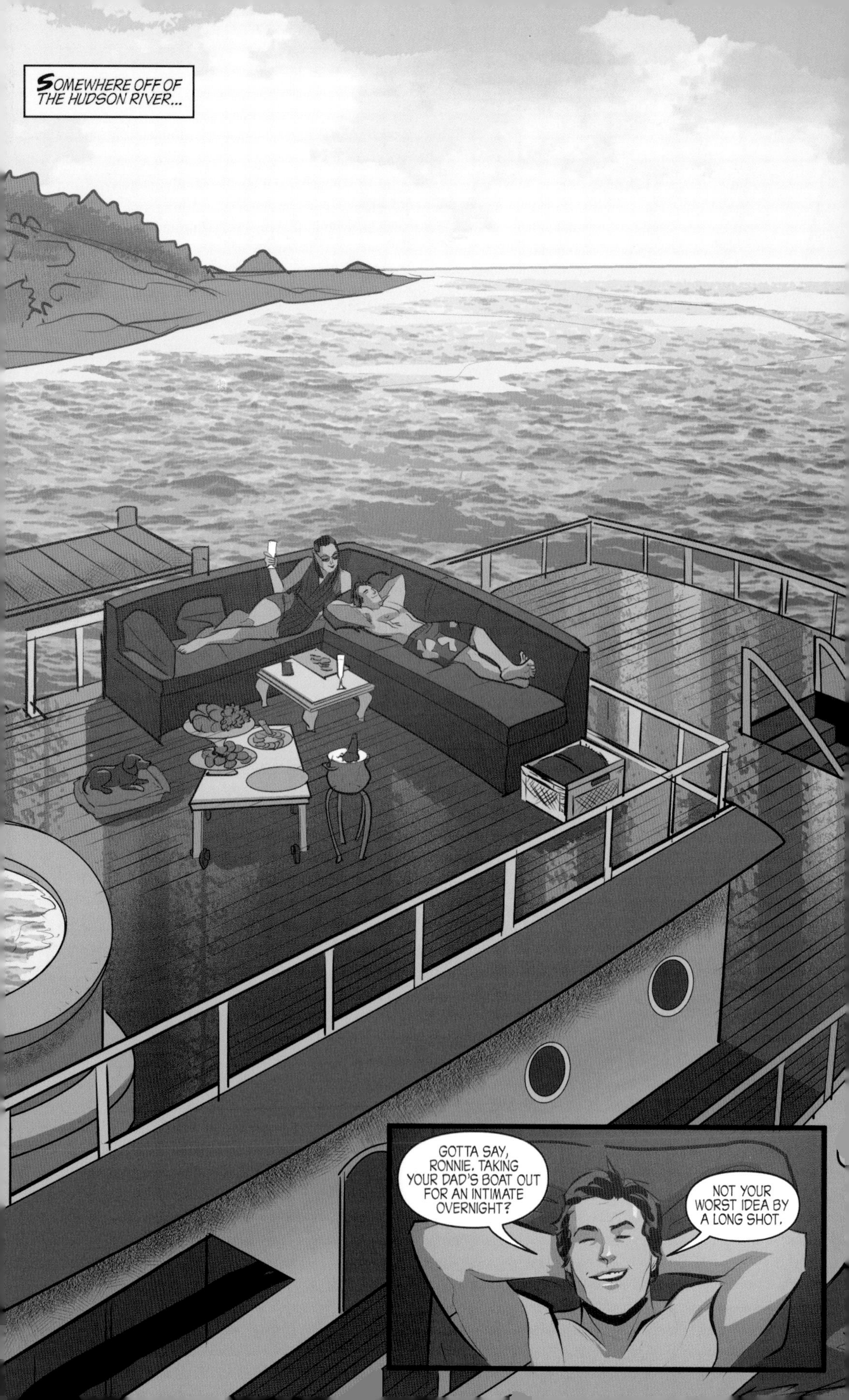
SOMEWHERE OFF OF THE HUDSON RIVER...
GOTTA SAY, RONNIE. TAKING YOUR DAD'S BOAT OUT FOR AN INTIMATE OVERNIGHT?
NOT YOUR WORST IDEA BY A LONG SHOT.

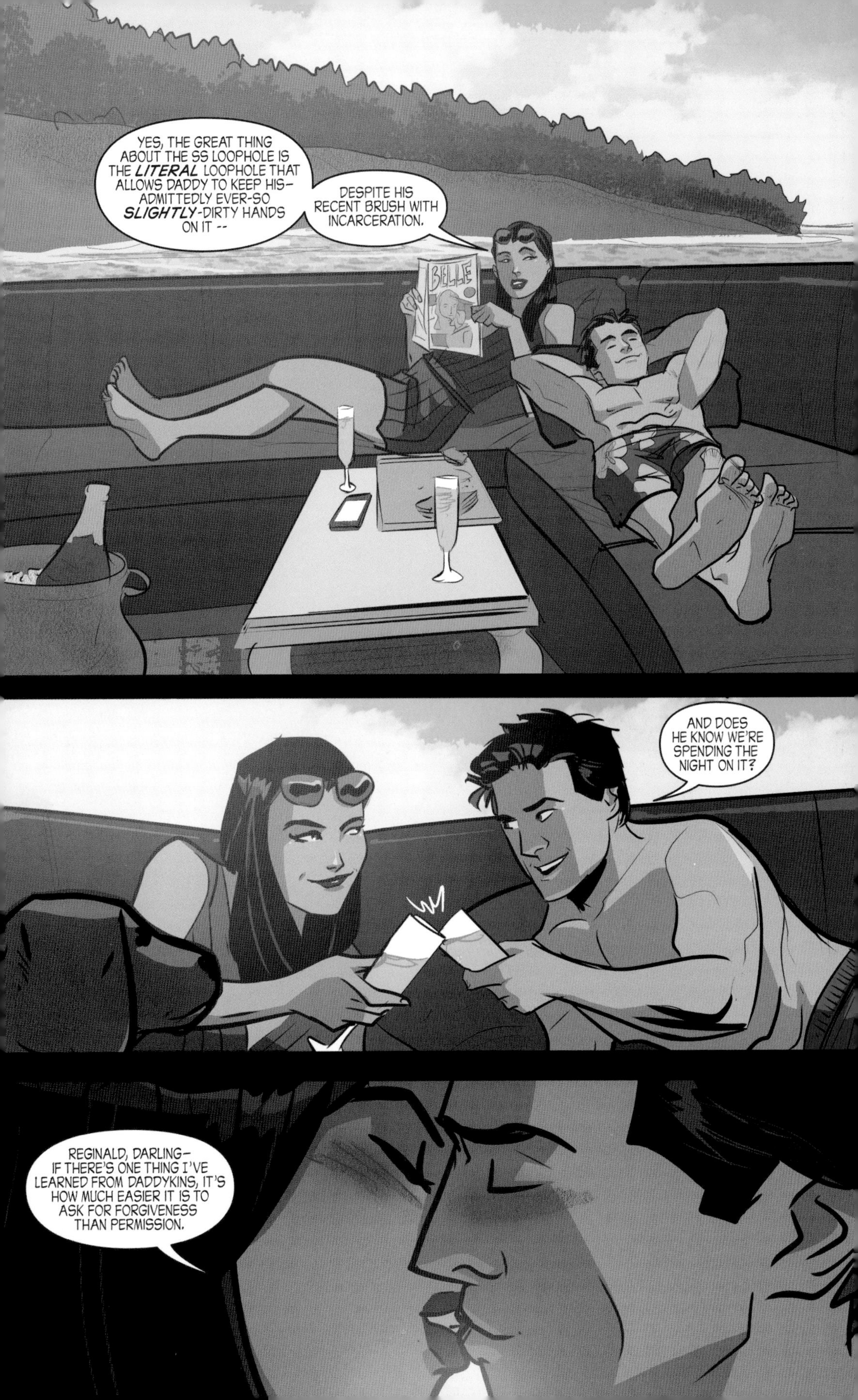
YES, THE GREAT THING ABOUT THE SS LOOPHOLE IS THE LITERAL LOOPHOLE THAT ALLOWS DADDY TO KEEP HIS-- ADMITTEDLY EVER-SO SLIGHTLY-DIRTY HANDS ON IT --
DESPITE HIS RECENT BRUSH WITH INCARCERATION.
BELLE
AND DOES HE KNOW WE'RE SPENDING THE NIGHT ON IT?
REGINALD, DARLING-- IF THERE'S ONE THING I'VE LEARNED FROM DADDYKINS, IT'S HOW MUCH EASIER IT IS TO ASK FOR FORGIVENESS THAN PERMISSION.

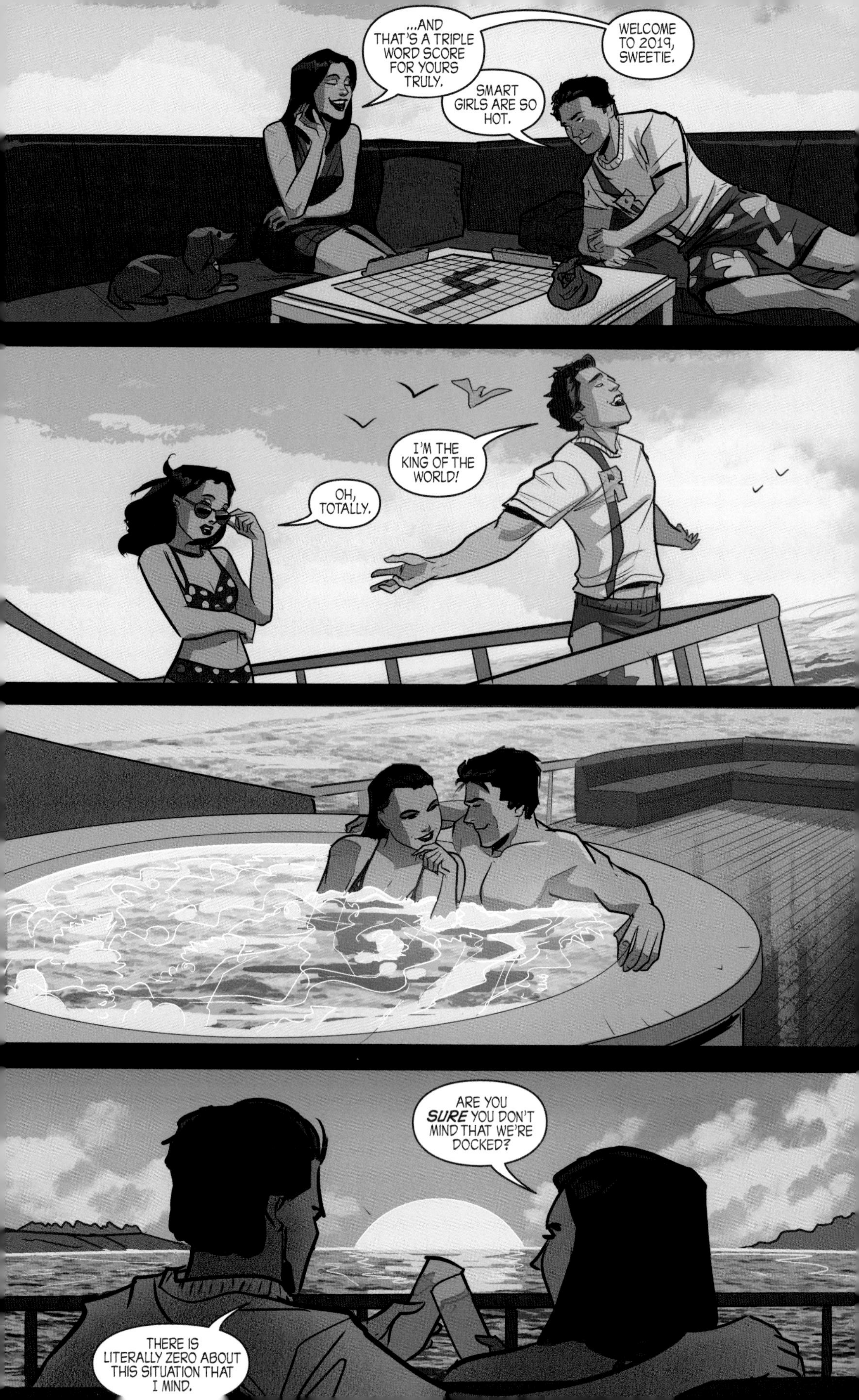

...AND THAT'S A TRIPLE WORD SCORE FOR YOURS TRULY.
WELCOME TO 2019, SWEETIE.
SMART GIRLS ARE SO HOT.
I'M THE KING OF THE WORLD!
OH, TOTALLY.
ARE YOU SURE YOU DON'T MIND THAT WE'RE DOCKED?
THERE IS LITERALLY ZERO ABOUT THIS SITUATION THAT I MIND.

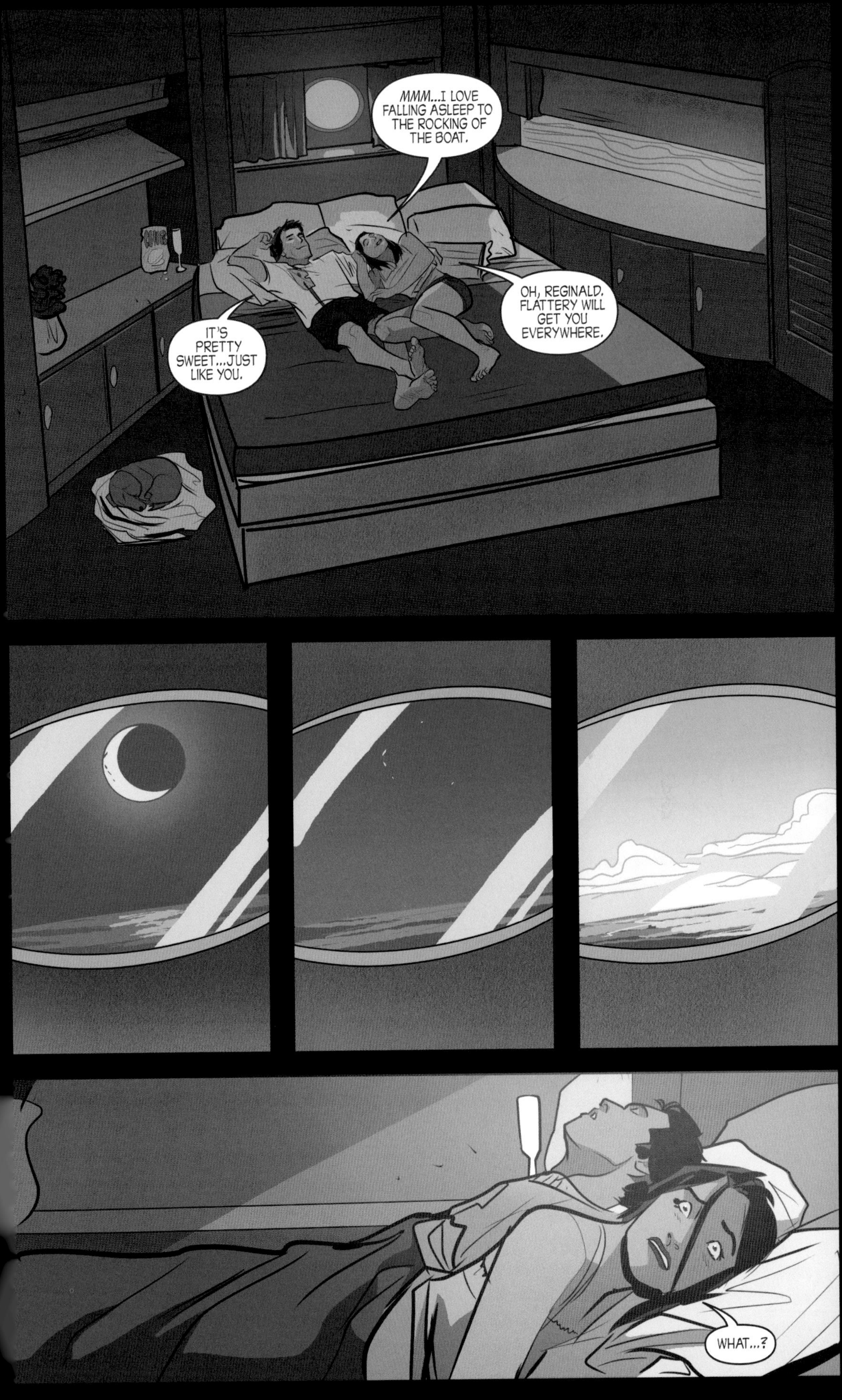
MMM...I LOVE FALLING ASLEEP TO THE ROCKING OF THE BOAT.
IT'S PRETTY SWEET...JUST LIKE YOU.
OH, REGINALD. FLATTERY WILL GET YOU EVERYWHERE.
WHAT...?

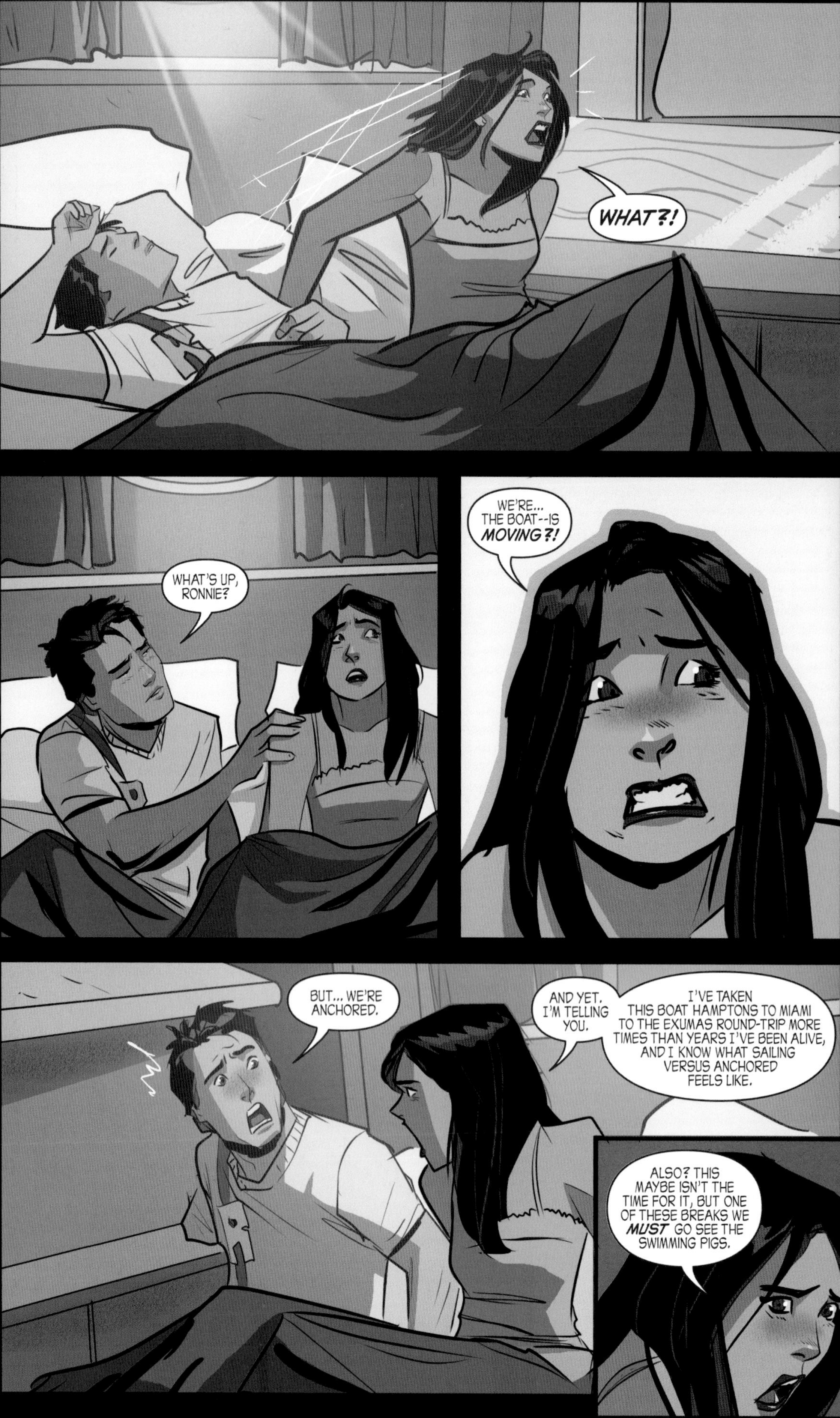
WHAT?!
WHAT'S UP, RONNIE?
WE'RE... THE BOAT--IS *MOVING?!*
BUT... WE'RE ANCHORED.
AND YET. I'M TELLING YOU.
I'VE TAKEN THIS BOAT HAMPTONS TO MIAMI TO THE EXUMAS ROUND-TRIP MORE TIMES THAN YEARS I'VE BEEN ALIVE, AND I KNOW WHAT SAILING VERSUS ANCHORED FEELS LIKE.
ALSO? THIS MAYBE ISN'T THE TIME FOR IT, BUT ONE OF THESE BREAKS WE *MUST* GO SEE THE SWIMMING PIGS.

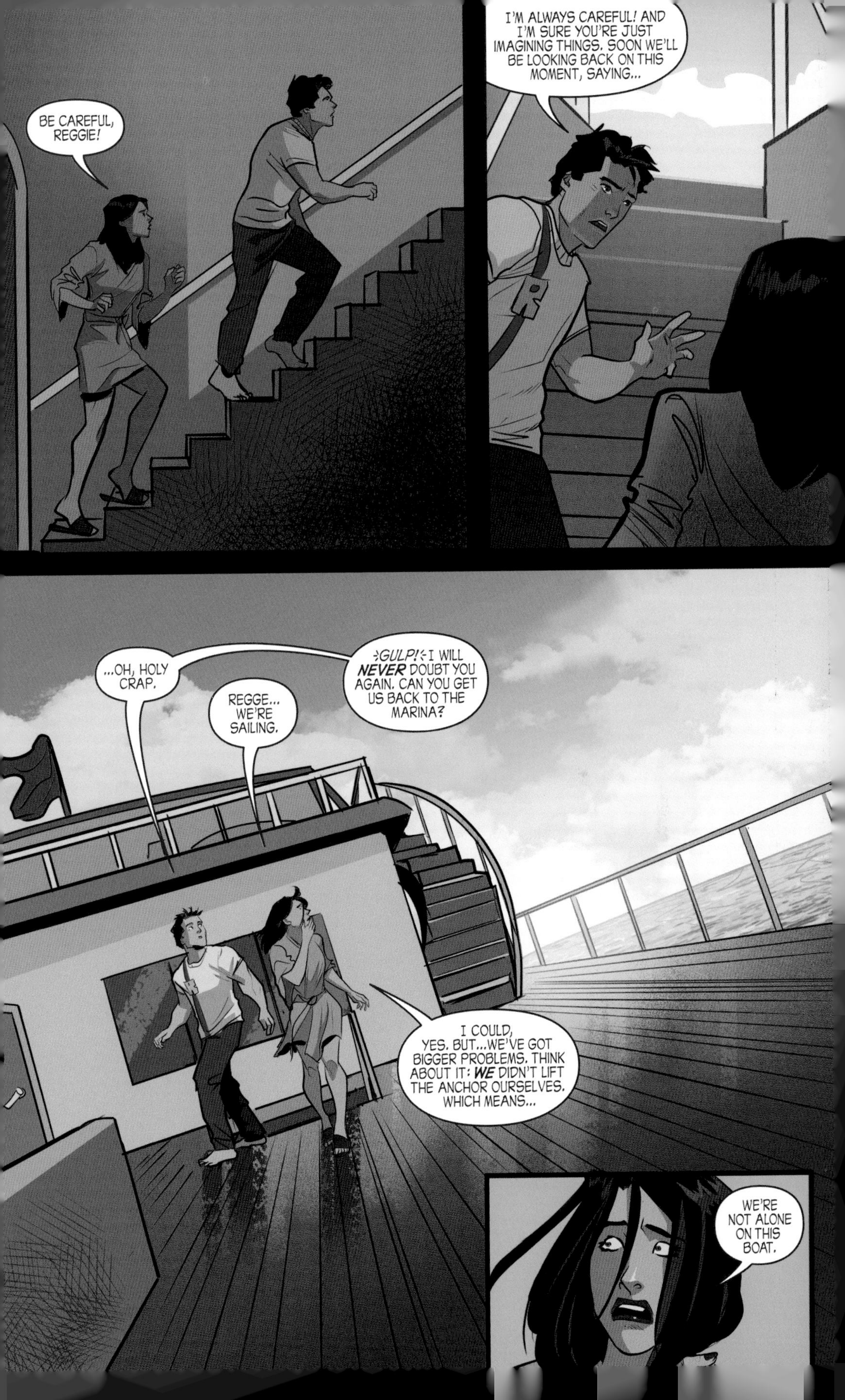
BE CAREFUL, REGGIE!
I'M ALWAYS CAREFUL! AND I'M SURE YOU'RE JUST IMAGINING THINGS. SOON WE'LL BE LOOKING BACK ON THIS MOMENT, SAYING...
...OH, HOLY CRAP.
REGGE... WE'RE SAILING.
GULP! I WILL NEVER DOUBT YOU AGAIN. CAN YOU GET US BACK TO THE MARINA?
I COULD, YES. BUT...WE'VE GOT BIGGER PROBLEMS. THINK ABOUT IT: WE DIDN'T LIFT THE ANCHOR OURSELVES. WHICH MEANS...
WE'RE NOT ALONE ON THIS BOAT.

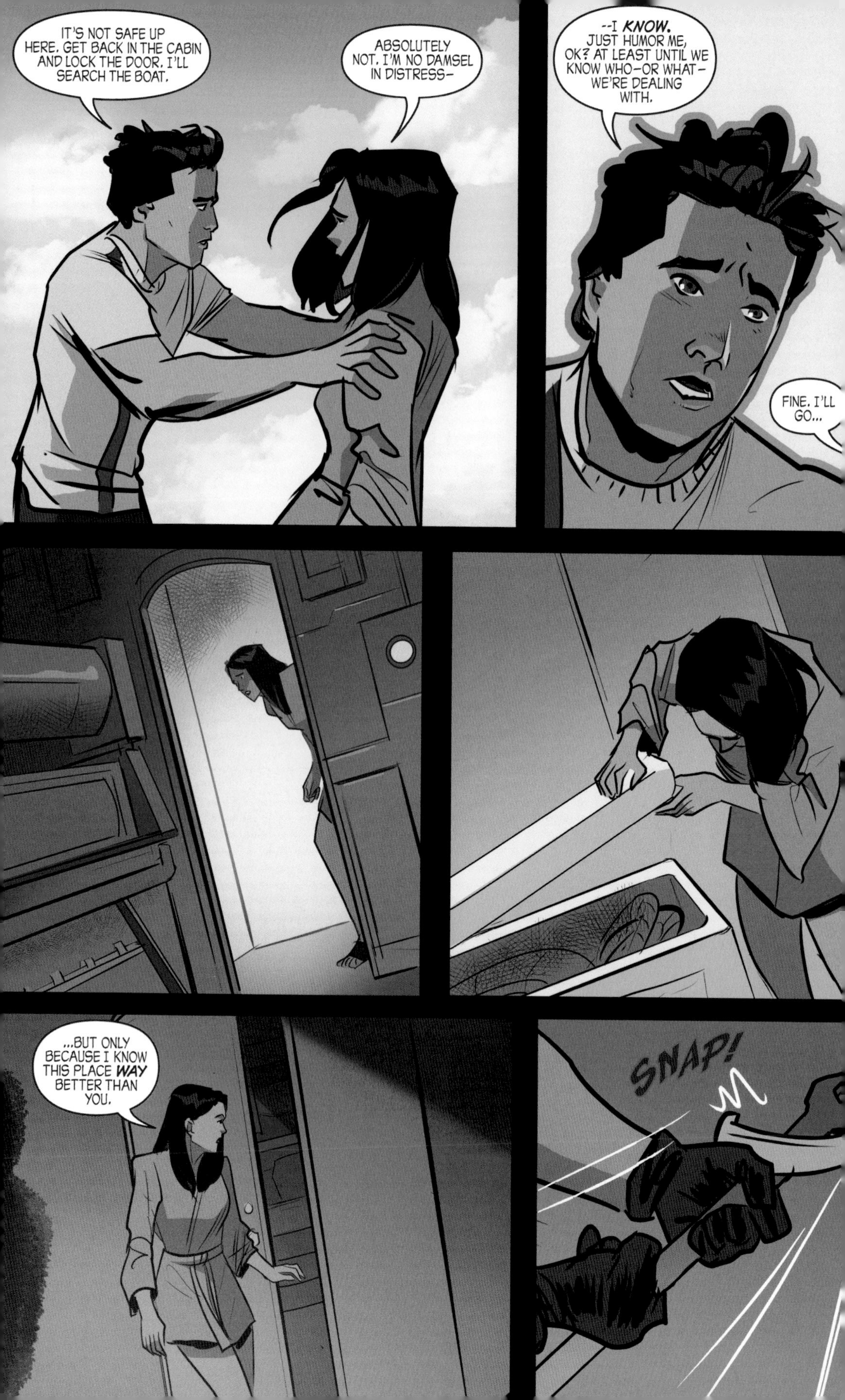
IT'S NOT SAFE UP HERE. GET BACK IN THE CABIN AND LOCK THE DOOR. I'LL SEARCH THE BOAT.
ABSOLUTELY NOT. I'M NO DAMSEL IN DISTRESS–
--I **KNOW.** JUST HUMOR ME, OK? AT LEAST UNTIL WE KNOW WHO–OR WHAT–WE'RE DEALING WITH.
FINE. I'LL GO...
...BUT ONLY BECAUSE I KNOW THIS PLACE **WAY** BETTER THAN YOU.
SNAP!

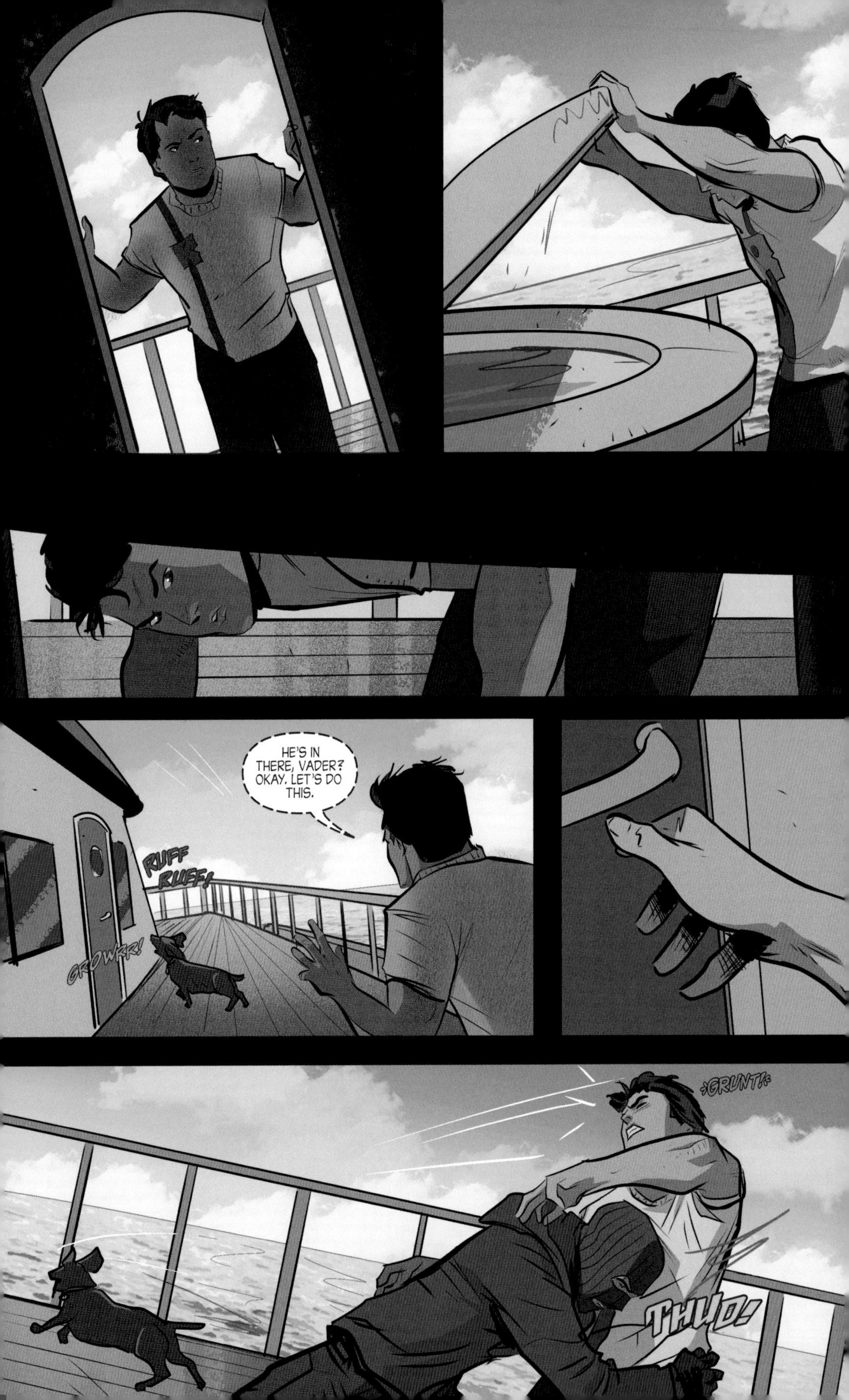
HE'S IN THERE, VADER? OKAY. LET'S DO THIS.
RUFF RUFF!
GROWRR!
GRUNT!
THUD!

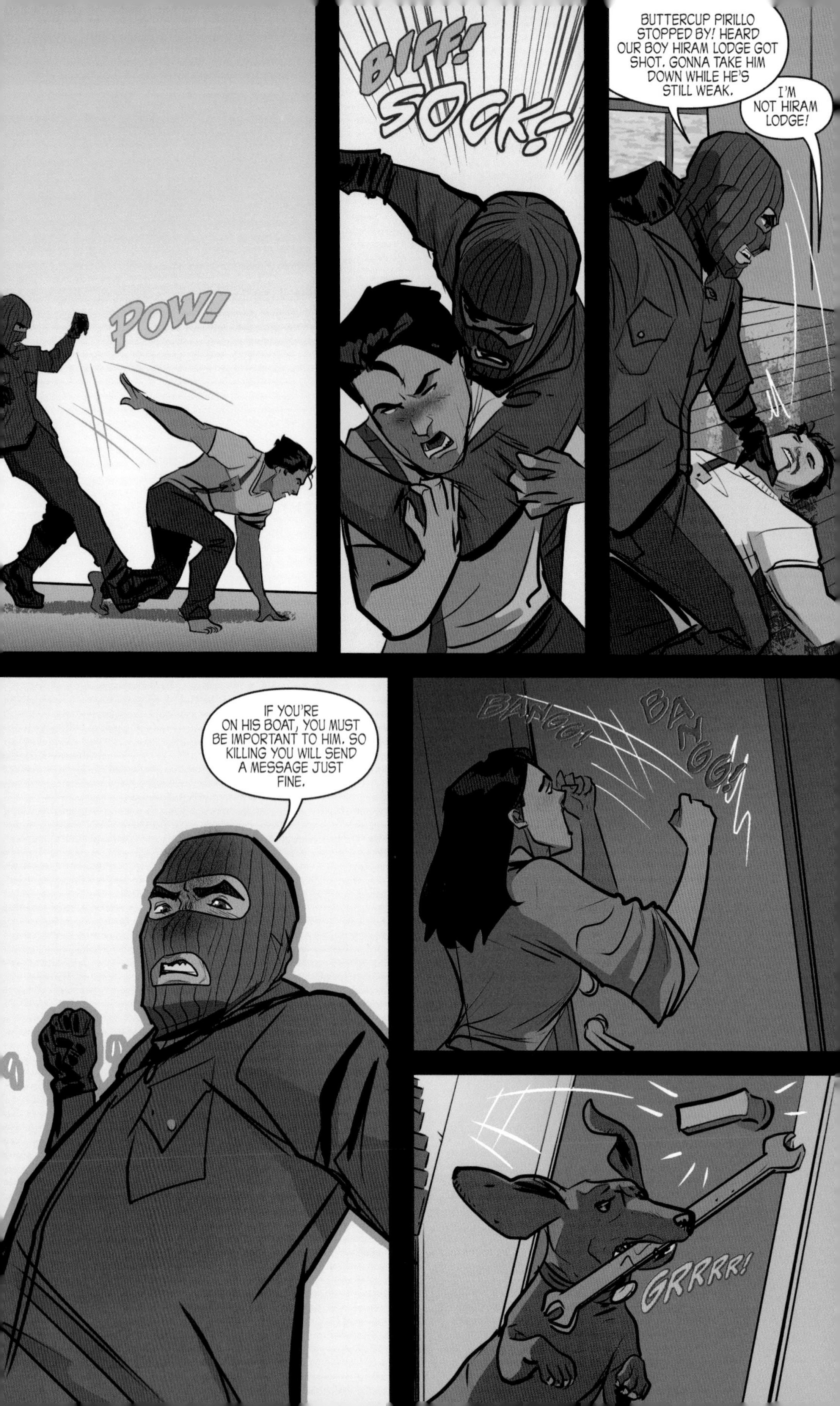
POW!
BIFF!
SOCK!
BUTTERCUP PIRILLO STOPPED BY! HEARD OUR BOY HIRAM LODGE GOT SHOT. GONNA TAKE HIM DOWN WHILE HE'S STILL WEAK.
I'M NOT HIRAM LODGE!
IF YOU'RE ON HIS BOAT, YOU MUST BE IMPORTANT TO HIM. SO KILLING YOU WILL SEND A MESSAGE JUST FINE.
BANGG!
BANGG!
GRRRR!

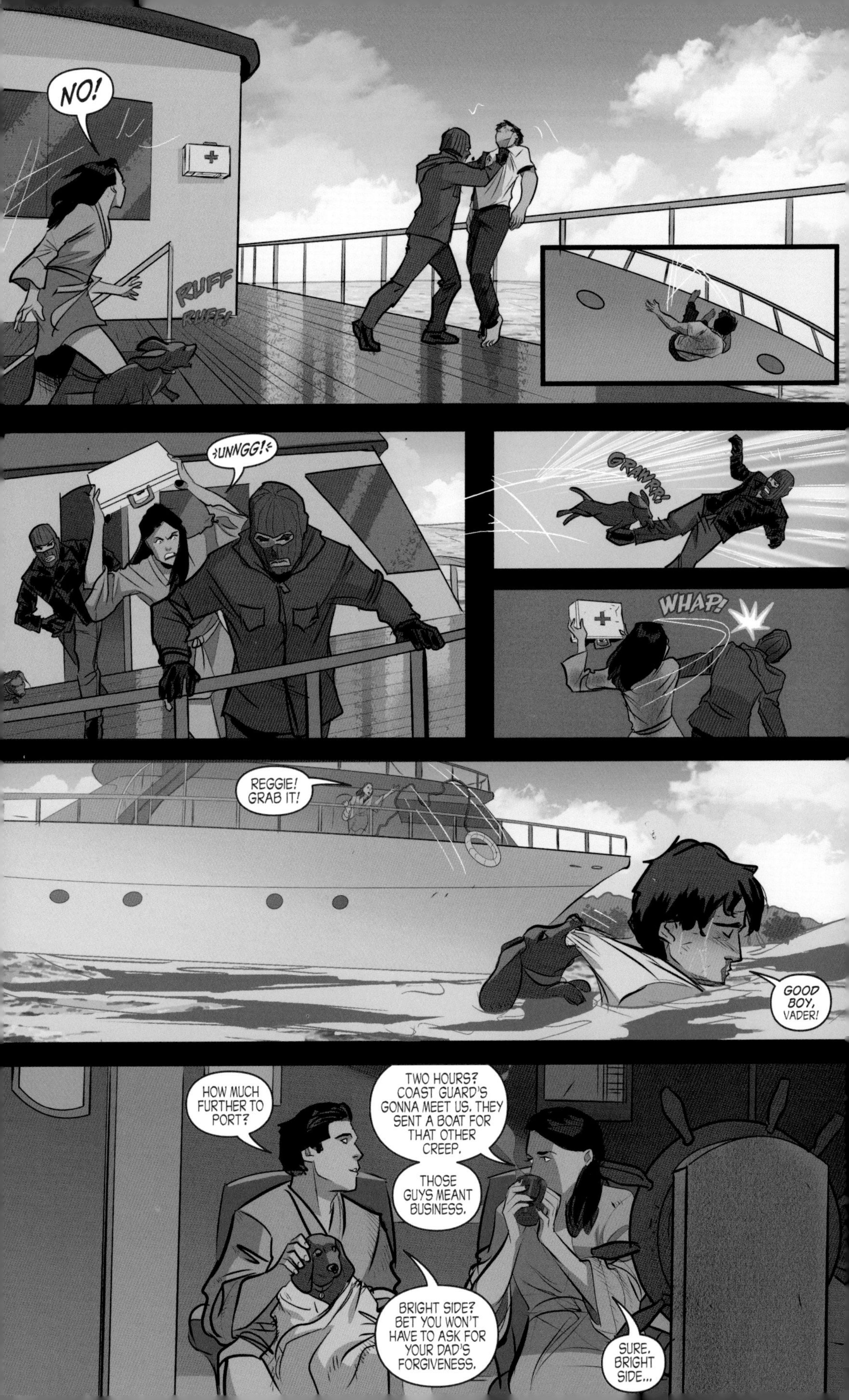
NO!
RUFF
RUFF!
UNNGG!
GRAWRR!
WHAP!
REGGIE! GRAB IT!
GOOD BOY, VADER!
HOW MUCH FURTHER TO PORT?
TWO HOURS? COAST GUARD'S GONNA MEET US. THEY SENT A BOAT FOR THAT OTHER CREEP.
THOSE GUYS MEANT BUSINESS.
BRIGHT SIDE? BET YOU WON'T HAVE TO ASK FOR YOUR DAD'S FORGIVENESS.
SURE. BRIGHT SIDE...

CHAPTER NINE

LADY SINGS THE BLUES

WRITER:
MICOL OSTOW

ART:
THOMAS PITILLI

COLORS:
ANDRE SZYMANOWICZ

LETTERS:
JOHN WORKMAN

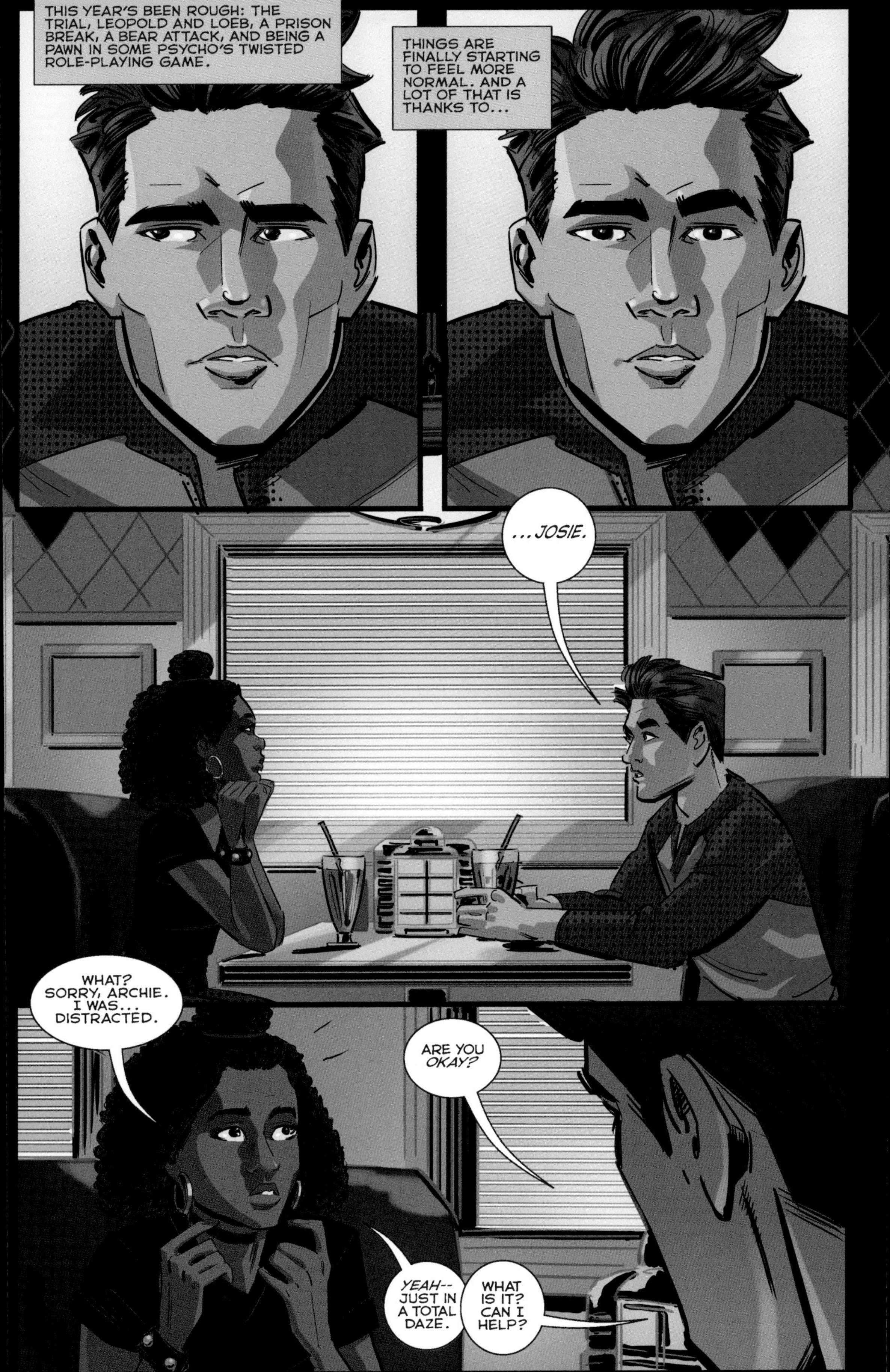
THIS YEAR'S BEEN ROUGH: THE TRIAL, LEOPOLD AND LOEB, A PRISON BREAK, A BEAR ATTACK, AND BEING A PAWN IN SOME PSYCHO'S TWISTED ROLE-PLAYING GAME.
THINGS ARE FINALLY STARTING TO FEEL MORE NORMAL. AND A LOT OF THAT IS THANKS TO...
...JOSIE.
WHAT? SORRY, ARCHIE. I WAS... DISTRACTED.
ARE YOU *OKAY?*
YEAH-- JUST IN A TOTAL DAZE.
WHAT IS IT? CAN I HELP?

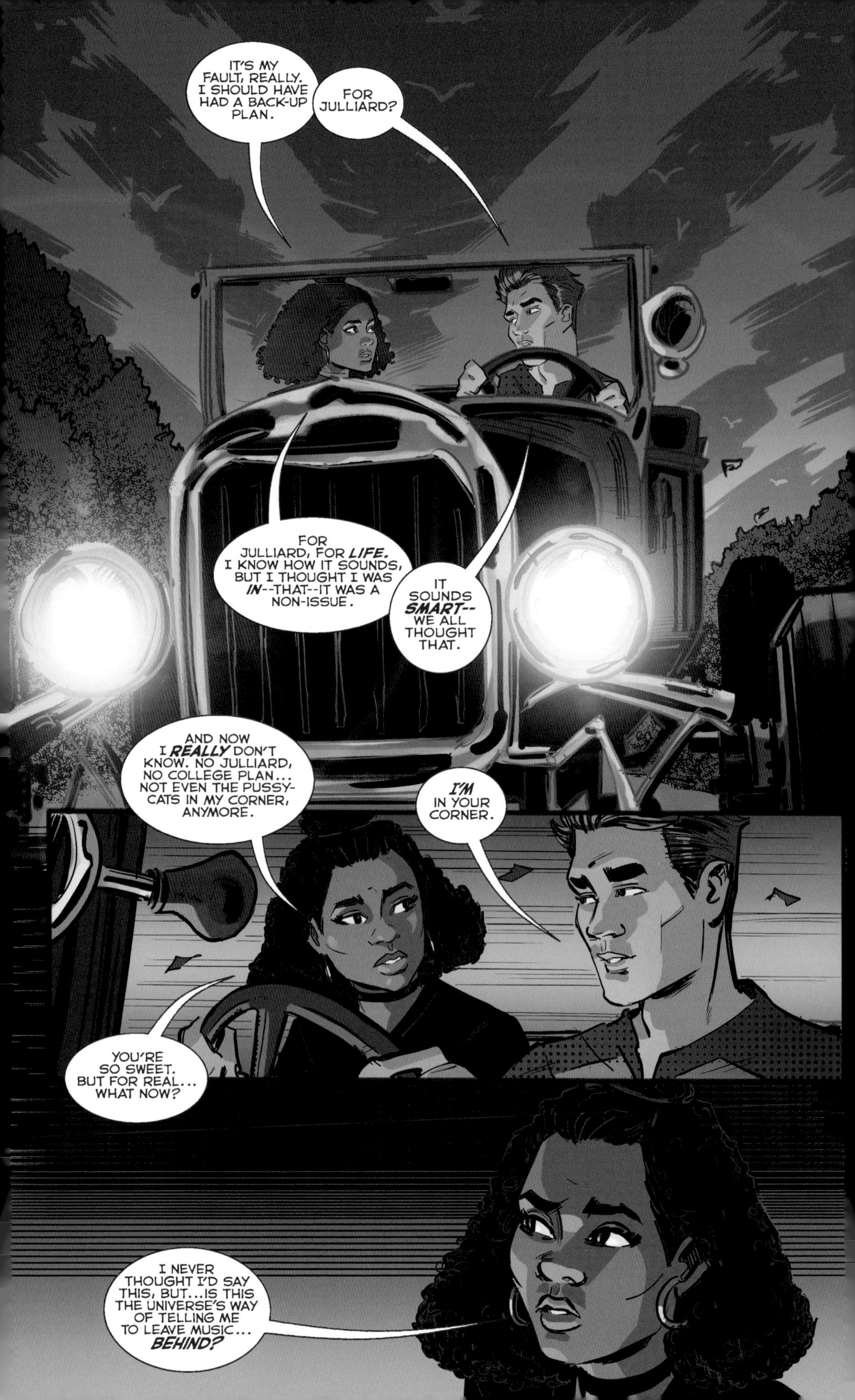
IT'S MY FAULT, REALLY. I SHOULD HAVE HAD A BACK-UP PLAN.
FOR JULLIARD?
FOR JULLIARD, FOR *LIFE.* I KNOW HOW IT SOUNDS, BUT I THOUGHT I WAS *IN*--THAT--IT WAS A NON-ISSUE.
IT SOUNDS *SMART--* WE ALL THOUGHT THAT.
AND NOW I *REALLY* DON'T KNOW. NO JULLIARD, NO COLLEGE PLAN... NOT EVEN THE PUSSY-CATS IN MY CORNER, ANYMORE.
I'M IN YOUR CORNER.
YOU'RE SO SWEET. BUT FOR REAL... WHAT NOW?
I NEVER THOUGHT I'D SAY THIS, BUT...IS THIS THE UNIVERSE'S WAY OF TELLING ME TO LEAVE MUSIC... *BEHIND?*

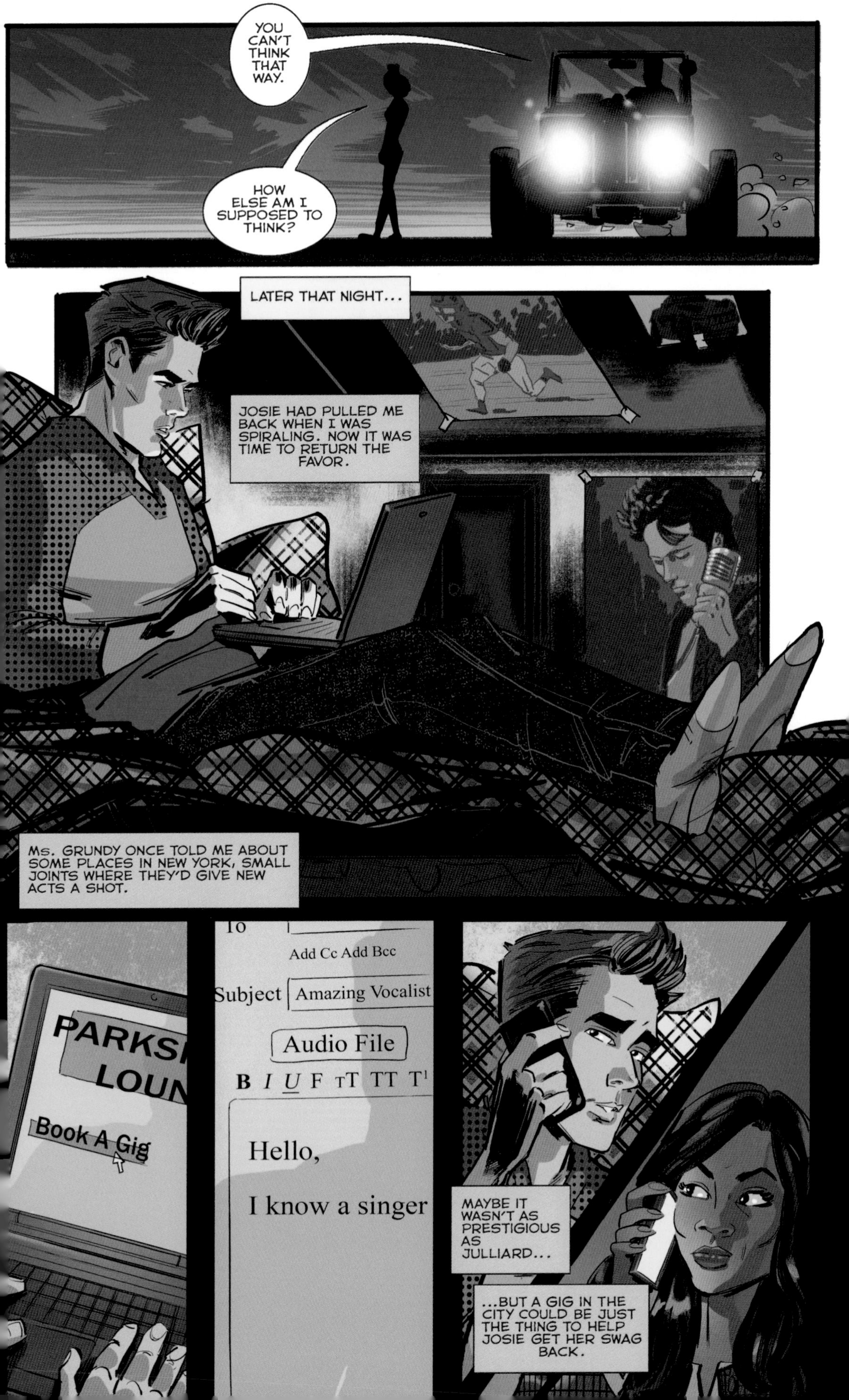
YOU CAN'T THINK THAT WAY.
HOW ELSE AM I SUPPOSED TO THINK?
LATER THAT NIGHT...
JOSIE HAD PULLED ME BACK WHEN I WAS SPIRALING. NOW IT WAS TIME TO RETURN THE FAVOR.
Ms. GRUNDY ONCE TOLD ME ABOUT SOME PLACES IN NEW YORK, SMALL JOINTS WHERE THEY'D GIVE NEW ACTS A SHOT.
PARKS
LOUN
Book A Gig
To
Add Cc Add Bcc
Subject Amazing Vocalist
Audio File
B I U F TT TT T
Hello,
I know a singer
MAYBE IT WASN'T AS PRESTIGIOUS AS JULLIARD...
...BUT A GIG IN THE CITY COULD BE JUST THE THING TO HELP JOSIE GET HER SWAG BACK.

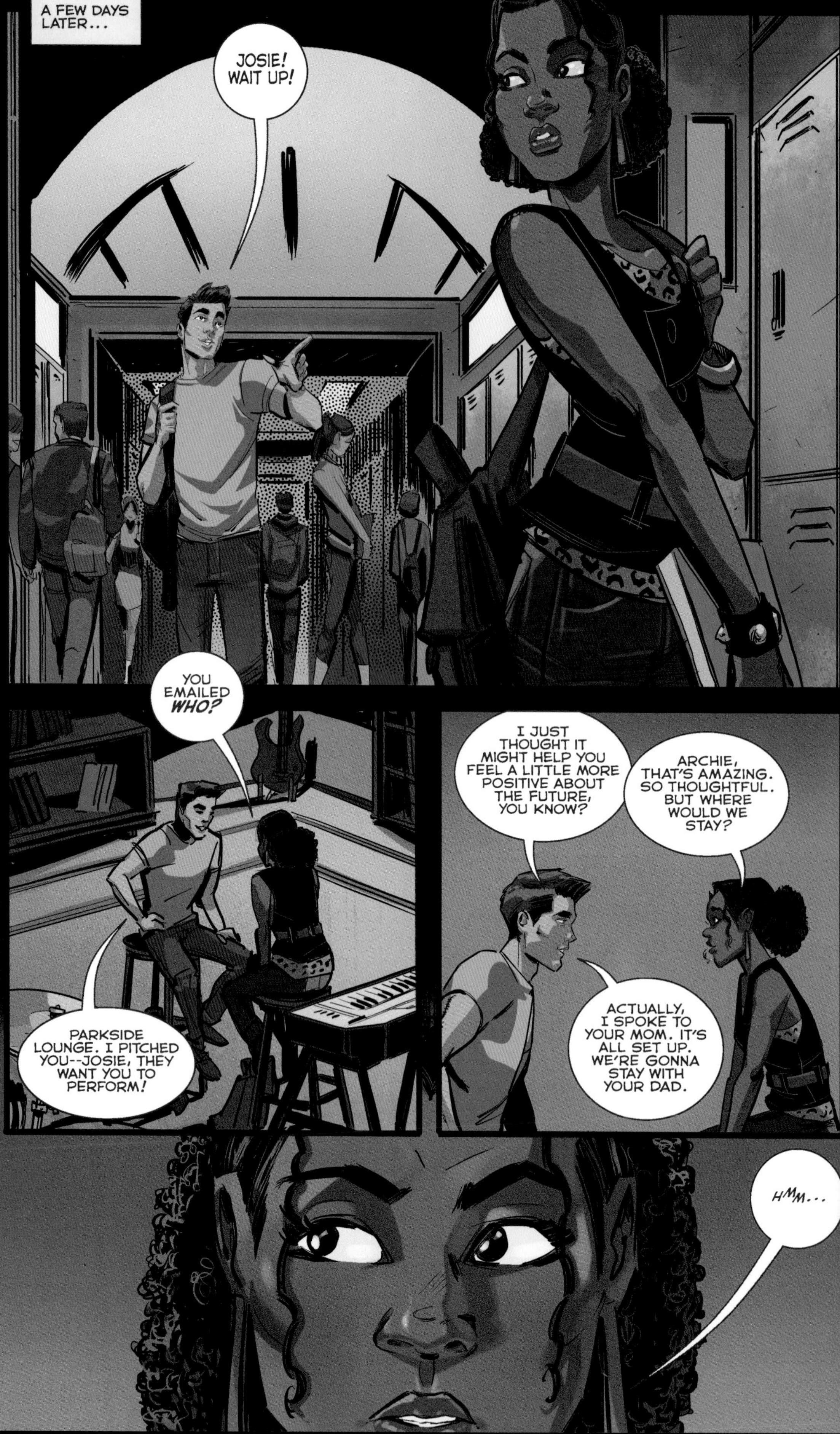
A FEW DAYS LATER...
JOSIE! WAIT UP!
YOU EMAILED WHO?
PARKSIDE LOUNGE. I PITCHED YOU--JOSIE, THEY WANT YOU TO PERFORM!
I JUST THOUGHT IT MIGHT HELP YOU FEEL A LITTLE MORE POSITIVE ABOUT THE FUTURE, YOU KNOW?
ARCHIE, THAT'S AMAZING. SO THOUGHTFUL. BUT WHERE WOULD WE STAY?
ACTUALLY, I SPOKE TO YOUR MOM. IT'S ALL SET UP. WE'RE GONNA STAY WITH YOUR DAD.
HMM...

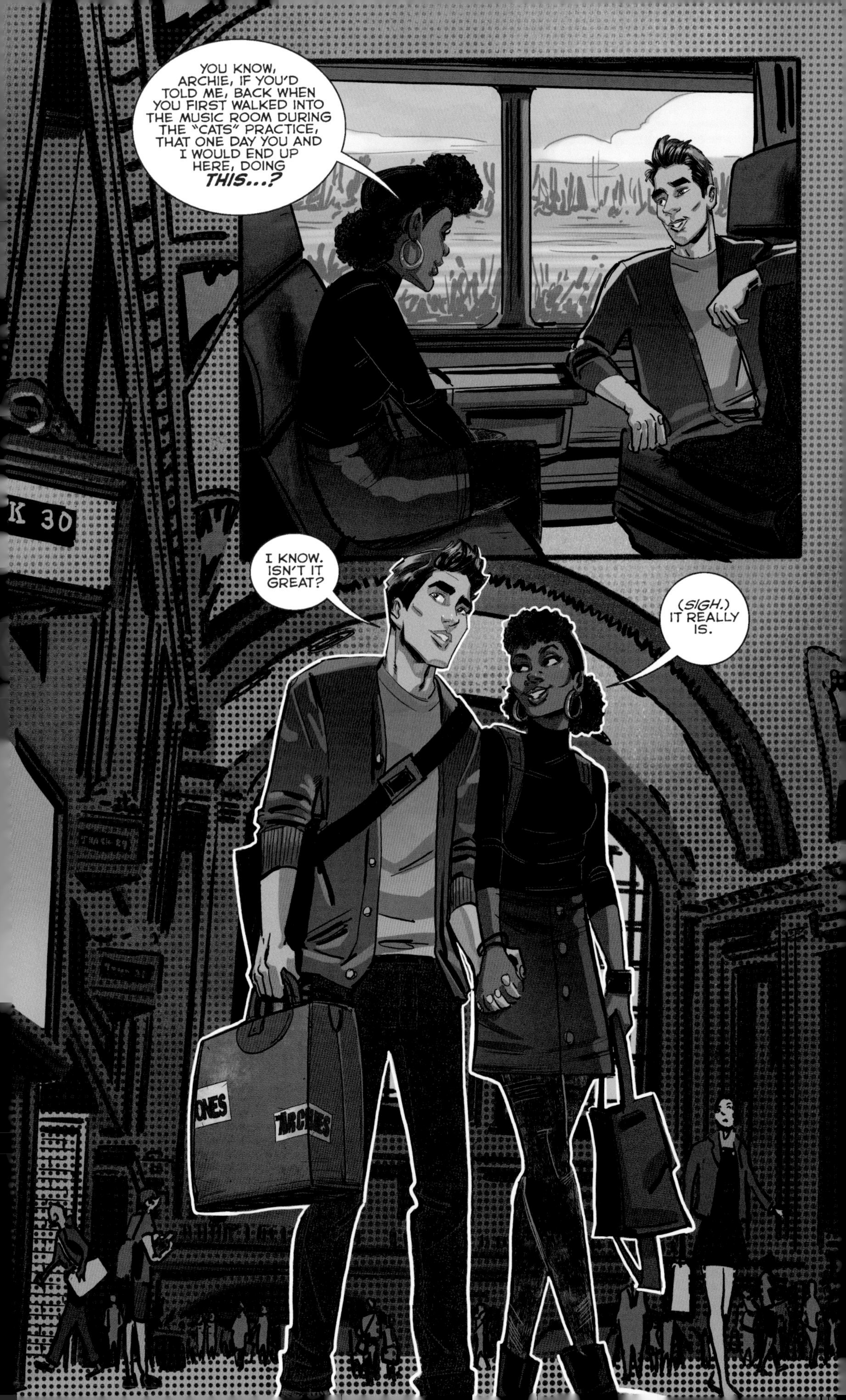
YOU KNOW, ARCHIE, IF YOU'D TOLD ME, BACK WHEN YOU FIRST WALKED INTO THE MUSIC ROOM DURING THE "CATS" PRACTICE, THAT ONE DAY YOU AND I WOULD END UP HERE, DOING ***THIS...?***
I KNOW. ISN'T IT GREAT?
(*SIGH.*) IT REALLY IS.
K 30
ONES
ARCHIES

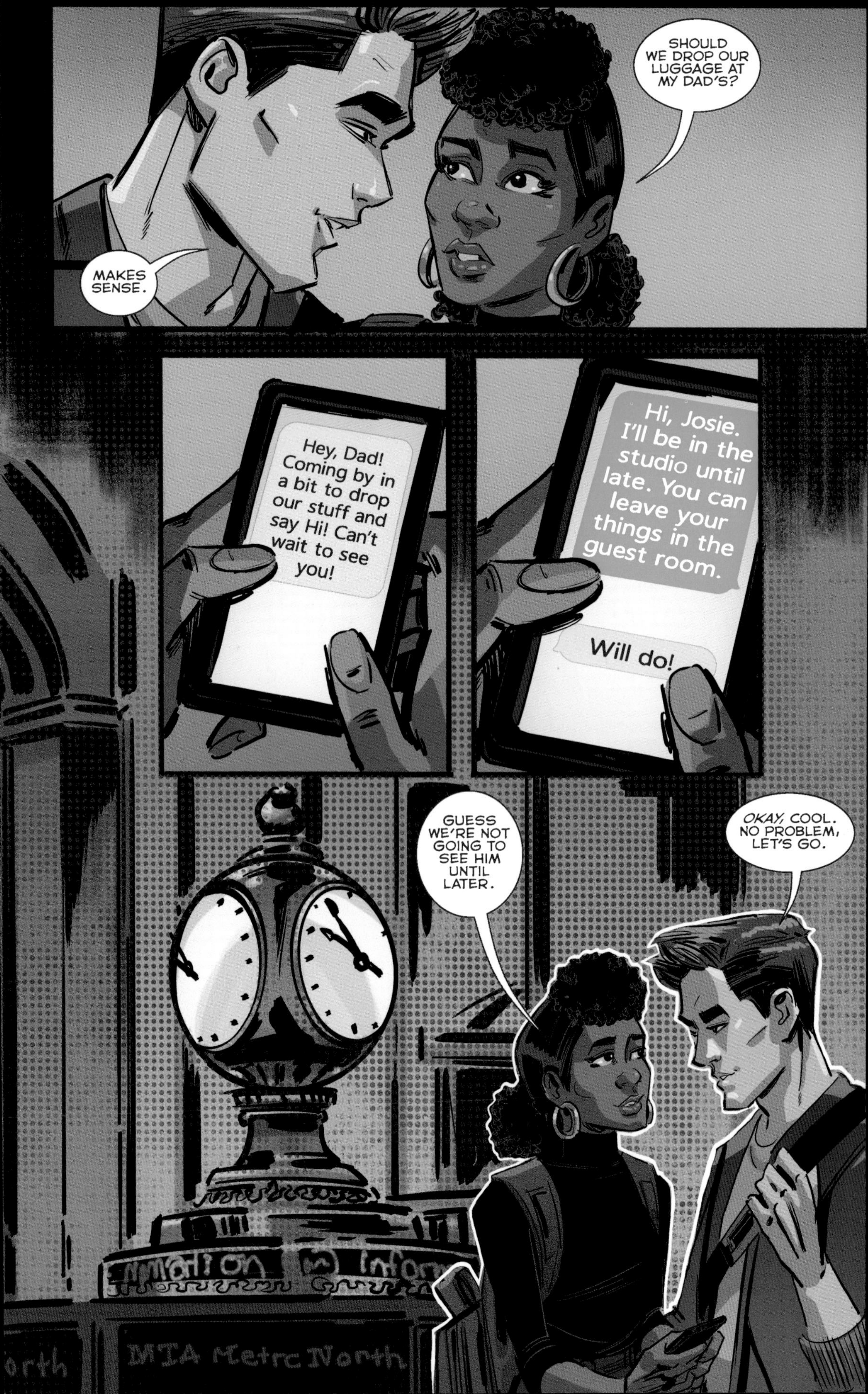
SHOULD WE DROP OUR LUGGAGE AT MY DAD'S?
MAKES SENSE.
Hey, Dad! Coming by in a bit to drop our stuff and say Hi! Can't wait to see you!
Hi, Josie. I'll be in the studio until late. You can leave your things in the guest room.
Will do!
GUESS WE'RE NOT GOING TO SEE HIM UNTIL LATER.
OKAY, COOL. NO PROBLEM, LET'S GO.

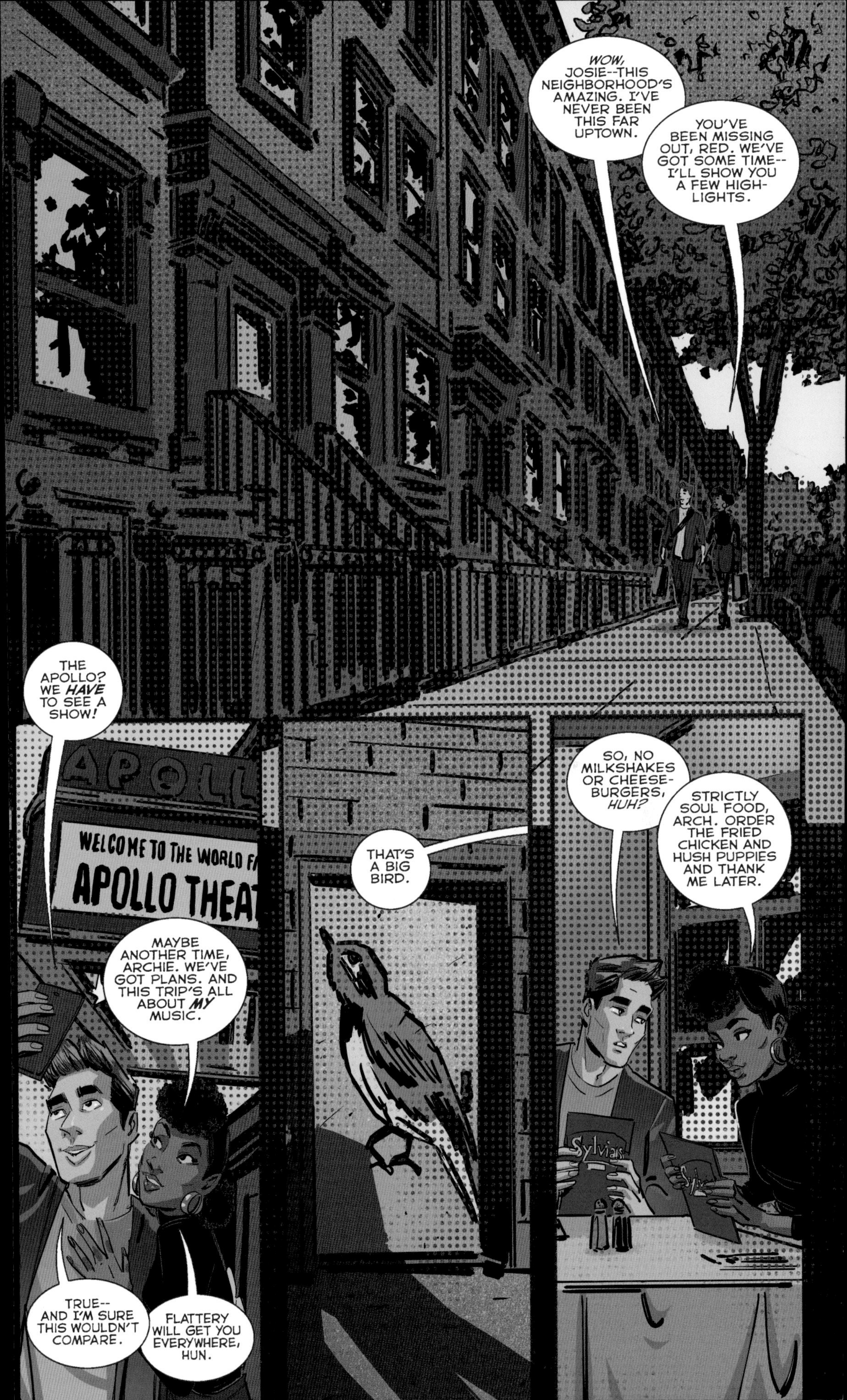
WOW, JOSIE--THIS NEIGHBORHOOD'S AMAZING. I'VE NEVER BEEN THIS FAR UPTOWN.
YOU'VE BEEN MISSING OUT, RED. WE'VE GOT SOME TIME--I'LL SHOW YOU A FEW HIGHLIGHTS.
THE APOLLO? WE *HAVE* TO SEE A SHOW!
APOLL
WELCOME TO THE WORLD FA
APOLLO THEAT
MAYBE ANOTHER TIME, ARCHIE. WE'VE GOT PLANS. AND THIS TRIP'S ALL ABOUT *MY* MUSIC.
TRUE--AND I'M SURE THIS WOULDN'T COMPARE.
FLATTERY WILL GET YOU EVERYWHERE, HUN.
THAT'S A BIG BIRD.
SO, NO MILKSHAKES OR CHEESEBURGERS, *HUH?*
STRICTLY SOUL FOOD, ARCH. ORDER THE FRIED CHICKEN AND HUSH PUPPIES AND THANK ME LATER.
Sylvia's

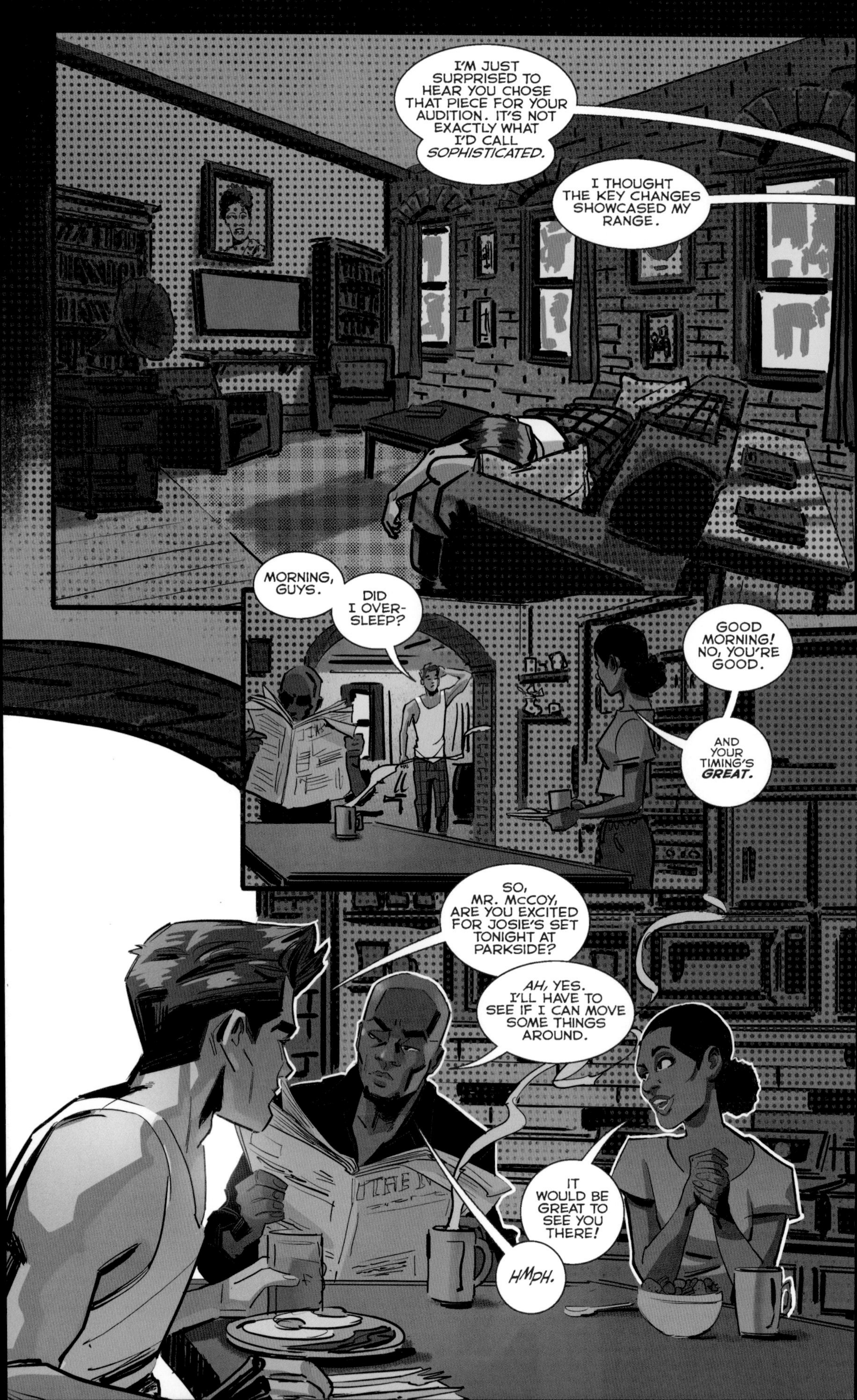
I'M JUST SURPRISED TO HEAR YOU CHOSE THAT PIECE FOR YOUR AUDITION. IT'S NOT EXACTLY WHAT I'D CALL *SOPHISTICATED.*
I THOUGHT THE KEY CHANGES SHOWCASED MY RANGE.
MORNING, GUYS.
DID I OVER-SLEEP?
GOOD MORNING! NO, YOU'RE GOOD.
AND YOUR TIMING'S ***GREAT.***
SO, MR. McCOY, ARE YOU EXCITED FOR JOSIE'S SET TONIGHT AT PARKSIDE?
AH, YES. I'LL HAVE TO SEE IF I CAN MOVE SOME THINGS AROUND.
IT WOULD BE GREAT TO SEE YOU THERE!
HMPH.

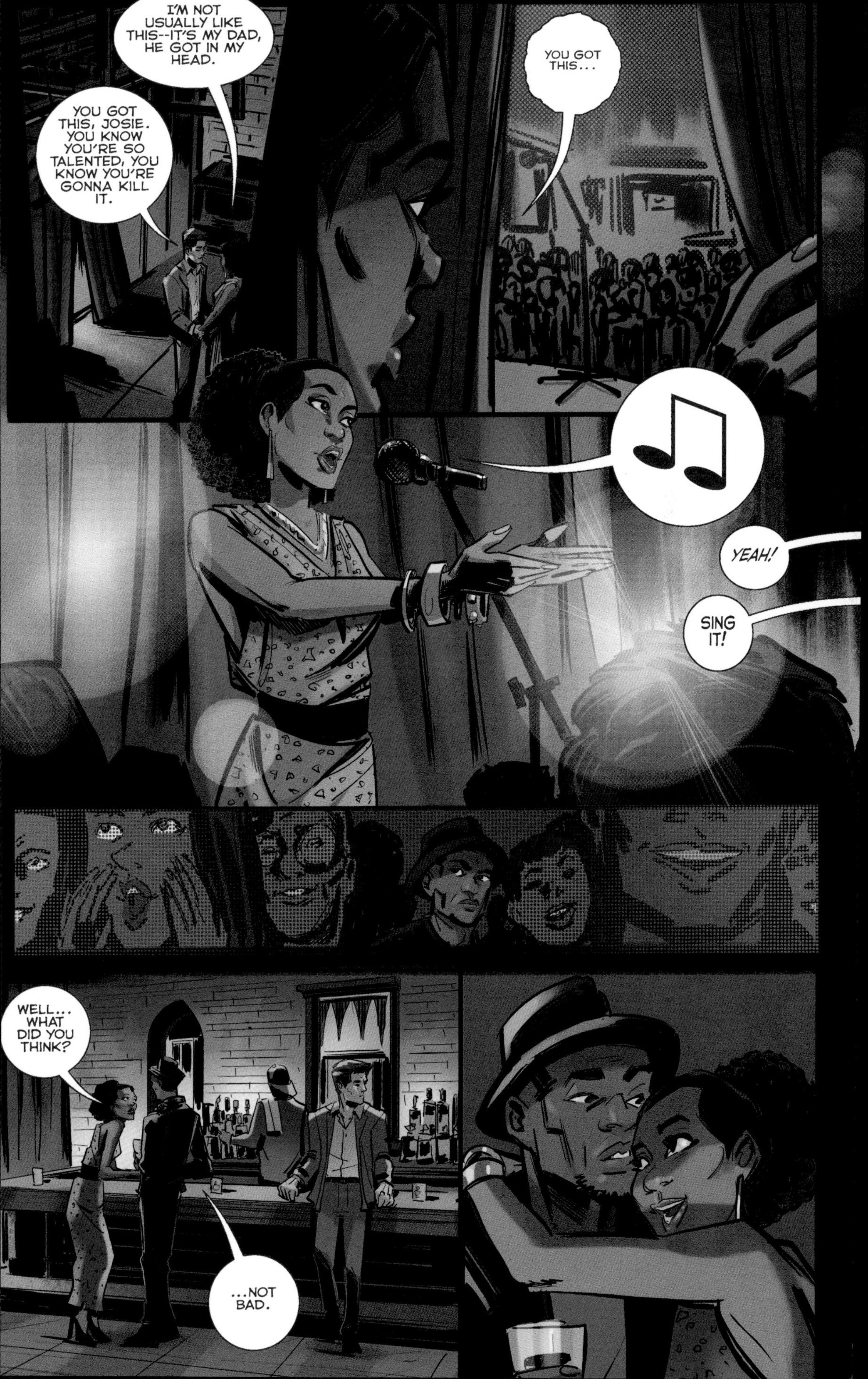
YOU GOT THIS, JOSIE. YOU KNOW YOU'RE SO TALENTED, YOU KNOW YOU'RE GONNA KILL IT.
I'M NOT USUALLY LIKE THIS--IT'S MY DAD, HE GOT IN MY HEAD.
YOU GOT THIS...
YEAH!
SING IT!
WELL... WHAT DID YOU THINK?
...NOT BAD.

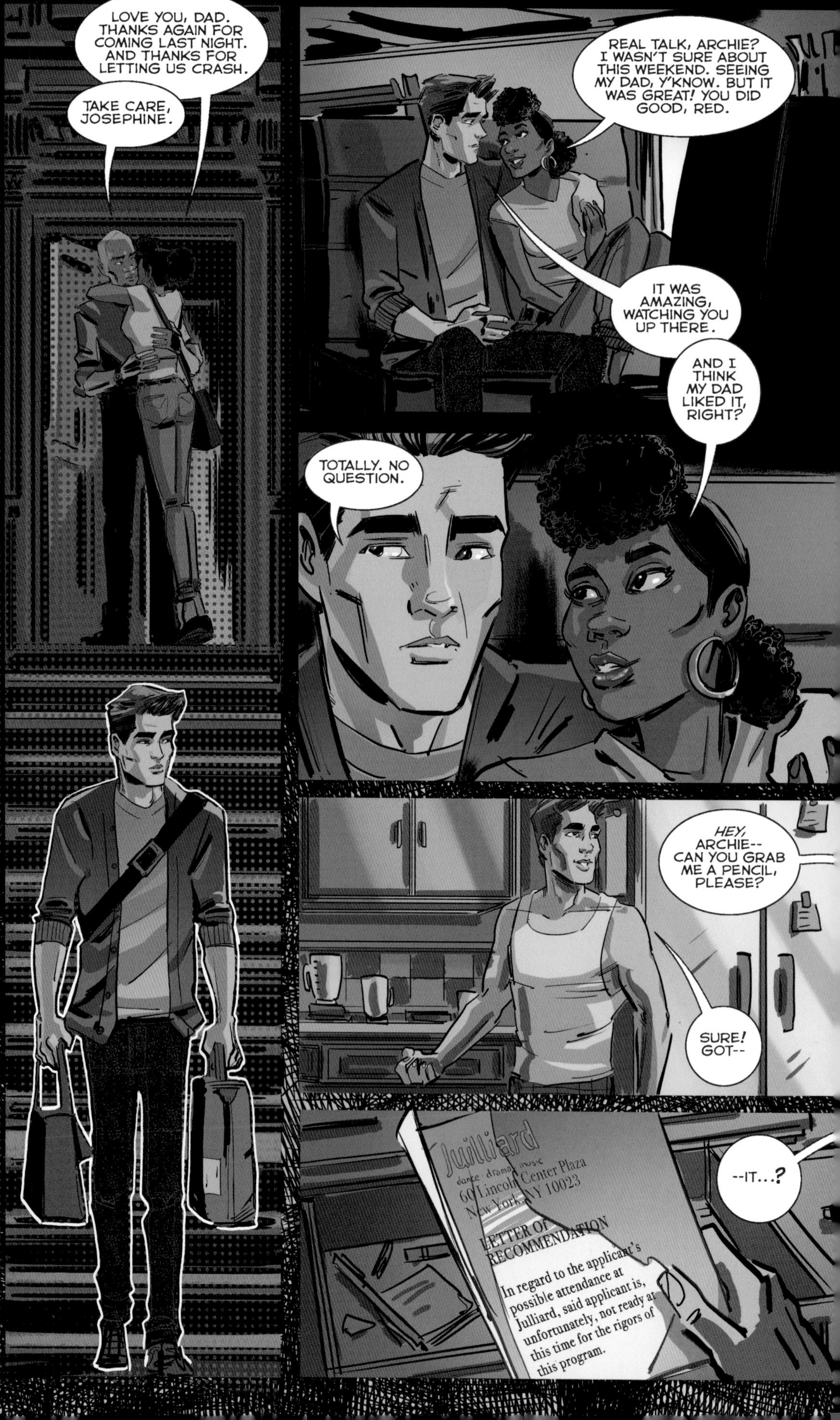
LOVE YOU, DAD. THANKS AGAIN FOR COMING LAST NIGHT. AND THANKS FOR LETTING US CRASH.
TAKE CARE, JOSEPHINE.
REAL TALK, ARCHIE? I WASN'T SURE ABOUT THIS WEEKEND. SEEING MY DAD, Y'KNOW. BUT IT WAS GREAT! YOU DID GOOD, RED.
IT WAS AMAZING, WATCHING YOU UP THERE.
AND I THINK MY DAD LIKED IT, RIGHT?
TOTALLY. NO QUESTION.
HEY, ARCHIE-- CAN YOU GRAB ME A PENCIL, PLEASE?
SURE! GOT--
--IT...?
Julliard
dance drama music
60 Lincoln Center Plaza
New York, NY 10023
LETTER OF RECOMMENDATION
In regard to the applicant's possible attendance at Julliard, said applicant is, unfortunately, not ready at this time for the rigors of this program.

CHAPTER TEN

INTO THE WILD

WRITER:
MICOL OSTOW

ART:
JOE EISMA

COLORS:
MATT HERMS

LETTERS:
JANICE CHIANG

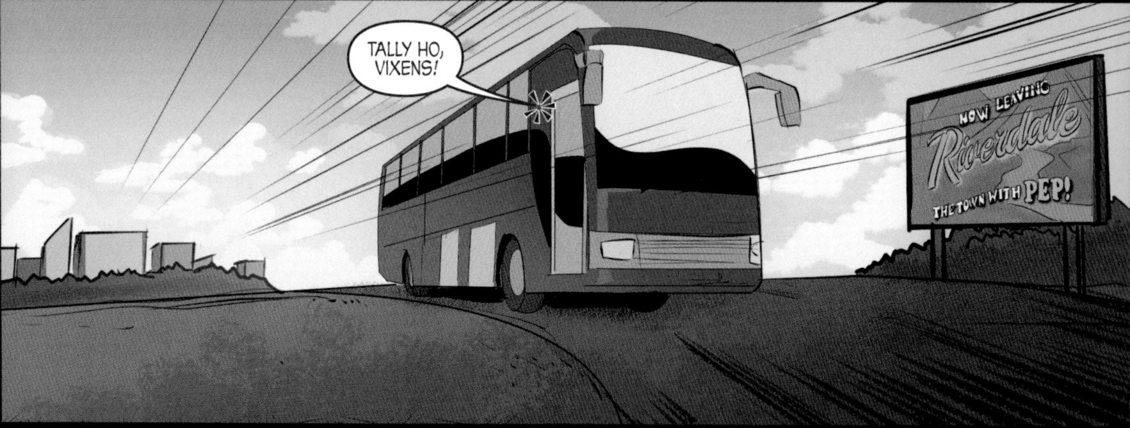
TALLY HO, VIXENS!
NOW LEAVING Riverdale THE TOWN WITH PEP!

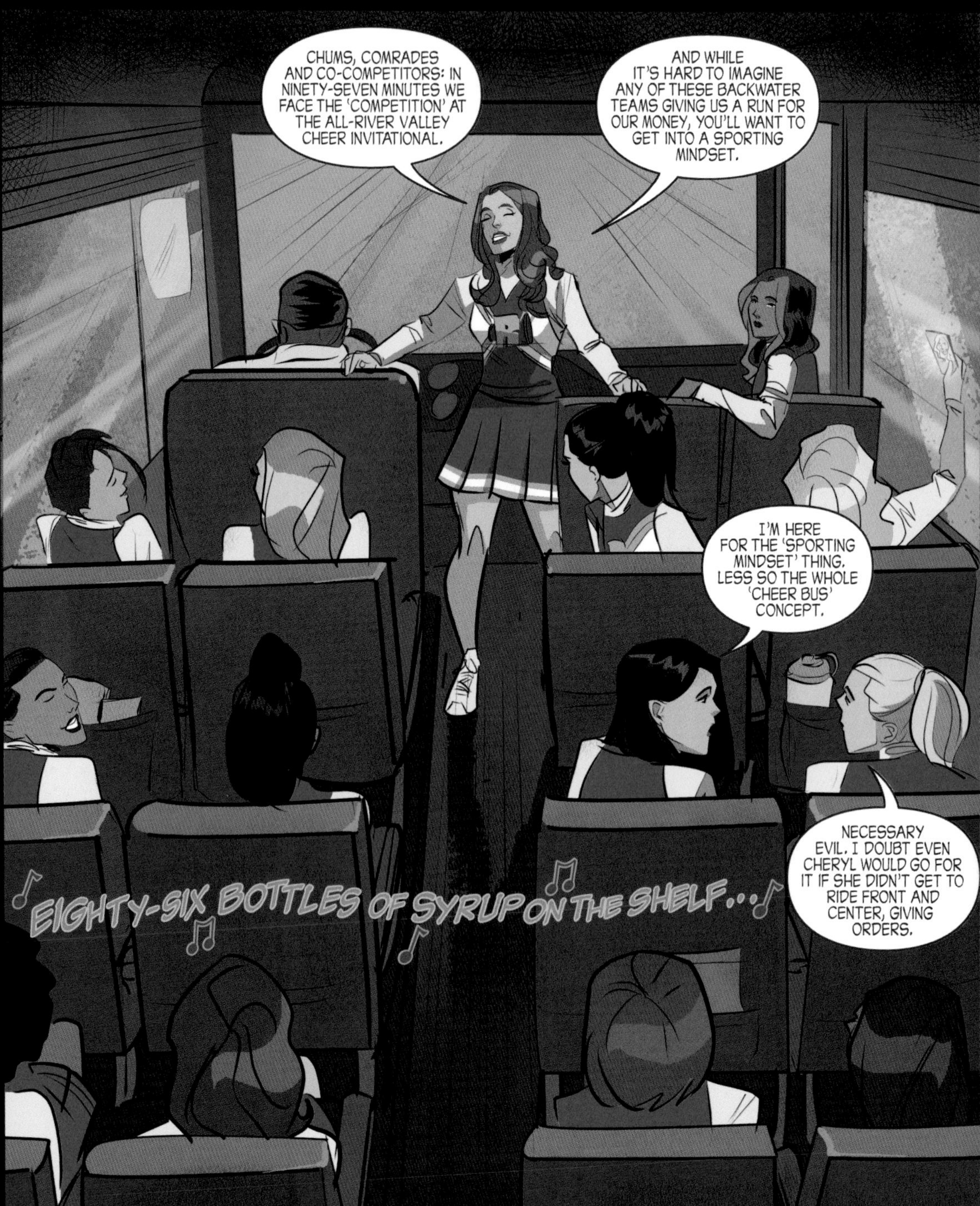
CHUMS, COMRADES AND CO-COMPETITORS: IN NINETY-SEVEN MINUTES WE FACE THE 'COMPETITION' AT THE ALL-RIVER VALLEY CHEER INVITATIONAL.
AND WHILE IT'S HARD TO IMAGINE ANY OF THESE BACKWATER TEAMS GIVING US A RUN FOR OUR MONEY, YOU'LL WANT TO GET INTO A SPORTING MINDSET.
I'M HERE FOR THE 'SPORTING MINDSET' THING. LESS SO THE WHOLE 'CHEER BUS' CONCEPT.
NECESSARY EVIL. I DOUBT EVEN CHERYL WOULD GO FOR IT IF SHE DIDN'T GET TO RIDE FRONT AND CENTER, GIVING ORDERS.
EIGHTY-SIX BOTTLES OF SYRUP ON THE SHELF...

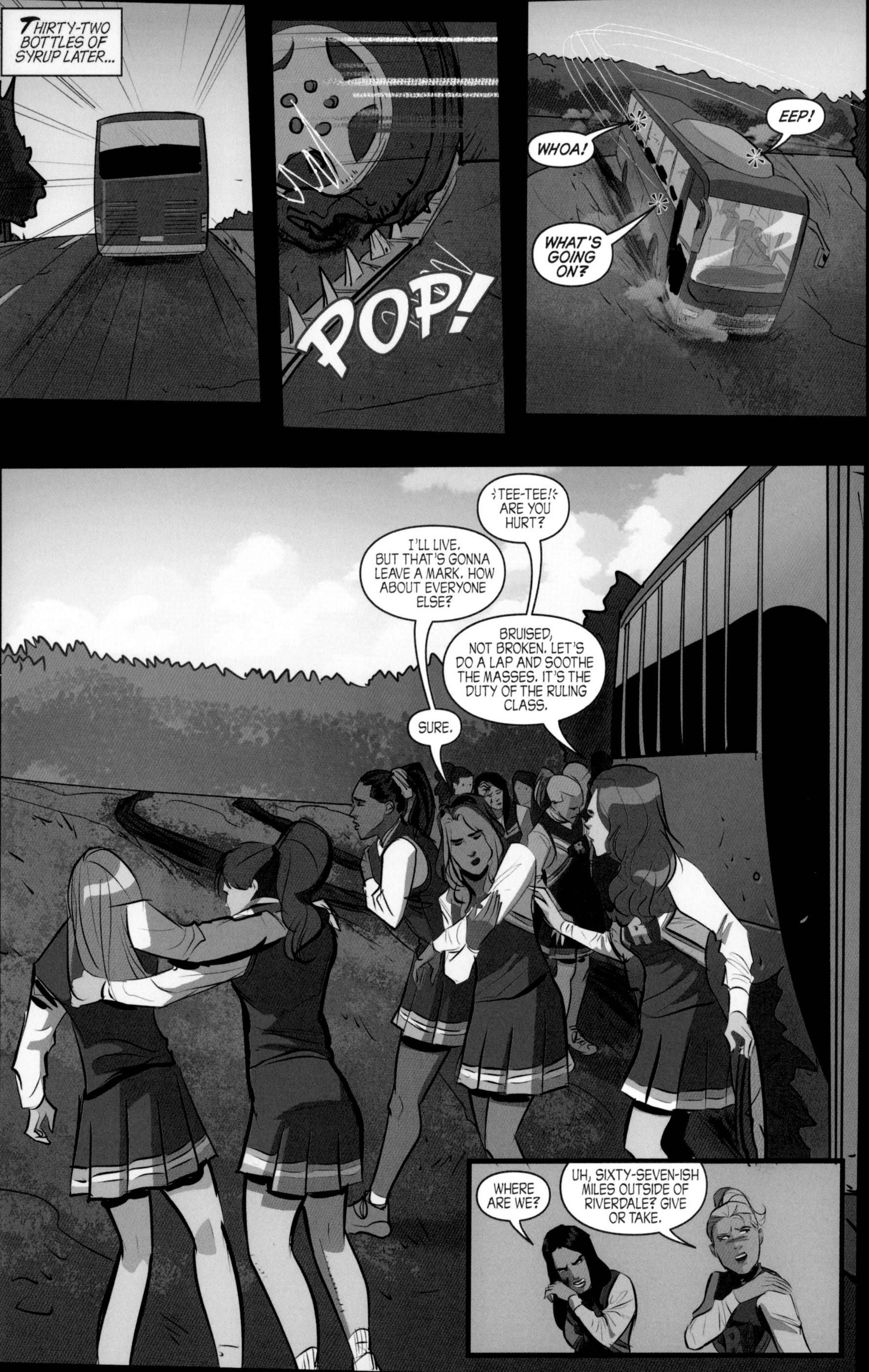
THIRTY-TWO BOTTLES OF SYRUP LATER...
POP!
WHOA!
EEP!
WHAT'S GOING ON?
TEE-TEE! ARE YOU HURT?
I'LL LIVE. BUT THAT'S GONNA LEAVE A MARK. HOW ABOUT EVERYONE ELSE?
BRUISED, NOT BROKEN. LET'S DO A LAP AND SOOTHE THE MASSES. IT'S THE DUTY OF THE RULING CLASS.
SURE.
WHERE ARE WE?
UH, SIXTY-SEVEN-ISH MILES OUTSIDE OF RIVERDALE? GIVE OR TAKE.

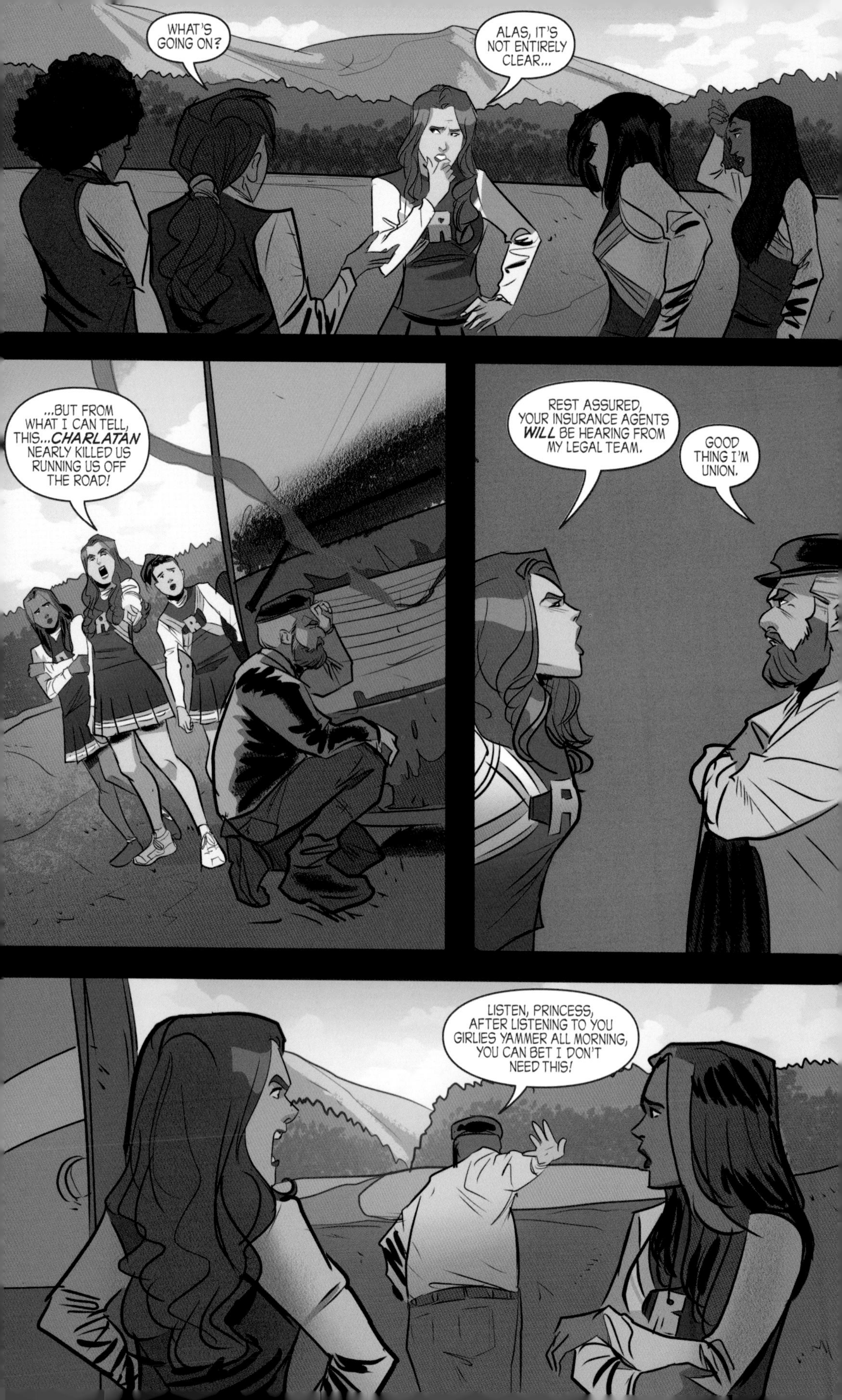
WHAT'S GOING ON?
ALAS, IT'S NOT ENTIRELY CLEAR...
...BUT FROM WHAT I CAN TELL, THIS...CHARLATAN NEARLY KILLED US RUNNING US OFF THE ROAD!
REST ASSURED, YOUR INSURANCE AGENTS WILL BE HEARING FROM MY LEGAL TEAM.
GOOD THING I'M UNION.
LISTEN, PRINCESS, AFTER LISTENING TO YOU GIRLIES YAMMER ALL MORNING, YOU CAN BET I DON'T NEED THIS!

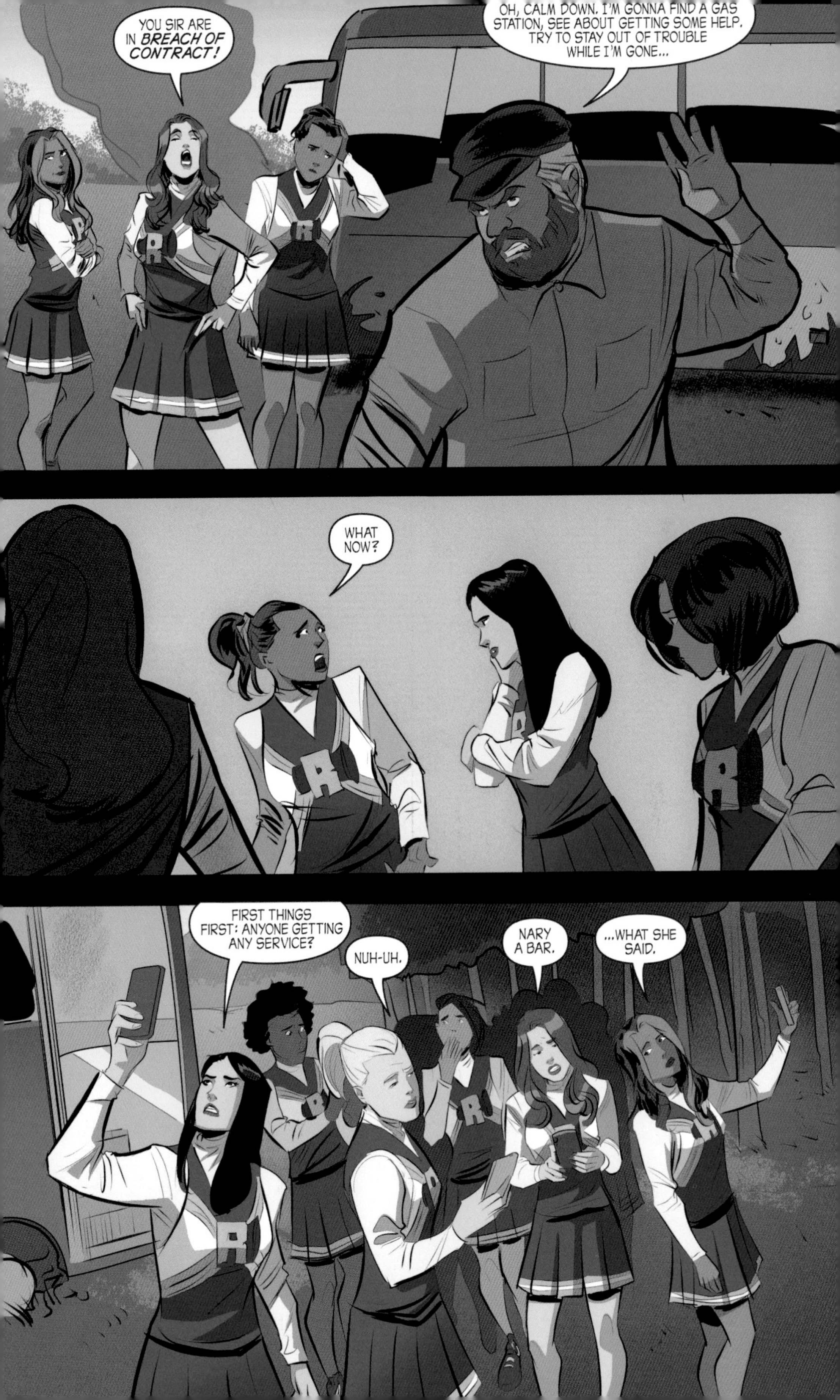
YOU SIR ARE IN BREACH OF CONTRACT!
OH, CALM DOWN. I'M GONNA FIND A GAS STATION, SEE ABOUT GETTING SOME HELP. TRY TO STAY OUT OF TROUBLE WHILE I'M GONE...
WHAT NOW?
FIRST THINGS FIRST: ANYONE GETTING ANY SERVICE?
NUH-UH.
NARY A BAR.
...WHAT SHE SAID.

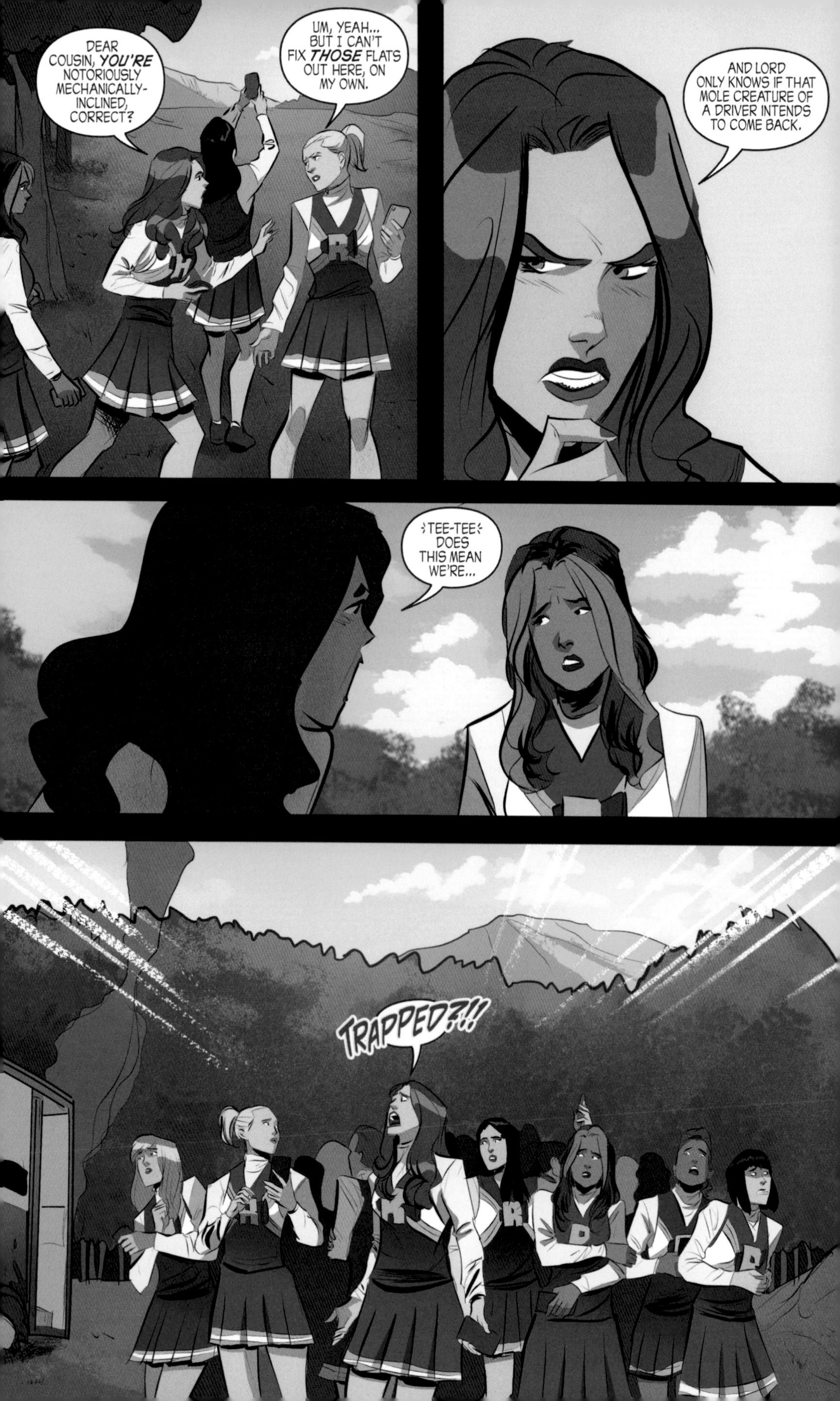
DEAR COUSIN, YOU'RE NOTORIOUSLY MECHANICALLY-INCLINED, CORRECT?
UM, YEAH... BUT I CAN'T FIX THOSE FLATS OUT HERE, ON MY OWN.
AND LORD ONLY KNOWS IF THAT MOLE CREATURE OF A DRIVER INTENDS TO COME BACK.
TEE-TEE DOES THIS MEAN WE'RE...
TRAPPED?!!

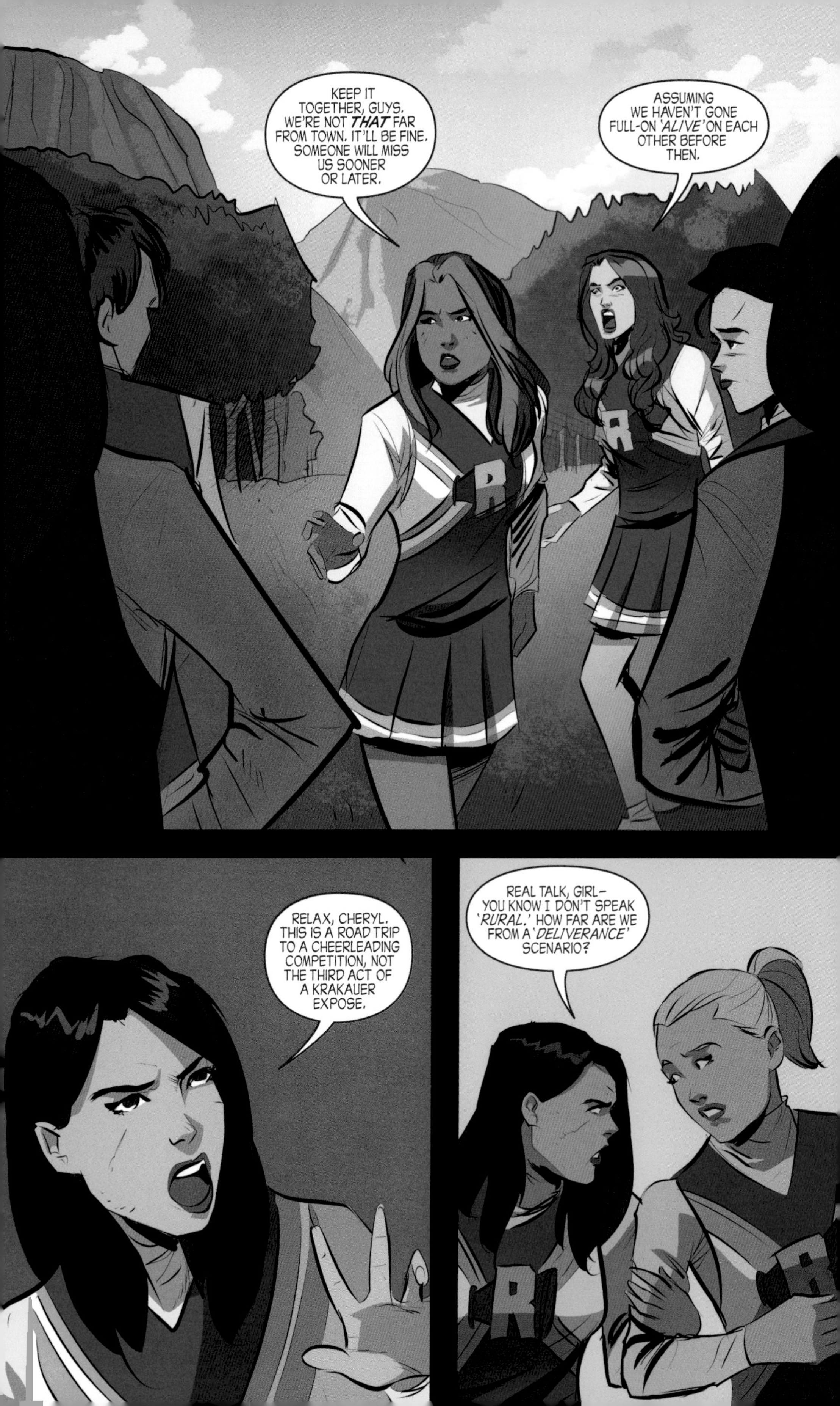

KEEP IT TOGETHER, GUYS. WE'RE NOT *THAT* FAR FROM TOWN. IT'LL BE FINE. SOMEONE WILL MISS US SOONER OR LATER.
ASSUMING WE HAVEN'T GONE FULL-ON '*ALIVE*' ON EACH OTHER BEFORE THEN.
RELAX, CHERYL. THIS IS A ROAD TRIP TO A CHEERLEADING COMPETITION, NOT THE THIRD ACT OF A KRAKAUER EXPOSE.
REAL TALK, GIRL– YOU KNOW I DON'T SPEAK '*RURAL*.' HOW FAR ARE WE FROM A '*DELIVERANCE*' SCENARIO?

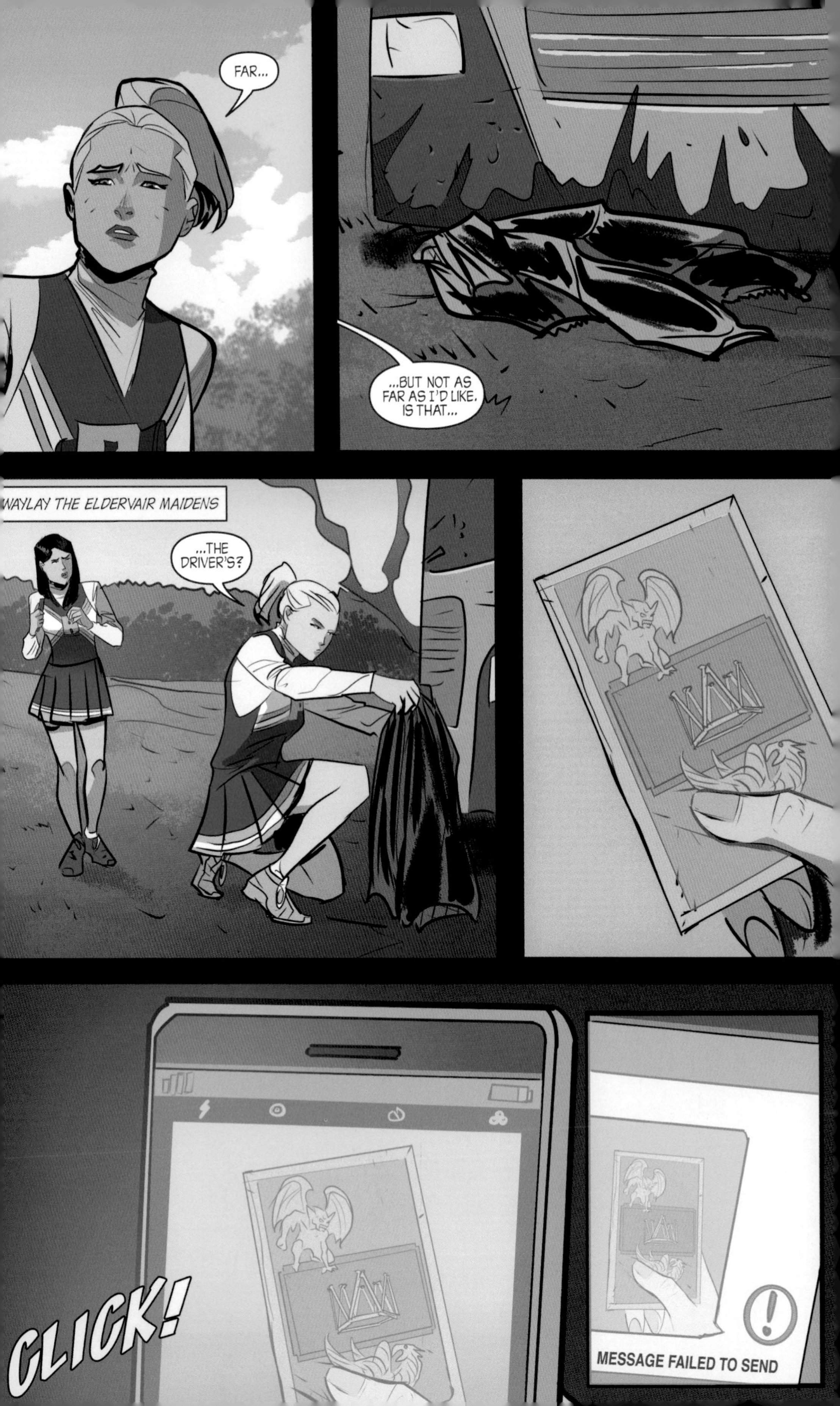
FAR...
...BUT NOT AS FAR AS I'D LIKE. IS THAT...
WAYLAY THE ELDERVAIR MAIDENS
...THE DRIVER'S?
CLICK!
MESSAGE FAILED TO SEND

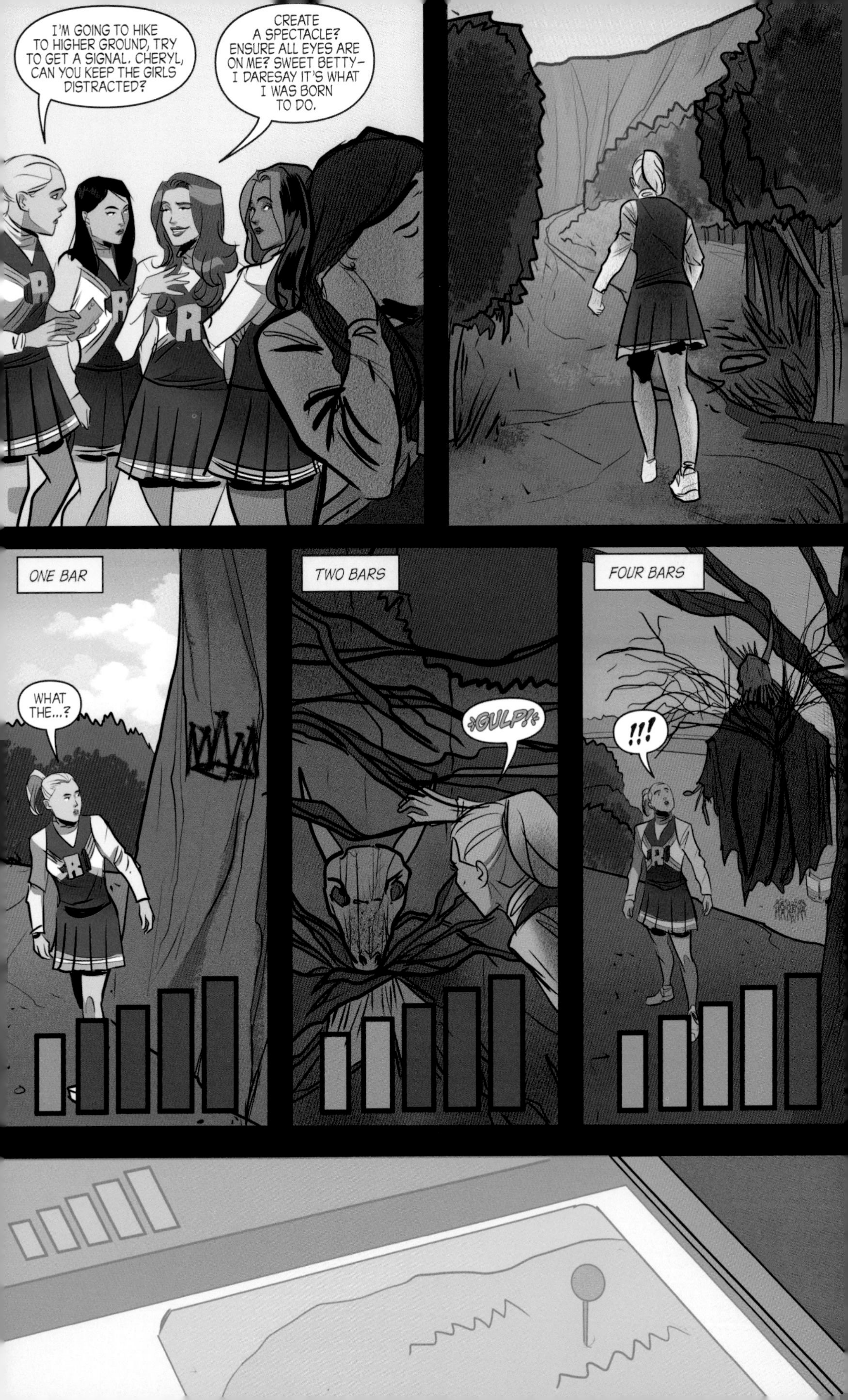
I'M GOING TO HIKE TO HIGHER GROUND, TRY TO GET A SIGNAL. CHERYL, CAN YOU KEEP THE GIRLS DISTRACTED?
CREATE A SPECTACLE? ENSURE ALL EYES ARE ON ME? SWEET BETTY– I DARESAY IT'S WHAT I WAS BORN TO DO.
ONE BAR
WHAT THE...?
TWO BARS
GULP!
FOUR BARS
!!!

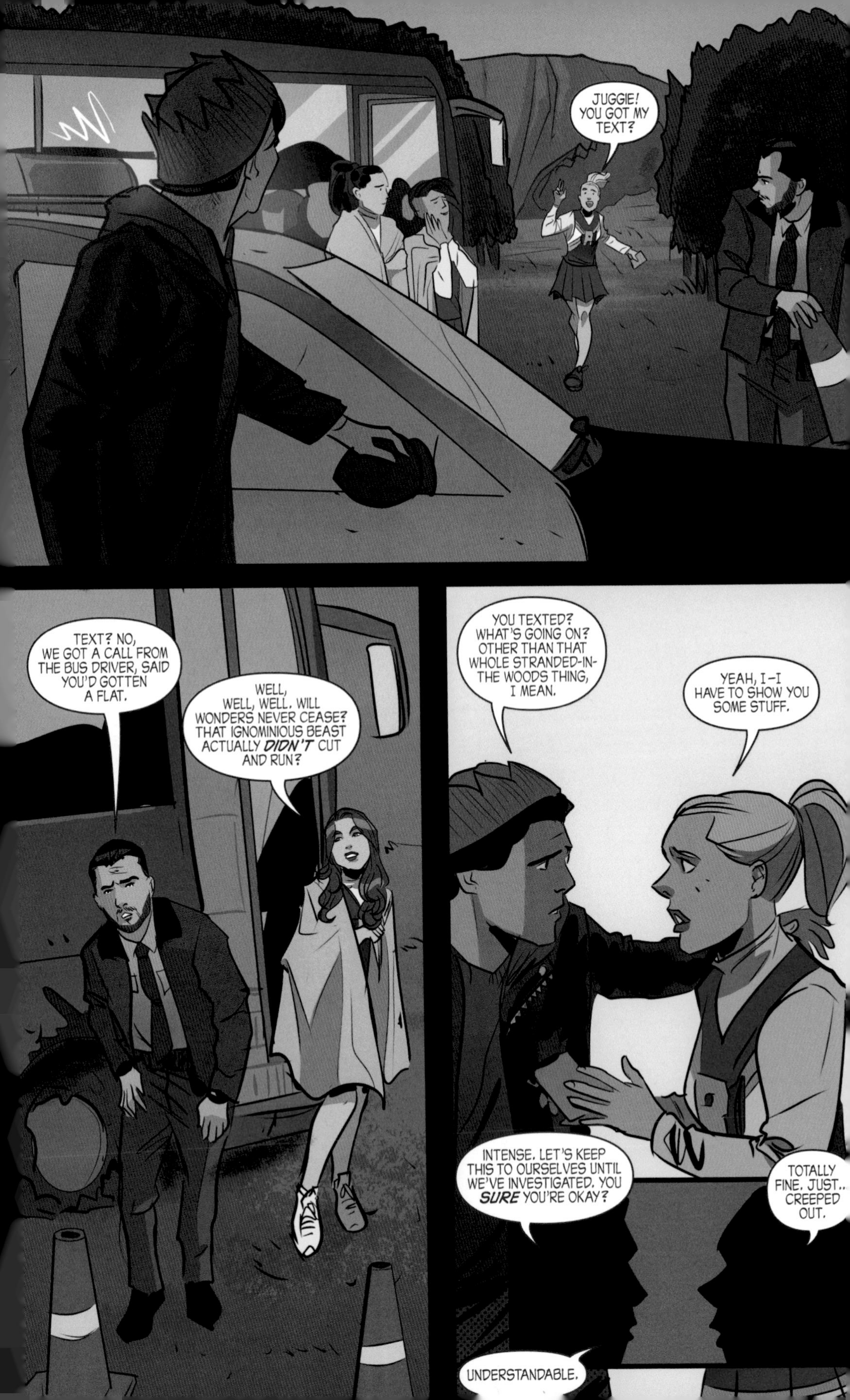
JUGGIE! YOU GOT MY TEXT?
TEXT? NO, WE GOT A CALL FROM THE BUS DRIVER, SAID YOU'D GOTTEN A FLAT.
WELL, WELL, WELL. WILL WONDERS NEVER CEASE? THAT IGNOMINIOUS BEAST ACTUALLY DIDN'T CUT AND RUN?
YOU TEXTED? WHAT'S GOING ON? OTHER THAN THAT WHOLE STRANDED-IN-THE WOODS THING, I MEAN.
YEAH, I-I HAVE TO SHOW YOU SOME STUFF.
INTENSE. LET'S KEEP THIS TO OURSELVES UNTIL WE'VE INVESTIGATED. YOU SURE YOU'RE OKAY?
TOTALLY FINE. JUST... CREEPED OUT.
UNDERSTANDABLE.

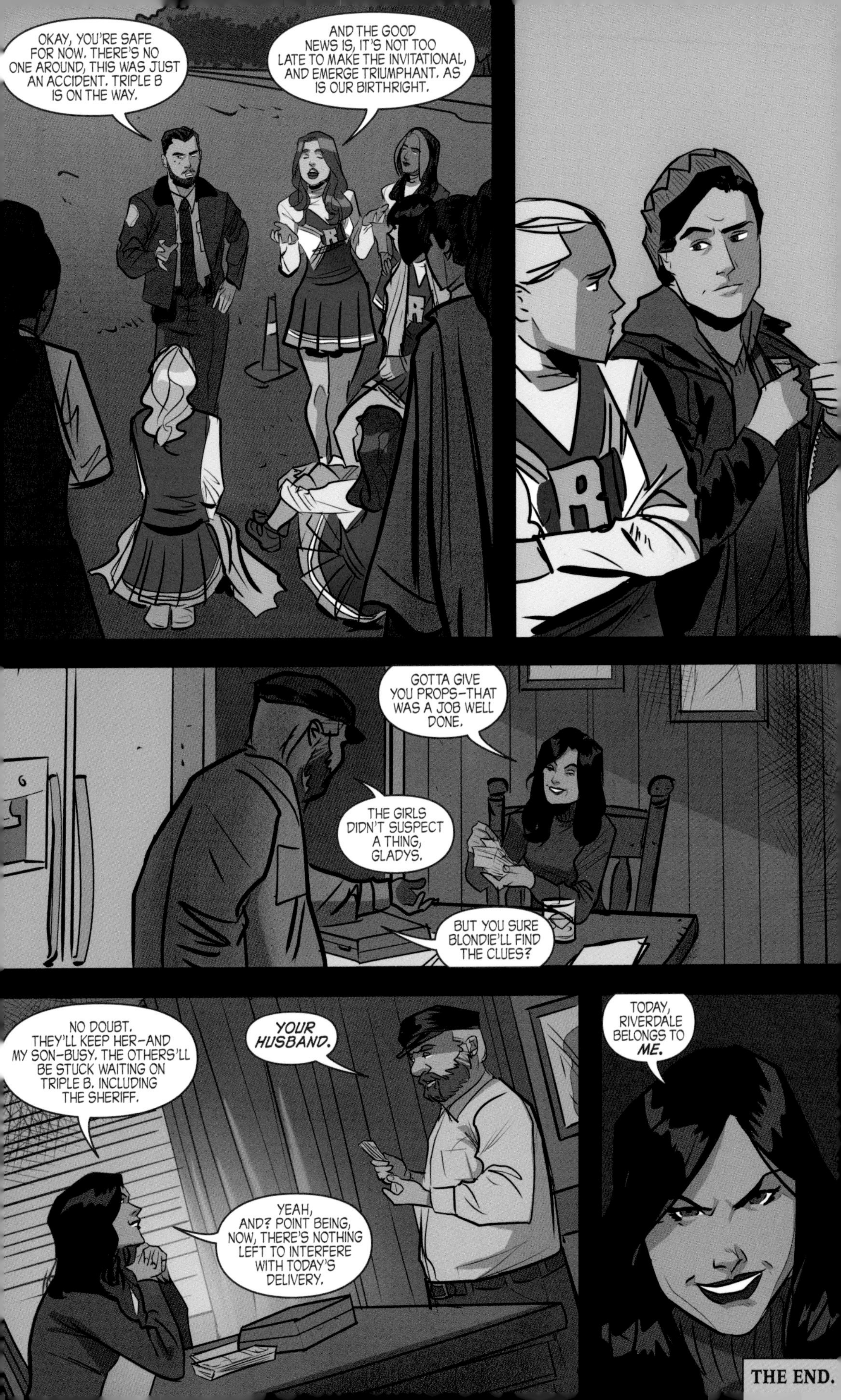
OKAY, YOU'RE SAFE FOR NOW. THERE'S NO ONE AROUND, THIS WAS JUST AN ACCIDENT. TRIPLE B IS ON THE WAY.
AND THE GOOD NEWS IS, IT'S NOT TOO LATE TO MAKE THE INVITATIONAL, AND EMERGE TRIUMPHANT. AS IS OUR BIRTHRIGHT.
GOTTA GIVE YOU PROPS–THAT WAS A JOB WELL DONE.
THE GIRLS DIDN'T SUSPECT A THING, GLADYS.
BUT YOU SURE BLONDIE'LL FIND THE CLUES?
NO DOUBT. THEY'LL KEEP HER–AND MY SON–BUSY. THE OTHERS'LL BE STUCK WAITING ON TRIPLE B. INCLUDING THE SHERIFF.
YOUR HUSBAND.
YEAH, AND? POINT BEING, NOW, THERE'S NOTHING LEFT TO INTERFERE WITH TODAY'S DELIVERY.
TODAY, RIVERDALE BELONGS TO ME.
THE END.

ISSUE ONE MAIN COVER

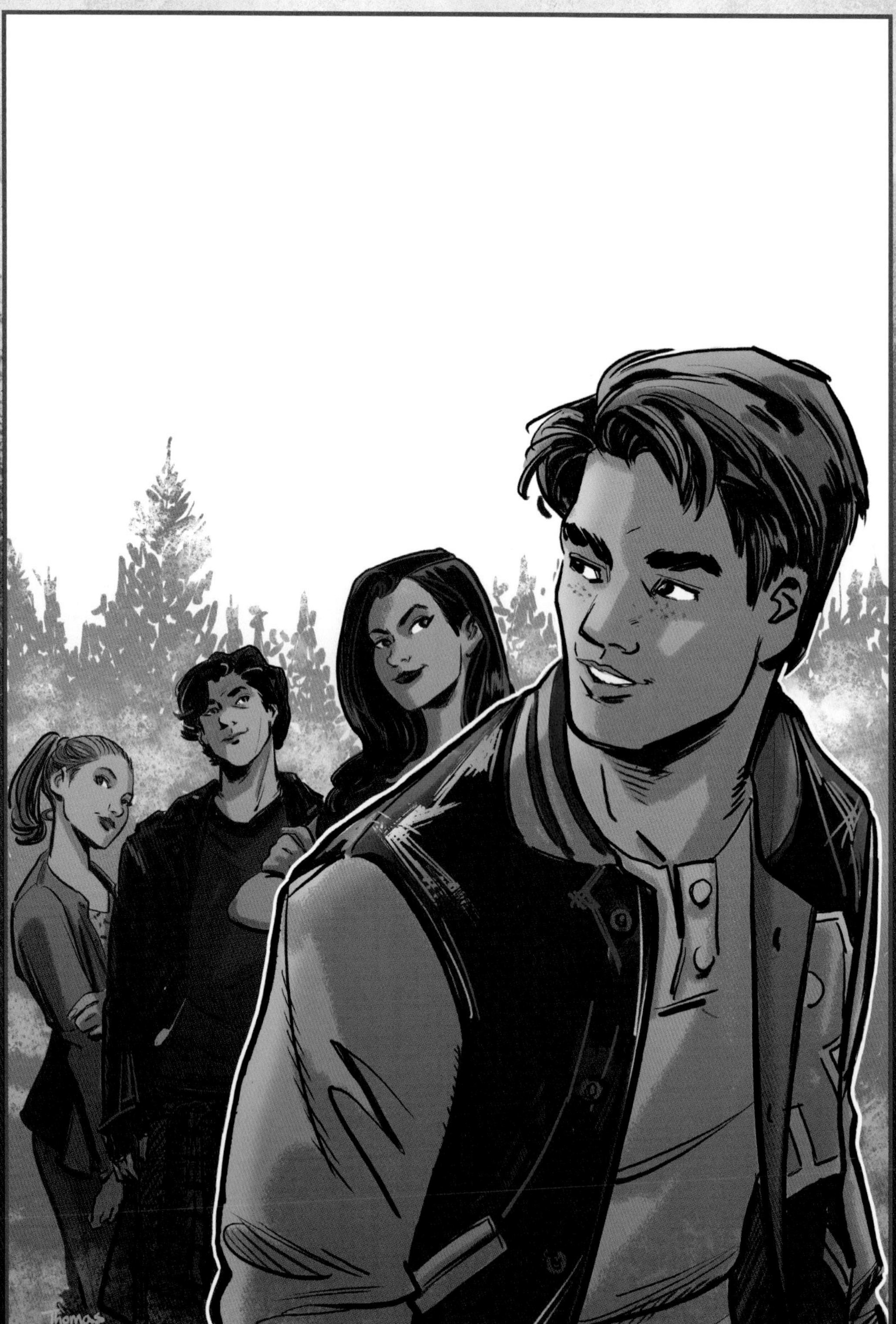
Thomas
Pitilli '18

COVER ART BY THOMAS PITILLI

ISSUE ONE VARIANT COVER

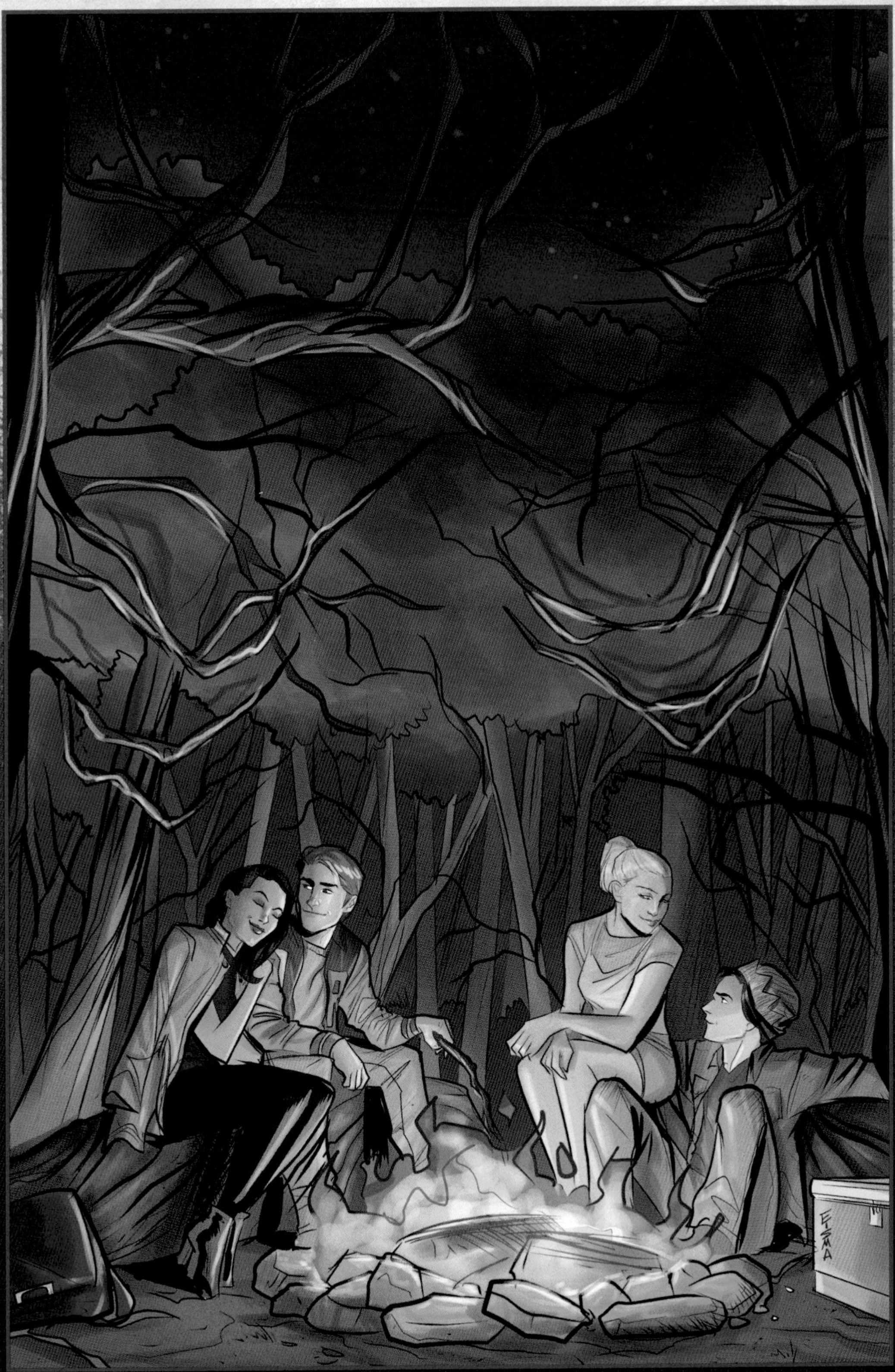
EISMA

COVER ART BY JOE EISMA

ISSUE TWO MAIN COVER

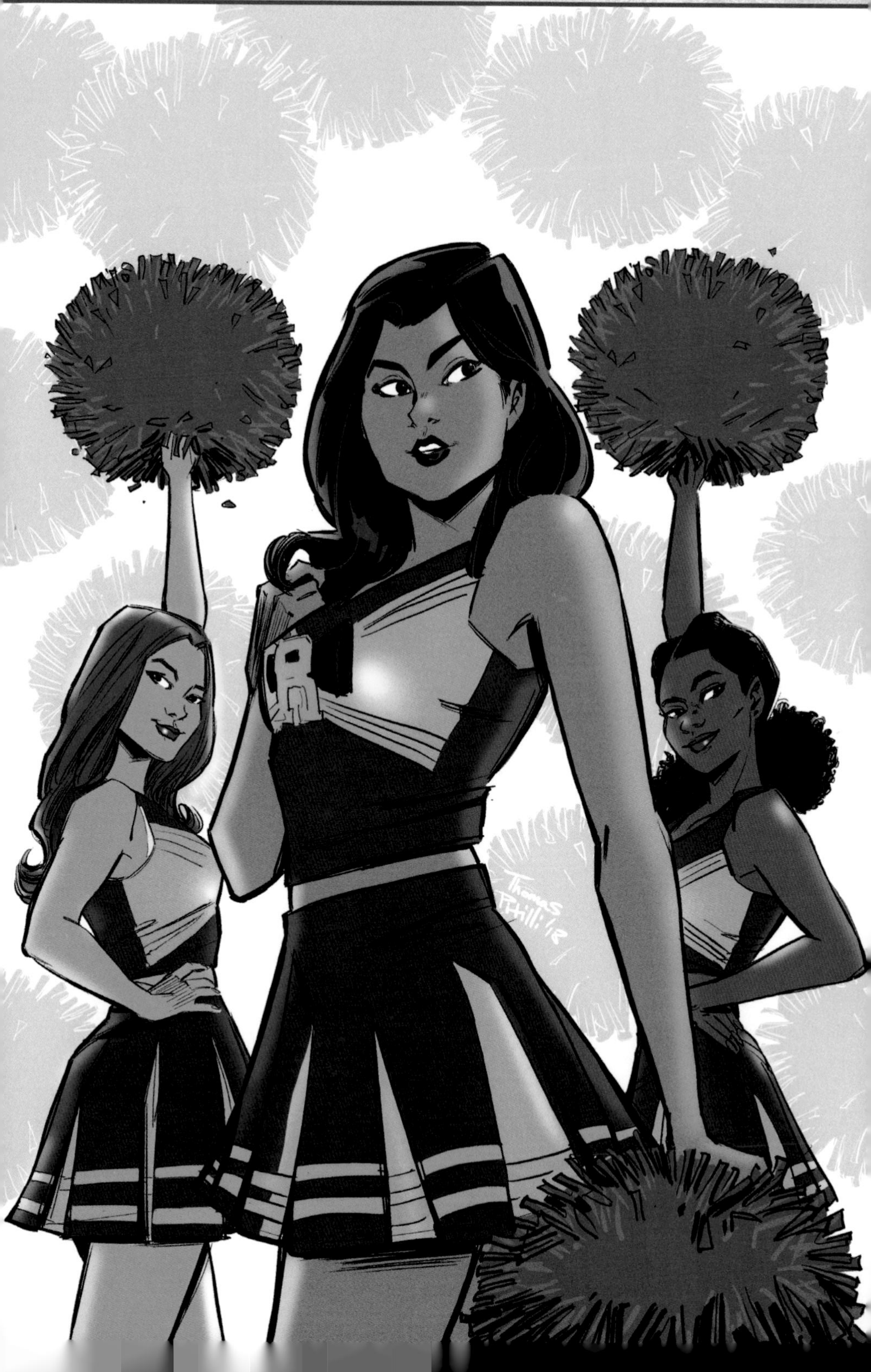

ISSUE TWO VARIANT COVER

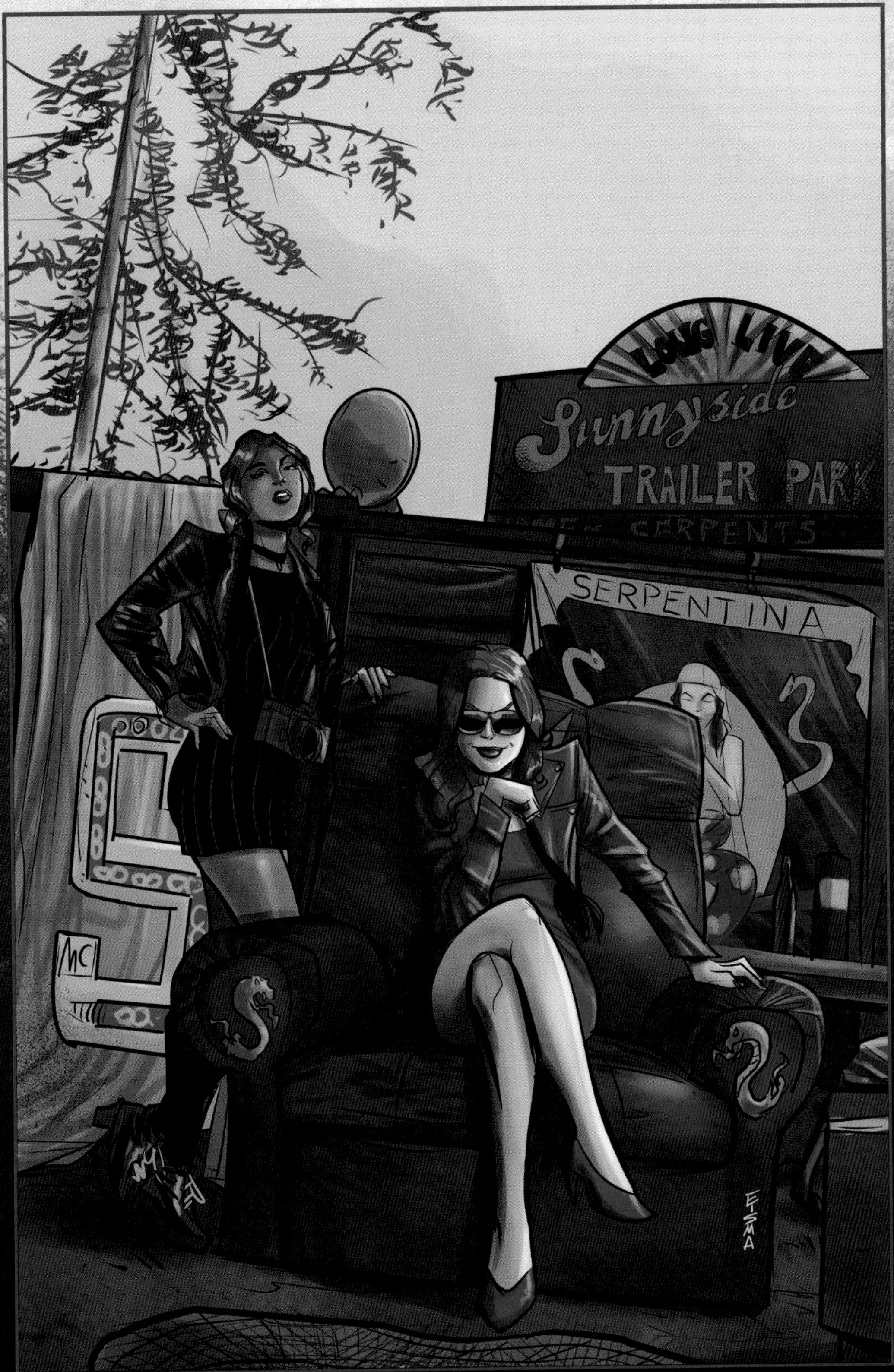
LONG LIVE
Sunnyside
TRAILER PARK
SERPENTS
SERPENTINA
EISMA

COVER ART BY JOE EISMA

ISSUE THREE MAIN COVER

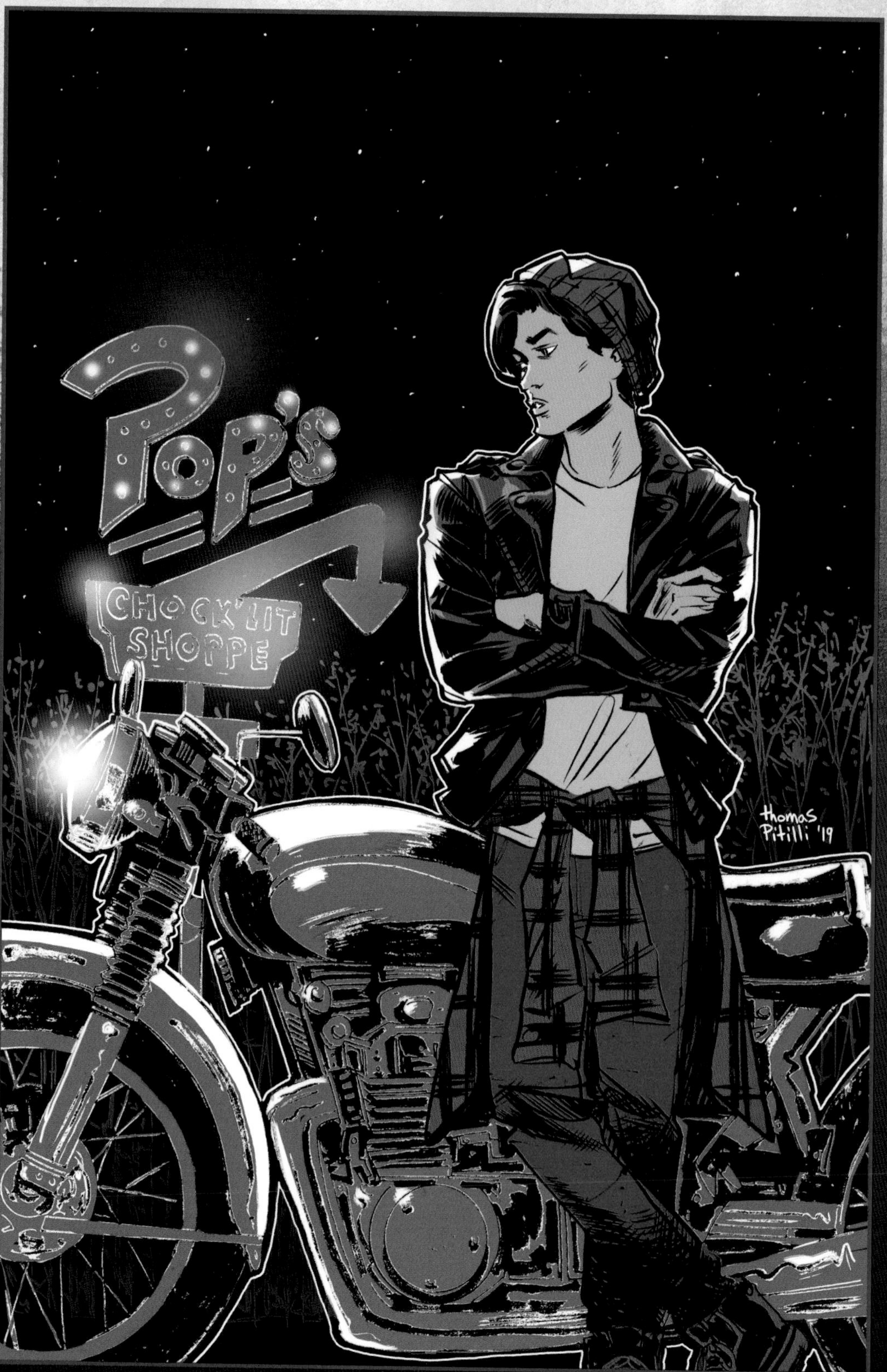

Pop's
CHOCK'LIT SHOPPE
thomas Pitilli '19

ISSUE THREE VARIANT COVER

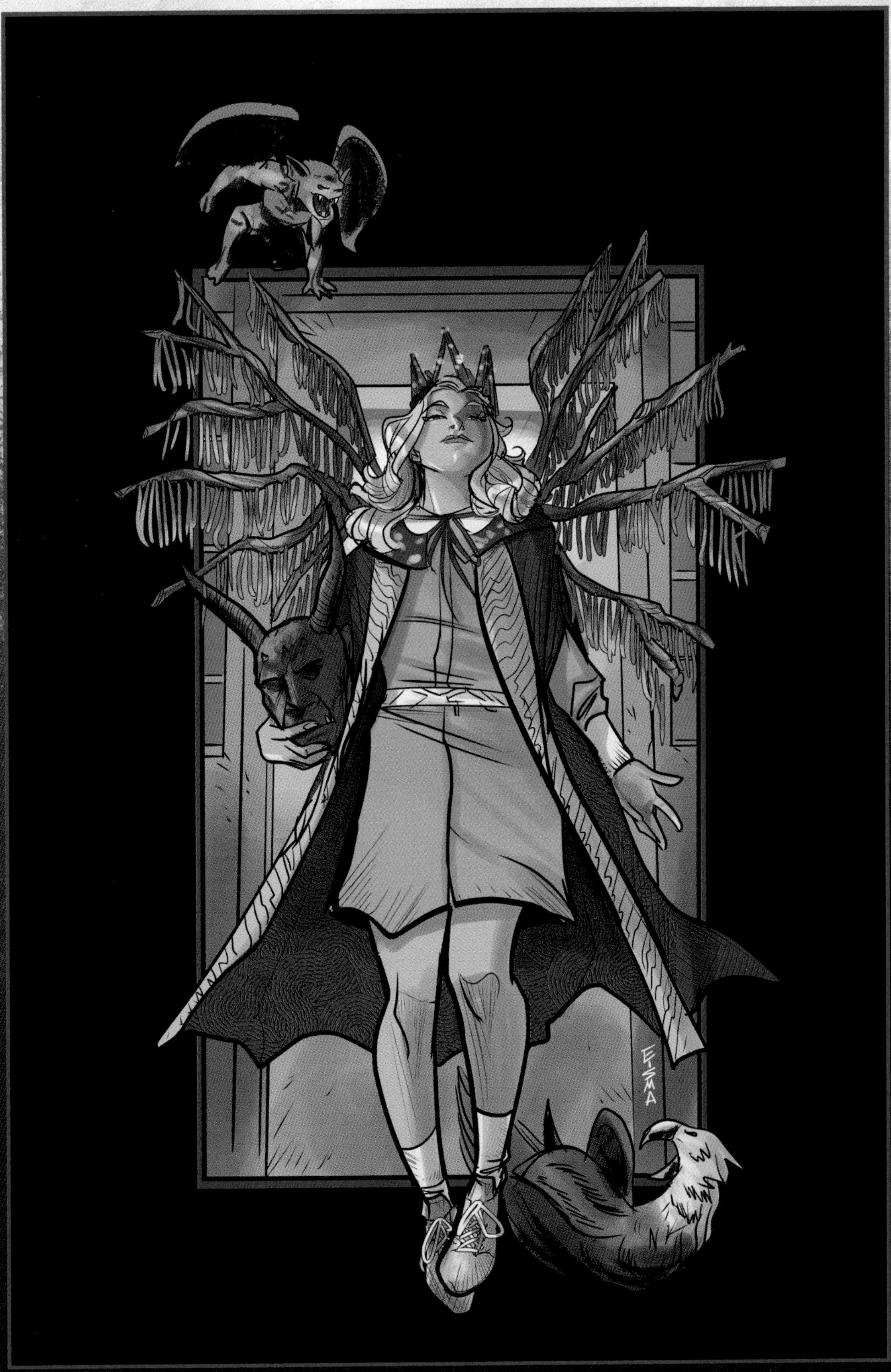
EISMA

COVER ART BY JOE EISMA

ISSUE FOUR MAIN COVER

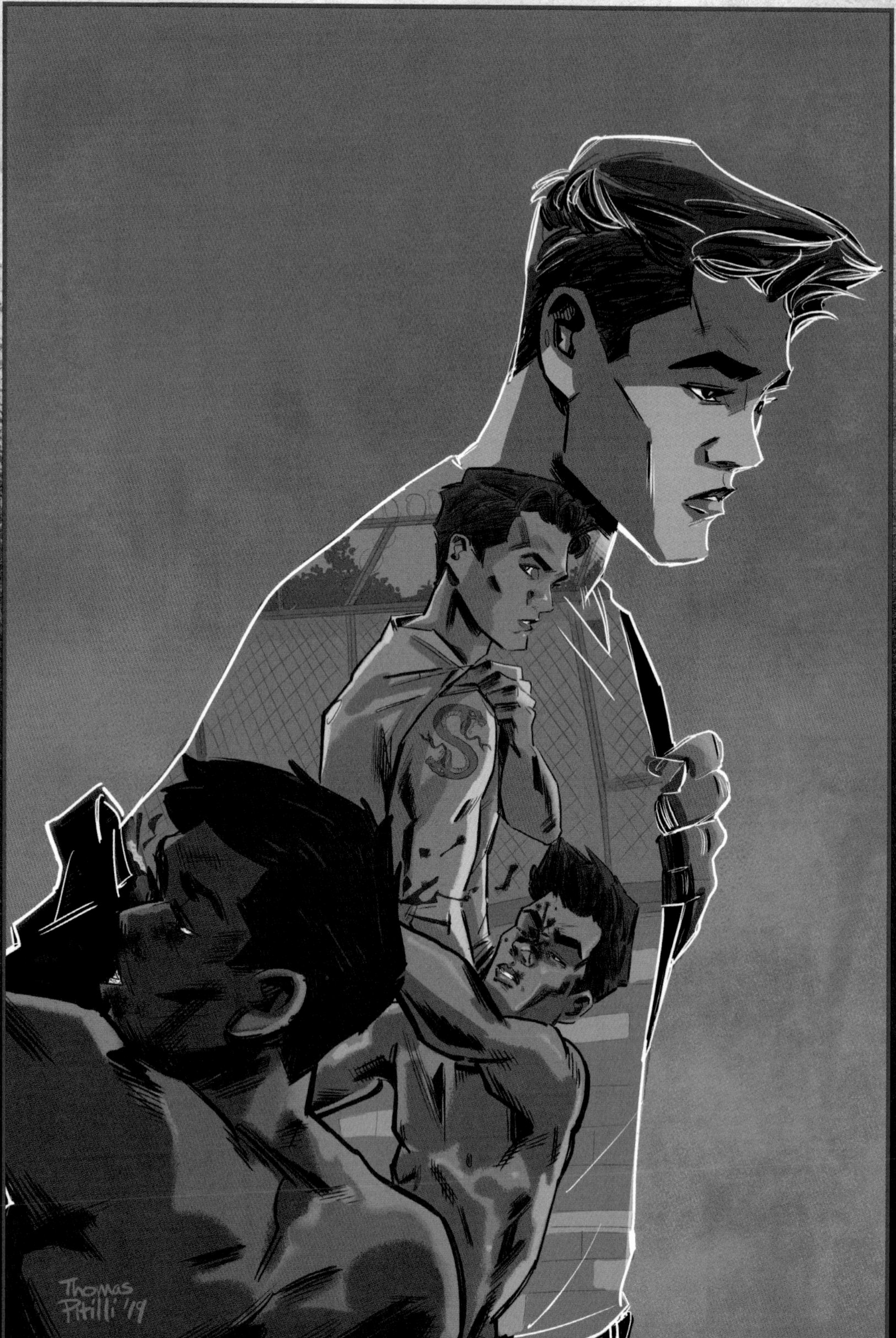
Thomas Pitilli '19

COVER ART BY THOMAS PITILLI

ISSUE FOUR VARIANT COVER

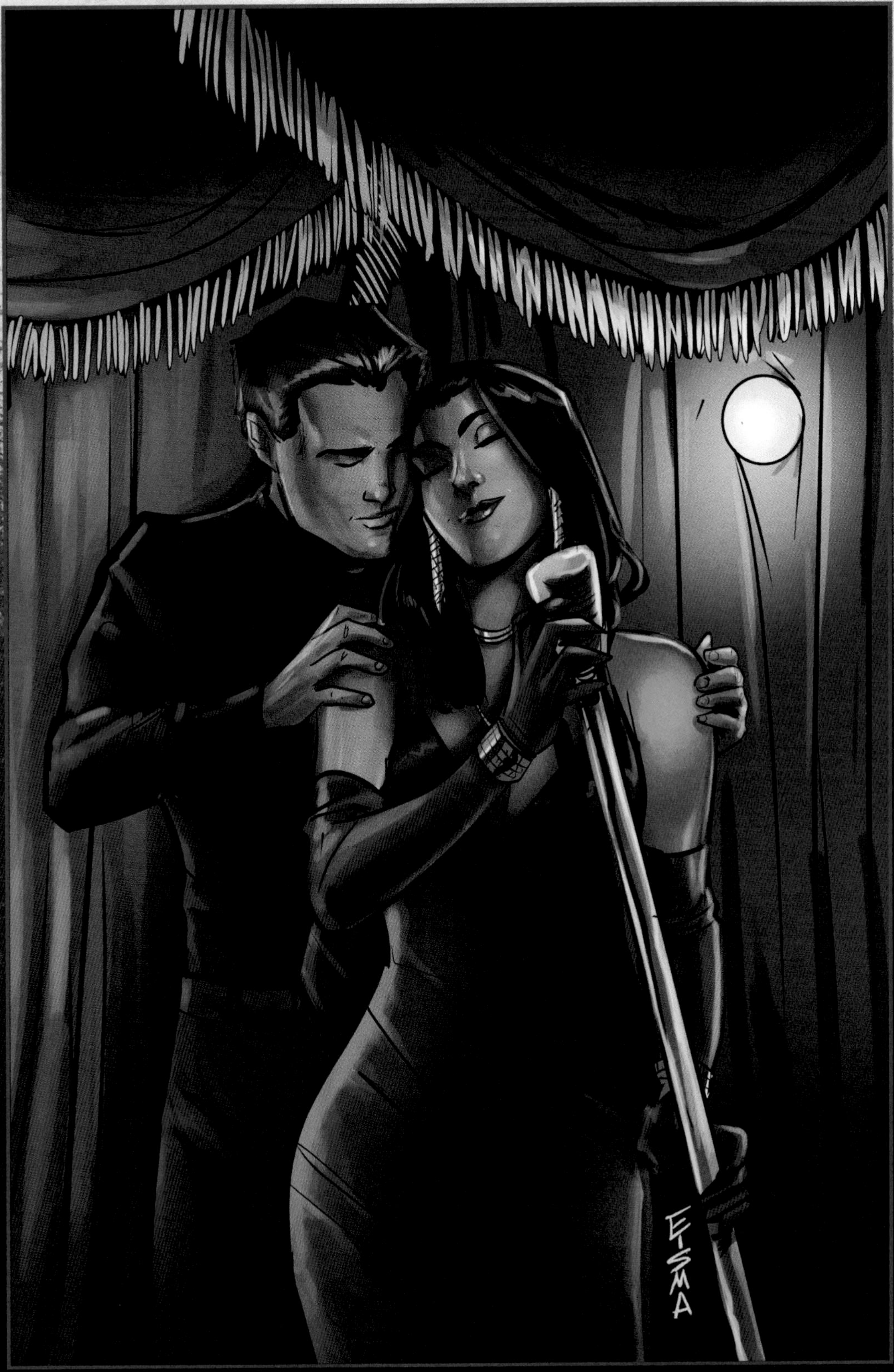
EISMA

COVER ART BY JOE EISMA

ISSUE FIVE MAIN COVER

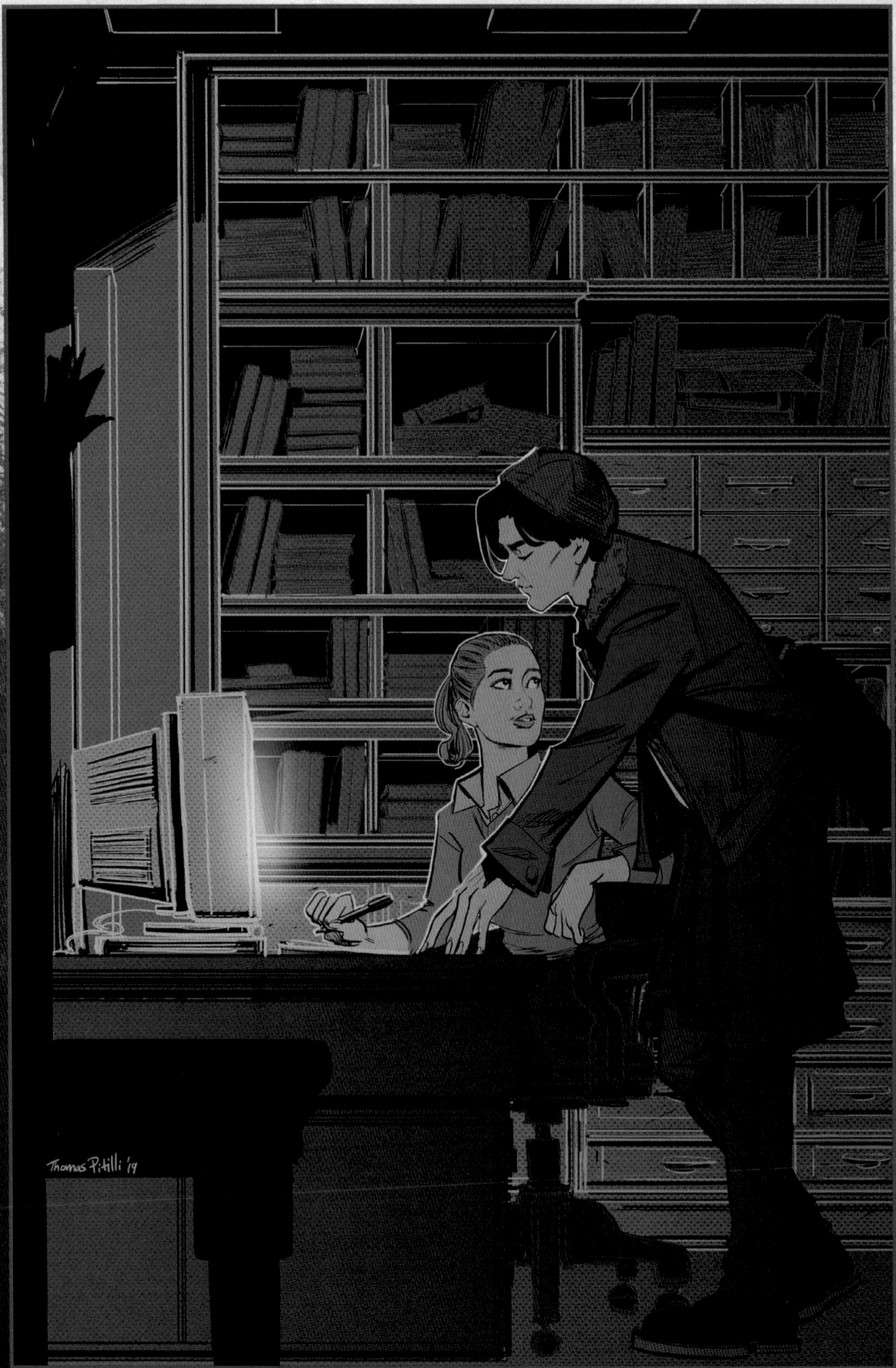
Thomas Pitilli '19

COVER ART BY THOMAS PITILLI

ISSUE FIVE VARIANT COVER

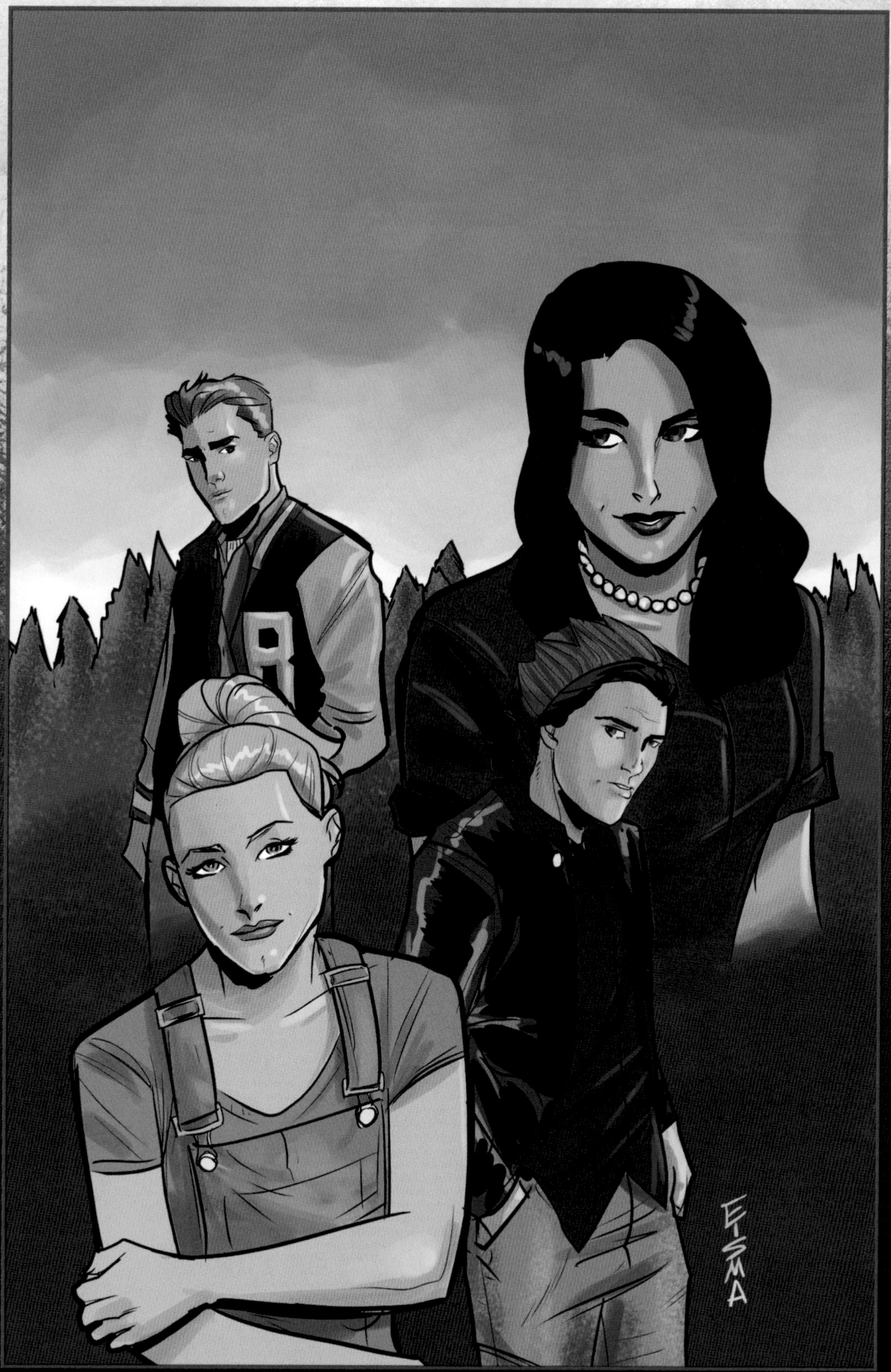

EISMA

COVER ART BY JOE EISMA

BONUS COMIC

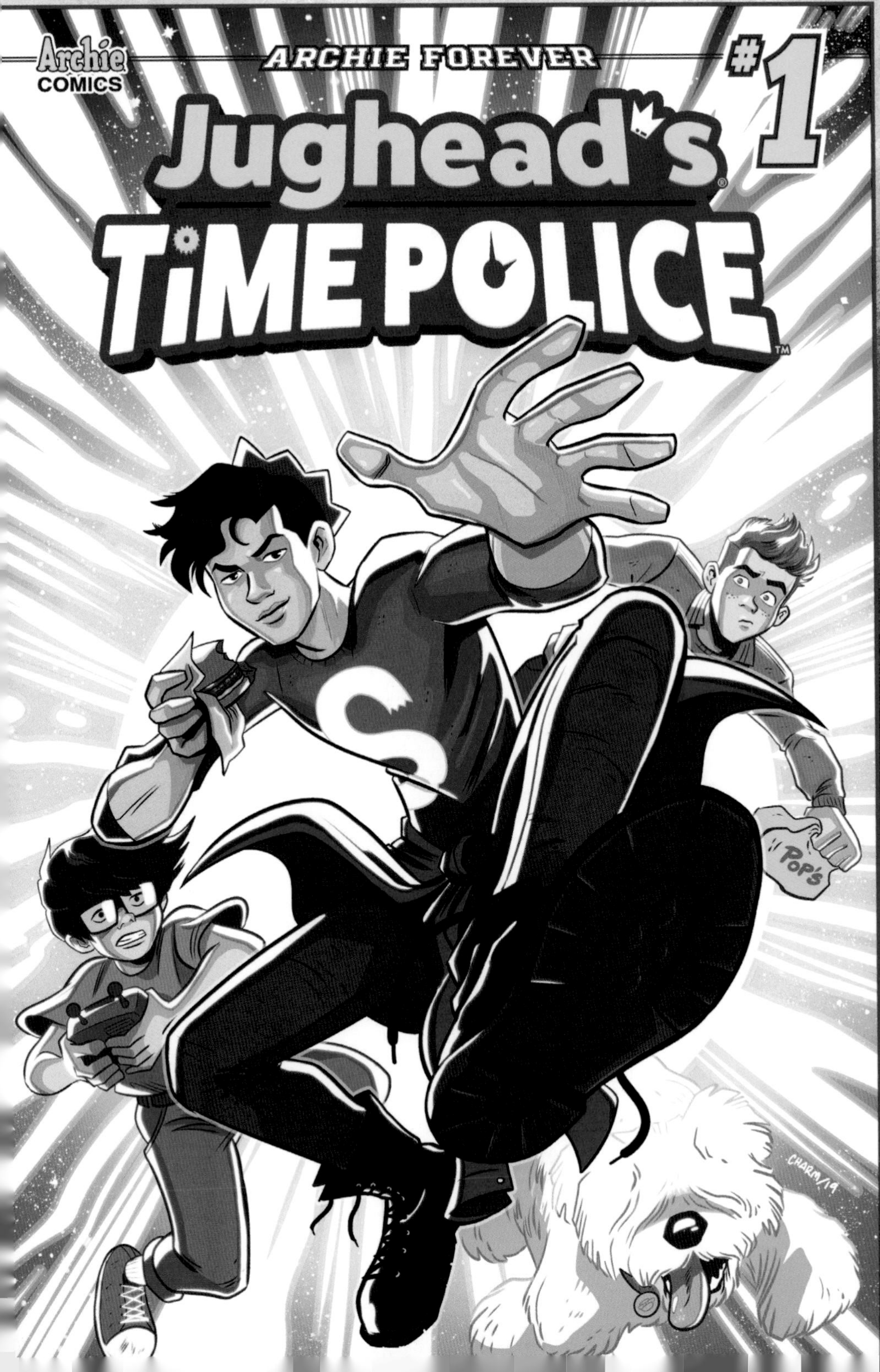
Archie COMICS
ARCHIE FOREVER
#1
Jughead's
TIME POLICE
POP'S
CHARM/19

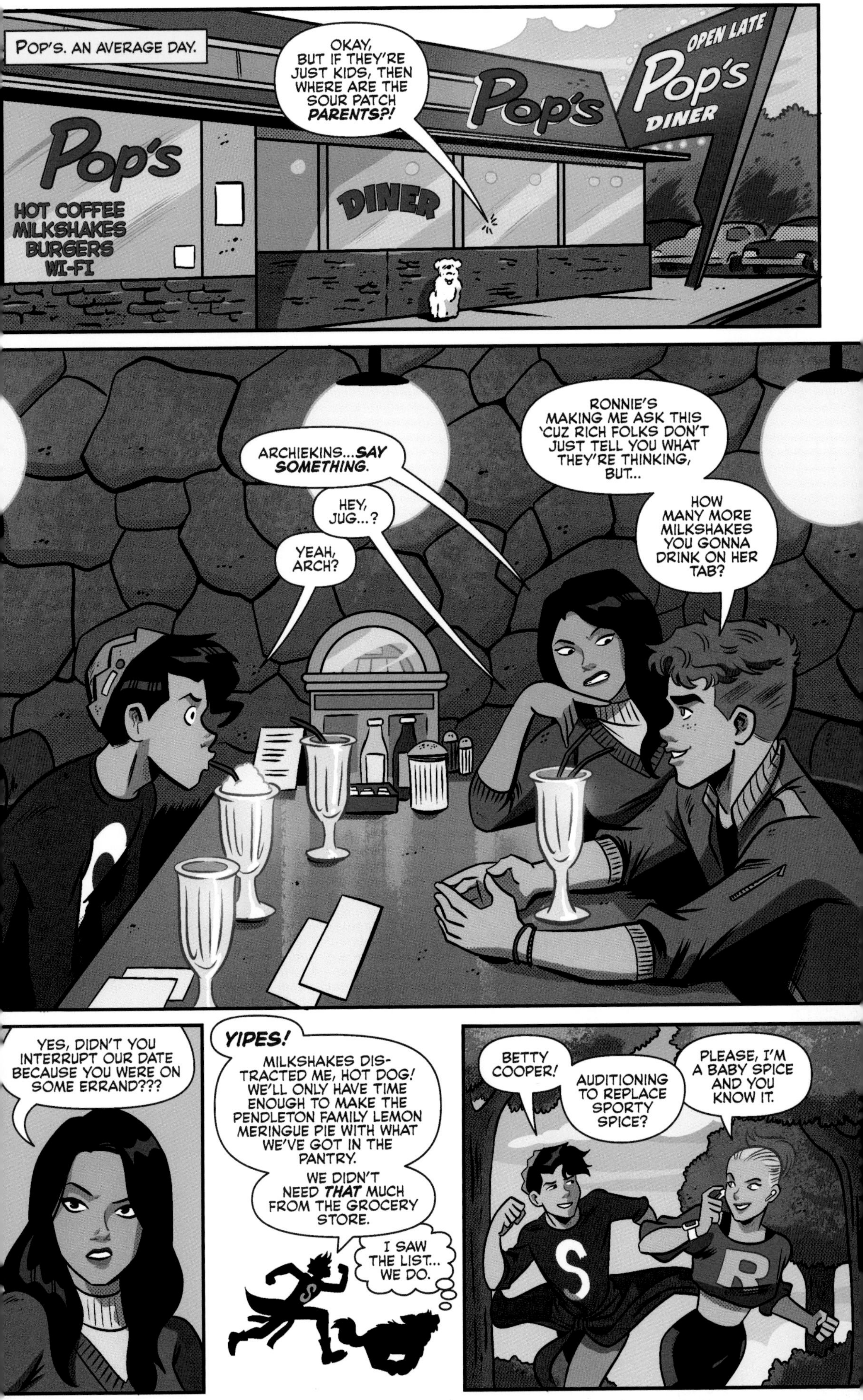
POP'S. AN AVERAGE DAY.
OKAY, BUT IF THEY'RE JUST KIDS, THEN WHERE ARE THE SOUR PATCH PARENTS?!
Pop's
OPEN LATE
Pop's
DINER
Pop's
HOT COFFEE
MILKSHAKES
BURGERS
WI-FI
DINER
ARCHIEKINS...SAY SOMETHING.
HEY, JUG...?
YEAH, ARCH?
RONNIE'S MAKING ME ASK THIS 'CUZ RICH FOLKS DON'T JUST TELL YOU WHAT THEY'RE THINKING, BUT...
HOW MANY MORE MILKSHAKES YOU GONNA DRINK ON HER TAB?
YES, DIDN'T YOU INTERRUPT OUR DATE BECAUSE YOU WERE ON SOME ERRAND???
YIPES!
MILKSHAKES DISTRACTED ME, HOT DOG! WE'LL ONLY HAVE TIME ENOUGH TO MAKE THE PENDLETON FAMILY LEMON MERINGUE PIE WITH WHAT WE'VE GOT IN THE PANTRY.
WE DIDN'T NEED THAT MUCH FROM THE GROCERY STORE.
I SAW THE LIST... WE DO.
BETTY COOPER!
AUDITIONING TO REPLACE SPORTY SPICE?
PLEASE, I'M A BABY SPICE AND YOU KNOW IT.

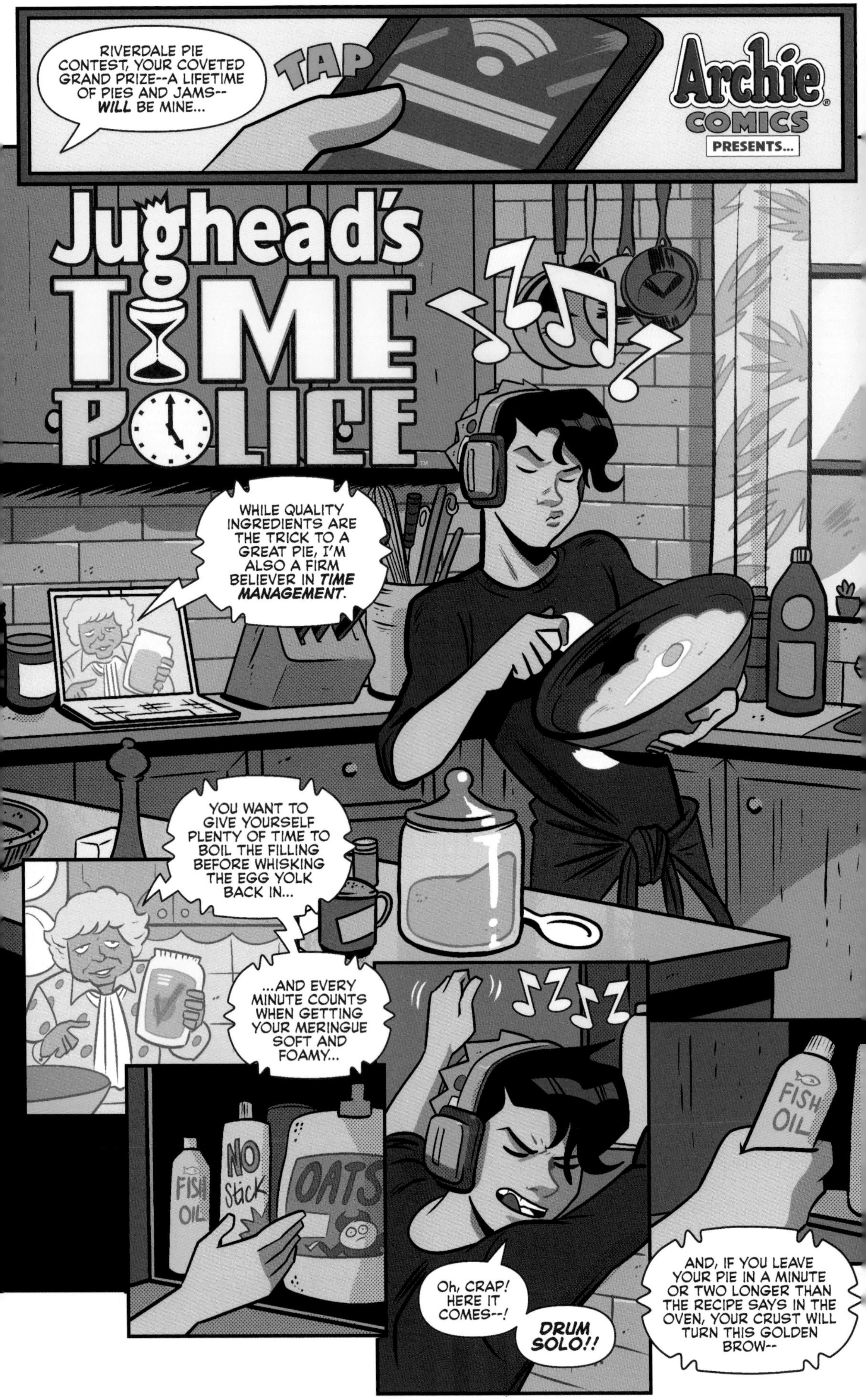

RIVERDALE PIE CONTEST, YOUR COVETED GRAND PRIZE--A LIFETIME OF PIES AND JAMS-- WILL BE MINE...
TAP
Archie COMICS PRESENTS...
Jughead's TIME POLICE
WHILE QUALITY INGREDIENTS ARE THE TRICK TO A GREAT PIE, I'M ALSO A FIRM BELIEVER IN TIME MANAGEMENT.
YOU WANT TO GIVE YOURSELF PLENTY OF TIME TO BOIL THE FILLING BEFORE WHISKING THE EGG YOLK BACK IN...
...AND EVERY MINUTE COUNTS WHEN GETTING YOUR MERINGUE SOFT AND FOAMY...
FISH OIL
NO Stick
OATS
FISH OIL
Oh, CRAP! HERE IT COMES--!
DRUM SOLO!!
AND, IF YOU LEAVE YOUR PIE IN A MINUTE OR TWO LONGER THAN THE RECIPE SAYS IN THE OVEN, YOUR CRUST WILL TURN THIS GOLDEN BROW--

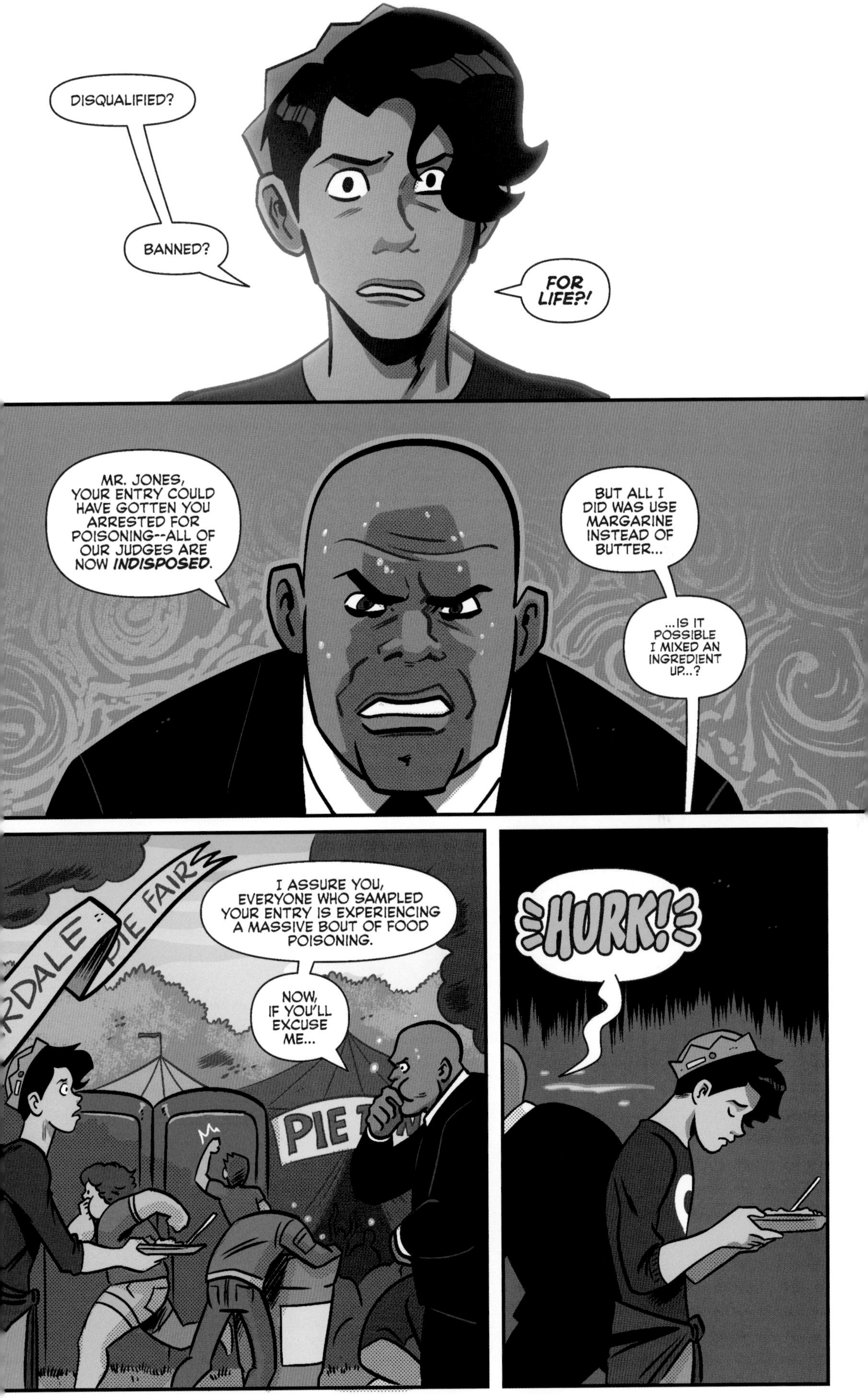
DISQUALIFIED?
BANNED?
FOR LIFE?!
MR. JONES, YOUR ENTRY COULD HAVE GOTTEN YOU ARRESTED FOR POISONING--ALL OF OUR JUDGES ARE NOW INDISPOSED.
BUT ALL I DID WAS USE MARGARINE INSTEAD OF BUTTER...
...IS IT POSSIBLE I MIXED AN INGREDIENT UP...?
RDALE PIE FAIR
I ASSURE YOU, EVERYONE WHO SAMPLED YOUR ENTRY IS EXPERIENCING A MASSIVE BOUT OF FOOD POISONING.
NOW, IF YOU'LL EXCUSE ME...
PIE
HURK!

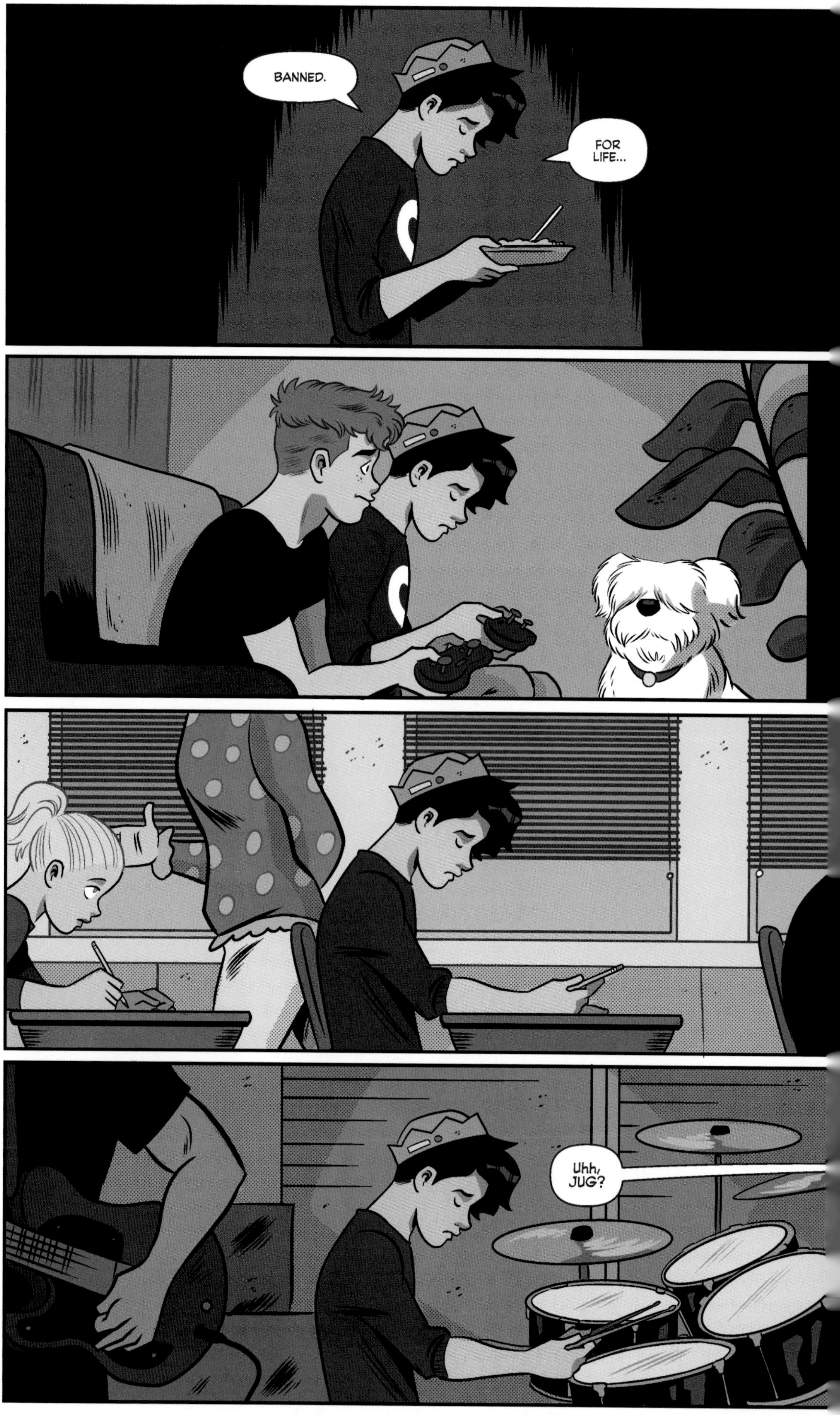
BANNED.
FOR LIFE...
Uhh, JUG?

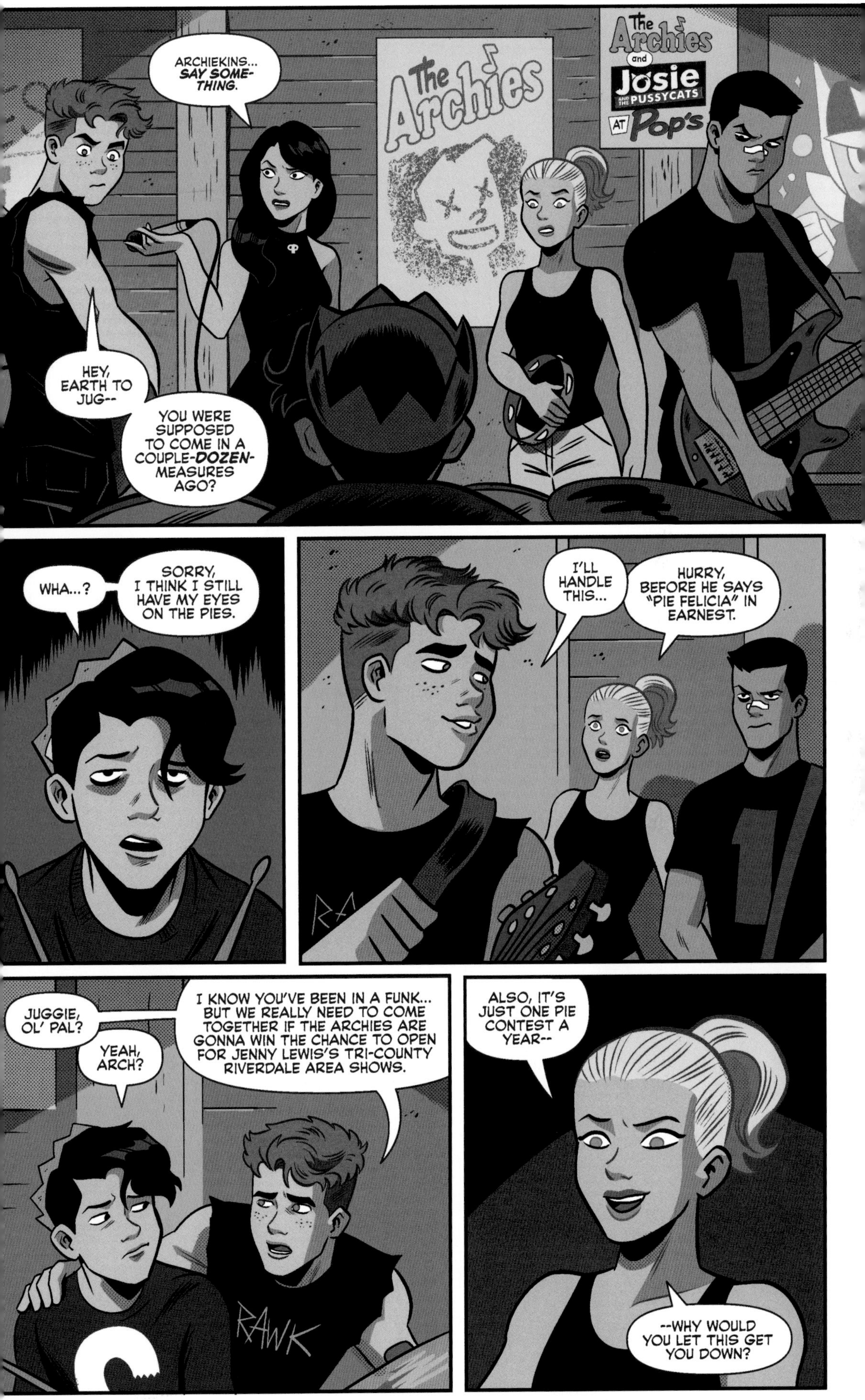

The Archies
The Archies and Josie and the Pussycats at Pop's
ARCHIEKINS... SAY SOME-THING.
HEY, EARTH TO JUG--
YOU WERE SUPPOSED TO COME IN A COUPLE-DOZEN-MEASURES AGO?
WHA...?
SORRY, I THINK I STILL HAVE MY EYES ON THE PIES.
I'LL HANDLE THIS...
HURRY, BEFORE HE SAYS "PIE FELICIA" IN EARNEST.
JUGGIE, OL' PAL?
YEAH, ARCH?
I KNOW YOU'VE BEEN IN A FUNK... BUT WE REALLY NEED TO COME TOGETHER IF THE ARCHIES ARE GONNA WIN THE CHANCE TO OPEN FOR JENNY LEWIS'S TRI-COUNTY RIVERDALE AREA SHOWS.
RAWK
ALSO, IT'S JUST ONE PIE CONTEST A YEAR--
--WHY WOULD YOU LET THIS GET YOU DOWN?

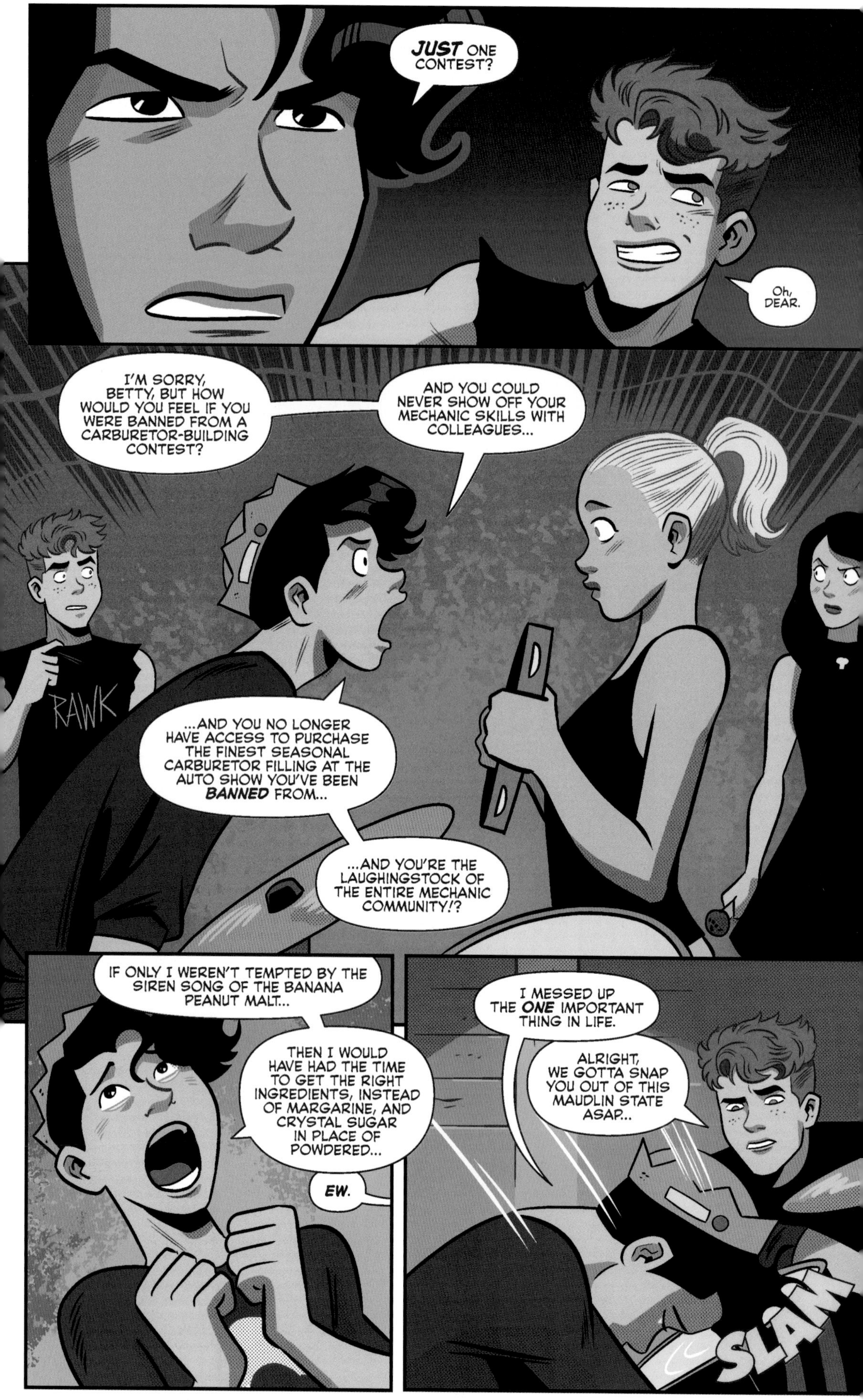
JUST ONE CONTEST?
Oh, DEAR.
I'M SORRY, BETTY, BUT HOW WOULD YOU FEEL IF YOU WERE BANNED FROM A CARBURETOR-BUILDING CONTEST?
AND YOU COULD NEVER SHOW OFF YOUR MECHANIC SKILLS WITH COLLEAGUES...
RAWK
...AND YOU NO LONGER HAVE ACCESS TO PURCHASE THE FINEST SEASONAL CARBURETOR FILLING AT THE AUTO SHOW YOU'VE BEEN BANNED FROM...
...AND YOU'RE THE LAUGHINGSTOCK OF THE ENTIRE MECHANIC COMMUNITY!?
IF ONLY I WEREN'T TEMPTED BY THE SIREN SONG OF THE BANANA PEANUT MALT...
THEN I WOULD HAVE HAD THE TIME TO GET THE RIGHT INGREDIENTS, INSTEAD OF MARGARINE, AND CRYSTAL SUGAR IN PLACE OF POWDERED...
EW.
I MESSED UP THE ONE IMPORTANT THING IN LIFE.
ALRIGHT, WE GOTTA SNAP YOU OUT OF THIS MAUDLIN STATE ASAP...
SLAM

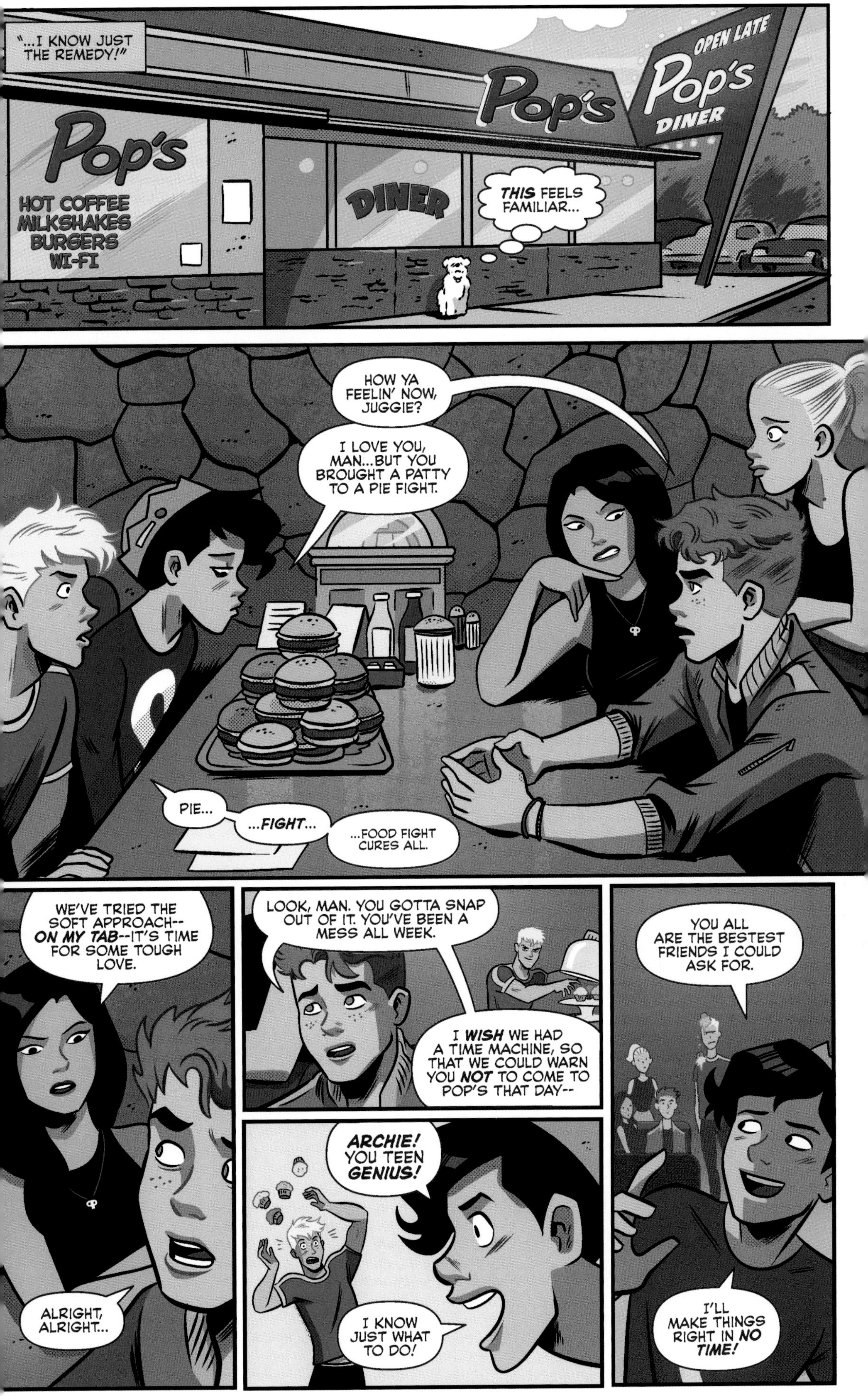
"...I KNOW JUST THE REMEDY!"
OPEN LATE
Pop's
DINER
Pop's
Pop's
HOT COFFEE
MILKSHAKES
BURGERS
WI-FI
DINER
THIS FEELS FAMILIAR...
HOW YA FEELIN' NOW, JUGGIE?
I LOVE YOU, MAN...BUT YOU BROUGHT A PATTY TO A PIE FIGHT.
PIE...
...FIGHT...
...FOOD FIGHT CURES ALL.
WE'VE TRIED THE SOFT APPROACH-- ON MY TAB--IT'S TIME FOR SOME TOUGH LOVE.
ALRIGHT, ALRIGHT...
LOOK, MAN. YOU GOTTA SNAP OUT OF IT. YOU'VE BEEN A MESS ALL WEEK.
I WISH WE HAD A TIME MACHINE, SO THAT WE COULD WARN YOU NOT TO COME TO POP'S THAT DAY--
ARCHIE! YOU TEEN GENIUS!
I KNOW JUST WHAT TO DO!
YOU ALL ARE THE BESTEST FRIENDS I COULD ASK FOR.
I'LL MAKE THINGS RIGHT IN NO TIME!

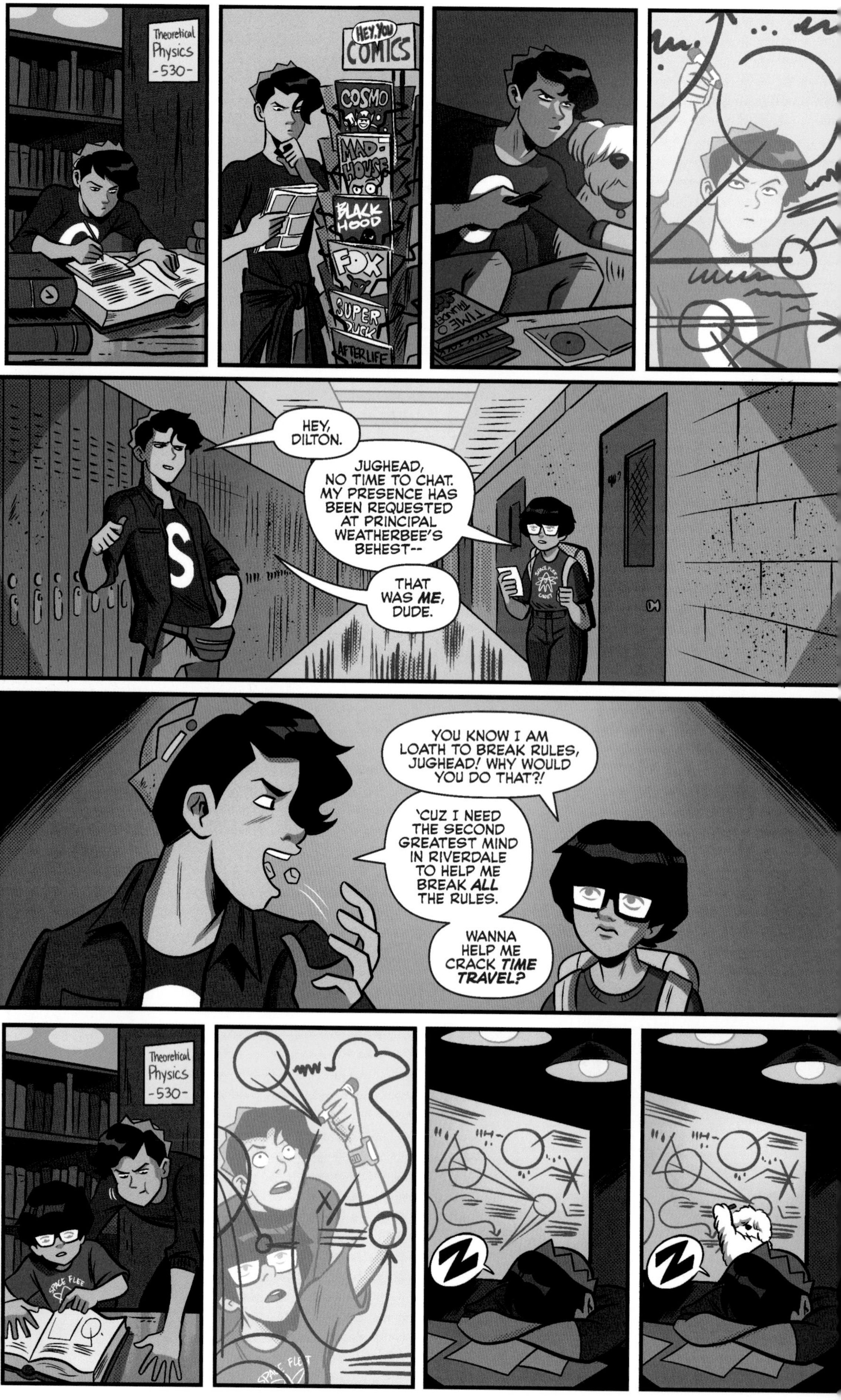
Theoretical Physics -530-
HEY, YOU COMICS
COSMO
MAD-HOUSE
BLACK HOOD
FOX
SUPER DUCK
AFTERLIFE
TIME
HEY, DILTON.
JUGHEAD, NO TIME TO CHAT. MY PRESENCE HAS BEEN REQUESTED AT PRINCIPAL WEATHERBEE'S BEHEST--
THAT WAS *ME*, DUDE.
YOU KNOW I AM LOATH TO BREAK RULES, JUGHEAD! WHY WOULD YOU DO THAT?!
'CUZ I NEED THE SECOND GREATEST MIND IN RIVERDALE TO HELP ME BREAK *ALL* THE RULES.
WANNA HELP ME CRACK *TIME TRAVEL?*
Theoretical Physics -530-
SPACE FLEET
Z
Z

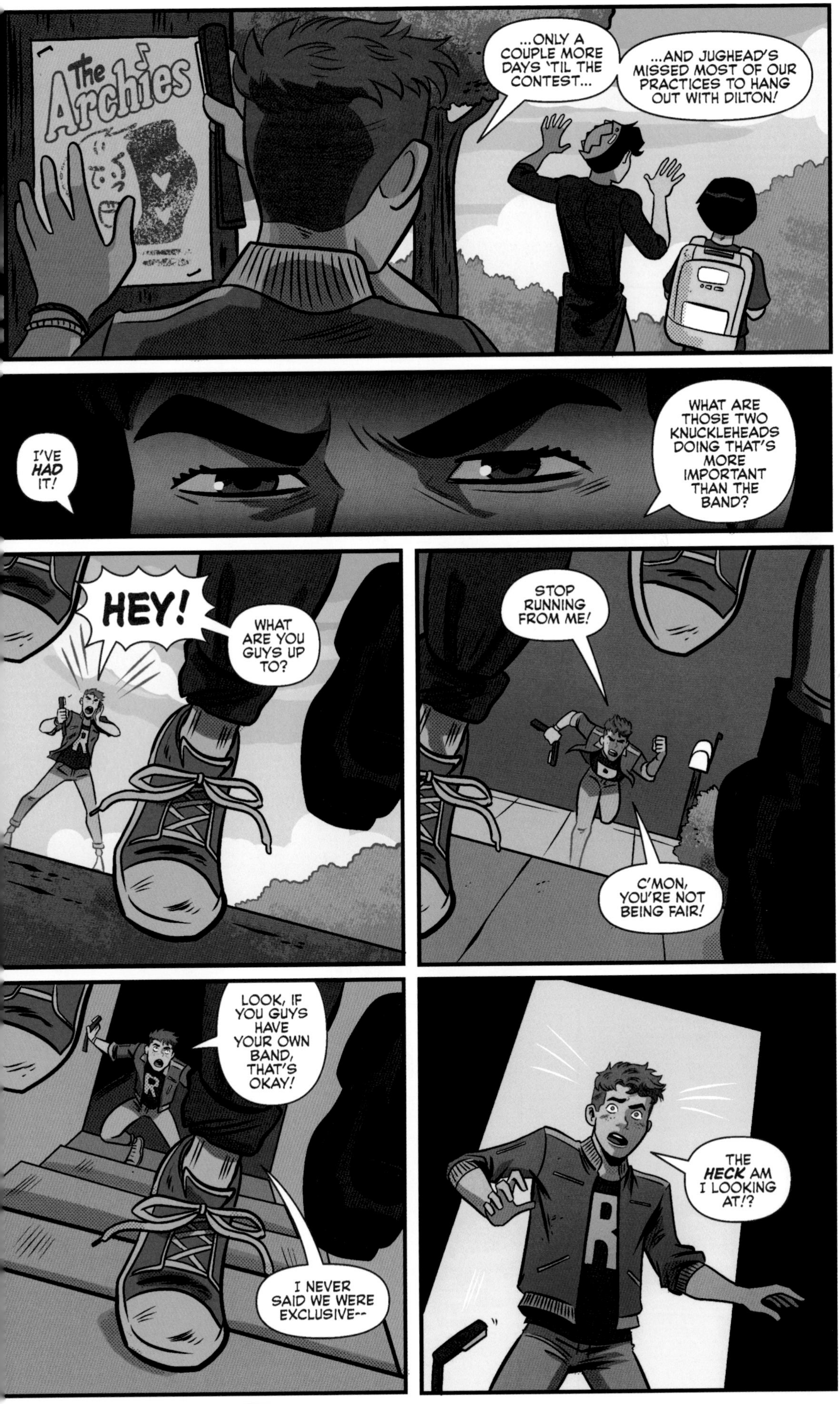
The Archies
...ONLY A COUPLE MORE DAYS 'TIL THE CONTEST...
...AND JUGHEAD'S MISSED MOST OF OUR PRACTICES TO HANG OUT WITH DILTON!
I'VE *HAD* IT!
WHAT ARE THOSE TWO KNUCKLEHEADS DOING THAT'S MORE IMPORTANT THAN THE BAND?
HEY!
WHAT ARE YOU GUYS UP TO?
STOP RUNNING FROM ME!
C'MON, YOU'RE NOT BEING FAIR!
LOOK, IF YOU GUYS HAVE YOUR OWN BAND, THAT'S OKAY!
I NEVER SAID WE WERE EXCLUSIVE--
THE *HECK* AM I LOOKING AT!?

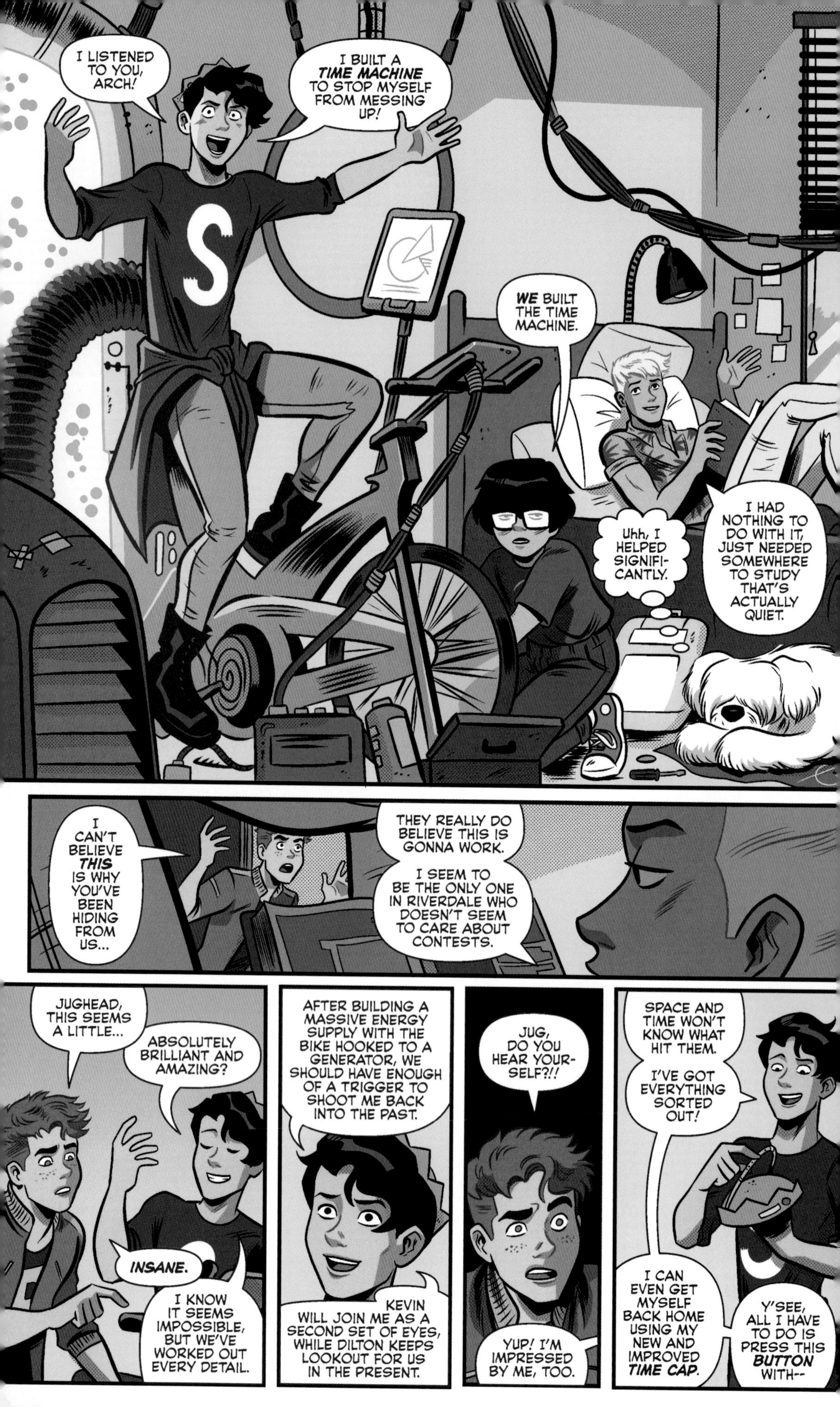
I LISTENED TO YOU, ARCH!
I BUILT A *TIME MACHINE* TO STOP MYSELF FROM MESSING UP!
WE BUILT THE TIME MACHINE.
Uhh, I HELPED SIGNIFI-CANTLY.
I HAD NOTHING TO DO WITH IT, JUST NEEDED SOMEWHERE TO STUDY THAT'S ACTUALLY QUIET.
I CAN'T BELIEVE *THIS* IS WHY YOU'VE BEEN HIDING FROM US...
THEY REALLY DO BELIEVE THIS IS GONNA WORK.
I SEEM TO BE THE ONLY ONE IN RIVERDALE WHO DOESN'T SEEM TO CARE ABOUT CONTESTS.
JUGHEAD, THIS SEEMS A LITTLE...
ABSOLUTELY BRILLIANT AND AMAZING?
INSANE.
I KNOW IT SEEMS IMPOSSIBLE, BUT WE'VE WORKED OUT EVERY DETAIL.
AFTER BUILDING A MASSIVE ENERGY SUPPLY WITH THE BIKE HOOKED TO A GENERATOR, WE SHOULD HAVE ENOUGH OF A TRIGGER TO SHOOT ME BACK INTO THE PAST.
KEVIN WILL JOIN ME AS A SECOND SET OF EYES, WHILE DILTON KEEPS LOOKOUT FOR US IN THE PRESENT.
JUG, DO YOU HEAR YOUR-SELF?!!
YUP! I'M IMPRESSED BY ME, TOO.
SPACE AND TIME WON'T KNOW WHAT HIT THEM.
I'VE GOT EVERYTHING SORTED OUT!
I CAN EVEN GET MYSELF BACK HOME USING MY NEW AND IMPROVED *TIME CAP*.
Y'SEE, ALL I HAVE TO DO IS PRESS THIS *BUTTON* WITH--

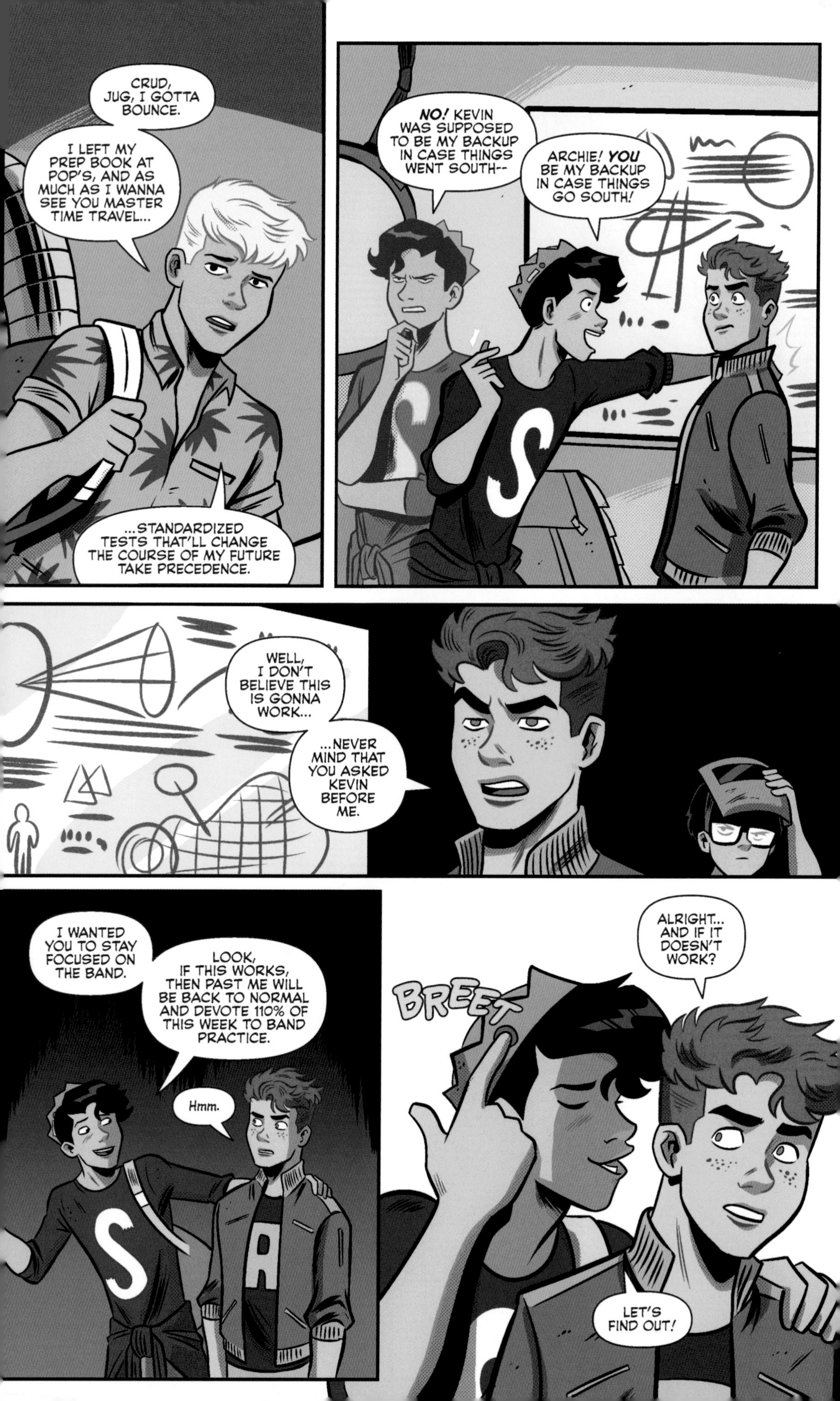
CRUD, JUG, I GOTTA BOUNCE.
I LEFT MY PREP BOOK AT POP'S, AND AS MUCH AS I WANNA SEE YOU MASTER TIME TRAVEL...
...STANDARDIZED TESTS THAT'LL CHANGE THE COURSE OF MY FUTURE TAKE PRECEDENCE.
NO! KEVIN WAS SUPPOSED TO BE MY BACKUP IN CASE THINGS WENT SOUTH--
ARCHIE! *YOU* BE MY BACKUP IN CASE THINGS GO SOUTH!
WELL, I DON'T BELIEVE THIS IS GONNA WORK...
...NEVER MIND THAT YOU ASKED KEVIN BEFORE ME.
I WANTED YOU TO STAY FOCUSED ON THE BAND.
LOOK, IF THIS WORKS, THEN PAST ME WILL BE BACK TO NORMAL AND DEVOTE 110% OF THIS WEEK TO BAND PRACTICE.
Hmm.
ALRIGHT... AND IF IT DOESN'T WORK?
BREET
LET'S FIND OUT!

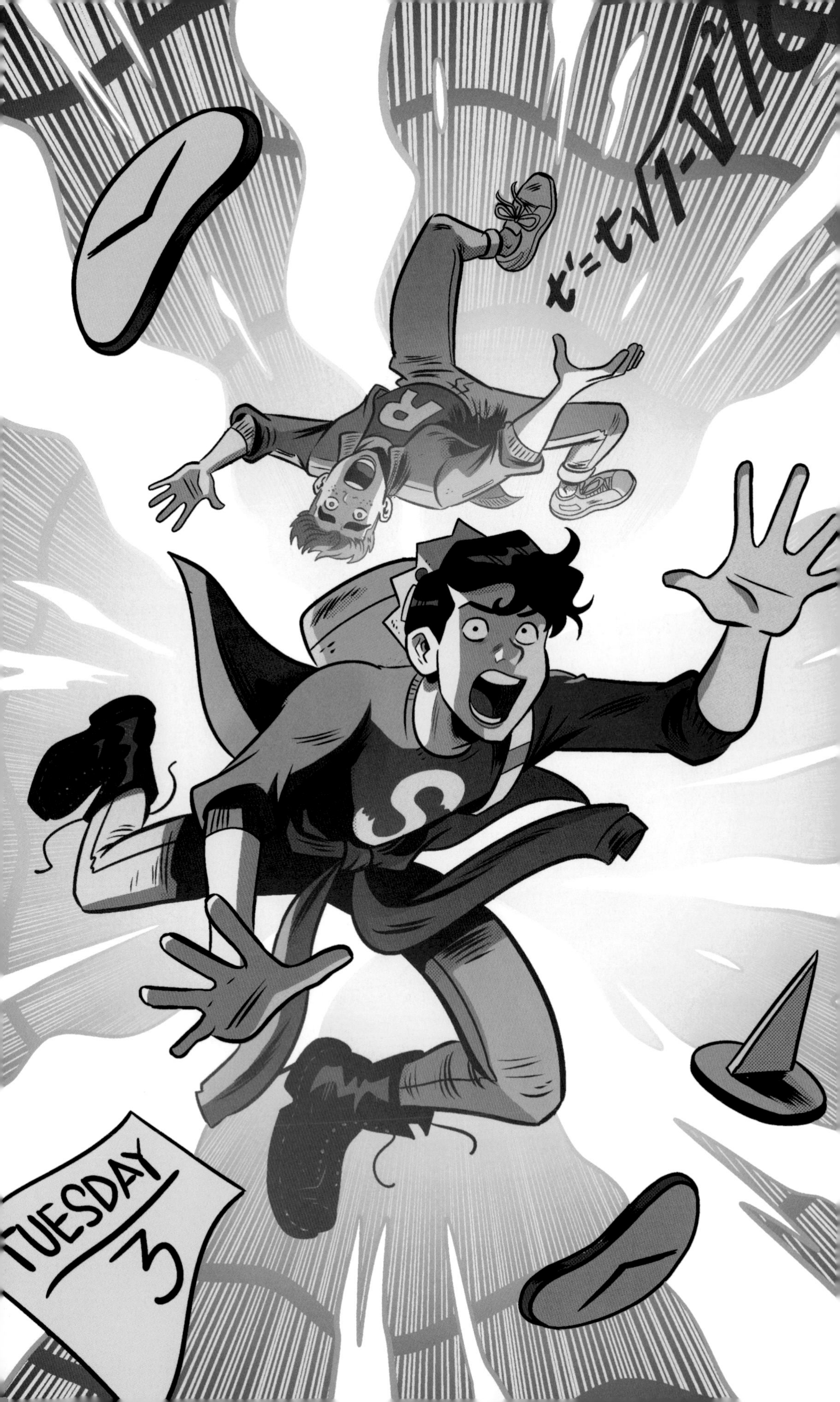
TUESDAY
3

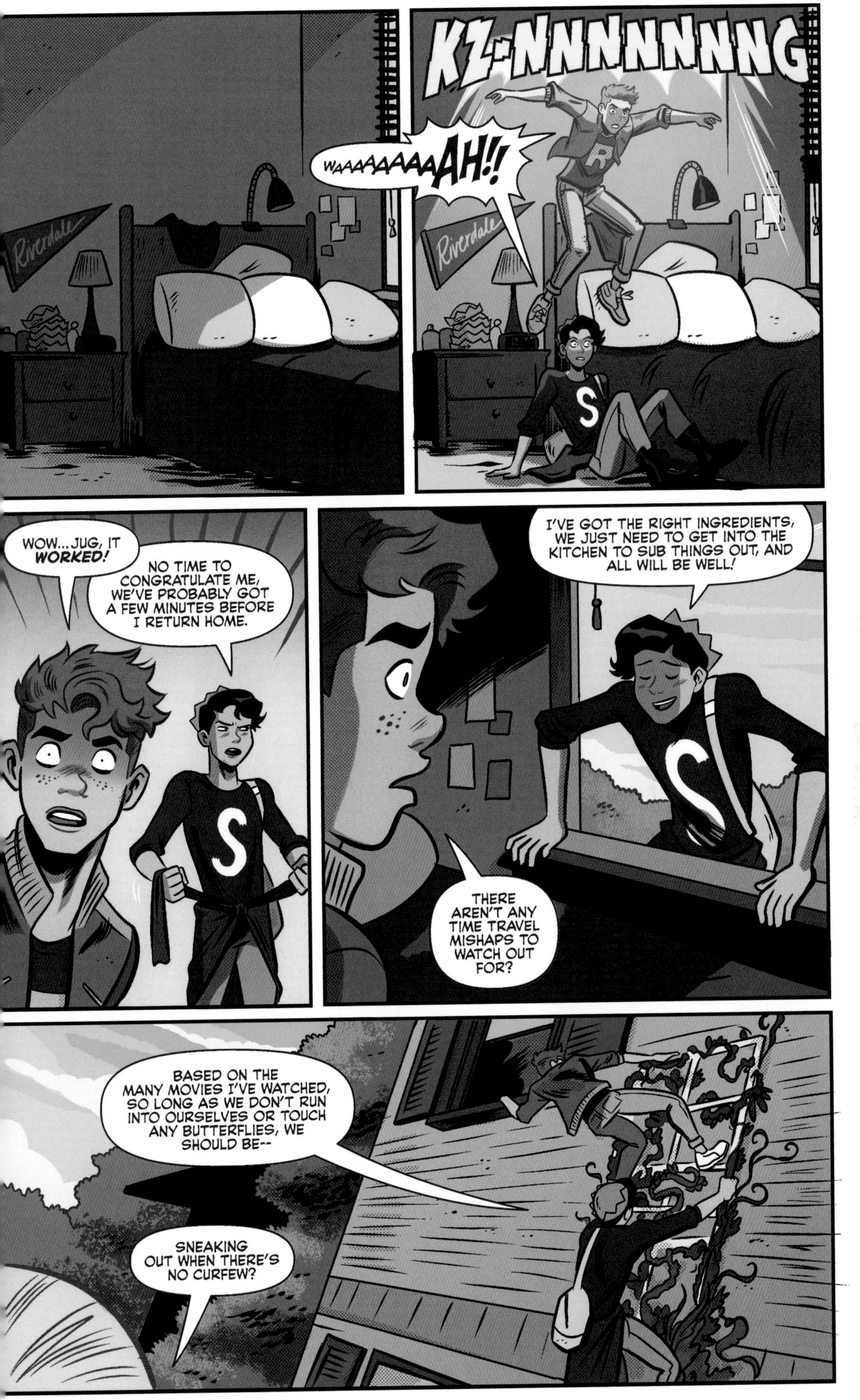
KZ-NNNNNNNG
WAAAAAAAAAH!!
Riverdale
WOW...JUG, IT WORKED!
NO TIME TO CONGRATULATE ME, WE'VE PROBABLY GOT A FEW MINUTES BEFORE I RETURN HOME.
I'VE GOT THE RIGHT INGREDIENTS, WE JUST NEED TO GET INTO THE KITCHEN TO SUB THINGS OUT, AND ALL WILL BE WELL!
THERE AREN'T ANY TIME TRAVEL MISHAPS TO WATCH OUT FOR?
BASED ON THE MANY MOVIES I'VE WATCHED, SO LONG AS WE DON'T RUN INTO OURSELVES OR TOUCH ANY BUTTERFLIES, WE SHOULD BE--
SNEAKING OUT WHEN THERE'S NO CURFEW?

ARCHIE, I THOUGHT I WAS MEETING YOU AND V AT POP'S BEFORE SHE TOOK ME TO KICK BOXING?

THAT'S WHY YOU WERE DRESSED LIKE THIS!

"WERE"?

IT'S VERY... FLATTERING.

Uhh, ARCHIE'S HELPING US WITH SOME LANDSCAPING.

'CUZ I'M LOOPY AND FOCUSED ON BAKING PIES.

YOU GUYS ARE *WEIRD.* SEE YOU AT POP'S, ARCH. I'LL TELL VERONICA TO WAIT.

NOT UNLESS HE CHANGES OUTFITS AND BEATS YOU THERE!

BYE, BETT-- *WHOA!!*

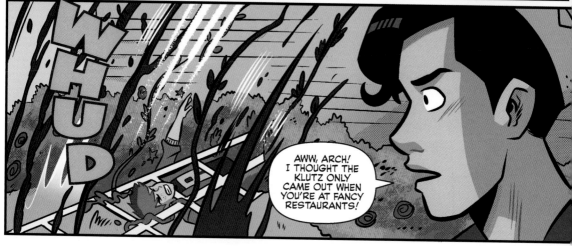

WHUD

AWW, ARCH! I THOUGHT THE KLUTZ ONLY CAME OUT WHEN YOU'RE AT FANCY RESTAURANTS!

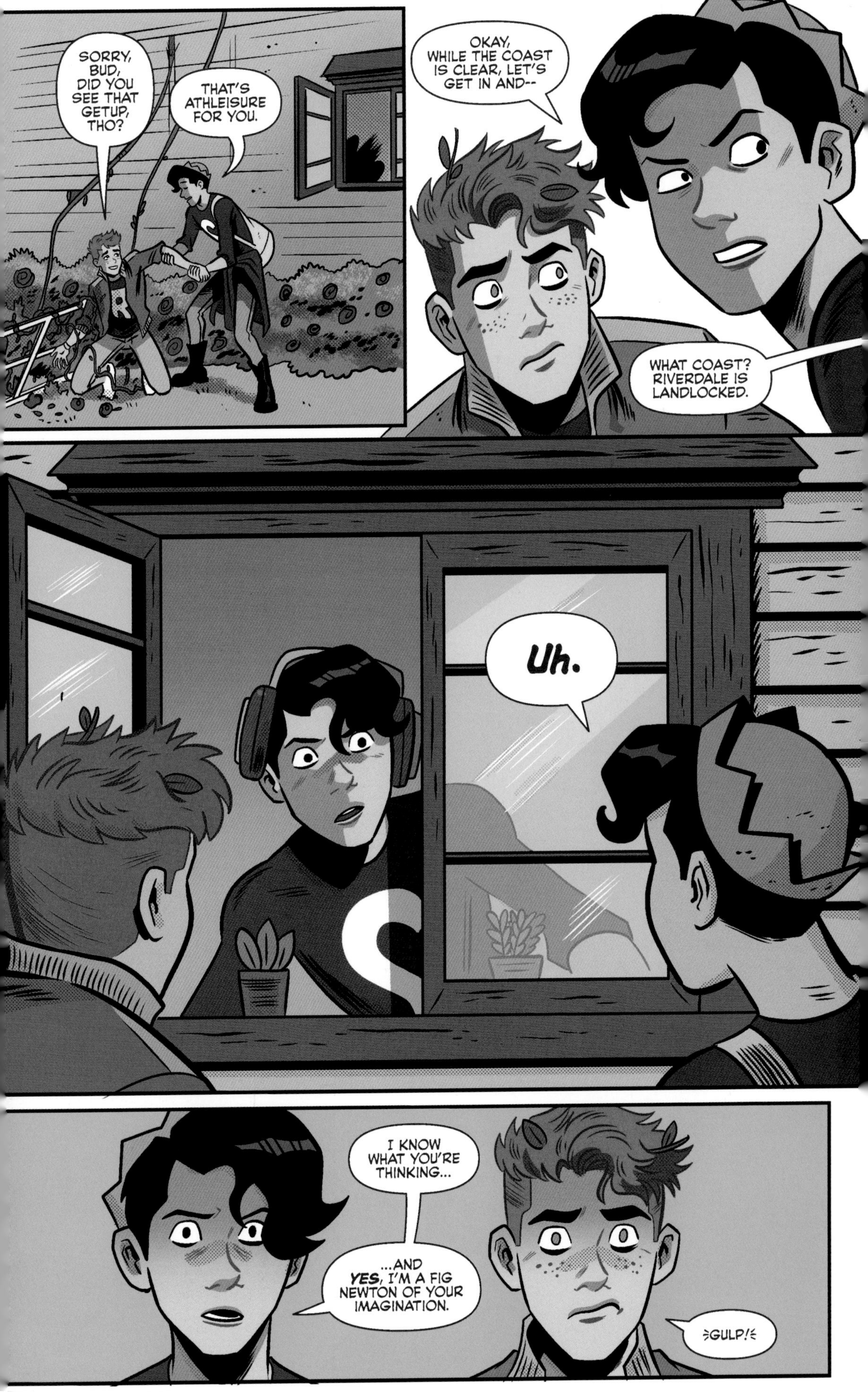
SORRY, BUD, DID YOU SEE THAT GETUP, THO?
THAT'S ATHLEISURE FOR YOU.
OKAY, WHILE THE COAST IS CLEAR, LET'S GET IN AND--
WHAT COAST? RIVERDALE IS LANDLOCKED.
Uh.
I KNOW WHAT YOU'RE THINKING...
...AND YES, I'M A FIG NEWTON OF YOUR IMAGINATION.
GULP!

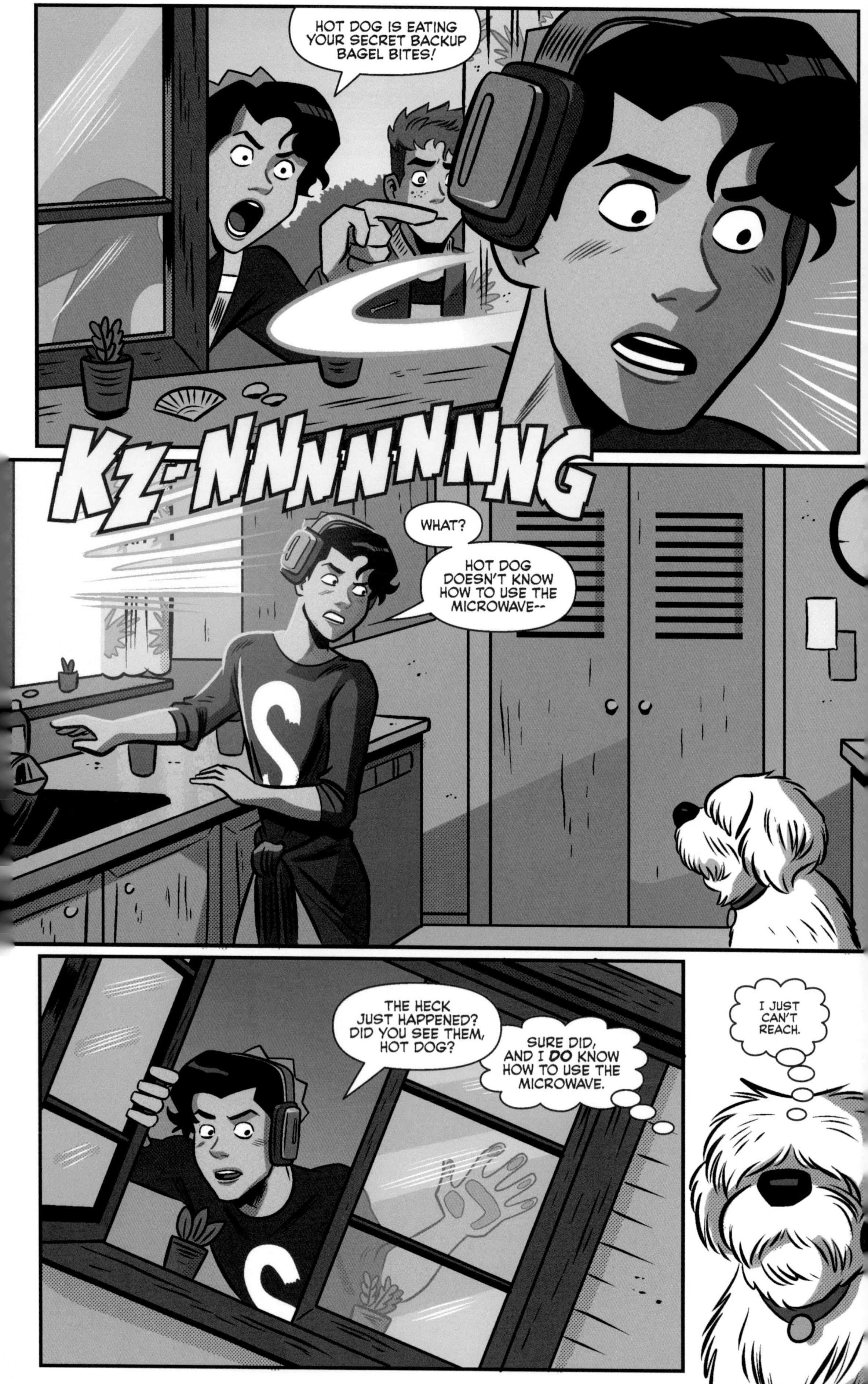
HOT DOG IS EATING YOUR SECRET BACKUP BAGEL BITES!
KZ-NNNNNNNG
WHAT?
HOT DOG DOESN'T KNOW HOW TO USE THE MICROWAVE--
THE HECK JUST HAPPENED? DID YOU SEE THEM, HOT DOG?
SURE DID, AND I DO KNOW HOW TO USE THE MICROWAVE.
I JUST CAN'T REACH.

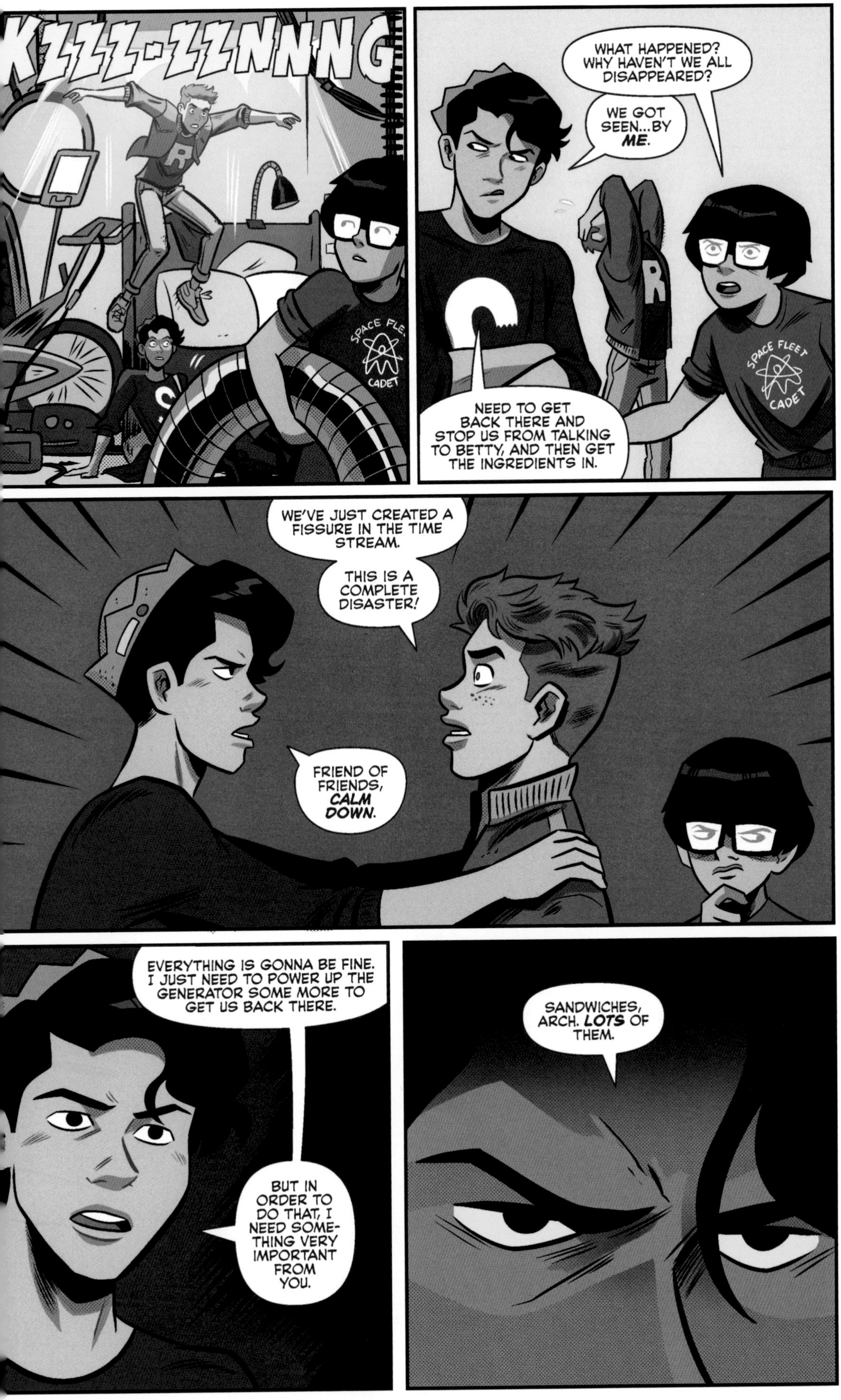
KZZZ-ZZNNNG
SPACE FLEET CADET
WHAT HAPPENED? WHY HAVEN'T WE ALL DISAPPEARED?
WE GOT SEEN...BY *ME*.
NEED TO GET BACK THERE AND STOP US FROM TALKING TO BETTY, AND THEN GET THE INGREDIENTS IN.
SPACE FLEET CADET
WE'VE JUST CREATED A FISSURE IN THE TIME STREAM.
THIS IS A COMPLETE DISASTER!
FRIEND OF FRIENDS, ***CALM DOWN***.
EVERYTHING IS GONNA BE FINE. I JUST NEED TO POWER UP THE GENERATOR SOME MORE TO GET US BACK THERE.
BUT IN ORDER TO DO THAT, I NEED SOMETHING VERY IMPORTANT FROM YOU.
SANDWICHES, ARCH. ***LOTS*** OF THEM.

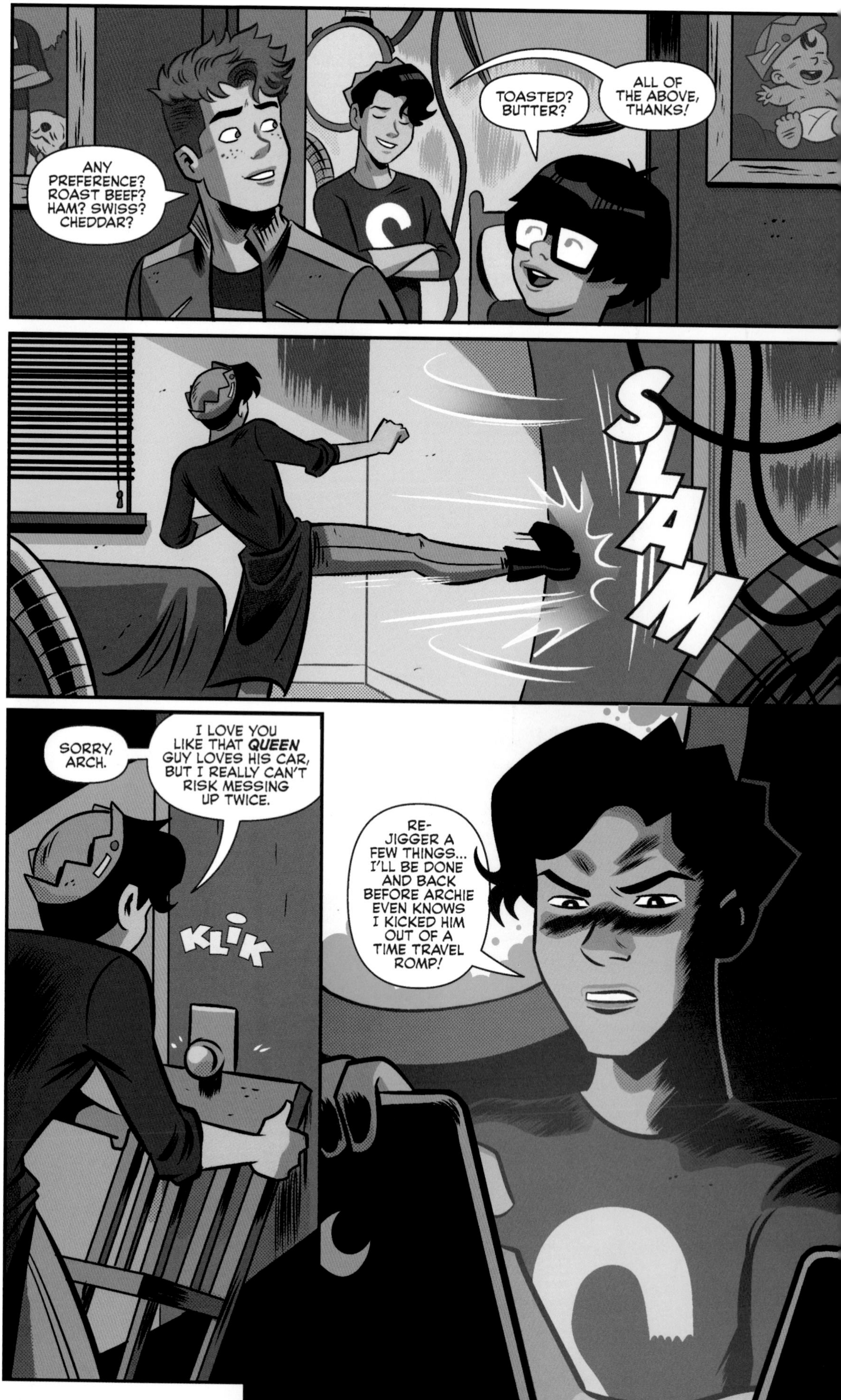
ANY PREFERENCE? ROAST BEEF? HAM? SWISS? CHEDDAR?
TOASTED? BUTTER?
ALL OF THE ABOVE, THANKS!
SLAM
SORRY, ARCH.
I LOVE YOU LIKE THAT QUEEN GUY LOVES HIS CAR, BUT I REALLY CAN'T RISK MESSING UP TWICE.
KLIK
RE-JIGGER A FEW THINGS... I'LL BE DONE AND BACK BEFORE ARCHIE EVEN KNOWS I KICKED HIM OUT OF A TIME TRAVEL ROMP!

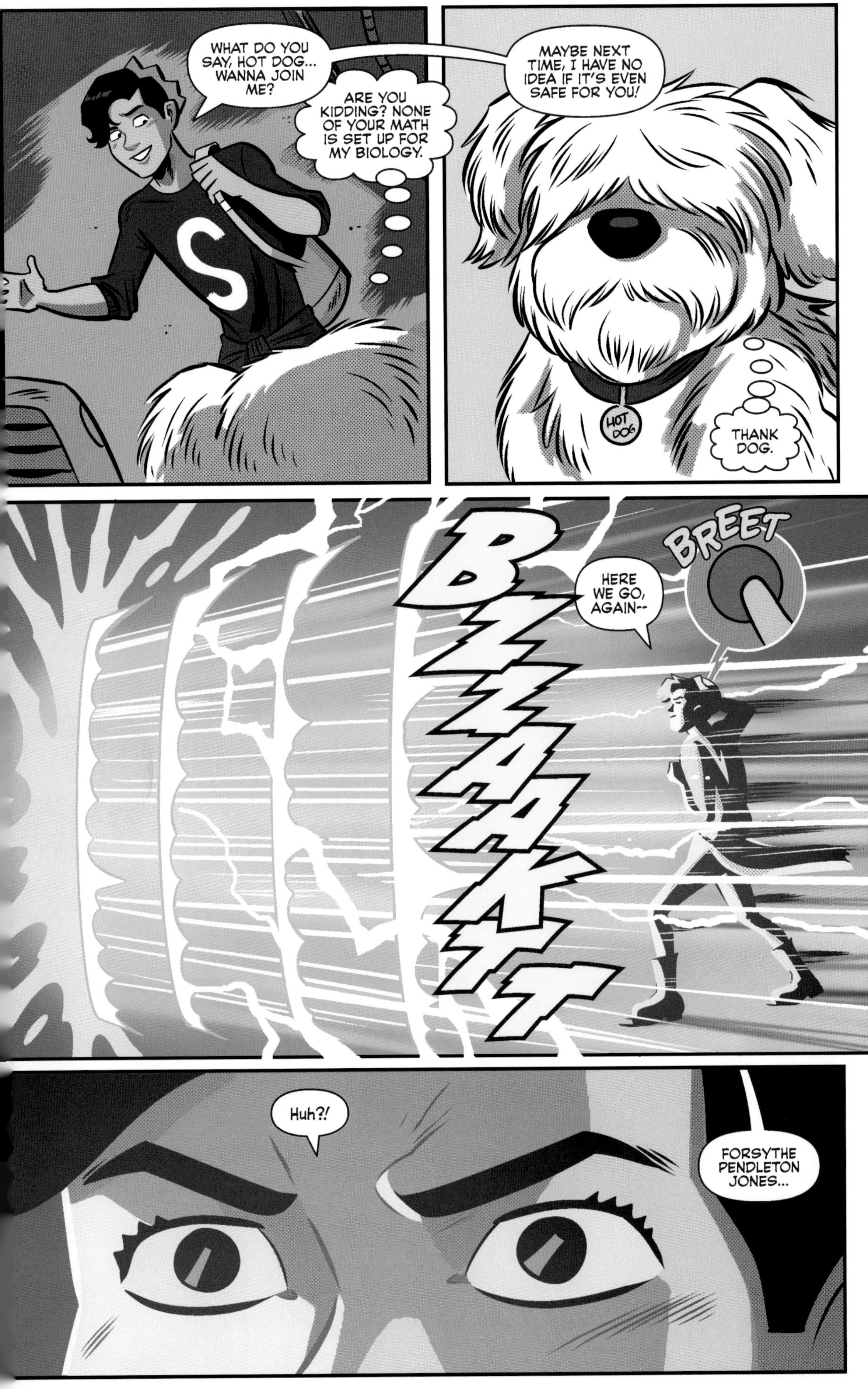
WHAT DO YOU SAY, HOT DOG... WANNA JOIN ME?
ARE YOU KIDDING? NONE OF YOUR MATH IS SET UP FOR MY BIOLOGY.
MAYBE NEXT TIME, I HAVE NO IDEA IF IT'S EVEN SAFE FOR YOU!
HOT DOG
THANK DOG.
BZZAKTT
BREET
HERE WE GO, AGAIN--
Huh?!
FORSYTHE PENDLETON JONES...

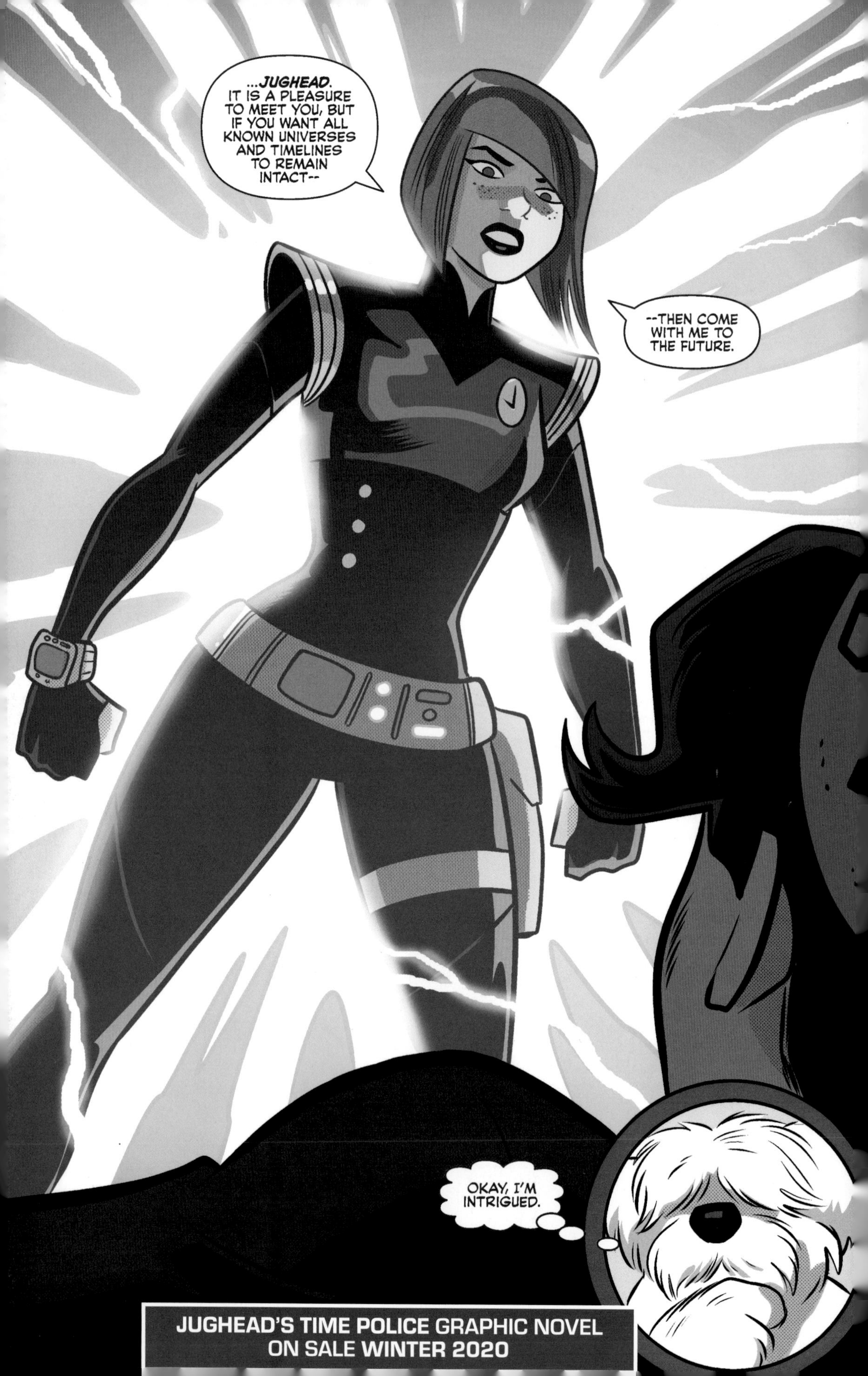
...JUGHEAD. IT IS A PLEASURE TO MEET YOU, BUT IF YOU WANT ALL KNOWN UNIVERSES AND TIMELINES TO REMAIN INTACT--
--THEN COME WITH ME TO THE FUTURE.
OKAY, I'M INTRIGUED.
JUGHEAD'S TIME POLICE GRAPHIC NOVEL ON SALE WINTER 2020